P.T.

"I ... Mar...

☆

Derek's head lifted abruptly from his pursuit of her lips. "I'd like to know why not."

Annalise braced her palms against his chest. "Because I'm marrying someone else. I'm engaged."

His temper exploded. "Engaged? You're *engaged?*" He gritted his teeth. "Give me one good reason why."

"I love him," she railed, pressed past all bounds.

"The hell you do!"

With a snort of impatience, he swept her up in his arms, crossed the room and settled them both onto the settee. "Derek," she managed to say at last, "you must let me up. The servants..."

"To the devil with the servants." His voice lowered. "I want you... and only you. It's time you knew just how much." His lips covered hers, and the kiss they shared was like liquid fire, igniting their desire for each other.

She turned her head away in a last attempt to evade him. But it was already too late...

"FIVE STARS—HIGHEST RATING!
An exciting tale of great adventure."
—*Affaire de Coeur*

☆

"FOUR AND A HALF STARS—HIGHEST RATING! All the hallmarks of Christine Monson's unforgettable romances are here—lyrical prose, intense emotions, wild adventures and sizzling love scenes... A first-class romance."
—*Rave Reviews* on *Golden Nights*

Also by Christine Monson

GOLDEN NIGHTS

Published by
WARNER BOOKS

CHRISTINE MONSON

A Time Warner Company

WARNER BOOKS EDITION

Cover design by Anne Twomey
Cover illustration by John Innis

Warner Books, Inc.
666 Fifth Avenue
New York, N.Y. 10103

Printed in the United States of America

First Printing: January, 1991

10 9 8 7 6 5 4 3 2 1

For John and Berna,
And my two best bears,
Jon and Jenni.

I

The Commissioner's Ball

*A**nnalise* Devon tensely smoothed the hoop skirts of her ball dress and watched her father, William Devon, and Derek Clavell as the dancers swirled past them on the vast teak floor of the residency of the commissioner of Kanpur. She wanted to know what they were discussing so intently. They had been closeted together often of late, and at times, their voices had risen as if angry with one another. The thought made her anxious. Her father was not given to quarreling and there was no man she would less see him quarrel with than Derek. They had always gotten on well together.

"Attractive, isn't he?"

"I beg your pardon?" Annalise's attention was diverted by Jane Witherton.

Her blonde curls damp from the humidity of Queen Victoria's India, Jane fanned herself vigorously. "Derek Clavell. He has such wicked, dark eyes. Whenever he comes into a room, the other men resemble a flock of sheep retreating before a wolf.'' Jane eyed her slyly, her blue eyes dancing with envy. ''He visits your parsonage quite often for a blade of such colorful reputation.''

''Colonel Clavell is a good friend of my father,'' Annalise responded, her slim, graceful body holding a trace of stiffness.

''Is he?'' Jane noted the flushed faces of the two men. ''I wish he were as intimate with *my* father.'' Her sly tone altered to one of cajolement. ''Why not take tea with me tomorrow? I do not know you half so well as I should like.''

Annalise clapped politely at the end of the waltz. Jane was so sure of herself as the belle of Kanpur that she did not trouble to be subtle. She had ignored Annalise completely until now, when she saw a possible route to Derek. Aristocrats in the East India Company's army were virtually nonexistent and so even if Derek had the temperament of a boar hog, he should be the catch of Kanpur. As it was, he was utterly charming when he liked . . . if blunt, and hot-tempered when he disliked. Glancing up at the tall, blonde beauty, Annalise wondered idly how the spoiled Jane would weather Derek's impatience with her affectations. Derek had many good qualities, but he was not tolerant of shortcomings in others. He went through servants like a cyclone. The ones who endured his furies would have died for him; the rest departed in quivers of fright and resentment. One either, she considered, hated or loved Derek Clavell. As a result, he had a few devoted friends and a great many enemies.

She started to make an excuse to Jane, then perceived she had no need, for Jane was preoccupied. Derek was walking toward them across the parquet floor clustered with dancers waiting for the next waltz. Jane straightened expectantly.

Oh, let him ask me to dance just this once, wished Annalise wistfully, knowing he would not. Derek did not trouble himself with schoolgirls.

Splendid in blue and gold regimentals, Derek bent over her hand. "May I have this dance, Miss Devon?" His dark, piercing eyes looked at her from a tanned, eagle's face with a predator's high-raked bones and a hard, resolute jaw. At least six feet four inches tall, his broad shoulders were exaggerated by gold epaulettes, and as big-boned as a Russian Cossack, Derek had an unconscious grace that belied his obvious strength.

"I . . . I should be delighted, Colonel Clavell." She accompanied him onto the floor as Jane stared after them, then turned to coldly accept a brevet captain's invitation.

As the strains of the "Imogene Waltz" wafted through the cream and gilt room, Derek led Annalise easily about the floor. Past them drifted women in gowns as varied in shade as summer tulips while the men in mess dress reflected the splendor of the British Indian Army. Naturally graceful, but unaccustomed to dancing, Annalise was a trifle stiff. Her rigidity gave her a strangely dignified air, as if she were an alert young owl on her first flight. Despite the heat and the raven hair sticking to her neck, she appeared cool and collected, her fine-boned, heart-shaped face reflecting none of her discomfort. Her face foreshadowed a drowsy sultriness that belied her alert, active spirit as Derek surveyed her.

Annalise was growing up into a beauty who looked very much like a seductive belle next to Jane Witherton. She was not old enough to be married, but in a year or two, Derek knew that William would need to secure her future. Yet finding a suitable mate among the many cantonment bachelors would be difficult. Most of the East India Company clerks and merchants were a shade too foppish for such a vibrant young woman. And it would be a shame if she married a soldier and was made a widow before she turned thirty. She had an elusive charm that wrapped a pool of tranquility about her.

Derek had first met her and her father on the Grand Trunk

Road. The fragile girl and frail old man, so alone in their stranded *ghari* cart, had tugged at his heart, and since then he had learned to admire their indomitable determination to be of service to anyone who needed their help.

He was particularly drawn to Annalise. Her silken way of moving seemed to frequently hover in his mind, as did her mysterious, feline face with those enormous, liquid eyes that seemed to look right through a man, then veil her thoughts as if she were comtemplating all she had seen. He knew she might well find him wanting in many ways, not the least for his many trysts among the ladies. He had not found a woman in India to suit him, just as he could not imagine a man suitable for Annalise.

With the flicker of a smile playing about his lips, Derek spoke close to Annalise's ear. "You look quite grown-up tonight, Puss."

At the use of the nickname, Annalise flushed. She knew well enough that her girlish blue tarlatan with its demurely scooped bodice and ribbon-sashed waist made her look younger than her age. Still, if she had worn Jane's sophisticated gold moire, Derek would have merely laughed at her outright. The glimmer of age-old instinct cast its subtle light through her eyes. She wagered he would not laugh if she put on a native, clinging sari.

"I'd give a sovereign for those thoughts," observed Derek with an intent look. "What are you thinking, you little witch?"

"I am not the child you imagine, Colonel," she replied, a note of indignation coloring her soft, liquid contralto. "Why do you persist in not letting me grow up?"

"Perhaps I am trying to protect myself," he teased. "You show every sign of turning into a raving beauty, you know."

"I do not believe that," she said in a stifled tone, the color flaring into her cheeks. "Please, tease the other ladies, if you like, but do not tease me."

"Why not? Have you no sense of playfulness?"

"I have too often heard you bait those whom you dislike."

A slow smile crossed Derek's lips. "I also bait those I like very much."

Her head came up abruptly, acute wariness concealing the irrepressible hope in her eyes. "Are you flirting with me, Colonel?" she murmured gravely, her voice unconsciously seductive.

He laughed outright. "No, indeed, Miss Devon. I should never do anything so daring . . . particularly with so serious a personage as yourself."

"You make me sound very dull."

He laughed, his teasing tone becoming ironic. "On the contrary, Miss Devon, you never bore me, which is a good deal more than I can say for most of the females in this room."

"What quality keeps a woman from boring you, Colonel?" asked Annalise curiously. According to gossip, Derek had been involved with a stream of women. None lasted more than a few months, and they came in all heights, shades, and descriptions. Although the transience of his affairs suggested otherwise, she wondered if at heart, he were not lonely.

"A woman must have intelligence," he answered flatly. "And honesty. If she has compassion as well, then the lack of other qualities can be tolerable. I have found, though, that most women are dishonest. Duplicity is bred into them from childhood."

"Then you mistrust them because they are taught to please men."

"Not only that, they are taught that they are inferior to men . . . and they spend the rest of their lives either rebelling or demonstrating the accuracy of the theory."

"What if a woman merely enjoys being herself?"

"Do you?" His bluntness made the question sound dubious.

"Yes, I think so. Certainly, I should not wish to trade places with you."

He looked taken aback. "Why not?"

"Oh, I think the reasons are rather obvious. For example, either way you turn, you have a brilliant future, whether you decide to stay in the military or return to your estates in England, yet you are restless and bored. From your ironic tone, you sound unhappy and incomplete as though nothing you ever strive for proves satisfactory, women least of all. I suspect you want a woman to be rather like a man, and yet I have never seen you pursue a homely woman." She tilted her head. "Do you not think your demands of women may conflict? You want them to be clever, yet pretty and . . . feminine. You want them to be forthright, yet mysterious and elusive. Is it fair to expect any woman to fulfill such contrary expectations?"

"That's quite a long speech from you, Oyster." The startled expression in his eyes faded to a gleam of cool amusement. His dark head lowered conspiratorially. "Can you keep a secret?"

"You know I can."

"There is such a woman . . . in England."

The blood drained from Annalise's face as her heart began to drum insistently. Stiffly, she followed Derek about the floor through a drifting, rainbow swirl of dancers as he told her about Marian Longstreet. "She's beautiful, a great lady, and a superb rider. You may never meet her, but . . ."

Annalise longed to clasp her hands over her ears and escape from the suddenly stifling room. Why was he telling *her*, of all people, about his prospective fiancée when he had told no one else? She could hardly bear the bright, expectant look in his eyes, the impatient hunger as he described Marian. La Longstreet was a redhead with milk-white skin and emerald eyes. Annalise was sure she would see beautiful Marian in her nightmares.

"She speaks French and German," Derek went on with innocent relentlessness. "She's perfectly trained to be the wife of a diplomat or statesman . . ."

"Is that what you want?" cut in Annalise in bleak desperation. "To be a politician?"

"Someday. I am not cut out to run an estate without some other interest; it's too quiet a life."

"Don't you like being in the military in India?"

"I love it . . ." he hesitated, "but you're right, I don't love being alone." For a moment, his brown eyes beneath their dark lashes were unshielded, their rare vulnerability twisting at her heart.

She got a firm grip on her emotions. "Then why not bring Miss Longstreet here?"

"I lead too risky a life to wish it on a woman . . . besides, Marian dislikes India."

Annalise's ears pricked with a tinge of uneasiness. A woman who loved a man would follow him anywhere. If Derek were her husband, she would be at his side if he were based in darkest Africa. "Did you invite Miss Longstreet to India?"

"Of course not. I haven't proposed yet, but I mean to do so when I return to England." He smiled engagingly. "I cannot have some other fellow snapping her up."

"Perhaps," said Annalise with a devilish flicker of renewed hope in her eyes, "she has already been snapped up."

The shadow that crossed his face turned the edge of her hope against her. "I hope not. Marian is all I have ever wanted in a mate."

I hate her! thought Annalise vehemently as the music ended and he led her off the floor. I may be wicked, particularly when we have never met, but Marian Longstreet sounds too perfect to be real.

She was still inwardly fuming when her father asked her for the next dance. After they had been some minutes on the floor, William cocked his head. "What is the matter, kitten? You're looking woebegone."

Annalise's chin lifted abruptly as a flush colored her face. She could hardly confess her uncharitable and immodest thoughts to William. "Nothing's the matter, Papa. I . . . my shoe is pinching." The half-lie tweaked her sense of guilt, for she was unaccustomed to being less than honest, particularly with William.

"I hope you are not in too much pain to yield me the next polka as well, Miss Devon," her father teased.

She laughed in spite of herself. "Why, Papa, you are reckless. Next, you will want to try the gavotte with Jane Witherton!"

"I shall leave that to Derek Clavell and the other young bloods." He eyed her with more shrewdness than she liked. "You would do well not to cultivate any notions about Derek, m'dear. He's too old and jaded for you."

Annalise caught her breath. "Colonel Clavell is only thirty, Papa." Her parry held a thread of anger that ran through her discomfort. "Besides, he's seasoned, not dissolute. And as for notions . . ."—her voice dwindled—"I'm very well aware of the distance between Colonel Clavell and myself."

William squeezed her hand. "I know, and you've been a model of self-control, as always. Sometimes, I think you may be too controlled for your age. I just don't want to see you hurt. Should Derek look your way someday, and he very well may, just remember that he is ambitious, and ambitious men don't marry simple clergymen's daughters."

"I shall remember, Papa," she murmured, "but I very much doubt if Colonel Clavell will ever display any interest in me." At her father's sharp look, she added lamely, "I'm far too young and peculiar, both in looks and habits."

Surveying his daughter's long limbs and lovely face, William suppressed a short laugh, his bright blue eyes amused. In a year or two, Annalise would look just like her mother, who'd had beauty enough to draw the attention of the emperor of China. He had never understood how Elizabeth could have been satisfied to be the wife of a dull missionary when she might have married a fortune, but then perhaps, like Annalise, he gave himself too little credit. Despite frequent hardship, Elizabeth had seemed entirely happy during their twenty years of ministry in China. He and Annalise had come last year to India after Elizabeth's death. She and Annalise were so alike: quiet, coolly graceful, studied in thought, yet utterly unpredictable. The sight of Annalise's swallow-wing brows darting above those liquid golden eyes, the proud *hidalga* nose, the heart-shaped face with its exotic planes, made him miss Elizabeth as if he had been dancing with her ghost. And yet, he was happy, too; happier than he had been in months of worry about his daughter's future, and glad to be alive. When the waltz was done, he insisted upon dancing the polka.

"Papa, do you think you should?" protested Annalise as he swung her out onto the floor.

"Should? I must! I feel perfectly splendid!" Minutes later, in the midst of a sprightly canter, he suddenly froze, then crumpled to the floor, his hand clutched to his left arm. As Annalise frantically knelt beside him, her tarlatan winging out, William twisted in pain, his body shuddering. In moments, Derek was at Annalise's side, but he was already too late. William made a choking sound as his body made a last spasmodic contraction, then he was dead, as still and apart from the gaity as a bit of discarded paper. In an agony of grief, Annalise pressed her trembling hand to her lips, forcing back the impulse to throw herself across his still form and scream that he was not dead, but the silence was like a heavy pressure across her heart and mind. He was dead, all his kindness and brave spirit had turned into this white, faded figure which bore so little resemblance to her bright, brave father. Even his soul was gone . . . into God's hands, where it would be safely kept until she followed him in death. If she saw him again . . . only what if she did not? What if her father and all the men of religion were wrong and nothing waited after death but black emptiness forever . . .

Then, she felt Derek gently grasp her shoulder in reassurance, and the tears that had threatened to spill from her eyes ceased. She took a deep, painful breath and fought back her growing fear with faith: the faith learned at William's knee. They would meet again; she knew that quietly in her heart. For the moment, she must go on living in the world and hold her head high. She closed her eyes, willing her heart to slow; then when her hand lowered from her lips to William's, it was steady.

II

A Fall From Pride

The funeral was held in the walled cantonment cemetery at dawn. Gray tinged the worn, tattered palm trees that stood outside the cemetery wall like disregarded mourners. With a black band on the sleeve of his uniform, Derek stood just behind Annalise as the simple wooden coffin was lowered into the earth. Although William's tenure in India had been brief, throngs of people attended the last rites. Annalise received them, her eyes weary from lack of sleep, but dry, as she was not given to public displays of emotion. Her throat was tight as she watched William's coffin being covered with dirt. The mourners slowly faded away to their carriages and horses. Could anyone ever really describe the finality of death? The living spoke of sharp, painful loss, but death was so much more awful than that. Her entire body felt like a black hole of grief, yet she knew worse was to come. Both her sorrow and the certainty of William's inheritance of a serene afterlife came and faded in waves. Now she was numb; the real grief had not yet begun. William had died so suddenly that the abruptness of his loss was like the sharp lash of a whip that struck whenever her mind turned to him. William had been such a loving man, and utterly without ambition. She could remember him with her mother wading through the paddies of China as they assisted their friends and converts in bringing in the rice crop. Her father had loved China, and would be there yet, had he not loved Annalise better. Her mother was buried in China, and after her death, William had changed. For the first time, he looked to his own end as a severance from life and all those dear to him. He understood the pain and bewilderment of those left behind. He began to anticipate the moment when Annalise must hear the hollow echo of the first clod of earth cast upon his coffin. Just as she was hearing it now . . . with inward horror and stinging grief.

When the last mourner took his leave, Annalise felt Derek's hand on her shoulder. His grip was warmly comforting, strong, and she ached to turn and bury her head against his shoulder. Instead, she forced herself to move away. At arm's length, she faced him. "Thank you for coming," she said softly.

"To know your father was a privilege. He was a gentleman." Derek's inflection broke the word *gentle man* into its true sense of kindliness and courtesy. "William had no hypocrisy or cant about him. I shall miss him."

"He liked and respected you. I believe he thought of you as the son he never had."

He walked her slowly from the grave, leading her mercifully away from the sound of the dirt being spaded into the gaping hole in the ground. "Did he discuss anything of the future with you?"

"No. He simply said he would make provision for me. I expect his barrister will make everything clear later this afternoon."

"Did he explain that he had appointed me executor of the estate?"

"Yes."

"And that I am to be your guardian until you marry or reach the age of twenty-one?"

She whitened. "He said nothing of appointing a guardian! I'm not a child."

Derek sympathized with Annalise's discomfiture. He had been startled himself when William had suggested his protectorship. "Annalise needs the protection, and you need the responsibility," William had informed him. "You've been in India too long, Derek. You're as civilized as a Tartar."

Derek took Annalise's arm. "You just turned seventeen last month. That's entirely too young to marry. Besides, for you to remain alone in India would not do. I want you to come home with me."

She stared at him. "You cannot be serious." Then gauging the adamant look in his eyes, she said abruptly, "The gossip would be extreme."

"Do you care? I don't."

Annalise was doubly uneasy. She had often been to entertainments in Derek's house, but she had never felt comfortable in it. The unimagined luxury of uncounted servants and lavish meals thrice daily had never put her at ease. The house, like Derek Clavell, was aggressively masculine, its walls covered with deep green leather and hunting trophies. She could almost smell Derek in the mellow scent of saddle soap and cinnamon that lingered about the generous rooms. "Surely, Father never meant . . ." she began.

"He didn't, but then he had no real idea of the trouble brewing in India. John Company has annexed half of the states of India by declaring their adoptive heirs invalid and having its army enforce suzerainty. Even the *badahur shah* in Delhi is ruler in name only. Over the years, the British East India Company has come to spend less time in making money in trade and more in its government as Raj. India resents British rule. The people fear their heritage is being threatened, and they are particularly touchy on the point of religion. I've even heard a story that the British are joined in a grand conspiracy to defile the Muslims and make the Hindus lose caste in order to form an army to send against the rest of Asia once India is absorbed into the empire. The charge is false, but there will be trouble, I fear.

"Besides, the arrangement of my guardianship over you would only be temporary, while I am off to the Afghan border. We would scarcely be spending more than a few weeks under the same roof."

"But what shall I do when you return?" she asked faintly.

"You will go home on the first ship from Karachi."

"I don't want to go home!" A healthy note of rebellion tinged her voice, although she was unsure of what she should do instead of returning to England. Her letters of inquiry regarding a governess's position in the cantonment had met with negative response, for she was considered to be too young to hold a position of such responsibility.

"Well, you cannot stay here. One day soon, all India may rise in insurrection. John Company is too small a giant to control the vast population of India. When the powder keg explodes, I want you as far away as possible."

"This cannot be what my father planned. He wouldn't . . ."

"He didn't. He wanted you to stay in India." He handed her up into his barouche. "But he also wanted me to use my best judgement. I should be a poor guardian if I let you run the risk of enduring a possible mutiny."

After prolonged argument as he drove her along the broad, pebbled cantonment avenue with its clapboard and stucco bungalows set in curved flower beds of marigolds and fuchsias, Annalise settled into numb despair. Her father would never have made Derek her guardian had he known that her attachment to him ran far deeper than a schoolgirl's infatuation. And to leave India . . . to return to stiff England and abandon all the bright color and adventure of the East . . .

Derek ignored her silence as they drove through the cantonment. She suspected he was used to dealing with recalcitrant females, but she could not summon the strength to fight him. Despite her knowledge of her father's weak heart, his death had occurred so suddenly that she was unprepared to deal with the abrupt cruelty of his loss. And now, to lose India as well . . . She stole a look at Derek's face. His darkly tanned features were set, adamant, yet a tiny frown lowering his strongly marked brows hinted at his preoccupation. For the first time since she had known him, Annalise sensed he was worried, and not entirely about her. Rumors had been circulating about a mutiny for some months now, but otherwise life had gone on as usual. There were no riots, no killings. From so many years in China, she knew there could be undercurrents of violence and tension beneath the Buddhistic calm of India's religious streams, but weren't rumors to be expected, when so few governed so many?

And yet Derek was not the sort of man who started at shadows. If the entire country rose, the English would be overrun and massacred.

She looked up at his sprawling house when the carriage halted at the end of the fenced walk lined with Shasta daisies. The familiar bungalow was handsome, its stuccoed walls roofed with terra-cotta tile, the arched windows finely trimmed with green, yellow, and black mosaic. Inside was a fortune in silver, fine paintings, and Moorish and Indian furniture. A rebellion would destroy it all: a way of life. So many women and children would die. So many men would die trying to protect them. Although she was not fearful for her own life, she was concerned for Derek. He would be far safer in the company of professional soldiers in a garrison than trying to guard her in an indefensible house. She touched his arm as he stepped from the carriage and turned to assist her. "I shall be glad to go to England, Colonel, if you think it wise."

Surprised at her demure acceptance, Derek led her into the house. He had assumed Annalise Devon had more grit than she was showing. Her father had fought him for weeks over her staying in India, yet she gave up the conflict with scarcely a whimper. Perhaps this guardian episode would not be the pesky nuisance he had expected. In a couple of months, Miss Devon would be off to England with his barrister to see her installed in a tidy town house. In a couple of years, she would be married and that would be the end of his obligations. Not that he wouldn't miss her badly; she had a winsome manner, with those lustrous golden eyes that promised to melt a man until he overflowed his boot tops, and that slim figure that moved with all the soundless grace of a cat. Unlike many misses, she was not frivolous, but then she was not much given to conversation. No chatter from Annalise Devon, and no proselytizing. William had more of a sense of humor than Annalise, yet there were times when her eyes held a sparkle of amusement at the oddest things . . . like the time his horse had started at a darting mongoose and dumped him on his posterior. She might have enjoyed seeing his dignity ruffled, but then he suspected she disdained pretense of any kind. She never wore jewelry on her plain, dark dresses, never even a ringlet in her smooth black hair, yet simplicity suited her. There was a quietude about her manner and movements that suggested a sense of inner peace that radiated to those about her. He often enjoyed her company, but of late she had avoided him. Perhaps she knew more than he assumed of her father's plans to appoint him her guardian, and disapproved William's choice. He could not say *he* approved of William's decision, but the two of them were stuck with it.

He handed Annalise from the carriage and walked her up the gravelled path to his bungalow. Inside, they met a modestly dressed, auburn-haired woman of middle age. "This is Mrs. Sarah Quill. I have engaged her as your companion until you sail."

Annalise stifled an inward sigh. Not only was she to be exiled, she must make drawing-room conversation for the next two months with a chaperone when she would have much preferred solitude. Nevertheless, she greeted the woman cordially. "I hope we shall become great friends, Mrs. Quill. Have you been in India long?"

"Forty years," replied Sarah Quill with an amused glint in her eye. "And I can affirm that a woman alone must tread a hard road in Asia, but then you must know that after so long in China."

Annalise liked Sarah Quill. A pleasant-looking, comfortably rounded matron with level blue eyes, she had a practical, no-nonsense way about her without being oppressive. They chatted pleasantly for a few minutes, then Annalise retired to her room before tea. She had been without sleep since her father died. The remainder of her childhood had died with him. The shock of his loss was beginning to wear off, and the pain of it was starting to seep into her consciousness. She desperately wanted the solace of sleep. Perhaps Derek had been not merely discreet in engaging Mrs. Quill, but wise in securing a companion to distract her from the harshness of her grief. She missed William badly. She was so accustomed to seeing him digging gleefully into the marmalade every morning as he described his projects for the day. She would often comment, "Father, you apply yourself to saving souls like a terrier." While he never intruded himself, people always wondered how he knew just the right moment to suggest God's assistance in their dilemmas. So often, he seemed to read her own mind, yet she wondered if he realized how much she cared for Derek. And why.

She understood that Derek had been brought up amidst great wealth and luxury. She had observed that he was spoiled and accustomed to having his own way, particularly with women; yet despite that flaw, he had been unfailingly kind to her father and her. Poor as proverbial church mice, she and William had little in common with Derek, yet he and William had gotten on splendidly. After having his squadron rescue their *ghari* cart from the mire of the road to Kanpur, he had made introductions for them throughout the cantonment and had teased several social patrons into making a generous donation to the mission. Baldly asserting that it was an Indian custom, he often sent them food in large, beribboned hampers on the pretext of celebrating some Buddhist or Hindu holiday to prevent their thinking of his gifts as charity. As often as not, William would throw a feast for all his native converts. Still, Derek never recognized his own virtues. He considered himself a selfish, trivial man. Every hostess in the cantonment wanted Derek at her entertainments; every mother hurled her marriageable daughters at him. His social calendar was packed, yet Annalise sometimes saw a wistfulness in his eyes that hinted at his loneliness.

Annalise removed her veiled bonnet, loosened her black clothing, and lay down on her bed veiled by mosquito netting. The sun was nearing noon and the heat approached that of an early summer morning. China had not been so hot . . . or so crowded. India sometimes seemed to be a ceaseless stream of people: Sikhs, Muslims, Hindus, Tamils, Pathans: all rivals and all suspicious of one another. Disease-ridden and dirty, India had few baths other than the rivers, and was increasingly resentful of English domination, yet Annalise loved its exoticism; its frequent dazzling beauty; its pageantry. She even loved curry. And she loved Derek, who would soon be as unreachable as her father. *I loathe cold, clammy England!* she raged inwardly as she lay stiffly on the linen slanted with stripes of hot sunlight from the blinds. *I shouldn't care if I never see it again. India is where*

Father and Derek are, and I want to be near them, not shelved like an unripened pomegranate until I turn twenty-one.

In time, frustration sank into grief for William, and she wept until teatime. When she descended the stairs, her eyes were puffy and swollen. Mrs. Quill nodded approvingly. "Best to let it all out. I was afraid you were one of those stoic sorts who cultivates an ulcer." She led the way to the conservatory where the grand piano filled a third of the room. "Colonel Clavell has gone to make certain preparations for his regiment to leave for Kabul next week. He sends his regrets." She sat down behind the waiting teapot. "He also asked me to tell you that a house will be available to you in London, and his solicitor at your disposal. You are to want for nothing."

"How very generous of Colonel Clavell," responded Annalise quietly as she took her seat. "He has always been most considerate."

"My husband was in his regiment. Since George's death two years ago in '54, Colonel Clavell has seen to it that Timmy and I have a roof over our heads. I don't know how many regimental widows he has provided for, but there must be a good number of them." Mrs. Quill poured the tea, then handed Annalise a cup. "Still, I have never known him to extend his generosity outside the regiment."

"He liked my father." Having no appetite for the small anise cakes dusted with powdered sugar, Annalise sipped her tea.

Mrs. Quill lifted an auburn brow. "Do you not imagine that he likes you as well?"

Annalise eyed her coolly. "I beg your pardon."

"You realize, of course, that there may be gossip, if Colonel Clavell provides a house for you."

"You appeared to have ignored any gossip," retorted Annalise crisply.

Mrs. Quill smiled. "Bravo. You will need that sort of

spirit in the future if you are to keep any company with Colonel Clavell. I would have joined you at your own house, but Colonel Clavell thought the memories might be difficult for you. As his house will be vacant for several months, he thought you might enjoy the change."

Then he should have asked me whether I should like the idea, thought Annalise, but said nothing. To fly in the face of Derek's good intentions would be unworthy of her. Her father had meant to accomplish something more than her comfort in appointing Derek her guardian, and until she understood what William had in mind, she had best play her part cheerfully. Then, if she disagreed with her father's assessment, she could politely withdraw.

The days until Derek's departure passed quickly, and Annalise was preoccupied with grief. The luxury of the large house, with its splendid paintings and trophies setting off the dark Asiatic furniture seemed alien, yet while she would have preferred the simplicity and cozy memories of her own bungalow, she was grateful for the company of the servants, Mrs. Quill, and the many officers who called. Derek was rarely there, and Annalise had the impression that he would have been gone more often, had he not felt an obligation to be with her. On his way out to an engagement one evening, he had touched her cheek in a teasing farewell. She bit her lip, waved goodbye, and thought sadly that he would see her as a child for the next twenty years.

Annalise rose before dawn to join Mrs. Quill and the house staff waiting on the steps to see Derek off to Kabul. More than one face was tear streaked in the flickering torchlight. She tried to hide her own fears as Derek clasped her hand in farewell. Stories of the Afghan border had begun to crowd her mind these last few days. Just twenty years ago, the British Raj had fought a bloody war with the Afghans and had been forced into a disastrous retreat that left fourteen thousand bodies rotting in the high passes of the Hindu Kush. Even in times of peace, the Afghans were a hard-fighting lot given to blood feuds and murder.

She caught his hand after he had swung up on his horse. "Do take care. I shall pray for your safety and that of your men."

He smiled at her impulsiveness. "We shall be grateful for your concern, but do not fret overmuch. We're a hardy lot, and used to rough treatment." Looking down, he squeezed her hand. "I've left Mrs. Quill with instructions to see to a new wardrobe for you. Your father would want you to wear bright colors again once your term of mourning is done. One day, I will introduce you to a round of eager officers."

She wondered how eager the officers would be once they learned she had no dowry. . . unless Derek meant to provide her with one in addition to a wardrobe. His very generosity might be an indication of his willingness to be rid of her. To be fair, one could not blame him. After all, she was not a relative, nor even a regimental widow, and Derek did not lead the sort of life that suited guardianship for a young woman. Quelling her uncharitable thoughts, she replied, "Please do not trouble yourself on my account, Colonel. Mrs. Quill and I shall be well occupied in teaching at the mission school."

He laughed ruefully. "So much sobriety may be excellent for your character, but it does little for the bloom in your cheeks. Still, I will not preach to a minister's daughter." He caught up his reins. "Goodbye, and do not forget, I want roast beef on my first night home." Touching his helmet, he nudged the horse into a trot to the head of the column of waiting riders beneath the tamarind trees. Annalise watched the squadron until they disappeared beyond the great wrought-iron gate, then turned to Mrs. Quill. "I shall want to stay exceedingly busy until the first letter arrives from Kabul."

Mrs. Quill smiled. "You have the makings of an excellent soldier's wife, my dear."

* * *

"So this is the Kyber Pass," Smathers murmured.

"Eh?" Derek questioned, still scanning the heights.

"The Kyber," Smathers repeated. "Do you know how long armies have been marching through here? The Greek general Hephaeston crossed here with part of Alexander the Great's army."

"Where did Alexander cross?" Derek asked absently. He and his sergeant major were riding knee to knee, reins held lightly in one hand, each man intently watching his side of the pass.

"Oh, somewhere to the north, through the mountains."

"Bloody smart bastard," the sergeant major muttered. He then quickly glanced back at Lieutenant Smathers. "Beggin' your pardon, sir, I meant Alexander, not yourself. I mean . . ."

"Steady, Sergeant Major. We know what you mean. Less than a mile now to the fort at Ali Masjid."

"That's good," the lieutenant said, with patent relief.

"Not really. We still must get through the narrowest part of the pass, just ahead. It will be tight."

"Tighter'n a virgin's arse," the sergeant major muttered, even more quietly.

The boulder-strewn slopes flanking the pass began to press inwards, narrowing their path. The river was gone now, replaced by a deep, rocky gully. The pass constricted the gulch and road to less than fifty feet across, with steep walls of rock rising on either side, hiding the hills and mountains above. Derek reached up to rub his neck as he walked his horse into shadow, his eyes still scanning the rock. He wished absently that Smathers would stop rattling on about Greek generals and listen. Derek was listening intently, trying to blot out the jingle of harnesses and creak of saddles. He also listened for the scrape of steel on rock and for the small rock slides set off by careless men taking position above them. Hearing nothing, he smiled grimly. That means, he thought, there is no one up there, which he doubted, having seen two turbans in the last half-hour, or there are no careless men up there, a different thing altogether.

The sunshine was eye-watering after the shade as they rode out of the narrows to see the short mud towers of Ali Masjid over the next hill. Their relief evident, the men of the vanguard started chattering again. Derek noticed a trickle of sweat running down the middle of his back. The sweat turned icy cold and the chatter died as they heard the crackle of musket fire behind them. Derek whirled his white mare on her haunches and saw the pass quickly choked with fleeing bullocks, camels, men, and horses. The entire baggage train was trying to get through the narrowest part of the entire pass, shouldering, pushing, shoving. A half-dozen bullocks were already lying broken and bellowing at the bottom of the gully. The musket fire continued. They were either thieves, intent on cutting out a few bullocks, or another Afghan tribe jealous of the wealth being delivered by the baggage train to the Zakakhel as tribute.

A bee zipped by Derek's ear and the sepoy behind him screamed and clutched his face, falling backwards over the tail of his horse. Derek caught sight of a half-dozen turbans on a rocky promontory overlooking their position. The attackers were too well organized to be bandits. "They are trying to cut the column in two and annihilate the rear guard," Derek shouted to Smathers and the sergeant major. Derek whipped his saber from his saddle scabbard and whirled it in a glittering arc around his head. Above the thrum of his circling blade, he shouted to his sepoys, "At them, my children! Let us thrash these brigands." He spurred his mare right up the rocky slope towards the small force sent to keep them from returning through the pass. With a deep-throated roar, the entire *risala* followed.

The sight of an entire cavalry *risala* impossibly charging up the slope directly at them so unnerved the Afghans that several turned heel and fled, heading higher into the hills. The rest worked frantically to reload their muzzle-loading *jezails*. The charge was impossible and quickly bogged down as the blown horses slithered back on their haunches in the talus. Derek jammed a horse pistol down each boot top and leaped from the saddle to a boulder the size of a kitchen table. A third pistol in his hand boomed and a turbaned head up the hill dropped from sight.

"Come, my children," he yelled to the sepoys dismounting all around him. "They flee before your fangs." Derek bounded up the hill, leaping from boulder to boulder where possible, scrambling up the loose scree between boulders, his heart hammering in his chest, his throat dry to cracking as he panted hoarsely. A bullet whipped an epaulette from his shoulder as he shouted with the last of his breath, "Come, lads, they can't hit anything with those *jezails*," and charged on. Two more sepoys dropped before the dismounted *risala* reached the top of the little round-topped knoll.

Two bundles of rags that had been men lay bleeding on the rock while a third tried to crawl away. A sepoy hacked and the wounded man lay still. "Bloody Gilzais," the sergeant major panted, toeing another body. "They're jealous, thieving bastards."

Derek, too, was breathing hard, leaning on his sword and looking around. The hilltop was well situated. While the mountains rose above and behind, the hill overlooked both ends of the pass. More importantly, they looked down on the Afghans on the other side of the pass who were pouring fire into the packed mob in the narrows. The ambushing Afghans were themselves about to be ambushed.

"Lieutenant Smathers, kindly take a dozen men to the edge of the hill and bring those tribesmen over there under fire. If we can sweep them from the ridge, our men will be able to get through the pass. It's a long range for pistol fire so gather up a *jazail* or two and send one man back down to the horses for all the carbines he can carry. Oh, send another man for the water bottles, if he can catch the horses. Sergeant Major, you and I will take the men we have left and form a perimeter here, to await the counterattack. We've got the high ground. Now we must hold it."

The crackle of gunfire from the edge of the little, round-topped hill began to whip across the exposed Gilzais below them. The surprised shouts and cries from the Afghans as they ducked and dodged for cover was audible above the melee in the pass. The sepoys, mounted irregular *hircarrahs*, and drovers lately caught in the pass by the Afghan fire from above, quickly seized the respite and pushed through toward Ali Masjid.

Derek and his men began to pile rocks up into a defensive position. There was an abundance of material and a crude barricade arose in front of each group of three sepoys. Derek paused to take a swallow of the warm, slightly foul water in the waterskin before surveying his own work. His father would have never approved of such sloppy construction back in Sussex, but for his purpose, "'t'was enough, t'will serve."

Commotion began above them. The sepoys rose from tending the wounded, collecting powder and shot from the dead, or frantically laying rock upon rock. They lay their carbines over the rocks, pistols beside them, squinting up the hill into the hot, searing sun, looking expectantly at the sound of cymbals and whistles growing ever louder.

"Look about you, lads," the sergeant major roared. "Nothing in the manual of arms says the bastards have to come from the place of most noise." But they did, a hundred or so, long black robes flapping like gigantic birds of prey, with long talons of bloody steel. Flags, fringed white silk with gold trim, with red and black devices, led the charging horde. There was time for two crashing volleys, which staggered the front rank of attackers, and the bulk of Gilzais were at the little rampart where bloody, frenetic work began.

"Stop 'em 'ere, lads. Stop 'em 'ere or else they'll murder us all as you try to run." The murder was being performed close at hand as the Afghans swarmed over the small stone barricade and into the closely packed British.

Derek whirled to face a second wave of black-bearded warriors cresting the ramparts. A ragged crash of musketry sounded behind him, a ball grazed his cheek and the wave of Afghan warriors tumbled at his feet. "Huzzah! Huzzah! Rah! Rah! Rah!" the old Rugby school cheer came from Smathers as he led the remains of his squad into the breach. The extra men stemmed the tide but momentarily, the Afghans losing momentum but not heart.

The rasp of gasping and ring of steel were the loudest sounds as shouts died for lack of breath. Smathers and Derek were fighting shoulder to shoulder, two against five, scientific training and old-school discipline pitted against natural talent and ferocity. The odds had been whittled to three to two when a backhand slash from a double-edged scimitar opened Billy Smathers' throat. In some corner of his mind, Derek had time to reflect, there goes two thousand pounds of education to a five-rupee blade. Derek caught the Afghan in the ear with a thrust of his saber, then went down himself under a slashing blow that took away his other epaulette and left his left arm numb.

The sergeant major loomed over him, an apparition with his face a mask of blood, swinging his carbine as a club. Two Gilzais turned their attention from Derek to attack the bloody mask but both went down under the madly swinging weapon. Derek scrambled up, saber on guard, standing back to back with the wild-eyed sergeant major. His vision began to narrow and grow gray. His breath was a rasping roar and his legs and sword arm were leaden. Back to back with the sergeant major and the last sepoy, they hacked desperately at anything before them. From behind him came yet another clash of cymbals and rattle of war yells as another group of bearded warriors swept towards them and green silk flags rose from the new direction. Derek stepped back, then uttered a hoarse cry as he stumbled into a rock crevice. Just as his leg snapped above the ankle, a *jezail* bullet bored into his back. At a sharp pain slicing into his brain, Derek pitched into a black well of silence.

After the conflict was done, two tall Pathans in flowing robes and black turbans stood over the pile of bodies heaped around the meager stone barricades thrown up by the British. Idly, they poked about with their swords. One with a henna-red beard spat on an upturned, dark face whose jaw had been cut away and whose eyes were unblinking in the harsh sun. "Gilzai dogs. This one has been taught not to steal rightful tribute from we Zakakhel." He turned to his companion who was staring thoughtfully at the fallen sepoys. "These British fight well. Too bad they were mostly dead by the time we got word the Gilzai dogs were nipping at them. Maybe we should take our rightful silver and let the survivors pass in peace."

The other one nodded, prodding at Derek's inert form. "We should take this one down to Peshawar. He is an officer and if he lives, we will get a silver ransom."

His companion looked dubious. "We should make a wager to guarantee at least some profit. Three coins says he will not make it halfway down this pass to Peshawar."

"Done."

III

Those Who Wait

"N*early* four months without a word," Sarah Quill railed. "How can you sit there so calmly?"

"Our anxiety will not speed Colonel Clavell's letters," replied Annalise with a tranquility she did not feel. She plied her needle to her cross-stitch with a steady, relentless hand. Distraction was the only way she could control her concern, which more than matched Sarah's. The linen represented hundreds of neat, precise stitches and hours of worry.

Sarah paced past the windows. "Colonel Clavell's being sent to Kabul should not matter so much, but to keep peace in the Kyber . . ." She shuddered. "The Afghans are never reliable."

"If one equates reliability with docility," Annalise replied evenly, "I suppose not . . . but Colonel Clavell expected the duty to be hazardous, and if there has been trouble, the dispatches may have been delayed. Then again"—she snipped off a tail of thread from a knot—"Colonel Clavell may merely be an indifferent writer."

"How well do you know him?" asked Sarah curiously.

"Not well at all. He was my father's friend."

Sarah came to sit beside her. Peering over her shoulder, she scrutinized the needlework of a Persian court scene. "Timmy and I might have starved if Colonel Clavell had not intervened in our behalf. We owe him a great deal."

"As do I, and as you say, so do numerous regimental widows about the settlement."

Sarah nodded. "Colonel Clavell has made certain they have passage home."

"He seems eager to send everyone home." Annalise rethreaded her needle. "He is convinced there will be trouble in India in the near future."

"I'm not," replied Sarah. "Our Indians aren't shifty like the Afghans. Why, we've given them sensible government, roads, railroads; improved their sanitation . . ."

"What if they don't want all these improvements? What if they just want life to go on as usual?"

"Life as usual includes *suttee* and *thuggee*: widows being burnt alive with their dead husbands, and stranglers murdering innocent people to exalt that heathen goddess, Kali. Surely, you don't think these practices should continue?"

"I think they're abominable, but I also see us as foreigners dictating to the native population, a population which does not wish to accept change. We are like a handful of yellow sand tossed onto a black, volcanic beach. Every morning at sunrise, we expect the entire beach to turn yellow." She took three stitches. "This seems particularly unreasonable when the yellow adamantly refuses to mix with the black. It's all rather one way, isn't it?"

Sarah regarded her soberly. "You *are* a rebel. Does Colonel Clavell support your notions?"

"I have no idea. My father did, and that is all that matters."

Sarah frowned. "You do like Colonel Clavell, do you not?"

"I think he is mule headed, arrogant, and spoiled; otherwise, he is delightful. My father liked him enormously, which is a great deal to his credit, but then Papa liked a great many people, particularly the Chinese, who have almost limitless patience. Papa was certain that every soul is perfectible, given time."

"So your father thought he could reform Derek?"

Sarah's use of Derek's given name caught Annalise's sharp notice. Sarah also sounded amused, which suggested she knew Derek extremely well. "Did you?" countered Annalise.

Sarah was taken aback. "Did I what?"

"Propose to reform Derek?"

Sarah flushed. "I suppose I do sound overconcerned about him . . . which may lead to misunderstanding . . ." She faltered, then added lamely, "He has been so very kind to Timmy and me. Thanks to this companionship position, we shall have our passage money back to England in a few months. He offered to give us the money outright after George died of cholera, but I wouldn't take it." She hesitated. "I didn't want to become dependent . . . start to care too much. There was no point in it, you see."

Annalise saw. The pair of them had the same problem. She touched Sarah's hand. "Don't worry. I shall never say anything . . . and I understand, better than you may think." Seeing Sarah's dismal face, she squeezed her shoulders. "Perhaps a letter may come today."

But none did; not the next day, or the next. The brutal heat of July changed to the suffocating heat of August without word.

Late in the afternoon of August sixteenth, when the heat

lay on the house like a stifling blanket, a dusty *ghari* pulled by two weary horses slowly rumbled into the courtyard. Ahmed Khan, Derek's syce, slid down from the box and bade the driver to lend him a hand. The two women, followed by a handful of servants, hurried into the courtyard, their hands shielding their eyes from the hot, harsh sunlight. As the women reached the *ghari*, Ahmed and the driver lifted out Derek's limp, unconscious form. Sarah knelt by his bandaged head with a muted cry. "He's been wounded!"

Ahmed nodded gravely. "The sahib has a broken leg, also a back wound from a Gilzai bullet. The Gilzais, may Allah blight their treacherous hearts, fell upon the sahib and his squadron in the Kyber Pass. The sahib and a few troopers gave the rest of us a chance to escape by holding off the Gilzais. The ones who escaped returned with reinforcements to carry away the wounded and cover the retreat. The sahib is very ill indeed."

Then why did the doctor send him home in this heat when he would have been better off in Kabul, Annalise wanted to demand, but held her tongue. Quickly, she guided the stretcher bearers to Derek's room with Sarah frantically following along behind them. When Derek was put to bed, Annalise ordered the driver to fetch the cantonment doctor, then asked Sarah to see that the servants brought cool water and lemonade in case Derek woke. Once Sarah was out of the room, she turned to Ahmed. "Why did the doctor in Kabul send the sahib home when he is so severely wounded?"

When he told her, she went pale. "Does the sahib know?"

"No, memsahib. He has been too ill to be inquisitive."

"Good. Say nothing to the other memsahib. I will tell the colonel myself when he is stronger. He will need to devote all his determination to healing."

She left Ahmed to undress his master, rather than offend

the syce's Muslim sensibilities, and met Sarah on the stairs with the basin of water. "Give Ahmed five minutes, then let him bathe the colonel. I shall send up some gruel at sunset." With that, she left Sarah to tend to Derek, knowing that being of service would ease her mind. She relieved her at midnight that evening. Near morning, Derek began to stir, his perspiring face half-obscured by its bulky bandage. Twisting, he threw off part of the sheet, baring his upper torso and hip. Truly, thought Annalise with a flush mounting in her cheeks, he is a magnificent man. Wide-shouldered, with a crisply curling black pelt covering his chest beneath its heavy bandage, Derek had a flat stomach and slim horseman's hips. Beneath the sheet stretched his long legs. A hard-muscled arm flung out toward her as he muttered something in Pushtu under his breath, then swore vehemently in the king's English. "Get fucked, you bastards!" he shouted, then began to mumble again, this time for water.

Quickly, she poured him a drink of water, then slipped her arm under his head. His head was heavy and difficult to lift, but she managed to get a little water down his throat. As he was drinking his eyes opened and he made an effort to speak. "Why . . . is it so dark? Where . . . what is happening?"

"It is night and you are safe in Kanpur. Most of your squadron is in Kabul." Her fingers closed over his.

He peered up at her, his eyes dazed with pain and grogginess from the laudanum the doctor had given him. "Is . . . that Annalise?"

"Yes."

His fingers tightened on hers. "You're like . . . the end to a foul nightmare. I feel . . . as if I were still dreaming, only now . . . I dream of angelic peace . . ."

She laughed softly. "Your dream is real enough, for I am no angel."

"You cannot know . . . what it was like." His face flushed

with fever, he struggled to continue. "They cut us to ribbons . . ."

"That is all over now. You must not try to talk any more, but rest and regain your strength."

He seemed not to hear her. "How . . . how many men . . . came back?"

"I will answer you in the morning if you will sleep tonight, but rest assured that many survived."

Despite his weakness, his grip did not lessen on her hand. "Stay with me for a bit. Talk to me about England . . . anything. I need . . . to clear my mind . . . think about ordinary life . . ."

She laughed. "I've never led an ordinary life by English standards. I spent my first fifteen years in China. My teething toy was an abacus."

Sweat from pain and heat bathed his brow. "Then tell me about China."

So she told him about spending her childhood in quilted pajamas, of seeing silkworms at their weaving, and the antics of her pet marmoset in Canton. At long last, his ragged breathing evened and he fell asleep.

The next weeks were an extension of the nightmare Derek had known in the Kyber Pass. Tossing on his bed, he was feverish the whole time. His leg caused him terrible pain but eventually began to heal; his back did not. Lying on his stomach, he developed rashes which broke open and became bed sores.

"Find me a sheepskin," commanded the doctor.

"You cannot be serious," Annalise returned. "He's already burning up."

"I don't want to cover him with it. Clean the sheepskin well and put it under him. The lanolin should afford him some relief."

The sores healed, but Derek remained feverish. One noon when the heat was oppressive, Derek uttered a muffled sound of pain as he stirred fitfully. His hair clinging damply to his brow, his dark-lashed eyes flickered open. Seeing Annalise as a silhouette with her back to the shuttered light, he lifted his head slightly. "Marian?" he whispered weakly in some confusion. "How did you come here?"

"I am Annalise," she said softly. "Don't you recognize me now?"

He gazed at her for a long time in dazed wonderment. "I am . . . in Kanpur?"

"Yes, and entirely safe." She took his hot hand. "You have been wounded, but you are healing now. All you need do is rest a bit and let us look after you."

He frowned slightly, still confused. "Where . . . where is Marian? She should be here."

Annalise touched his forehead. He was still feverish and half-delirious. The wound which had so nearly shattered his spine was seeping yellow liquid. "Marian is in England. Had you forgotten? She must be waiting for you to become well enough to write her."

"Write . . . for me," he whispered. "With my . . . love. Say I . . . haven't forgotten . . ."

"Don't trouble yourself," she reassured him with a pang of pain at his longing. "Surely, Marian is waiting for you and you will be together again."

He still did not seem to understand. "Marian, defy my father . . . and come away . . . to India with me. Too long . . . without you."

Now a bit bewildered herself, Annalise murmured, "Derek, I don't understand. I'm not . . ."

"Kiss me, Marian," he whispered urgently. "Now. Here. I need you . . ."

Before Annalise realized what was happening, his feverish fingers had tangled in her hair and were drawing her down to meet his heated lips. His kiss was ravenous, the kiss of a man losing the last thing he loved. Despite his weakness, his arms wound hard about her, his lips capturing hers as surely as if he had known her a lifetime. Her head spun, her wits careening away under the possessive certainty of his lips. Her hair came loose from its pins, and spilled down to cascade about his shoulders. Dizzy, yet stable as she discovered the certain center of her longing, she returned his kiss with an awkward, slowly growing ardor that intensified his passion. "Let me make love to you . . . one last time," he whispered huskily. "Meet me at the boathouse tonight."

"What? I-I cannot," Annalise stammered, her face flushed scarlet. "How can you think I . . ."

His face drew away from hers sharply, his passion-filled eyes narrowing as reality intervened with the clarity of a dash of ice water. "Who . . . the hell are you?" His eyes widened slightly. "Annalise! I'm . . . damned . . . well sorry. I must have been . . . out of my mind." Then his lips curved with a trace of dazed relish. "Annalise." He uttered her name softly, as if he were hearing it for the first time, sounding each syllable as if it were a sweet, lulling bell. "Angelic Annalise . . . my little guardian." Still wearing that quizzical, startled smile, he drifted back into sleep.

When he awoke, it was as if he had utterly forgotten the brief, intense kiss they had shared, and for that Annalise was grateful. She would have been mortified had he remembered her increasingly eager response. On the surface, she remained matter-of-fact, but that kiss lingered in her mind for many days. At the oddest moments, when she was sewing or giving directions to the servants, she would imagine his lips brushing hers. Her eyelids would flicker down as her reverie swiftly took her back to the fiery splendor of his embrace. Finally, she forcibly quelled her remembrance by reminding herself that it was Marian, and not herself, he had been kissing with such abandonment. To Derek Clavell, she was still the meek, modest missionary's daughter. She resolutely resumed that role once again.

Derek was continually in great pain, particularly in the summer's blazing heat. Suffering fierce headaches, he became increasingly feverish, tossing and turning fitfully on perspiration-damp sheets as the *punkah* fan scythed in its slow swing. Annalise and Sarah took turns reading to him when he was willing, but he paid scant attention to anything. At length, Annalise ordered *charpoy* placed on the upstairs verandah, so that he might sleep more comfortably at night. Their evenings were spent talking by the light of an oil lantern that drew myriad insects undiscouraged by the syce and his swatter. In the trees beyond the verandah the chattering of parrots and monkeys blended incongruously with readings of Milton and Thackeray. In time, Derek was able to struggle his way about his room with the aid of crutches, but the fragile furniture soon became scraped and scarred from collisions. "Damned useless leg!" he would swear and veer perilously off in another direction. "I feel like a bull in a china shop! When does this blasted splint come off?"

At last, Annalise could put off the day no longer. One early evening, when the swiftly fading day had left behind a brief purple dusk, she summoned the doctor to remove Derek's splint.

Refusing to let anyone assist him, Derek stumbled across the library, only to fall midway, his leg refusing to support him. The hastily set leg extended at a grotesque angle. "The devil take this useless leg!" he swore furiously as Annalise and Ahmed hurried to help him up. "I cannot even walk decently, far less ride a horse," he said between clenched teeth to the doctor. "How am I supposed to rejoin my squadron next month?"

"You have scant right to complain. You should be dead by now," the doctor retorted crisply, "but if I were you, I should resign my commission. You very likely have nerve damage from that spinal wound. The less active you are for the next several years, the better.'' He tossed the splint fragments on a nearby table. ''For all purposes, sir, you are an invalid.''

Moving between him and the doctor, Annalise took Derek's arm. ''Will you go upstairs now? I've had your valet lay out your night clothes.''

Distraught, Derek started to remark that she knew damned well he did not wear night clothes, but thought better of it. Such an intimate discussion might well prompt the doctor's inclination to gossip. The help Derek had accepted in coming down the stairs, he refused in mounting them, although the ascent was perilously awkward. Laboriously, he made his way up the stairs alone. ''It's too dangerous,'' Sarah protested when he brusquely rejected her arm.

''For God's sake, I'm a soldier,'' he snapped, shaking her off. ''What do you think I cut my teeth on?''

''Let him be,'' Annalise gently restrained Sarah. ''He needs to learn how to manage for himself.''

''But that's heartless . . .''

''Nonetheless, he's not a cripple in his mind. He must continue to do what he can,'' she murmured, then added so that her voice carried, ''Colonel Clavell is managing well enough alone, don't you think, Doctor?''

''Yes,'' conceded the doctor reluctantly, ''he has backbone . . . and stubbornness enough for any three men.'' He clicked the medical bag closed with a grimace. ''That fortitude will either be the life or death of him.''

Giving no indication of hearing them, Derek disappeared into his room.

At dawn the next day, Annalise dressed quickly and went up to the roof patio. As she expected, Derek sat on his *charpoy* facing the lightening horizon. Silently, she sat next to him and they waited for the sun to come up. Gradually, the great red orb inched above the horizon, filling the sky with a yellow and violet light. The parapets of the city beyond the cantonment took shape, became solid. The tinkle of a herd of belled goats came up from the cantonment's dusty road as they passed beneath the golden *mohur* trees. The city's minarets and onion domes took on a rosy glow while the sun's color deepened to a rouge that gave the *mohurs* a bronze tint. Wails calling the faithful to prayer sounded briefly from the minarets. In a few minutes, the sound of the goat herd's bells faded as it disappeared from view.

For some time, Annalise sat silently while Derek remained immobile. "I see the sun," he said at last, "but the rest might as well be nothing but a burning haze." His head turned, his dark eyes tormented beneath the bandage that still concealed the slice to his skull. "I'm as good as a cripple . . . and most of the time, my skull feels as if it's exploding."

"Then you must wear smoked glasses over your eyes until your vision clears. Straining them in the light can only make your headaches worse." She held out the crutches Ahmed had fashioned for him. "And until your balance is secure enough to use a cane, you need to use your crutches."

"I'm lamed . . . and all you can say is, 'use your crutches'?" he burst out. "I cannot walk a straight line . . . I . . ." Suddenly, he faltered, as if fearing he might break down.

"I understand that you were wounded only a few weeks ago and that you need time to heal. Perhaps if you can walk a little today, tomorrow you will walk more, and the next day more again. We have no way of knowing God's will."

Derek gripped his head. "What if tomorrow I'm still a cripple, a cripple with a gouging needle in his brain, and the next day . . ."

"Take each day as it comes."

His head lifted as if he were seeing her for the first time. "I feel as if I were hearing your father. At times, I wonder if you are not older than I."

"Girls grow up very quickly in Asia, Colonel," she replied softly, forcing away the stubborn memory of his kiss. "Even *feringhi* girls. And even a child can trust in God."

"Only a child can trust in God," he countered bitterly. "A man must trust in himself."

"What a terrible weight that must be," she murmured. "The Muslims have discovered a great truth when they say, 'As Allah wills.' "

But her words fell on deaf ears. In the next week, a letter from Sussex arrived stating that the baronet, Derek's father, was dying. Derek was urged to return to England posthaste. That same day, he resigned his commission and his last faith in God's mercy.

IV

Homecoming

"D*erek!*" Robert Clavell threw his arms about his brother as he descended from the train in Brighton. "You look wonderful," he lied gallantly.

Annalise liked Robert at first sight. Of medium height, with chestnut hair and warm brown eyes, he had a ready, genial smile and an inviting manner that immediately made her feel almost as welcome as Derek.

Derek embraced him gladly, then tousled his hair. "Always the diplomat. Still planning that tour of the Continent?"

Robert sobered, then shook his head. "Father's dead, Derek. He tried to hold on, but he didn't make it. Lung fever took him night before last. He will be buried tomorrow."

Derek's pale face became taut. He looked weary from the journey, the sun lines that had creased the corners of his eyes now faded. He leaned heavily upon his crutches, his creased gray linen suit giving him the suggestion of a scarecrow. Now, his gaunt features were strained with sharp regret. "Two months' passage from India. I was afraid we wouldn't reach home in time." His head bowed, he hobbled to the edge of the train platform beneath a canopy of fluid green willows and stood there for a moment, looking in the direction of Claremore. Distracted by grief, he collected himself with an effort before returning to the group. "I'm sorry, I've forgotten my manners. Annalise, this is my brother Robert. Robert, may I present Miss Annalise Devon. Her father and I became close friends in India, until his recent death. I feel I've twice lost a father."

"I am very glad to greet you, Miss Devon," offered Robert with an appreciative smile. "I only wish we could have met under happier circumstances."

"I am very sorry to hear of your father's death, sir. It must be very difficult for you and your brother," replied Annalise, brushing up her black bonnet veil. Despite the fatigue of the long journey, her magnificent amber eyes were filled with warmth and tender understanding, and Robert was taken aback at their beauty. She was one of the few quietly regal women who could wear black mourning crape as if it were a soigneé ball gown.

At the sight of her exquisite young face, Robert shot a quick, questioning look at his brother.

"Miss Devon is my ward," supplied Derek, leaning on his crutches. "I did not wish to leave her alone in India."

Robert looked startled, as if he could not imagine any sane father bequeathing so lovely a daughter to a rake like Derek. Then his smile widened as he gripped his brother's shoulder in jubilation. "The doctor in Kabul wrote us the worst, but you look fairly fit, if a bit white about the gills! What luck, you old terror! We were scared silly, I can tell you. If only Father could have known."

Derek nodded with a faint smile. "I was somewhat alarmed myself, but my health has been improving every day. My sight has cleared. If I could be rid of these blasted crutches and headaches, I'd be right as rain."

Robert threw his arm about his shoulders. "What are trifling crutches and head pains compared to your life? You're a fortunate man. I wish I could tell you just how glad I am to have you home." He led the way to the carriage, and all the way to Claremore House kept up a light, cheerful patter that Derek might have been glad to hear, had his head not been paining him fiercely. As the carriage rolled and swayed through the green Sussex countryside with its clouds of spring apple blossoms, his head began to ache with increasing severity until Robert's voice became a relentless knell that mingled with the sound of funereal bells. The loss of his father was a severe blow. They had parted on bad terms, and Derek now regretted it, although he had borne the grudge these past three years. Derek missed his father sharply, and his grief seemed to aggravate the torment in his head.

He winced as he saw the servants lined up on the manor steps, and the pleasure he first felt at the sight of the familiar, red brick Tudor mansion amid its grove of sycamores and chestnuts was reduced to the dread of having to endure a receiving line.

Annalise was in awe. Even accounting for every scullery maid and field hand who wanted to be present to welcome the young master home, there were an enormous number in the estate's employ. They included maids of every description, cooks and preps, a butler, menservants, a barber, a stoker, grooms, gardeners, hands, sweeps, and a pensioner or two; Robert knew them all. Annalise had thought Derek's Indian staff of twelve had been lavish but saw now he had been living simply, by his standards, not hers.

Derek moved through the entire line, his face growing increasingly pale and tense. Murmuring her greetings to all, enduring the wide-eyed stares of several as she was introduced as Miss Devon, Annalise followed him.

"And Bertha here," Robert announced, "is my latest find, a magnificent cook. She has prepared a wondrous luncheon to welcome you home."

Bertha's gap-toothed smile of welcome stiffened when Annalise broke in, "Derek, do you think you are able to sit through luncheon? Perhaps you might like to lie down a bit."

Derek turned to his brother. "Robert," he said briefly, "I should like to go directly into the house, and after I've paid my respects to Father, retire."

A puzzled expression momentarily crossed Robert's face, then he nodded as if suddenly understanding. "You must be frightfully weary after such a long trip. I keep forgetting you're barely out of a sickbed. I'm so used to seeing you hale and hearty and roaring down the house. Of course, Boggs can bring up your lunch." His smile widened. "I shall dine with Miss Devon and Miss Longstreet."

"The devil you will," rallied Derek with an effort. "Why didn't you say Marian was coming to lunch?"

Robert grinned as they entered the house. "She's not *my* fianceé to be. Beside, I was intent on Miss Devon." He flashed Annalise a merry grin as she darted him a sidelong glance. "You do still intend to propose to Marian, don't you?"

"You'll be the last to know," retorted his brother, leading the way through the magnificent foyer checkered with black and white tile. "I don't care to become the butt of one of your pranks."

Robert assumed an innocent air. "I was thinking of loosing a fox and hounds into the bridal bed, but with concentration, I can think of something livelier."

Annalise passionately wished they would change the subject. She had heard far too much of Miss Marian

Longstreet *en route* from India. As they walked down the wide hall, lined with mahogany and inset with statuary, she was again struck by the contrast of what she had once thought lavish in India: now it seemed tawdry and gilt compared to the splendor of Claremore. Derek was home. These were his family trappings, and the gulf between their stations suddenly was all too evident to her.

Derek was in no mood to hear Miss Longstreet discussed, particularly in a cavalier manner. "You haven't told me about Father, Robert," he intervened as they gave their wraps to the butler. "Your letter said he'd been in failing health for some time."

"He'd had an apoplectic seizure when I wrote, then another while you were on the way home. We expected yet another, but lung fever took him off suddenly. He had great difficulty with his speech, and the second seizure paralyzed his left side. In truth," Robert added soberly, "I think he was glad to make a quick end."

Pausing, Derek rubbed his brow and said nothing for some time, then spoke as if his head were paining him. "So you managed the estate while Father was ill?"

Robert nodded. "I haven't been half bad at it, either, for the scapegrace ruffian Father used to dub me."

"Responsibility . . . probably good for you . . ." Derek gripped his head, grimacing in pain. "The devil . . . I feel as if I've a scorpion inside my skull. Where is Father, Robert? I want to see him while I'm still on my feet."

Robert led them to the oak-arched chapel where John Clavell lay in all the state of a peer of the realm. Tall, massive candles burned at head and foot of the great ebony and gold coffin which rested on a black marble dais. The regalia of a Knight of The Garter lay upon his breast. A snowy mane of hair curved upon the brocaded pillow beneath his head while his strong Clavell nose jutted toward a red, green, and gold ceiling draped in the Clavell blue and gold. Centered by the drapery was a painting of Elizabeth I greeting the captains of her fleet after their victory over the Spanish Armada.

"He was a strong, stubborn old man," said Derek with an effort. "For three years, he consigned me to India over that spat."

"Telling him you'd marry Marian whether he liked it or not didn't sit well with him. Not that he had anything against her..."

"Was I mentioned?" Marian Longstreet swept into the chapel, her topaz, silk hoop skirt billowing. Annalise had the impression that she had been listening in order to make an entrance, but Marian Longstreet could have made a dramatic impression anywhere on her looks alone. Her flame-colored hair and bright-yellow dress made her resemble a mote of gold sifting into the room on a sunbeam. In her black mourning crape, Annalise felt like a drab, cinder-dusted sparrow.

Derek caught Marian's hand, his lips so near hers that he clearly wanted to kiss her. Only the awareness of their sober surroundings prevented him; that, and Marian's subtle restraint. Standing behind him, Annalise was glad he could not see the pain in her eyes, but glancing intently over his shoulder, Marian caught it. Annalise would have given anything to prevent her heart from being in her eyes at that moment. On Robert's face was a fleeting grimace of... was it distaste, disapproval? Remarkable the man who could disapprove of the beautiful Miss Longstreet.

"Derek," said Marian Longstreet with a note of soft huskiness in her low contralto. "You're so tall and tanned. You look so wonderfully..."

"Ill," said his brother succinctly. "Derek feels like hell. His head is giving him a fiendishly hard time, so why don't we all go to dinner and continue this conversation over the stuffed quail.'' He held out his arm to Annalise. ''Miss Devon, may I accompany you?''

''Miss Devon,'' said Marian Longstreet *en route* to the dining room, ''we haven't met.'' Her clipped tone indicated she was wondering who the devil Annalise was, keeping unchaperoned company with two of the most eligible bachelors in Britain.

Robert intervened. ''Miss Devon is Derek's ward. Her father recently died in India.''

''Then you and Derek have something in common,'' said Marian in the same crisp manner as they walked along a long, window-lighted hallway lined with Holbein and Gainsborough paintings, weapons and suits of inlaid Spanish armor. ''How terrible for you both.''

Annalise was beginning to share Robert's antipathy for Marian. Somehow she found herself saying, ''Colonel Clavell and I also have India in common, Miss Longstreet. India is quite different from England.''

Marian levelled a green-eyed stare at her that said, *cross swords with me, will you?* ''I gather India's rather poor and dirty.''

''Also unbelievably beautiful,'' intervened Derek, sensing an impending battle, and having no patience for it. ''I am not long away from India before I miss it.''

Swinging his crutches in brusque arcs, he led the way into the crimson and gold dining room with its long, dark mahogany table and high-backed chairs. A portrait of Charles II hung at the far end of the table, and dominating the near end was a portrait of Queen Victoria and Prince Albert with their spaniels. Annalise had the impression of walking into a train station as their footsteps echoed hollowly on the floorboards before reaching the heavy Brussels carpet. She found the house oppressive despite its beauty. Its very grandeur suggested a centuries-old tradition of pomp and show that radiated an imperious pride. Although she loved

Derek and found his brother appealing, she saw the arrogance of that old man in the flag-draped coffin in both their features. Even though they had India in common, Derek had returned to his element and she was now the one out of place.

Derek seated Marian, then gravely touching his father's empty chair, took the chair next to it for himself. Robert seated Annalise opposite them, then assumed the chair next to hers. "What are conditions really like in India now, Derek?" asked his brother as the butler served consommé.

"Turning dangerous. The Indians believe the fall of the Raj is at hand. One hundred years ago, Clive won control of India at Plassey. According to legend, the anniversary of the battle foretells the end of the company's control over India."

"But surely that's just an old wives' tale," protested Marian. "The Indians are superstitious children, and ready to snatch at any hope of having rule placed back in native hands."

"There are millions of Indians to every Englishman in India. An uprising could be catastrophic."

"But that's just it," said Annalise softly. "India is not Indian, but Hindu, Muslim, Buddhist, Pathan, and Sikh . . . a whole mixture of rival races and religions. What could ever unite them in an insurrection?"

"Nothing that I can think of"—Derek rubbed his head as he glanced at his soup, then pushed it aside—"but the Muslim priests are calling for a *jihad*, or holy war, at the same time the Hindus are complaining of defilement."

He paused as the servants brought in the main course.

"What do you think will happen?" asked Robert.

"I think there will eventually be a mutiny if English officers continue to look the other way and ignore native grievances."

"But surely they wouldn't dare," protested Marian indignantly with a sweep of her beringed white hand.

"They're primitives, aren't they? We English have given them laws, schools, the railway . . . What have they accomplished on their own in the past two thousand years?"

Derek smiled wryly. "Now you sound like a typical Downing Street hack, Marian."

"I think, Miss Longstreet, that Derek means the Indians prefer to do things in their own way, even if it takes longer," interjected Annalise, noting the whiteness of Derek's face. "Asians are rarely in a hurry, and philosophical about the passage of time."

"Exactly," said Derek, glad Annalise had relieved him of explanation. He felt as if a chisel were being driven into his skull.

Seeing that she was outnumbered, Marian smoothly changed the subject to one that threw her in a better light. "Must we talk of predictions of gloom and gore when the past year at home has been so splendid?" The various fêtes and parties that had spangled the season glowed again in her breathless description. She finished with a cool glance at Annalise's dingy black crape. "Did you know, Derek, that I was presented to the queen in June? I was dressed all in white—with a nosegay of white roses and lilies of the valley."

"Indeed"—his eyes lit briefly with pride in her striking beauty—"I should like to have been there."

She laughed. "Perhaps it's as well you weren't. In your splendid regimentals, you would have made Prince Albert look stodgy."

"I doubt it," he replied with a grimace. "I should have collapsed with an ice pack clapped to my brow. No competition, I think, for the prince."

Marian critically scrutinized the still fresh, livid scar on his brow. "Poor darling, that must have been quite a nasty gash. Do you still feel so dreadful?"

He avoided a direct answer. "Not so badly as I did while carrying a Gilzai bullet from a *jezail* . . . but I'm walking after the mess the doctors made getting it out, so I should say I'm fit enough."

Those same doctors had also warned you not to ride for a year, as have I, reflected Annalise, but at the way Derek's eyes had brightened at first sight of the verdant Sussex countryside, she knew he would spend not a fortnight longer out of the saddle. She hated to see him ride, when every step still cost him pain, but Marian and Robert could see nothing when Derek carried himself so erectly and hid his suffering. His back and leg were healed, and his vision had cleared, but his headaches still concerned her, for they seemed to be growing steadily worse. She sensed he had one now. Barely tasting his food, his knuckles white on the chair arms, he sat with uncustomary tension. Having learned to read the signs in India, she hoped he would retire before his pain grew worse.

As if reading her mind, Derek abruptly rose. "If you will excuse me, the journey tired me more than I thought . . . and I feel I should be with Father." Briefly, he caught up Marian's hand and touched it to his lips. "My apologies. Perhaps tomorrow afternoon, I shall be better." Taking up his cane, he started for the door.

Marian's husky contralto pursued him. "But surely I may join you, Derek. I've ridden so far and to see you for such a short time . . ."

Let him alone! Annalise wanted to cry. Can't you see how much pain he feels, both physically and for his father?

But Marian did not see, and Derek was not about to let her. Despite the cramped line of his shoulders as he turned, his brown eyes were eager. "Of course, come along if you like."

"In a little while, darling," Marian put him off as negligently as a cat toying with a mouse. "I must have dinner first. I'm famished."

Not as famished as I am for you, his eyes said, then

veiled with ill-concealed disappointment. With a nod, he turned and went to his father.

Marian's faintly contemptuous emerald gaze returned to Annalise. "I gather you're a missionary's daughter."

As if seeking a defensive weapon, Annalise took up a spoonful of her scarcely touched soup. "My father served both in China and India."

"Will you be living in London, Miss Bevins?"

"Devon, Miss Longstreet." Annalise gathered her courage and dignity. "There was some discussion of my living in London, but Colonel Clavell has not made a final decision, I believe." Not a lie, surely, when Derek had made no mention of her going to London since they had sailed from Karachi.

A sulfurous glint entered Marian's eyes, as if she had grown intent upon piercing the innocent serenity in Annalise's expression. "I am surprised you agreed to be . . . shall we say, Derek's protégée. You are markedly progressive in your moral attitudes for one brought up under the shelter of the cross, Miss Devon, unless you have wearied of the restraints of mission teachings."

"Marian!" Robert Clavell was as startled as Annalise by Marian Longstreet's bluntness. "How can you address Miss Devon in such a fashion?"

"Oh, I feel certain Miss Devon understands my meaning. After all, she cannot have been so long out of polite society that she does not understand that Derek's providing her support will be regarded in a very severe light."

"I cannot imagine why," returned Annalise with apparent tranquility, "when I am his ward and Colonel Clavell's assistance is kindly meant. To insult me is to insult him. As for my moral attitudes, I assure you they have not become in the least wearisome. And now"—leaving Marian to ponder her last oblique statement—"I should like to retire, as the journey has been a long one."

As she left the room, Annalise heard Robert's muffled, angry tone behind her. "Marian, must you ever play the cat behind Derek's back?"

"Surely," came back Marian's curt voice, "you noticed there were two cats loosed in the room?"

Instead of going to her room, Annalise went out on the bricked terrace for a breath of fresh summer air. Surrounding the estate, the Sussex countryside was a vivid, rolling green splashed with dandelions, wild daisies, and Queen Anne's lace. Sweeping off her ugly bonnet, she hurried down the terrace steps and ran, her skirts billowing across the sweet-scented lawn, past the formal boxwood hedge that was patterned upon the grass with its flower beds of crocuses, daffodils, and tulips. Marian Longstreet was indeed a cat, out to claw and hurt, intent on sending her scurrying away from the tangle of gossip that must ensue, even if Marian did not care to weave it. Oh, to be free of dependency upon anyone, free to go anywhere she liked . . . back to India, whose mysteries still eluded and fascinated her. Certainly, she did not belong here.

For nearly an hour, she half walked, half ran across the meadows beneath the great, fluffy clouds. From a distance, the great E-shaped manor house was set like a jewel in the countryside. An awesome house, designed to honor the great Queen Elizabeth. How proud Derek must be of Claremore . . . and how blind to the woman he planned to place at his side as baroness. She saw now why Robert disliked Marian; there was a streak of unfeeling cruelty in her, but then as Robert had intimated, perhaps Derek had never seen it.

Annalise stripped off her hoops and lay down upon the grass to gaze up at the sky. Lovely as Claremore was, she did not envy Marian her future possession, but only her position as Derek's wife. As for herself, she had acquired her father's taste for adventure and exotic climes. Sussex was much too sedate, too bucolic, too restful. Her eyes closed against the drowsy late-summer heat and droning bees as her mind went back to India with its great, gray bejewelled elephants and ornate Hindu temples, its sudden violence and sensuous beauty. She thought of jungles, dark, deep, and mysterious as Derek's eyes, nights black as his hair . . . and yet, what could it be like to make love with him? Her father had told her little of the physical act between a man and woman that lead to the bearing of children; although of an open nature, he could not be explicit with his only daughter. After seventeen years in Asia, she was no stranger to human nudity, but seeing Derek half-covered in bed had been something of a shock. He was a tall man, but unclothed, he seemed to be so much more impressive. Flushing at the remembrance, she flung an arm over her eyes. During the long months at sea, she had tried not to imagine him in any romantic way at all. She was a realist; Derek could never belong to her. To nurture a secret longing for him could only embarrass him, and hurt her. With more or less a doctor's detachment, she had thought of Derek as a patient when he was severely ill; yet now . . . the dark, crisp mat of hair on his chest seemed to curl against her cheeks, his shoulder seemed warm and strong against her temple. She could almost feel his arms about her, comforting and tender; feel his lips . . .

"Miss Devon . . ."

Startled, Annalise half turned on her side and pressed upward, her body curving through the meadow grass. "Mr. Clavell!" She shot a hasty, embarrassed glance at her discarded hoops.

"I'm sorry to have surprised you, Miss Devon." Robert looked a trifle embarrassed himself. "I should have given you some warning as I climbed the hill. Shall I leave?"

Her cheeks turning rosier, Annalise drew a little circle

with her finger. "No, but if you will be so good as to turn your back . . ."

Robert obliged, but with a lack of alacrity he knew Annalise Devon must find provoking, for he hated to lose sight of the long, lissome curve of her undisguised by fashionable paraphernalia. She was curvaceously made, and delicious for one so young. Robert wondered how Derek had kept his hands off her. She had long legs, sweetly curved hips, and a tiny waist that ripened into high breasts that fairly made his mouth water. Her black hair was caught high, and loosed about her brow in fine tendrils that snared the wayward breeze, sending the hair ruffling across her face to catch in thick, sooty lashes over eyes that reminded him of a golden cat's. Lying on her back in the long grass, she had made him think of a wild, young courtesan, waiting for her forbidden lover. In the black crape, she looked older than she was, and her ivory skin was like cream poured through the rose and gold of the pure Sussex light. There was a voluptuous quality to her face, the rounded chin, the Andalusian nose, and amber, smoldering eyes, but particularly the full mouth that might have seemed petulant had it not been so finely formed. She was very near to becoming a great beauty; how then had his brother said nothing of her in his letters . . . unless he was attracted to her himself. Robert wondered how Derek could not be; even Marian, with her stunning looks, would find her regency as reigning beauty in the county threatened once Miss Devon flowered into her full glory. Just now, she seemed still partly a child; he could hear her scrambling into her hoops. Finally, there was an agitated smoothing of skirts and silence.

"You may turn around now, Mr. Clavell."

Robert obliged, then offered a smile that held a pretense of shyness. He had the idea Annalise Devon was a bit in awe of his brother; he did not want her to be in awe of him as well. With a trace of chagrin, he viewed her traditional, bell-shaped silhouette. "I ventured to find you, Miss Devon, because I wanted to apologize for Miss Longstreet. She is rarely so blunt and ill mannered, but then, perhaps she views you in a competitive light."

Annalise was bewildered. "How can so beautiful and fashionable a woman possibly be concerned with me? Even if I meant to be her rival, I am in mourning."

"Black becomes you very well, Miss Devon. Miss Longstreet has every reason to be discomfited." He offered her his arm. "Will you walk back to the house with me? I should like to hear from your own lips how my brother has fared these past few months since his injury. I fear he will tell me that he is perfectly well, when he looks not at all well."

She accepted his arm. "I can tell you no more than your brother, Mr. Clavell. I know his head wound still pains him more than he expresses, but other than dissuading him from attempting more than his present strength allows, I can make no suggestions."

"So," drawled Robert as they descended the lushly grassed hillside, "you are his ally even within the bosom of his family. Rest assured that I only seek Derek's welfare. I have just lost a father; I should not care to lose a brother. Derek wrote me he had suffered mild injury while on campaign, yet his doctor wrote that he had been seriously wounded and suffered a broken leg, also that his head wound incurred perhaps the most alarming damage. Just how serious are these headaches?"

"In truth, I do not know, Mr. Clavell, as I am no doctor," she evaded. If Derek did not wish to concern his family, she had no right to circumvent his purpose. "Perhaps you should talk with Derek himself."

"Prying an answer out of Derek would be no simpler than trying to gain one from you," Robert scoffed with a grin that softened his appearance of irritation. "But I stand justly rebuked, Miss Devon. I shall remember you as a young lady who can well keep a secret, have I ever one to confide."

She gazed at him with serene innocence. "Why do you assume that I hold a secret, Mr. Clavell?"

"Because my brother wrote that you had become his confidant, his . . . how did he put it . . . small shadow. Imagine my surprise to find you a very lovely young woman."

Her gaze sobered. "Did you suppose me a mouse?"

He studied her with mischievous relish that reminded her of Derek. "Well, one does suppose missionaries' daughters to be excessively demure in looks and nature."

"And now that you have seen my hoops, you think otherwise."

Robert had the good grace to flush. "I *am* sorry about that, I assure you."

"One assurance is quite enough, Mr. Clavell." She smiled with a trace of his own mischief. "Hoops are quite detestable instruments, are they not?"

He laughed. "As detestable as you are disarming. I confess I find you more of a kitten than a mouse."

"Oh, I am very nearly a full-grown cat according to Miss Longstreet, Mr. Clavell. Surely, you noticed it was she who emerged from our meeting at dinner displaying scratches. Why don't you like her?"

Uncomfortable at being on the receiving end of the questioning, Robert dodged. "Don't I?"

"No," said Annalise coolly, "you don't. She does pounce for the throat, doesn't she?"

"I should say Marian is direct, yes," agreed Robert slowly, "particularly with pretty women, but she rarely unsheathes her claws so blatantly. Your spending so much time with Derek must have alarmed her."

"Did the baronet ever forgive Derek for his vow to marry her?"

"No. While Marian was sweet as butter to Father, he regarded her as overly enterprising, despite her looks and money. He foresaw difficulties between her and Derek. They are well matched in violent tempers and strong wills. In some ways, perhaps Father supposed they were too much alike, but Marian has a selfish streak that Derek lacks. Derek can be self-centered, but he's not mean. Now there's nothing to stop his marrying Marian." Robert hesitated. "Ah . . . perhaps I've said too much."

She studied his worried face. "You love him very much, don't you?"

He smiled wryly. "When I don't covet the baronetcy. All Claremore is Derek's now, and I love Claremore, too."

"You're very honest."

He laughed. "Nothing subtle about a Sussex farmer."

"What do you plan to do now that Derek is baronet?"

"Stay on as long as he'll let me, I suppose . . . which won't be long once Marian moves into the house. She loathes me. You've heard the old saw, 'women always hate their husband's best friends'? Well, I'm not only Derek's brother, but his best friend. I know where all the proverbial bodies are buried, and that includes quite a few skeletons belonging to Marian."

"But I gather that she's quite popular locally."

"Few people have seen Marian as you saw her today. She doesn't bother concealing her claws in front of me, because she knows I know she's got them." A look of wicked delight entered his eyes. "She certainly hated you on sight. We should have a lively time of it until you depart for London." He paused, then added firmly, "I say, may I call on you there?"

"In London?" Annalise was startled as she picked up her skirts to cross a freshet cascading down the hill. "Why ever would you want to do that?"

"Because I think I should like to know you better. If

you're to be whisked off after the funeral, I shall have little chance of that. Say yes, Miss Devon." Like Derek, there was no entreaty in his tone, only certainty of his charm and attractiveness. "If you will tell me all about the mysteries of the East, I shall tell you all about the mysteries of Sussex." He gave her an engaging grin, his brown eyes dancing.

"When I am no longer in mourning, Mr. Clavell, I should be glad to see you," replied Annalise with genuine pleasure. She was not certain yet, but she thought she liked Robert Clavell. He certainly seemed to be his own man, and no miniature of his brother. As they talked their way down the hill, her good impression mounted.

Then, as they crossed the boxwood-patterned lawn, she saw Marian emerge from the house. Derek was just behind her. As Marian started to cross the terrace toward her waiting carriage, Derek caught her hand, then tugged her to him. Precariously balanced on his crutches, he kissed her, and a pain shivered through Annalise's soul. How could he love Marian, with her icy green eyes and malicious heart? He could not know her and kiss her so fervently . . . and yet, if there were no Marian, there would be another woman. Only a great lady of his own rank and background could have a place in his life. She was like a simple sparrow pining after a hawk.

Derek, hearing her and Robert approach, lifted his head. Marian turned to look over her shoulder. She cast a triumphant look at Annalise. "Robert, Miss Devon, you will be first to know that Derek and I mean to become engaged a year from today and married shortly thereafter. I hope you will congratulate us."

A knot tightened about Annalise's heart as she looked at Derek. Despite the head pain that cast a pallor over his features, he looked like a sublimely happy man. "Marian," he gently chided, "we agreed not to tell anyone until the engagement reception."

"But Robert is your own brother," Marian said as if wounded, "and Miss Devon can certainly be trusted to be discreet . . ." Her cool green eyes looked directly into Annalise's amber ones. "Can you not, Miss Devon?"

"Of course," replied Annalise levelly. "I shouldn't think of telling anyone."

"I knew we could count on you," was Marian's sweet reply. She turned again to Derek. "I shall see you tomorrow, darling. Do try to get some rest. The funeral services are likely to be tiring."

Derek nodded as if he were too weary to argue. Clasping her lightly, he kissed her forehead. "Until tomorrow."

Marian took Robert's hand as she descended the steps, summoning him to help her into the carriage. Derek, Annalise, and Robert stood watching the carriage fade down the drive beyond a stand of oak and chestnut trees that set off the sycamores nearer the manor. "I'm sorry to welcome you home to such a reception, Derek," said Robert, glancing toward the family graveyard a short distance from the house. "I'm sure Father would have given a great deal to have been here to welcome you today."

Annalise caught Robert's meaning if Derek did not.

Derek rubbed his brow as if it pained him "I should have given much to see Father again . . . settle old accounts."

"You know," said Robert as he and Annalise accompanied Derek up the red brick steps, "Father would have been most displeased by the promise of this engagement."

"Father's displeasure is no account anymore, is it?" bit out Derek. "Don't play devil's advocate, Robert. I'll take no chastising from you when I refused to accept it from him." He limped into the house alone, and the door slammed.

V

Pairs

The funeral the next day was held under the pouring rain in a sea of black umbrellas. Derek's face was strained, closed as if shutting out his father's awful loss. As the great black coffin was lowered into the ground, Annalise longed to go to him, but Marian stood at his side, her face fierce and waiting. Now she was done with the old baronet's disapproval and Claremore was at her feet, just as its new master was within her reach. When the service was done, many of the mourners returned to the house, where the servants brought out cold meats, cheeses, fruits, and bread. The old baronet had known a great many people; the house was full. After an hour, Annalise noticed that Derek was gone from the crush, leaving Marian to stand beneath the family portraits in the mahogany-lined library as she greeted various people. It was easy for them to suppose her portrait would soon join those of Derek's ancestors. At the other end of the room, Robert was filling the role of host, so Annalise, worried that the strain of the day was probably proving too much for Derek, went to find him.

When she tapped softly at his study door, there was no answer, then as she turned away, a terse command to enter. Slipping into the green and gold room, she saw Derek sitting by the rain-wet window. His cheeks were glittering with tears. "What is it, Derek?" she murmured gently. "How may I help you?"

"No one can help now. No one could have helped when Father and I quarreled," he replied huskily. "We were close, he and I. Sometimes, we almost seemed to hate one another."

She went to stand by his chair. "Were you very alike?"

"Very." He smiled crookedly. "I inherited my winning disposition from him. He was quicker to take offense than any man I know."

"And perhaps kinder, when he wanted to be?"

He looked up at her. "You understand grief, don't you? The unfinished hopes, the things said and unsaid. The hideous, eternal loss." He was silent for a moment. "But you and your father never quarreled, did you? I have rarely seen two people more supportive of one another."

"That doesn't mean we didn't disagree. I'm sure that had I fallen in love without Father's approval, he would have been most concerned."

"Would that have changed anything?"

"I should never have married against my father's wishes." She hesitated. "Still, love is not so easy to extinguish. While I trusted my father's judgement, I might not have been able to put an end to my affection so easily."

"How do you know that, never having been in love?"

She gazed at him. "How do you know I have never been in love?"

"You're too young, too . . ." He started to say virginal,

then thought better of it, particularly as her eyes held a curious light. "Have you been in love?"

"I think so. It is sometimes painful, is it not?"

He nodded, then his head lowered and he gripped his temples with his hands. "I cannot . . . I cannot forget the things I said to him. The vitriol he poured upon me. We loved each other until that moment, then twisted the love until it was hideous, like a broken animal. Now all that bitterness can never be undone."

Because of Marian Longstreet, thought Annalise as his pent-up pain continued to gush out. That woman has done a great deal of damage at Claremore and may do more if she is as truly heartless as she seems. Yet who am I to say that she does not love Derek or that she does not mean him well. Surely, she cannot see only the vast acres and fortunes of Claremore when Derek is so worthwhile a man.

Unable to bear the stricken look on his face, she did not move away when he brokenly caught her about the waist and buried his head against her. Gently, she stroked his hair as he wept, the years of bitterness and rancor seeping like pestilence emerging from a long-festering wound. "Don't punish yourself," she murmured. "I'm certain your father was as eager as you to settle your differences. Robert says the baronet tried very hard to live until you came. In his heart, he must have known you wished to be reconciled as well. You're a good man, and a loving son. He knew that."

"I wish I could believe it," he replied in a stifled voice. "He told me when I left for India that I was a stubborn, reckless ingrate, and that if I thought he'd welcome me back like the prodigal son, I'd have a long rot in hell." Lifting his head, he pushed his hair back. "He was more correct than he knew."

"Is your head still hurting?" she asked with a trace of anxiety.

He nodded. "I didn't sleep last night. I tried brandy, but

it seemed to make the pain worse. At the funeral, my skull was pounding like an anvil.'' He let out his breath. ''I keep thinking that any day now, my headaches will ease.''

She sat on the carpet at his feet. ''You're nearly well now. Surely, the pain will fade in time.''

He laughed sharply. ''You're very supportive. I can still see you and your father now, mired in the mud of the Grand Trunk Road and certain Providence would relieve you.''

''And Providence arrived in a 3rd Cavalry uniform and rattling a saber.'' She smiled. ''I though you were the most awesome, impatient angel I had ever seen.''

''Patience would have seen you landed in the Ganges. What you needed was a quick hand and a head for physics . . .''

They went on talking for some time until Derek's eyes began to close as he rested his head back in his chair. She had hoped she could relax him enough to dose off. Quite often aboard ship, she had gently distracted him so that he could sleep, but she was not sure the method would prove effective a good deal longer. Dark circles were carved beneath his eyes and his face was drawn with the unrelenting pain. Just as his eyes shut and she rose to leave the room, Marian's voice sounded crisply behind her. ''I wondered where you were, Derek. Miss Devon.''

Thoroughly awake now, Derek raised his head. ''Marian. Has everyone gone?''

''Indeed not.'' Marian looked at Annalise. ''Miss Devon, you are wanted downstairs. Robert and I cannot manage alone.''

''Playing hostess is not Miss Devon's responsibility,'' responded Derek, getting awkwardly to his feet. He gave Marian a tired wave. ''I shall come down. I should never have left you alone.''

Marian went to take his arm, her tone dulcet. ''I shouldn't think of your venturing downstairs when you are so clearly unwell. Why not nap for an hour while Miss Devon and I see to our guests?"

He shook his head, and picking up his crutches, headed for the door. Annalise followed Marian, who fell into step just behind him. Annalise could cheerfully have kicked her.

The last guest left at ten o'clock that evening, and thanking him for coming, Derek shook his hand. When at last, Derek tried to mount the stairs, his lame leg collapsed and he desperately caught at a chair to keep his balance. Robert hastened to his side to support him. "Sorry," breathed Derek. "Strength just . . . gave out."

To her credit, Marian looked worried as Robert and a footman helped Derek up the stairs. "I . . . I didn't think he was still so ill," she told Annalise in a muffled tone. "It's been four months since he was wounded."

"He was seriously wounded," returned Annalise gravely. "I believe we should send for a doctor. His condition is worsening."

Instantly, Marian descended the stairs and summoned a servant to go into Brighton and fetch a doctor. She does love him, thought Annalise with relief. Surely, she loves him . . . unless she just wants to keep him alive for the title and property he will bring. She chided herself for the distinctly uncharitable thought. Still, to have him marry a woman who might see him only in terms of acreage was an alarming prospect.

The next morning, a servant returned with the doctor: one Dr. Whyte, with whom they shared a congenial breakfast while waiting for Derek to rise. Derek had slept badly and was barely civil as the doctor poked, prodded, and thumped him. "The army life certainly made a mess of you," Whyte announced at last.

"I've always enjoyed your bedside manner, Doctor," Derek retorted. "Tell me something I don't know."

Dr. Whyte tapped him on the shin with his knuckle and

Derek winced. "This is as botched a job as I have ever seen. The leg must be rebroken to set properly."

Derek's jaw was tight. "And if it is, will I be able to walk normally?"

Dr. Whyte shook his head. "I can promise only that if it is not rebroken, Your Lordship's leg will remain twisted. It may be that the pressure is affecting your spine and the nerves that go to the brain. Or, it may very well be that the spinal wound has not healed so benignly as it appears. I could probe for splinters . . ."

"Indeed not!" protested Marian. "The doctor in India wrote that he had done everything possible. Mend his leg if you like, but leave his spine alone. You could kill him by poking about."

Robert agreed, though Derek was inclined to accept the doctor's suggestion. He was willing to take any risk to end the headaches, but at last surrendered to Marian's pleading that she could not bear to risk losing him.

It was settled; after he recovered his strength, his leg would be rebroken and set. But somehow as the weeks passed, Derek seemed to have no time for the doctor. In time, he was able to discard his crutches and use a cane, but his gait was an awkward shamble compared to his former energetic stride. With Robert at his side, he went about the estate having repairs made, settling differences among tenants, conferring about crops and fields, the price of corn, the chance of rain. From dawn to dark he worked, and put off being incapacitated again. A month went by, then another, and still he made no effort to send Annalise back to London despite Marian's subtle pressure. When Robert questioned him about it, he replied, "It's better that Annalise remain here where she has some semblance of family about her. After all, she recently lost a father too."

Although pleased at Derek's decision, Robert could not help wondering. When Derek would tolerate no one else's company, he would permit Annalise to come to him. Often, they said nothing to one another, yet a subtle tension tugged between them like a physical force. Annalise was like the sister the two brothers had never had, yet there was something more than mere fraternal affection to their relationship. Robert would have been jealous, were he less assured that his brother had eyes only for Marian Longstreet. He was jealous of his brother's company, when Derek preferred to ride only with Annalise. "I won't have you see me crawling on and off a horse, Robert. Miss Devon once held my head while I vomited with pain. She has been my nurse, and more, a friend as faithful as her father."

Derek himself could not have explained what he felt for Annalise, although one day, he had occasion to question his conscience. They were riding to the north, the day warm and bright, the sun copper. All day they had ridden along the stone fences, with Derek looking for encroaching thistle and weak spots in the walls caused by burrowing groundhogs. Annalise, laughing at his stories of garrison life until she cried, was distracted from the cold seeping through her fox muff. Suddenly, Derek's bay stallion jumped a low ditch and the fatigue of the long day caught up with him. Derek fell headlong, his bad leg unable to grip the saddle. Swiftly, Annalise dismounted with her heart in her throat and ran to his side. Stunned, he lay unmoving, his leg throbbing with pain as she anxiously dropped to listen for his heartbeat. Her black hair was a swirl over his chest, her young breasts brushing him, and dazedly, he felt a wave of unbidden desire creep over him. Her face was as near to his as a lover's, her body arching over him. The concern and compassion in her eyes filled him with both an unexpected longing and enchantment. He fought back the impulse to entwine her in his arms, taste those parted, frightened lips, and reassure her he was very much alive: too much so for comfort, for his sex was beginning to stir. Careful not to touch her, he slowly lifted his head. "An eight-year-old boy could have managed that ditch better," he told her faintly. "Thank God, Robert wasn't here. He'd never let me live down such a tumble."

"Never mind Robert. Are you all right?"

Woozily, he sat up and tried not to look into those worried golden eyes that were sending his senses singing. "I was in the light cavalry, remember? I was weaned flying over a nag's crupper." He extended an arm. "Help me up, will you?"

She reached down to him, then at his sudden weight, lost her balance and fell across his body where she felt the unmistakable evidence of his interest. The concern in her eyes altered to startled wonder and a touch of fright that quickly faded into a kind of tranquil waiting that touched a sense of longing in him. All his life he had waited for such a look of trust and serenity on a woman's face, only to see it now in a near child's. Without thinking, he kissed her, gently, with a soft caress of welcome. Her lips were yielding, unpracticed, yet held such a sense of certainty that he felt he was one with her. All the nights when she had nursed him, all the dusky twilights when they had talked of India and the far, misty reaches of Asia returned to him now as if she were the life companion for whom he was born. Longing to be joined to her, he tightened his arms about her, only to feel the quick thud of her heart against his. Remembrance of her youth, his responsibility for her shuddered through him like a warning. My God, what was he doing? William Devon had given her to him to protect, not seduce! Paling with shame, he thrust her away and struggled to his feet. "My apologies . . . I forgot myself. I assure you I shall not be so remiss again." The curt, stern note in his voice was meant for himself, but in her own embarrassment at being thrust away so suddenly, Annalise assumed it was directed at her.

"The fault was equally mine, Colonel . . ."

He cut her off abruptly. "Indeed, it was not. You have had no experience in these matters, and I have taken grievous advantage of your ignorance. I should not have kissed you."

Annalise's embarrassment faded as her eyes flashed. "Experienced or not, I liked it . . . so much so"—she drew herself up bravely—"I should not mind if you cared to do so again."

"What a brazen little baggage you are!" Derek burst out, then scowled at her. "I should take you over my knee and remind you that you are supposed to be a lady . . ."

"I *am* a lady, and I think the only lady who does not enjoy being kissed by an attractive man must be dead." Briskly, she brushed off her skirts and marched to her horse.

Stupefied, Derek stared at her as she mounted. "Did your father teach you nothing of decorum in your mother's absence?"

"What has decorum to do with the pleasure of a kiss?" Annalise looked genuinely bewildered. "We simply wanted to kiss each other and did so. It's not as if we made love in Winchester Cathedral."

"What do you know of making love?" he bellowed.

She nodded toward the grassy knoll they had just vacated. "Wasn't that making love?"

"As a cricket cage is like your Winchester Cathedral, and I'll thank you not to bandy about places of religion so coolly."

Her eyebrow raised. "You *are* conservative. God isn't going to strike us down because we kissed one another, you know."

He brusquely mounted his horse. "The issue isn't a mere kiss, but where the kiss can lead."

"But where can a kiss possibly lead besides additional pleasure?" Annalise regarded him blankly.

In face of such provocative innocence, Derek subsided into a brooding silence for the remainder of their ride. For the rest of the afternoon, he pondered the dilemma their embrace had precipitated, and after dinner, called Annalise into his study. "I have decided to send you to London by week's end," he said bluntly. "I have not lived up to my responsibilities to you and your father by keeping you here at Claremore so long."

Distraught, she was silent for a moment, then asked softly, "Then why did you keep me here?"

Derek rose from his desk. "Because I was selfish. Your presence gave me . . . comfort. You also remind me of India, of which I am very fond."

She stood quite still. "But you are not fond of me?"

He hesitated. "You . . . you are like the daughter I have never had . . ."

"You are not old enough to be my father," she shot back, "and that was not a father's kiss this afternoon. Even I know enough to realize that. Are you still feeling guilty because you kissed me?"

"It's not as simple as that, Annalise. My intentions toward you are no longer . . ."—Derek struggled for the right word, then gave it up—"honorable."

The darkness of her eyes impenetrable, she watched him like a child who has just been slapped and is waiting to see if another blow is warranted. "You could not possibly be dishonorable, Colonel. Impatient, hurtful, yes; but never dishonorable. I would trust you with my life, just as my father did."

"It appears your father was as naive as you," he replied tiredly. He had rationalized his attraction this afternoon, but dared not tell Annalise so. How could he explain that he had wanted to love her because he wanted Marian so badly: Marian, who was so elusive an aphrodisiac to his senses. Marian, who had not given herself to him since his return from India. Her excuse was that he had never possessed a virgin, and despite all her past experience as his lover, she wanted to appear virginal to him on their wedding night. The notion was titilating . . . with one marring aspect. His dreams were full of her, yet every time he thought of making love to her, the disapproving image of his father disrupted the idea, and now, when he imagined making love with Annalise, *her* father cropped up.

"Annalise," he began again, "your father entrusted you to me. He meant me to care for you in his stead, and when the time comes, see to it that you are married to a respectable husband: that, I intend to do. This coming Monday, you shall leave for London. I shall see that you are comfortably established. Believe me, one day you will come to see the wisdom of my decision."

Annalise's dark head lifted. "I see only that I am to be sent away as if I had done something shameful. I felt no shame when I kissed you . . . only that it was sweet and good. You are turning that moment into something sordid. And as for London, I beg you, do not send me there. I should be miserable, and most particularly so, alone. Let me stay here at Claremore until I can return to India. On my part"—her lips trembled—"I swear I shall commit no such offense as you envision again, only I beg you, do not send me away to live among strangers."

At the rare tears that darkened her eyes, Derek hesitated. Why should he place his own guilt upon her? She was right; she had kissed him in all innocence, just as naturally as Eve might have once kissed Adam in Eden. The idea of sin had never occurred to her. She made him feel small, and no one had done that since he was a child. If anyone deserved punishment, it was himself. Not only Annalise's welfare, but her happiness was his responsibility. If anyone were to exercise control, he was the one to do so. "Very well," he finally relented. "You may stay at Claremore for a time, but do not think of returning to India until any possible mutiny is settled."

"Thank you, milord." Annalise's fingers tightened on the handkerchief she had compressed to a ball. Her knees felt weak with relief. She would never so much as touch his hand again if it meant being banished from Claremore. From Derek. On the day she saw Derek married to Marian, she would be glad to go to London to hide her hurt. Only now, William's loss was still too recent for her to face the loneliness of a world without him. She must be brave; she must, for all too soon Derek would be lost to her forever. Only now she had something precious to take away with her: the memory of his kiss, willing and tender.

"And now," Derek added, resuming his chair, "perhaps you can tell me if you would care to attend a hunt Wednesday next."

"I do not ride well enough to hunt," Annalise began awkwardly, aware that Marian was an expert horsewoman.

"We're merely going after grouse. Are you a decent shot?"

"I do not shoot at all," replied Annalise, "but I should enjoy joining the hunting party. Thank you for inviting me."

He laughed. "You may not thank me after seeing the bog into which we mean to venture."

The bog was indeed intimidating, with a blanket of bramble and wan trees that pierced the dawn mist like outstretched hands. Fourteen were in the party, and soon the women's skirts were heavy with mud as were the high-laced hunting shoes of the men. Derek managed surprisingly well, leading Marian and the others through the murk with Robert and Annalise bringing up the rear. No one spoke, and in the silence, their surroundings held a clammy, oppressive stillness. Finally, they crossed the bog and the gamekeeper loosed the black-and-white spaniels who scattered, sniffing at the ground, disappearing and reappearing through the mist. For two hours, they awaited results from the dogs, without luck. Finally, the packs were broken open, and bread, cold meat, and cheese, along with tepid tea dispensed. "Well, what do you think of grouse shooting?" inquired Robert laughingly from his seat at Annalise's feet.

"I feel as if we were trooping about the bogs of Ireland expecting to meet a banshee," Annalise replied with an expressive wave of her hand and a teasing smile. "Surely, you don't really do this for amusement."

"Don't you hunt tigers in India for amusement?" queried Robert, his eyes showing a dancing light of flirtation.

Annalise laughed. "You must ask your brother about tiger hunting. I have never had the honor of pursuing Old Stripes through the bamboo."

"You have indeed led a sheltered life if you have done no hunting, Miss Devon," inserted Marian. "I should think being a fair shot would be mandatory in India."

"I have never had the opportunity to learn to shoot, Miss Longstreet. My father was opposed to killing."

"If you intend to return to India, Miss Devon," said Derek, "you must learn to use a gun for personal protection. The situation there is becoming too perilous to ignore."

Robert sat up straight in some alarm. "Surely, you're not thinking of leaving us, Miss Devon."

At his evident interest, Derek abruptly intervened. "Rest easy, Robert. Miss Devon should be with us for some time. Certainly, she shall not return to India before any danger of rebellion is past."

"Begging your pardon, Miss Devon," said Robert, his relief mingled with a touch of gaiety, "but I cannot imagine why your father chose such an ill-tempered blackguard as my brother as your guardian."

"I have wondered that myself," put in Marian with a lifted brow. "Derek has so few fatherly inclinations." She made a little *moue* at Derek's dry expression.

"Colonel Clavell saved our *ghari* cart from slipping into the Ganges *en route* from Calcutta to Kanpur," Annalise explained. "I will tell you of it someday. My father considered him the best of men."

"I shouldn't wonder if the old gentleman did not mean to reform you, Derek," mischievously commented his brother. "They say the responsibility for children does wonders for maturity."

"There may be truth in that," retorted Derek. "I have certainly noticed you do not treat Miss Devon like a child."

Marian, piqued by the concentration of attention on Annalise, intervened. "I think we should all go shooting mountain goats in Switzerland this summer . . . although I dare say Miss Devon is not accustomed to climbing."

"I dare say I can follow anywhere you lead, Miss Longstreet," replied Annalise evenly. "The province of Szechwan where I grew up is extremely mountainous."

"It's settled then," said Robert, jumping up. "I shall teach Miss Devon to shoot."

"Miss Devon is my responsibility, Robert," Derek fired back at his brother. "Remember my need of maturity?"

"Shouldn't I teach Miss Devon to shoot?" hastily intervened Marian. "Learning from another woman might be more palatable for her."

Annalise finally ended all the bickering with a quiet, matter-of-fact opinion. "I believe Colonel Clavell should teach me to shoot. After all, I shall be obliged to fire at men, not grouse, and Colonel Clavell is the only one of us who has had that kind of experience."

Derek's triumphant glance at his discomfited brother drew a jealous glare from Marian; but Derek failed to notice. He was inwardly wincing from the pain that had been mounting in his head since first rising. His skull throbbing like a scarlet drum, he could only hope the hunt would be quickly ended. After brunch, they all set out again, fanning widely over the daisy-strewn field. The grass was straw colored, still flecked with sparkling dew, while the silence held only the low hum of insects. The sky was overcast to the north, but rapidly clearing to the east, with patches of blue skirting the sullen clouds. Suddenly, the dogs went rigid by a clump of brush. Robert and Marian quickly approached the dogs. With a whir of wings, two grouse took to the air in a brown blur. The guns whipped up and fired.

Even as the grouse plummeted to the earth, Derek went to his knees, the explosive sound issuing from the guns clamoring in his skull. Pressing his hands to his temples, he let out a strangled cry of pain. A shotgun seemed to have been put to his head and fired point blank, its charge echoing through every raw nerve ending. Through a red haze, he saw Annalise bending down to him, her face filled with anxiety, coming closer . . . then obliterated by a black veil.

When Derek regained consciousness, his head was resting in Annalise's lap. She was bathing his brow with cold water from a flask while the rest of the hunting party crowded close with anxious mutters. Robert bent worriedly over her shoulder while Marian looked down at his inert form, her concern mixed with horror.

"What happened?" Derek whispered.

When Marian told him, he struggled to rise, but Annalise pressed him down. "The gamekeeper has gone to fetch a carriage. You shouldn't try to walk, you look much too dizzy."

For the next hour, Derek kept protesting he was well enough to stand, but his slurred voice and unfocussed eyes made Robert insist he stay still. Both Robert and the gamekeeper were required to assist Derek into the carriage when it arrived. Marian joined him quickly.

Robert waved the driver toward the house. "Annalise and I will see our guests back," he called.

Derek struggled up to wave as the carriage pulled out, and he saw Robert's head bent to Annalise's as if they were talking intimately together. Startled at his sharp pang of jealousy, he closed his eyes and tried to listen to Marian. Her stream of anxious questions as to his welfare was distracting, but the image of his brother close to Annalise still burned against his eyelids. His brother had a familiar look; he had worn it himself when he had fallen in love with Marian. She was a potent aphrodisiac of which he could not get enough; why then should he be jealous of Robert's attentions to Annalise? He might rationalize that his reaction displayed the protectiveness of a brother, except the small core of magnetism drawing him toward Annalise was far from fraternal.

He had always been fond of her, but he knew he was more than that as of late. He must concentrate on Marian, for he was certain that if he could lure Marian back into bed, he would promptly forget about Annalise. His ward was practically a child, after all . . . in spite of the surprisingly rounded young body that pressed against his when he had so foolishly kissed her. Marian was no child, and her snug loden jacket showed that quality off to perfection. Forcibly, he tore his mind from Annalise and applied it to Marian. "Darling"—he kissed Marian's earlobe—"why don't we meet at the boathouse tonight? We've another eight long months until we can announce our engagement. Were I a priest, I should conduct the ceremony with good grace rather than suffer celibacy as a bridegroom."

Marian laughed, relieved that he was coherent. "You are a cockerel! Scarce awake, and already crowing." She stroked his cheek. "I am as impatient as you, my love, but you are not yet well enough to entertain such an escapade."

"Marian, I'm going daft. Why pretend to be a virgin, for God's sakes, when we've been sleeping together for years?"

"Most of those years you spent in India," she reminded

him blandly. "You cannot expect to find me the same woman after so long. Besides, I do not suppose that you passed all that time alone. England is not so far from India that I have not heard of *nautch* trollops. Besides"—she laughed—"I like to see you pant. You're far too used to having your wicked way with the ladies. When we are married, I want you to remember how hard I was to get; thereby you shall work all the harder to keep me, and not flirt with all the London actresses and ballet dancers."

Derek sighed. "Miss Longstreet, you are diabolically cruel."

"Not entirely." She stroked his jaw. "Think how eager we both will be . . ." she whispered in a sibilant purr that heated his blood.

Virgins: he cared nothing for virgins. Give him an experienced vixen like Marian any day. And the sooner the better!

During the month of May, Derek recovered from his fainting spell, but his headaches increased in frequency until the pain was so unrelenting, he feared he must lose his mind. Stoically, he completed his duties in managing the spring planting, but when not so occupied, he kept to his room and retired early. Even Annalise was banished from his company and Marian came to Claremore less and less.

On the first of June, at the dawn's light, Derek awoke with a splitting head. Apparently, this day was not beginning with a gradual increase of pain as usual. The afternoon promised agony, unrelieved by an engraved invitation from Marian to a formal "surprise" gathering that evening at Briarwood. After trying to find Robert to go in his stead, Derek rode over to the west barns with the steward, trying to decide which needed repair before the harvest. All morning, he wrangled with the steward, who thought money grew alongside the chestnuts.

Exhausted, he decided to try to ease his aching head by punting on the river. Soon he found that the effort of rowing was making his head worse, and lying back in the boat, he drifted down river. The green leaves of the trees overhead reminded him of Marian's eyes, the swirls of grass at the water's edge of her waving hair . . . and yet the water itself, cool and deep and blue reminded him mysteriously of Annalise: all shadows and quietly flowing currents, sunlit ripples of sapphires and molten Indian gold. With his eyes closed, he could imagine her hair like night, slipping through his fingers; feel the brush of her lashes, like midnight butterflies, against his cheek; hear her voice. Abruptly, he sat up. A peal of tinkling laughter sounded across the water from a bend of willows on the far bank. Through a veil of green he saw her white leghorn hat dipping low across the water over the gunnel of a boat. He heard Robert's voice, low and cajoling. Then he saw their heads draw together, the hat stop its lazy drift and poise for a long moment of a kiss that roused all his envy and anger. Swiftly, before they saw him, he applied himself to the oars and sped upstream despite his headache.

That afternoon, after lunch, a servant summoned Robert to the study. Robert's cheery, "Fine day, isn't it?" was abruptly interrupted.

"What are you thinking of?" Derek exploded. "Miss Devon is my ward, not your personal concubine! How dare you compromise her as you did this morning!"

"You compromised Marian Longstreet years ago, and I'll wager my intentions are more honorable with Annalise Devon than yours with the women you've kissed over the years. How many is it, Derek? Be honest. You must have stopped counting after fifty."

"Annalise Devon is different, and I bloody well ought to knock you down for that remark about Marian."

"Try it," responded Robert curtly. "I'm not the 'little' brother you left behind when Father packed you off to India. Annalise has never permitted me a kiss before, and I don't flatter myself that it was due to anything more than feminine curiosity. In fact, she as much as told me so, although I can't imagine who she can have been comparing me to, for she clearly had little experience.'' Robert casually examined his fingernails. "And frankly, I don't think fisticuffs are called for over Marian. Father was right about her, you know. She isn't good enough for you. She's calculating and shallow . . .''

Derek's eyes narrowed into furious slits. "One more word out of you and I'll pound you to a pulp, 'little brother.' You've developed a mind foul as a gutter.''

"At least I have a mind,'' snapped Robert. "It isn't tied up in so much of a bullet-creased snarl that I can't think straight.'' At the look of startled hurt on Derek's face, Robert hesitated, then let out his breath in regret. "I'm sorry, Derek. I didn't mean to say that, but I think you ought to know that I have only the best intentions toward Miss Devon. Surely, I cannot be blamed for kissing her. Only a blind man could forego that pleasure.''

"From now,'' Derek bit out, "you will be exactly that: blind. Unless you mean to wed Annalise, leave her alone, or you'll leave Claremore.''

Now Robert was angry. "You mean that, don't you? When I've kept the whole place going these past few years.''

"What are your intentions toward Miss Devon, Robert?''

"I don't know! I just wanted to kiss her . . .''

"Then don't, until you do know, and approach me first. I stand in her father's stead, Robert, and he was a good man, just as Annalise is an unsophisticated, innocent young woman. I won't have her sullied just because you want a convenient plaything.'' With that, Derek left the room as Robert gazed bemusedly after him.

Robert thought Derek more scrupulous than her father would have been. It was if he were a man in love rather than a guardian. A small, wry smile crossed his lips. He would not be asking his brother's permission before kissing Miss Devon again . . .

Marian's surprise proved to be a small concert to which all the local families of social consequence were invited. The music room was crowded. The pianist reigned as the lion of London's season and Marian was beside herself at having lured him into the country. He chose a noisy piece of Beethoven's to quiet the crowd.

Their skirts spread like richly colored bouquets of tulle, tarlatan, and glacé, the women sat cooling themselves with fans of ivory filigree and silk while the men sat stiffly in their black and white evening clothes, longing to retire to their cigars. The evening was hot, the Venetian doors thrown wide to capture the last twilight breeze. Bending heavily over the stone terrace balustrade were great peonies, wafting their fragrance through the summer air. Fragrant with Parisian perfume, Marian sat in the front row beside Derek and her father, while Robert and Annalise sat by Mrs. Longstreet. Marian was all in white, while Annalise wore her old blue tarlatan that, this time, failed to make her look as young as usual.

By the time the pianist began an equally noisy piece by Liszt, Derek knew he had made a mistake in attending. As the pianist pounded, the agony mounted until perspiration beaded Derek's brow. The vehement music aroused the terror that had been steadily growing for months; what if he finally went mad? In his mind, the music became an earsplitting cacophony that tore through him like physical blows. The figures in the audience seemed to develop scarlet haloes, while his own body bore a nimbus of agony. At that moment, or perhaps it was another, for he was no longer distinctly aware of anything, he saw Robert levelly look at him, then deliberately cover Annalise's hand with his own. Without thinking, impelled by pain and detonating rage, he went for Robert's throat. Chairs overturned and splintered while people scattered as he bore Robert to the floor. With his fingers locked around Robert's neck, they grappled in a blaze fomented by his tortured brain. He felt hands grab at his shoulders, tear at his hair, then a heavy blow at the back of his skull resounded hellishly before pitching him headlong into darkness.

Derek awoke surrounded by utter silence. As his vision cleared, he saw the wary face of a strange man bent over him, then gradually Annalise and Marian drifted into blurred view. He was in a strange bedroom and his head was hurting so badly he could scarcely think, far less speak with coherence, but when he remembered dimly what had happened, panic compelled him to try to struggle upright. "Robert! Where is Robert! Is he all right?"

Robert moved forward between Annalise and the doctor, then drew his hands from his coat pockets with a lopsided smile. "I'm a bit bent, but otherwise no damage done. The question is: how are you? We half expected you to be demented."

Derek grasped his offered hand. "I must have been demented . . ." Confused, he dropped Robert's hand to rub his throbbing forehead. "I *was* insane . . . for a minute . . . I wanted to kill you." He focussed on Robert's bruised neck. "Good God, I might have. What the devil . . . ?"

Seeing the confusion mounting in his pain-filled eyes, the stranger at his elbow pressed him down. "I am Dr. Sothby. My advice to you now is to rest until we can have a carriage brought round to take you to the hospital. I should like to keep you under observation for a few days."

"So you think I might be going mad, too."

"Not necessarily, but it's possible. You seem lucid enough now, but you did give a number of people quite a scare."

Derek's eyes narrowed. "Can I leave the hospital when I like?"

"If you behave in a sane manner for a week, I should think you capable of going home." He paused. "Your head hurts you a good deal, doesn't it?"

"My head . . . and back now. Whole left side."

Dr. Sothby nodded. "I should like to make a complete examination tomorrow. Miss Devon tells me you were wounded some months ago in the Kyber. Nasty occupation: professional soldier. I don't envy you, sir."

"I resigned my commission before coming home . . . I . . . if you don't mind, I should like some brandy."

"I think not, sir. Alcohol is the worst possible remedy for an aching head. If any painkiller is warranted, I shall so advise you after my examination. I should judge you have had altogether too much laudanum since returning home."

Derek nodded and sank back upon the pillows. While Dr. Sothby went to summon a servant, Marian bent over him. Her face was stiff with worry and patent nervousness. She almost looked as if she feared he would leap up from the bed and swing from the bell cord. "Don't worry, darling. I shall come every day to see you."

Too distracted to believe he would be free in a week, Derek looked past her at silent Annalise, whose dark eyes echoed the pain in his own. *I am here whether you prove mad or sane,* she seemed to say. *As long as you need me . . . as long as you let me stay by you.*

VI

The Abdication

A *week* later, Derek returned home a changed man, silent and pale after Dr. Sothby's guided tour about the local Bedlam with its chains, dark coffinlike seclusion boxes, and shrieking, wretched inmates. He arrived with a quiet, burly body servant with hamlike hands. "For protection," Derek commented shortly to Annalise and Robert. "Yours, not mine."

Early the next morning, Annalise was in the dimly lit hall when Robert came out of the library. After closing the door behind him with exaggerated care, he leaned back against the library's mahogany doors, his eyes closed. Wondering if he were ill, Annalise hurried to him, her soft leather heels making a muted sound on the marble. His eyes flashing open, Robert stepped away from the doors. Swiftly, he drew her with him to the conservatory with its long grand piano and pale-blue wall panels of olive wreathes and urns.

"Derek proposes to cede me the title," he told her in a tense voice.

Annalise was shocked. "Surely, not as an apology . . . !"

"No. I'm to be his heir in case of death or by reason of insanity. If Derek continues as he is, he can expect further attacks such as the one at Briarwood, but the alternative is just as grim. Dr. Sothby believes an operation on Derek's back may relieve pressure on the nerves damaged in India. He does not expect Derek to survive. Derek holds the opinion that he is no longer fit to carry the responsibilities of the baronetcy. He most fears the surgery will leave him alive but either mad or incompetent and unable to bequeath the title."

Pausing, Robert looked thoughtful. "I wonder what he plans to do about Marian. She visited him only once last week and if I'm not wrong, seems to be deuced well afraid of him."

"She must have been very shocked by his behavior. He has always been gentle with her." Annalise looked worried. "I do hope she visits him here. He needs her badly now."

"Did you know he struck me because of you?"

"What?" Her eyes widened in disbelief. "Why should he?"

"That same morning, he warned me to stay away from you. He must have seen us kissing on the river. When I took your hand at the concert to show he could not dictate to me, he reacted like an angry bull." He watched her closely. "Why do you think that is?"

"Why did you want to provoke him?" she countered.

"To see whether he was thinking like a father . . . or a lover."

Her brows nearly met in an angry frown. "How dare you play such games . . . as if I were some tawdry prize. I resent your behavior very much, Robert. You had no right . . ."

"I had every right. The next baroness of Claremore will

wield a good deal of power. As heir apparent, I am in a precarious position."

She glared at him, her anger mixed with disbelief. "You supposed he would marry me? Even if he cared for me in that fashion, which he does not, you are foolish to assume he should stoop to a level of society that he must consider beneath him. You insult me, sir, as well as your brother!" Turning on her heel, she left him staring after her.

By God, the little wench had a temper, mused Robert. What an interesting twist to her; he would have to explore it.

But he was to have little chance to explore anything with Annalise. Intent on keeping Derek's spirits up, Annalise was so often with him that Robert had no time with her. She was like a fierce little terrier, ready to defend Derek from anyone who threatened to upset him. Robert had to send her to Dr. Sothby's for a potion to get some time alone with his brother. "It's too risky, Derek," he warned. "I want a live brother, even if it costs me the baronetcy."

"That's fraternal of you," replied Derek with a wry smile as they walked together in the garden. "Will you keep me in a silk-padded cell in the attic?" He gripped Robert's shoulder. "I appreciate your concern, Robert, but don't you see I would rather be dead than live like a murderous idiot, a threat to everyone I love? If you love me, support me in my choice. Sothby seems like a good man, certainly better than the doctors who pieced me together in India, although I suppose I should thank them. They kept me alive when I should have by all odds died." He paused. "Let me do what I must, Robert. If there's a chance to live decently, I want it."

Robert looked at him, his worry mixed with resignation. "If you must, you must, but I don't mind saying I don't like it. I just lost a father; I don't want to lose a brother as well.

When you came home alive, I though God had blessed this house, after all. To lose you twice would be hell."

"If I lose my faculties, you will lose both me and the baronetcy as surely as if I were banished to hell . . . for I will be in hell, Robert."

Marian was no more pleased than Robert when she found Derek alone that afternoon in the garden, but expressed herself more forcefully. "Give up the baronetcy just because you had a temporary seizure? You *are* mad!" For nearly an hour, she stormed to and fro until the crunch of her impatient footsteps on the gravel walks hurt his head. "How can you think of relinquishing your heritage, your birthright? Do you want to be a mere country squire, parcelled off to some petty farm while your brother takes your place in the House of Lords? What will happen to all your ambitions, to *our* ambitions?"

Furious when she could not change his mind, Marian stormed back to Briarwood in a rage.

Only Annalise was reconciled to the operation. The evening before Derek was to go into surgery, she sat quietly with him in the library. For a long while, they sat companionably without speaking, both gazing into the fire while its flames flickered upward like the tendrils of a tropical flower. India, with all its bright, mysterious passion and splendor, appeared to them in the flames with turrets and minarets shaped by the licking gold-red firelight. "How alien and exotic the fire seems in this English darkness," murmured Annalise. "India is so very distant."

Derek regarded her dark, delicate silhouette lined by the firelight. Her features were pensive, her eyes faraway beneath their long, shadowing lashes. "Do you miss it much?"

She evaded a direct answer. "I have been happy enough at Claremore."

"With an ill-tempered tyrant who attempts to throttle people for after-dinner entertainment?"

"You were not yourself. The Colonel Clavell I kno kind and gentle beneath his hard exterior."

"And you think that after tomorrow's operation, he will return to you," he observed ironically.

"He is here now," she said softly, "and tomorrow is in God's hands."

His voice softened. "You have the faith of your father. Would that he were here now . . . I could do with one of his uplifting sermons."

"Then why did you never attend one of them while he was alive?" she returned teasingly. "You are very late to church, sir."

"Perhaps because I do not believe that God spends much time in church. Why should he listen to a parcel of hymn singers when children are wailing from hunger in the streets of Calcutta? Perhaps God is where he is needed . . ." he paused, "just as you are. You have been a blessing to this house, Annalise."

She looked startled. "But I have done nothing."

He leaned forward, the firelight sculpting the bleak, rugged planes of his hard face. "The quietude of your spirit is a blessing. I think that serenity helped me to make my decision. To you, everything is in God's hands and happens for good reason. I have lost much of late, but the peace in your face promises it was all for the best, even if it stems from the peace of a child."

Her lashes lifted, her amber eyes mysterious. "I think we both know I am no longer a child, Colonel."

He, too, remembered his kiss, and sat back in his chair, his eyes grave. "I should not have taken such advantage of your trust. You may be sure I will not do so again."

"I liked being kissed, Colonel." Her eyes were level. "I should be very sorry to think I should not be kissed so again . . . whoever the gentleman might be."

He eyes her intently. "Why did you kiss Robert?"

"I wanted to see if I should like his kiss as much as yours," she answered simply.

He laughed shortly. "And did you?"

She tilted her head thoughtfully. "His kiss was more . . . to the point than yours."

He frowned in puzzlement. "Was I so timid?"

"Less timid than tentative, or perhaps explorative."

"And Robert's was not . . . explorative."

"Oh, no," she replied soberly. "He knew exactly what he wanted."

This time he did not laugh. "You are not to kiss him again," he said tersely.

"Oh, I had very little to do with it," she said noncommittally. Then she asked, "Will you be buying another mare at the horse fair in Chicester?"

Derek was not to be diverted. "Did you enjoy my kissing you?"

"Oh, I did not assume you were serious, so I have tried not to think very much about it." She folded her hands demurely in her lap. "After all, baronets do not kiss ministers' daughters with a view to marriage."

Derek let out his breath explosively. "You are certainly cool about that probability." His mind flicked to another tack. "Why the devil should a man marry every woman he kisses? A kiss is just . . . a paltry kiss."

"Then why did you attack Robert merely for holding my hand?" she pointed out.

His voice and temper went up a notch. "Because I told him not to; that's why!"

"But I'm not a porcelain figurine and Robert is not a two-year-old child. Why should you intervene?"

"I'm responsible for you," he answered, exasperated.

"But you're not my father. Surely, you don't mean to insult my judgement."

He rose abruptly. "Kissing Robert is very ill advised, and

you're too young to contemplate a serious relationship with any man. While I am your guardian, you will heed my wishes."

She stood up as well. "I didn't think guardianship ceded you the rights of a property owner. I don't belong to you, Colonel, whatever arrangement you and my father devised. I shall, however, endeavor to be more discreet about my private affairs."

Derek's nose nearly met hers. "Does that mean you intend to do your kissing behind the bushes?"

"It means I shall let you know whenever I mean to be serious about a man, and mind you, I shall not be asking for your approval."

"And I was thinking you were a quiet, tranquil little piece," he burst out in exasperation. "Didn't your father ever teach you anything about filial duty?"

"No more than your father taught you when you became engaged to Marian Longstreet. You do recollect why you were sent to India?"

His guns spiked, Derek watched her march from the room. You little baggage, he thought, his anger mixed with admiration, you trimmed me as neatly as a gunnery sergeant disciplining a puny *jawan*.

The doctor was still in the house at noon the next day. Sothby had taken over the parlor for Derek's operation. "The parlor affords the best light and I can control the atmosphere here as well as at the hospital." Annalise was unsure what he meant, for he had closed all the parlor windows and the room reeked with the unfamiliar stench of carbolic acid and chloroform. The operation had been an agonizing ordeal, and Derek's scream when his leg was rebroken still seemed to echo about the house. Mercifully, he lost consciousness afterward and was oblivious when the doctor began the dangerous surgery on his back. Annalise sat outside the door in misery. "I lost my temper and quarreled with Derek last night, Robert," she muttered worriedly. "He could die still upset by all I said to him."

"Do you want to apologize?"

"No . . . I'm just sorry I made him angry."

His own concern evident in his eyes, he took her hands. "Don't worry then. Derek has spent most of his adult life being angry. Once Father began to groom him for the baronetcy, he rode him ruthlessly. I dare say your quarrel was a mere spark to the conflicts they used to have." He paused, then his eyes narrowed shrewdly. "What did you quarrel about?"

Her quick flush told him all he wanted to know as she backed away. "A private matter. I told him he was being altogether too proprietary."

"Derek takes surrogate fatherhood quite seriously. I must say I'm relieved. Before he went to India, he was as wild as you can imagine." Worriedly, he stared at the closed parlor door. "Apart from his roaring temper, he's as fine a brother as a man could want . . . what's taking Sothby so blasted long?"

The wait was long. When the door finally opened, Sothby looked exhausted, the front of his apron bloodstained. Annalise and Robert rose from their chairs almost as one. "He survived the operation," said Sothby. "I took a mass of splinters out, drained and excised the old wound. Only time will tell whether he will survive the fever or even whether I have done any good. He must have absolute bed rest and no disturbances for at least a month. I'll send over a trained nurse from the hospital."

Derek hovered between life and death for a long week. Robert stopped by Derek's bedroom whenever he could escape his estate duties and sat with his brother during the long evenings. Annalise alternated with the nurse by his bedside, bathing him hourly to keep the fever down. In a few days' time, she looked no less haggard than Derek, so white and still in his bed. Heavily drugged with laudanum, he was scarcely aware of her and when he spoke her name faintly, his speech was slurred.

"Don't try to talk," she said softly. "Just rest for now. I shall be here if you need me." And she was. At times, the nights merged with those nights in India when Derek lay moaning on his bed under the mosquito netting, and Annalise would awaken from a drowsy stupor by Derek's bedside, wondering where she was.

Marian came twice to speak briefly alone with Derek, but she never lingered. In the third week, Sothby ventured to suggest that Derek might survive, and on one of her visits, Marian ventured to suggest to Derek that he resume the baronetcy.

"Take back what I gave Robert, when it means so much to him?" Derek shook his head. "I think not. And besides, it's much too early to decide such a step."

Marian was adamant. "The baronetcy is yours by right, Derek, and the doctor says you're doing wonderfully. He expects the relieved pressure on your spine will reduce your headaches. In a few months, you should be completely well. It's absurd to give up your birthright."

But Derek refused to discuss the matter, although he would wait for Marian's visits as if she were the sun on a black day, and Annalise would try to reassure him that Marian would soon reconcile their differences. As if fighting his own weakness, he struggled to forget his disappointment and tried to concentrate on becoming well.

One day as he reclined in the chaise longue by his bedroom fire, he caught Annalise's hand and indicated for her to sit on the edge of the chaise. "Tell me, little oracle, if you were in love with a man, would you shun him?"

"I am not Marian, Colonel," she said quietly. "I cannot say what she would do."

"I asked what you would do." His eyes were intent and dark with pain, whether from his headaches or Marian's abandonment, Annalise could not tell. Surely, her own feelings could not matter to him so much.

"If I loved a man unwisely, then I should stay away, but if not, then nothing should separate us," she replied, then added in a muffled tone, "provided he loved me in return."

"And if you believed he did not?"

She gave him a long look. "Then I should guard my heart very carefully."

He stared into the fire. "Marian believes I do not love her enough to reclaim the baronetcy. Being a baroness means more to her than I realized."

"Must you then choose between her and Robert?"

He smiled crookedly. "Solomon rarely had a more difficult judgement."

"Do you care as much for Marian as you do for Robert?"

He was silent a moment. "Yes, I do. Each, in a different way, is dear to me. I have known Marian since childhood. I think we have always known we were meant to marry. Only in India"—his rueful smile turned a trifle puckish—"I sometimes forgot."

Annalise laughed. "Perhaps you might forget again."

"You sound like my father."

"Our last quarrel was over a similar problem from your direction. Shall we each be at ease with our respective fathers and produce no more advice?"

His smiles were rare these days, but the shadow of one crossed his lips. "Your father was one of the best men I ever knew."

Her smile was gentle. "He was very fond of you . . . and very proud. You have great courage, Derek, or you would not be alive now."

"Tomorrow, I mean to walk," he said flatly. "And by the end of next week, I mean to walk up the steps of Briarwood to tell Marian she will have to settle for being a colonel's wife in the company's army. *That* is where *I* belong."

Climbing the steps at Briarwood with his crutches was as difficult as climbing the side of the Kyber Pass and the results were as disastrous. Derek returned to Claremore in a daze and had the driver and his footman carry him back to his room on a chair. Annalise held his hand as they proceeded down the long, oak-panelled hallway.

"Marian won't go to India," he muttered to Robert who was at his shoulder. "The engagement is off. She said if I loved her, I wouldn't take her to that cholera-ridden, pestilential heat."

They set his chair down at the door of his room. He turned to Annalise. "I want to be alone." Then he hobbled through the double doors.

"Doesn't sound promising for the jungle, does it?" quipped Robert as he closed the doors behind them.

"Oh, do be serious," said Annalise sharply. "He's enduring this for you."

Robert sagely shook his head. "Oh, I think he's looking after himself; he just doesn't know it."

"He's lost his career, his health, his birthright, and now Marian. I fear for him."

"Come now," Robert cajoled. "He is better off without her, you'll see."

A week passed before Derek ventured from his room. If he was glad to have lost Marian, he gave no evidence of it. Now, he would often have his footman and driver carry him out to the garden instead of making the effort to hobble across the gravel paths. His condition deteriorated and in the morning, he spent long hours asleep on the chaise in the dim library. An active, vital man, he was particularly constrained by crutches and resented Annalise requiring that he visit with her. Listlessly, he listened to her read to him while walking or sitting in the garden. For her sake, he made a pretense of interest, but she sensed his mind was on Marian.

One afternoon, they sat alone in the garden while she read to him in the shade of a massive chestnut tree. Their heads and shoulders dappled by the sunlight sifting through the leaves, he lay quietly on the grass with his head in her lap while the poetry of John Donne shimmered through the boxwood hedges, formal, clustered rosebushes, and lilacs. ''I think Donne would call you the lady of the shadows,'' murmured Derek when she had finished *The Canonization*.

She tilted her head. ''Why such a sad entitlement?'

''Because the shadows of your eyes beneath their lids are the most delicate violet,'' he mused, ''and you have a Renaissance face . . . like a heroine out of Dante. Lying here, I feel as if we were together in a sunlit garden of four hundred years ago, with the centuries halted for the fall of a phrase.

'Then as an angel, face and wings
Of air, not pure as it, yet pure doth wear,
So thy love be my love's sphere;
Just such disparity
As is 'twixt air and angels' purity,
'Twixt women's love and men's will ever be.' ''

She laughed a trifle self-consciously. ''I fear you have your Donne and Dante a trifle mixed. Dante might have called me solemn and dark . . .''

''As the wings of night,'' he murmured. ''Loveliness as fair as the midnight star.''

She smiled. ''Rosy sunlight has not left you entirely, I think. Matters may be yet reconciled with your lady.''

''I'll not go begging to her . . . or Robert,'' he said abruptly. ''Nothing is settled. My head still hurts like the devil and I could go berserk in the next hour, with both of them better without me."

"You still fear you will be sent to an asylum?"

"Whatever happens, I won't end up in an asylum."

She looked at him sharply. "You wouldn't harm yourself."

He closed his eyes. "Why should I?"

Noting the noncommittal tone of his voice, she was filled with silent fear. Careful to register nothing, she thought desperately. Short of locking him up, there was no way of assuming he would not try to put an end to his life. Then, a possibility occurred to her. Derek had many painful needs now, and she was capable of filling only one of them. Slowly, deliberately, she bent her head and kissed him.

Startled, he flicked his eyes open. "What the devil . . ."

"No devil," she murmured. "I merely thought you should be reminded that not everything is predictable. As long as you are alive, anything is possible: even that you may be well again and that a woman may love you."

For a long moment, he looked up at her. "Did you kiss Robert in this fashion?"

She laughed softly. "Most certainly not." Then added with a mischievous sparkle in her eye, "No kisses are the same; even a novice quickly learns that fact." She traced his lips wonderingly as if seeing them for the first time. "Of course, that kiss just now was disappointing."

"I saw nothing wrong with it," he asserted swiftly, "though it was deuced brief."

Seeing the half-shy invitation in his eyes, she kissed him again lingeringly, as though tasting a luscious but possibly threatening fruit. "Yes, there is a great improvement when one's kiss is returned," she said softly. "Your lips taste like the apple you ate an hour ago."

"Yours taste of peace," he breathed. "I think I find my appetite returning."

She laughed. "No fear. I shall be fond of you even as a portly gentleman."

His eyes darkened with both wariness and attraction. "Are you fond of me now, as a shambling wreck?"

"You are dear to me, as my father was." She evaded his eyes dancing with impudence and a touch of the same wariness as her own.

"Somehow kissing you reminds me I am not your father," he teased. "I wonder why."

"Perhaps I should help you think of a reason." Her head bent once more over his. The kiss was innocent at first, yet filled with the age-old instinct of a woman: a knowledge that grew with every passing moment.

In mid-kiss, Derek suddenly gripped her shoulders and pressed her away. "Don't . . . Annalise, you don't realize the effect you're having on me. Your father made you my responsibility . . . "

"Have you considered that Father made you mine as well?" When he looked puzzled, she added softly, "Father saw that we were both alone. I needed someone to look after me, while you needed someone to look after you."

He was thoughtful for a moment. "I see what you mean. I have wondered what he had in mind, but we're an unlikely pair, you and I."

"I don't think I fully understood myself what he intended until now."

He sat up. "Whatever he intended, he didn't mean for you to be involved in a liaison. I upbraided Robert for taking such liberties with you."

"Robert's intentions are a great deal more honest than yours," she said levelly. "He has never lied about his feelings, even in pretense of being noble."

"You imagine my pretense?"

"I know about the *bibi gurh* of women behind your house

in Kanpur," she replied wisely. "Its tropical flowers are surprisingly voluptuous."

"You are not a *bibi*," he retorted.

"But I am a woman," she shot back, "even if I am a minister's daughter."

He laughed shortly. "You haven't the faintest idea of what it means to be a woman. You're scarcely out of school."

"School is a matter of learning, is it not?" She leaned toward him again, her dark eyes lustrous with subtle invitation. "Teach me . . ."

"Not on a dare," he breathed. "I should never be able to stop with a single lesson."

She smiled. "Have you ever thought that I might have something new to teach you?"

He grinned. "Frankly no."

This time, her smile held a glimmer of challenge. "Rest assured, I am like no other woman you have ever known, milord, whereas you are as shy and safe as a lamb."

This time he kissed her firmly and with an intensity that dispelled any notions about his temerity. Judgement seemed a dim, dull shadow next to the vibrance that leaped between them. Her head slipped back, her throat arching beneath his kisses. Determined to teach her not to meddle with his passions, he pressed her down, then slowly, surely, lost the path of his intent and found the thread of longing, leading him as if he were a child lost in a dark, threatening forest. Her lips were wine, they were life, they were light promising an end to his despair. He kissed her as if she were hope itself, the promise of a day filled with glorious sun. The sun brightened through the chestnut leaves, spangling them with motes of flickering gold. Living flame twined in the light, pulsed with promise of delight yet unborn, then slipped into the waning glow of the afternoon.

VII

The Affair

That evening, Derek moodily listened to Annalise playing Chopin. Robert was out, gone to a campaign meeting for election to the House of Lords, and Derek could not help wishing he were in Robert's place. Fruitless now, to think of all the things in life he should have done to accomplish his ambitions, but one mistake he would not make, as he had come so perilously near to doing, was to enter into an affair with the young, unwary Annalise. She was so trusting, so tender, and he had been so nearly swept into the current of passion with her. He could sense her lips on his even now, alluring, undeceiving, all that he could want in a lover. . . and yet, that was all he could promise her: a liaison that could end only in unhappiness and disenchantment.

They were from two different worlds, and Marian: stormy, willful Marian, still ruled his heart. He could not get Marian out of his thoughts, and yet, so quickly, Annalise had slipped into her place, calmly moving her aside as if she were chaff on the wind. Annalise was like that wind, elusive, cool, twining about him, then slipping away. After they had left the garden, she had become a demure, distant stranger again; thoughtful, as if she shared his misgivings.

"Annalise," he said quietly, when she finished the melody she had been playing, "we must talk."

Smoothly, she closed the piano with an unconsciously graceful gesture and waited.

"I owe you an apology," he began gravely. "I never should have kissed you today."

"Perhaps the discussion should begin the other way around. I kissed *you* . . . but I am far from sorry for it." She smiled softly. "I have been wanting to kiss you for a very long time."

"Annalise"—his voice was muted—"you must not confuse compassion with love. I am not the man for you, not for any woman. The future that confronts me is too unpromising to share with anyone I care for. The last manhood I have would be erased, should I destroy your innocence."

"I am not a blind waif you must shepherd through life. One day, I shall become a woman, whether or not you are my teacher. As for compassion, I do not think I spend it unwisely. You are a good man, who has given much of his time and self to others. Infirmity does not lessen your attributes. The Derek Clavell I care for, did not die in the Kyber."

"No, he died when he attacked his own brother." Derek caught up his crutches and headed toward the library door. "Do not hope for a tomorrow with me, Annalise; there is none."

"You will have a tomorrow, Derek," she called softly after him. "Whether I mean to share it or not is a matter of *my* choosing."

The next day, Derek brought in a male nurse from

Brighton and politely but firmly shut Annalise out of his personal life. No longer did he ask her to play the piano and read to him, or do any of the small, caring services she had been wont to perform. Together, they had been able to bring a measure of peace to one another; apart, they were bleakly and finally alone.

Derek had been silent of late and appeared much the same as always, but Robert was quick to notice a change in Annalise. She seemed to fade, like a bright wildflower that bloomed too soon to escape the last frosts of winter. Unaware of what had passed between her and his brother, Robert attributed her sadness to his own neglect. Hoping to cheer her one bright morning as they walked under the chestnuts, he invited her to accompany him to London on business. "You might wish to do some shopping and see the sights. We shall be staying with my Aunt Gertrude, so even Derek can rest easy about the proprieties."

"Of course, I would love to go. I've been thinking of traveling to London for some days now. When shall we leave?"

Taken aback by her ready acceptance, he temporized. "Ah . . . I was thinking of the day following tomorrow. Don't you want to ask Derek?"

"No, why should I?"

"Well, perhaps I should let him know."

"As you wish."

Derek's release of wrath brought on a fierce headache. "That does it," he muttered, clutching his head as he berated Robert. "She can go, but I'm sending a note to Gertrude to provide permanent quarters for that little mutineer. You"—he fixed his brother with an unyielding stare—"will stay in an inn."

En route to London, the trip was not as delightful as Robert had hoped. Having anticipated a pleasant time alone with Annalise to press his suit, he could not understand her friendly but distant reaction. "Robert," she said firmly, "you have assumed the duties of baronet. Nothing can be the same as it was. I have learned to my rue that one kiss does not make a lifelong attachment."

Not realizing she was referring to the excitement of discovery and awakening passion under these very chestnuts with Derek, Robert mistakenly assumed she was referring to his kissing her in the boat. Remembering the tender, tentative brush of her soft lips under a parasol while drifting on the river, he protested, "But Annalise, although I may have been neglecting you of late due to the press of duty, I have certainly not forgotten you or that kiss; far from it."

"No matter," she replied calmly. "I am accompanying you to London not to further our relationship, but to visit an old friend of my father's, Professor Sanderville. Professor Sanderville stayed with my family for some months in China when I was twelve years old. He should have been my guardian, had Derek not been appointed in his place. He will not know of my father's death, and I would break the news to him gently."

Two days later, Robert's heartfelt protests grew in vehemence as they neared the outskirts of London, but he delivered her to Professor Sanderville's as requested. Best not to have Annalise about, he decided with regretful resignation, when he and Gertrude discussed her future exile from Claremore.

Professor Sanderville swung from delight at Annalise's arrival to great sorrow at the news of William's death, but reacted with shrewd assessment at her request for suitable semipermanent lodging in London. "I can afford no more than the simplest flat," she advised him, "and I shall need it for only a matter of months. I want to miss the rainy season upon my return to India. Father and I found travel at that time impossible."

"Why not come with me to India in September?" queried

Professor Sanderville. A little man with a snowy wealth of mutton-chop whiskers, he had bright blue eyes like shiny marbles stuck in a round, pink ham. "You may be having difficulties keeping the young Clavell brothers at bay, but I cannot be accused of ulterior motives. I'm old enough to be your grandfather. What a pity that William died so young." To Martin Sanderville, anyone under forty was underripe.

Across town, the regal, white-haired Lady Annandale, Gertrude Clavell-Downing was equally forthright with Robert. "You shall send Annalise Devon here to live with me. I won't have you and Derek bickering over her like a bone with not a pure intention between you. You're both spoiled and too much used to having your own way. That poor chick hasn't a chance of escaping without her feathers mussed."

When she met Annalise after her visit to Professor Sanderville, Gertrude was much less inclined to dub her a poor chick. "Good afternoon, Lady Annandale," murmured Annalise with a small curtsey perfected in after-church receiving lines. "I am so very happy to meet you at last."

Chic Gertrude cupped her chin. "You're a pretty sprig. I can see why my nephews are taken with you.'

"They might as easily be taken with a sister," amended Annalise smoothly, "for they have extended me all the kindnesses of elder brothers."

"I dare say their motives are not entirely brotherly," said Gertrude dryly. "Their habits are altogether too self-interested for that."

"I have found them the best and most honorable of hosts, Lady Annandale. My own father could hold them up to no reproach."

I dare say not, thought Gertrude, as he's conveniently deceased. "That's a very self-possessed young woman," she affirmed to Robert after Annalise retired to her room to freshen up before teatime. "A pity she's a commoner. She might have made a very fair duchess." She tapped her fan against her cheek. "You may be quite sure I shall waste no time in removing her from Claremore."

"Not too far away, Aunt," begged Robert with a roguish grin. "There's a shortage of eligible duchesses in Sussex."

Gertrude arched an ironic brow. "Has Marian Longstreet retired to Scotland?"

"Indeed not. She and Derek had a furious row. The explosion could be heard all the way to Wales."

"I take it she resented being deprived of the duchy."

"The phrase she used was, 'I damned well won't be buried in India.'"

"Pish," said Gertrude. "India isn't the issue. It's Claremore she's always wanted"—she frowned—"but I could have sworn she wanted Derek as much."

"He's a changed man, Aunt. As I told you, he embarrassed her mightily at the concert and his operation has not yet made him regain his feet in earnest."

"And you say he's the one who ordered Miss Devon to London." The fan began to tap again. "Perhaps I may pay a visit to Claremore before Annalise vacates the estate." She eyed him. "Just how serious are *your* designs on her?"

He flushed slightly. "Well . . . I . . . wasn't thinking of marriage."

She made a short, ironic sound of dismissal. "That's honest, at least. What about Derek?"

"I didn't know he was interested in her at all."

"So he's serious enough to keep his mouth closed, at least." The fan flicked open. "I shall definitely have to visit Claremore."

Annalise thought London the dirtiest, most confusing, handsomest city she had seen, for it was filled with surprises. "As Ben Johnson says," Robert remarked as they rode home after a frenetic week, "when a man is tired of London, he is tired of life."

At Claremore, they were greeted by a welcome surprise

when Derek left his crutches at the top of the verandah steps and walked down to meet them. Although he used a cane, and his face was white with strain, he managed the descent capably. Robert let out his breath as Derek negotiated the final step. "Bravo!" He clapped Derek on the shoulder. Derek swayed, but kept his balance. "I knew nothing would keep you off your feet!"

Annalise was silent, her bright, tender eyes speaking for her as Derek looked down at her. Erect with pride, she smiled up at him, then took his arm opposite Robert, and they mounted the steps.

That night, Annalise was awakened by a sound: low, distorted, agonized. At first, she thought an animal had somehow wandered into the house—a dog, even a wolf, perhaps. Then she recognized the sound as human, emerging from the depths of misery. The groan came again. Sweeping back the covers, she rose swiftly and covered her long linen nightgown with a cashmere shawl, then went silently out into the hall. The house was dark, the moonlight sifting beneath Derek's door opposite hers. Behind the door came the fall of a candlestick; she could hear it rolling across the bare floor until it was halted by the carpet. She knocked gently. "Derek. Derek, let me in. Are you all right?"

There was a long silence, then a muffled cry. The door abruptly jerked open. Derek was half dressed, his torso bare, his hair rumpled from tossing in his bed. Clearly, he had gotten no sleep. "Go away," he rasped. "I don't need you . . ." As he closed the door, he half-twisted away as if shrinking from some unbearable light. Gripping his head, he curled into himself.

She caught his arm and led him toward the bed. "Lie down. You're unsteady on your feet."

He tried to pull away, but the pain in his head contorted like a bent shaft of iron. Gasping, he went to his knees.

With a low cry, she went down beside him to cradle his head to her breast. Blindly, his arms went about her, clung to her as if she were his last refuge. "Derek ... oh, my poor darling," she whispered, kissing his forehead, then his eyes. "It's all right, I'm with you. I won't go away as long as you need me."

He buried his face between her breasts, breathed lilac and the soft, sweet smell of female. Felt the untouched, young curves of her luring him despite the blinding pain in his head. Then the agony came again, worse than before and he made a dull sound of despair in his throat. Gently, gently, she held him through the long hours while the pain racked him, until, like a red, glowing sea, it ebbed and sank away into the sands of fearful memory. Exhausted and unable to reach the bed, he sank down upon the floor and drew her down beside him, clasping her to him like a precious talisman. Silently, they lay entwined while he slept until the light of mauve dawn glinted through the windowpanes. Awakened by a strand of her hair across his cheek, Derek turned on his side and stroked her raven tresses back to spill across the Persian rug. Her eyes drowsily opened to find him gazing down at her as if she were some fair, fabulous gift he had just discovered. Slowly, ever so gently, his lips covered hers as his hand slipped down her long curves. Startled, breathless, she felt him caress her breast, explore the length of her inner thigh. She needed no further lessons in love to know he desired her, longed to be one with her... as she did with him.

Love and compassion overcame her first instinctive fright, and gently, she unfastened her gown for him, eased his way by arching under his caresses, let him know that her heart and body welcomed him. His lips found the pale, bare skin between her breasts, the high, pink roses at their crests, made her shudder and thrill at the flushing tingle throughout her body when he tasted them. Her throat was his Nile, her breasts the lilies floating upon it. Slowly, he unfastened the remainder of the gown, his kisses grazing the untouched perfection of her slender form. The dawn caressed her body with a gold-pink light even as his own fingertips wonderingly traced the shadows that it made upon her ivory skin. At long last, he found the dark, curling fleece between her thighs, and kissed her there as if finding a delicate, priceless secret. Aware she was a virgin, he ventured slowly, his expert caresses languid, yet exploring her body as a connoisseur would a lovely painting, tantalizing himself, putting off the moment of supreme understanding.

Finally, when she was breathless with dazed, half-fearful anticipation, he opened himself with a single, quick gesture that gave the lie to his patience before his hands slipped down her sides as his tongue darted gently inside her, its delicate flick sending rouged waves of heat through her, inundating her like a fiery sea. Then his body came over her, surged inside her at the moment the heat wave crested, mingling sharp pain and delight together, so that her cry was that of a child being born, and a mother yielding to that life and all the pleasure that gave it shape.

Slowly, the pain ebbed as his body receded from hers, only to pulse within her again and sweep the pain away. His eyes were dark, holding hers as if he would never have enough of her. Gently, so gently, like foam upon the crest of swirling water, he moved within her as if they had been one since the beginning of time. Eons seemed to pass, with the ancient knowledge of love re-creating itself, reshaping their bodies and souls with a quickening, musical rhythm. Annalise felt her mind spin away. Derek was loving her. Her. He was inside her, joined to her, the very beat of his heart quickening to match hers, even as his body was quickening, soaring, taking her with him, higher, the foam spilling away from them in specks of spume, higher to the sun itself, where they were wreathed in searing, perfect light. The light burst inside Annalise's soul, streaked outward in a spinning nebula that made her cry out against Derek's lips. With a low sound of exaltation, he buried his face against her shoulder and found his own splendid release. Their lovemaking ended like a still, ecstatic sigh, a single breath in the stillness.

Sometime later, Derek cradled Annalise's silky head against his shoulder and carried her to the bed, where he lay beside her, stroking her gently until the dawn had brightened the sky into full morning, clear and blue-white like a polished mirror that reflected their joyful, newborn discovery of one another. Although he longed to love her again, Derek knew Annalise's virginal body was as yet too tender to endure his renewed passion. Soon . . . soon she would be healed and be his alone. He delighted in her innocence, cherished her as if she were adorned in diamonds with a purity rivaling the Grail of King Arthur. Gently, silently, he carried her back to her room and laid her on the bed. There, he kissed her lingeringly and coaxed the tendrils of hair back from her brow. "Thank you," he whispered. "You have become my dream of hope. I turned to you in pain and you answered me in joy, like a limitless, hovering spirit. God give me the strength to be worthy of your gift."

After he left her, Annalise lay for a long while with a shy, wondering smile. Derek had made her a woman and she would never be a child again. He had blessed her with his tenderness and his seed. Somehow, she knew her father would not be shamed by her choice of a lover. Derek was a good man, for all his temper and autocracy. He was brave and tender, loving and kind.

But he would not marry her. She must have no delusions on that score, whatever beatification she cared to bestow upon their lovemaking. While worthy enough in her own light, she was, after all, no Marian. She had walked out upon a very narrow ledge and the fall would be long if she made a misstep. As she progressed out upon the ledge, it would narrow until she had no choice but to step into perilous space. Taking Derek as a lover could only prove disastrous, she reminded herself ruefully. Their making love did not mean he loved her, and with time, he could only grow weary or embarrassed by her as a mistress. Still, she had given herself to Derek not only impulsively, but with certainty that he was the man with whom she wished to share her virginity. She had never thought she would know this moment, and brief as it might be, she reveled in it.

Robert, too, could not help wondering why Derek so strongly discouraged his company when they went boating on the river two days later. For the first time, he thought Aunt Gertrude might have been right about Derek's intentions. With a slight frown, he watched the boat dwindle around the bend and disappear in a sunny haze along the willows. Jealousy tripped lightly through his mind like a small demon, jabbing at memory after memory of Derek's quiet attention to Annalise. How like Derek to vault over the fence after the lamb, while deluding the rest of the wolf pack into pursuing other game. Robert frowned again, flicking sharply at a thistle with his ebony-tipped cane. Annalise was delectably charming and nothing like the simpering, ringleted little idiots who too often bid for his attention. Still, a minister's daughter . . . it was really too bad of Derek to seduce a minister's daughter. Robert thought he had better write Aunt Gertrude and advise her to pay a call sooner than she had intended.

Derek and Annalise beached their boat a few miles below Claremore in a sun-dappled dell and spread a linen cloth over the grass. Cheese, fruit, and wine from the picnic hamper were neglected as Derek pressed Annalise down beneath him and slowly covered her face and throat with lingering kisses. "Bother the food; I've been hungry for you," he whispered. "This moment has been in my mind for days."

"And mine," she murmured. "Today alone has seemed like an eternity. Derek, hold me . . . love me now."

Derek needed no second bidding, but took his time slipping off her hoops and unbuttoning her bodice, savoring each moment, each bit of ivory flesh and white lace that escaped the fastenings of her dress. Smoothly, the camisole lacings slipped free, and her amber eyes reflected the glow in his own as he surveyed the exquisite bounty that was his. Fascinated, he undressed her until she was naked as Venus, pure and pagan. Long and silky, she luxuriated beneath his caressing hands, arched toward him on the sweep of white linen as he unclothed himself and came to her. Magnificently made, his long brown body covered her pale one, his sex warm and probing. Still, he held himself back, touching her everywhere, discovering each small path the sunlight made between the leafy shadows on her skin. He found the curling dark mound that still kept secret the pink flower of her womanhood. Opening her thighs, he made love to her, giving to her, pleasuring her until she moaned softly and her fingers tightened in his thick, black hair. A little, guttural, animal cry escaped her as his tongue probed deeper, finding her source, making her twist and cry out for the release only his manhood sheathed inside her could fulfill. Only then did he enter her, and even then, with delicious, tantalizing slowness so that she felt the entire length of him, slowly burying deeply within her. He filled her so that she ached with the size of him. Annalise wrapped her legs about Derek with age-old instinct and caught him close, hearing the hum of a nearby bee like the underlying note in a summer symphony. Derek's fingers buried in her hair as he moved inside her, tasting her lips in slow rhythm with the swirling drive of his body. Their cadence increased as their heart-beats quickened, the music of their senses interplaying with the rush of the breeze from the water and rustle of the meadow grass. The sun was growing hot on their bare skin and the tree's crusty gray bark. Tiny flecks of perspiration began to appear on Derek's hard-muscled back as he reveled in the smooth feel of Annalise under him. Not wanting to end their loving, he drew out their sensuous joining until he saw Annalise's eyes grow murky with sensation, her lips part with breathless joy as she gave herself wholly to him. He delighted in her freshness, her naive lack of reservation. Untutored in love, she was teaching him a boundless freedom between a man and a woman that he had never known.

Marian was a skilled and knowledgeable lover, as clever and adroit as an art dealer showing off a masterpiece, but spontaneous, she was not. Nor were the women he had known in India. The females of the *bibi gurh* had been harlots since puberty; beneath their spangles and jewel-colored silks, they were cold and practiced. As for the Englishwomen he had known, they were too concerned about tomorrow to enjoy today. They were very aware of their status and what their lovers thought of them. Only in Annalise had he found an unselfish delight in giving that offered endless pleasure to both lovers. Although reared in the shadow of the church, she was not ashamed of her body and the joy she exchanged with him; indeed, she seemed to revel in physical love and all that it offered. Although experienced with women, Derek felt as if he were discovering the splendors of love for the first time . . . as if he were as virginal as Annalise.

As his heart healed, so did Derek's body until days at a time passed before he experienced a twinge of a headache. Gradually, his pain passed altogether. His back healed cleanly and long walks brought strength back to his horseman's legs. Claremore was overjoyed, for Derek was well liked, but Robert, though happy for his brother, was also disturbed. Derek now spent most of his time with Annalise and they did little to hide their blossoming love until at length, Robert addressed the problem to Annalise. "I cannot help but be concerned," he told her one day after summoning her to the library. "I have grown fond of you, as has Derek, but I feel I am in clearer possession of my faculties. Derek will never marry you; you surely know that."

She looked at him levelly. "You feel that Derek is wrong to love me?"

"I do not wish to be cruel, but do you believe he loves you?"

"Perhaps not, but he needs me," she replied slowly. "I never hoped for more from him."

Robert rose, his face distraught. "But this is monstrously unfair to you, and in a strong sense, unfair to Derek, for it makes him selfish." He came to her and placed his hands carefully on her shoulders. "I hope you have not gone too far with this attachment." When she made no reply, his voice lowered. "Have you, Annalise?"

"I am not ashamed of loving Derek," she replied at last. "I would do nothing differently than I have done." Head high, she continued to meet his eyes as he swore under his breath.

"I feared as much." His hands dropped from her shoulders. "Damn Derek. He should have known better..."

"Derek had little more choice than I," she said softly. "We were both driven together by pain and need. Of late, we have given each other peace as perhaps no one else could have done."

"But this peace cannot last! Don't you see that? As Derek heals, he will turn increasingly to the life and companions he has known since childhood...to the station in life to which he was born. This can only hurt you cruelly, and in the end Derek will blame himself for both his part in the liaison and your pain. Besides," he paused, "he may very well give you a child. Have you any right to damage the well-being and prospects of one who has had no say in the matter of his birth?''

''If a child is born, I shall care for it with all the love I have shared with Derek,'' she replied. ''I feel that Derek, too, would love any child of mine, even if we could not live together.''

''So you're satisfied to be his mistress until such time as Derek feels like tossing you aside,'' he said harshly. ''That offers you naught but the dregs of the life you might have had. I care for you, Annalise; you know that. You deserve better.''

''Would you have offered me better, Robert?'' she queried evenly. ''When you kissed me, were you thinking of making me baroness of Claremore?''

He flushed. ''I admit I am no better than Derek . . . but since you first came here, I have seen the loving care you have given him. I've seen your bravery . . . your fineness of character. Were it up to me, I should have chosen you over a hundred women to be my wife . . .''

''But it is up to you, Robert, just as it is up to Derek. You imply I am no more fit to be a mistress than a wife. That yields me little credit for quality of character, even humanity. As society gives no heed to me, why should I pay heed to it?''

Robert was shocked. ''Did your father teach you this?''

''Father taught me to be honest. I shall never love another man as I do Derek, and this time in my life will never come again. Perhaps I am the selfish one, but I mean to cherish every hour I have with him.''

Robert gave up on Annalise and turned to admonishing Derek, but had no more luck with his brother. ''I've no intention of sending her away now,'' retorted Derek. ''She has given me happiness and hope. Should I now banish her to shame and discredit? Annalise has my protection for as long as she wants it.''

Stymied, Robert sent for Gertrude, who came and did nothing. "Let the affair run its course," she advised him calmly. "There are always ways to speed the course. In a month, the year of mourning for your father will be done. We shall give a round of entertainments that include all the marriageable young ladies in the district. Derek has always had a roving eye, and Miss Devon may prove sensitive to exposure."

Robert frowned. "I don't want her hurt. She deserves better."

"My dear boy, better she is hurt now, before the matter is further complicated by a child," Gertrude told him flatly. "The sooner Miss Devon retires from the scene, the better."

VIII

The Tables Turned

Gertrude was as good as her word. While she was entirely civil to Annalise during her stay at Claremore, she had Robert give a hunt promptly at the end of the proscribed month and invite Marian. Annalise did not ride well and was forced to stay behind while Marian rode off at Derek's side. All gaiety and flirtation, clearly delighted to see Derek completely recovered, Marian focused her considerable charm. The look on Annalise's face as they rode off gave Robert a pang of guilt, but he banished his misgivings. Gertrude was right; the affair had to end, both for Annalise's sake as well as Derek's.

As for Derek, he was not quite as vulnerable to Marian's wiles as Gertrude thought him. He had not forgotten who had been the one to end their engagement. Still, he admired Marian's flaming hair swept back from her face beneath the seductive veil of her riding hat. Slender, tiny-waisted in her gray Eugenie habit with its smart epaulettes, she gave him a fleeting look of approval. The black jacket of his riding attire fit his broad shoulders superbly, while the tan breeches were a smooth line down his sleekly muscled legs. Letting her horse stretch out as the huntmaster sounded the horn, Marian flashed him another glance of gay challenge when he nudged his own horse into a run. Always, they had been competitors as well as lovers, and he thought that her mock defiance of him was perhaps much of the reason he had fallen in love with her. Marian was never demure. Always self-possessed up to the moment she lost her temper, she lived life with the zest reflected by her vivid coloring.

As the horses stretched out, he followed the red flag of Marian's hair rather than the huntmaster. The rolling Sussex countryside was vibrant under the bright yellow morning sun. The yapping little beagles and rally bassets sounded eagerly down a fence line, then cut down a meandering stream with the hunt in pursuit. To his slight surprise, Marian soon veered off the course and led him into a copse of trees, where she swiftly dismounted and walked into a clearing, swinging her crop against her boot. "Darling, you look marvelous," she told him as he swung off his horse. "I've nearly gone berserk wanting to see you, but I thought you wouldn't want to see me."

"Berserk, eh?" He cocked an ironic brow. "Poor you."

She pulled off her hat and shook out her hair. "Don't be nasty, Derek. Breaking our engagement hurt me as much as it did you."

"I heard how distraught you were. Gossip travels in a country backwater like Sussex. You've scarcely missed a gathering in six months, particularly when a certain gentleman from London was present. I gather said gentleman: an earl, mind you, is quite smitten."

She came toward him with a smile that was half-apologetic,

half-tantalizing. "I was trying to bury my heartache. You really said some dreadful things to me when we parted, Derek." Her voice softened and became lulling. "I've tried to tell myself that you were ill, and that pain affected your mind; otherwise, I know you never would have turned on me like that . . ."

He did not bother to placate her. "Reliable sources also claim you met the earl while I was in India. You continued to see him after I came back. Did you expect me to fawn at your feet?"

She drew herself up. "If that's the way you want it . . ." When he smiled at her coolly, she whirled on her heel and started for her horse. Before she managed two steps, he caught her, spun her around, tangled his hand in her hair, and kissed her hard, with a relentless force she had merely guessed was in him. "Why did you do that?" she whispered when his head lifted.

"I wanted to remember why you got into my blood," he breathed harshly. "Now I remember." Abruptly, he let her go and remounted his horse. Leaving her to make her own way back, he disappeared among the oak trees.

Gertrude, seeing Marian's envious look when Derek paired off with Annalise at the hunt breakfast, took Marian aside. "My dear girl, I think it's time you learned you've had some competition."

"That little mouse?" scoffed Marian. "She may be pretty to a moderate degree, but Derek could never take a psalm singer's daughter seriously."

"He has taken her, and more than seriously," said Gertrude pointedly. "They have been conducting an affair of late, if I do not miss my guess. You would do well to set a mousetrap, if you care to catch the cat."

The pitying condescension that Derek had almost erased with his sultry kiss, now completely vanished with the evidence that he had not been languishing without feminine succor. Marian's temper matched her fiery hair. Not one to take defeat lightly, she decided to bring up her cannon.

The moment Derek left Annalise's side, Marian approached her. "Miss Devon, I have missed your company at Briarwood. I am inviting Robert and Derek to a ball at summer's end. I hope you will also attend."

"But, of course, if it will please you," replied Annalise softly. "You are so kind to invite me."

"It will be my pleasure," returned Marian with a subtle smile. "Be sure of it."

Annalise smiled up at Derek, and stretched her bare arms outward as she lay in the grass of a meadow hilltop overlooking Claremore. "I feel as if I were lying upon a cloud in heaven," she murmured happily. "Do you think God could despise us when he permits us such joy?"

"Not when he permits angels like you to walk the earth." Derek outlined her mouth with a blade of grass. "I think I can never have enough of you."

Annalise said nothing. Derek had spent little time with her these past weeks since the hunt. His mind seemed to be elsewhere, and she suspected it was with Marian. He had attended several soirees, but had never once invited her to go with him. She was hurt, more than she would ever let him know, but it was no more than she had expected. Now that he was well, he was returning to his old way of life . . . in which she had no part. She had expected this, but not so soon. She had not imagined the grief she had begun to feel; like a gray, cold rain, it inundated her, and her whole being shivered beneath its pitiless deluge. Still, she would allow Derek to sense none of her anguish. For him, she was, as ever, his strong, succoring spirit. The separation, when it came, would be clean, like an amputation made by a surgeon. There would be no mess, no bother. She would simply walk out of his life as if she had never been more than a calm memory.

He buried his head in the curve of her neck, and she wondered what he was thinking. So much of late, he was as silent as she, as if his mind, like hers, was troubled.

Derek closed his eyes, feeling the brush of Annalise's hair against his eyelids; it spun away like an emperor's silk sleeve, airy, disappearing to nothingness. Too often, he feared she would disappear the same way, wafted into an abyss of forgetfulness; only he would never forget her, forget the gossamer of her yielding body, the velvet of her kisses, the spindrift haze of their days together. Marian was more real than Annalise, somehow permanent despite her feckless, if temporary desertion. He wanted Marian back, and yet if she came back, he must forever lose Annalise. A future without Annalise was like a barren waste, empty and futile. It was to protect Annalise that he had attended his social engagements alone, reveling in his renewed interest in life, but feeling as if he were a man visiting a solitary isle where all was amicable, but somehow foreign, and without love.

Yet never once had Annalise said she loved him. Her every gesture spoke the word, yet never had she uttered it. She could so easily be like Marian, her affection a passing whisper in the wind. And yet, something deep inside him told him it was not so, that she could be his alone, if only he would take her to him and keep her close as the beat of his heart. Dipping his head, he kissed her, slowly, tasting her like the clear, sparkling freshet of a summer brook. He longed to say the word *love* to her, yet could not, no more than could she. They were worlds apart.

He spoke to her now with his body, their only words were caresses, with kisses like a dewy wine, intoxicating, lingering. She wound her arms about him like a skein of air, a playful breeze, binding him close, her lips making him dizzy with satiety; and when he entered her, he ventured into paradise.

Slender and perfect, she came into his arms as if seeking a cradle, a haven, protected, yet exhilarating. She made his senses sing and his body fit to hers as if born to it. When the moment came, that rare explosion that vibrated through both their senses like wild, ethereal crescendo, he clasped her tightly to him as if fearing her loss; putting off the moment of their brief parting until they could be one again. The clouds furled overhead while the world spun beneath them, yet they were time itself, which could not pass so long as they were joined together.

"What rare delight and contentment we've shared," he breathed at last. "How could you know so instinctively how to please me? I feel that I've passed into some impossible realm of bliss, yet fear that any day, it may be snatched away and I will be once again in that dark abyss of misery and self-pity where you found me." He smoothed her hair. "I must have you ever near me. Promise me to remain at Claremore as long as I have the power to make you happy here."

"You have only to need me, Derek," she said softly. "Whisper my name, and I shall come to you, and if we are far apart, I shall hear you with my heart."

"I shall hold you to that promise." Gently he traced her lips. "When the Gilzais left me for dead in the Kyber, little did they know they were leaving me to a happier life than I had ever known. I wish . . ." He hesitated, wanting to speak the words of betrothal for which she must have longed, yet he could not. Silence wrapped him like a smothering, merciless blanket. For all her sweetness and winsome grace, Annalise had no place in the severe social strata at Claremore. Hers was a quieter, gentler place, where faith and trust alone held sway. Not for Annalise was the hypocrisy and narrow combativeness of caste, the bitterness of rejection.

Troubled, Derek wondered how he would ever be able to keep her without exposing her to the ridicule and slanderous gossip of his own set. Whether he married her or not, she would be a defenseless target.

And yet, when he kissed her, the nectar of her lips banished his dark thoughts, leading him to put aside any idea of sending her away. He could only think of caressing her and sheltering her in his arms. This time, this joy was theirs, jewelled like a rajah's diadem. With the regularity of pretty, fanciful mechanical birds, their stolen moments passed, with their tiny screws revolving slowly, inevitably winding down.

So the days passed and the last day of summer neared, the roses billowing on their stems in the garden at Claremore while the first swallows began to wind their way south to Africa and India. Gertrude extended her stay, and while she pretended indifference, she let Annalise know that she was distastefully aware of her liaison with Derek. "I am surprised, Miss Devon," she told her dryly one afternoon as they took tea together on the verandah, "that you can so far have forgotten your upbringing as to entertain a love affair with my nephew. I am certain your father would be appalled."

Although shocked at Lady Annandale's bluntness, Annalise kept her outward composure. "My father is dead," she replied quietly, "therefore his opinion is of no consequence, but were he alive, he would approve of my loving Derek. He did not approve of virtue cloaked in hypocrisy." Watching the white clouds kite over the long expanse of lawn, with its avenue of poplar trees, she set down her teacup. "I would have preferred marriage, but as that cannot be, I have accepted the gift of love that God has given me."

Gertrude's pale blue eyes were cold. "Has Derek ever said he loved you?"

"Never," said Annalise softly, "and he never shall. He is

too much a gentleman to lead a woman to yearn for the impossible."

"Do you think he loves you?"

Annalise was silent for a long moment. "I do not think he knows. Only a few months ago, he was in love with Marian Longstreet. I doubt if his mind and heart can be so swiftly changed as to forget her."

Gertrude studied her. "You are a matter-of-fact little idealist. I wonder if you will be able to deal with the facts of eventual abandonment. Social censure is not a pretty thing to endure, particularly when one is alone. A man may walk away unscathed, while a woman is pelted with every stone of ridicule and contempt."

"My self-esteem does not have foundation upon the censure of others, Lady Annandale. People may say what they like at the end; I shall have had the beginning and the middle."

Gertrude smiled in spite of herself. "Cheeky devil! You're sure enough of yourself to have made a creditable Clavell. Odd, you don't look as if you have a good deal of sand to you, and while I've grown too old to be surprised, I look forward to seeing how you manage to extricate yourself from this mess." She saluted her with her cup. "To your fortitude."

Annalise smiled wryly at her. "And your entertainment."

The night of the Briarwood ball was a grand parade of silks and satins, ostrich and maribou, pearls and powdered shoulders. Marian, dressed in a gown of cream tulle garlanded in seed-pearl-traced lilies about the full skirt, greeted her guests at the foot of a winding marble staircase. Gertrude arrived on Derek's arm, while Annalise was escorted by Robert. Gertrude had refused to let Annalise out of the house in her old blue tarlatan frock. "If gossip is going about," she vowed, "I won't have Derek accused of cradle robbing." She had insisted Annalise wear one of the new dresses Derek had bought her: a rose Alençon lace fitted with a basket-weave tracery of fern-green velvet leaves and roses. About Annalise's creamy throat was Gertrude's triple strand of Balinese pearls clasped by a heart-shaped diamond parure. The net capturing her chignon was sprinkled with tiny diamonds that caught the blazc of candlelight like stars. Looking at least five years older than she was, and ravishingly lovely, she drew the attention of the guests like a magnet. She also drew their comments. Murmurs circulated about such a beauty residing unattended with two young bachelors who were not known for their celibacy. Marian, jealous at the buzz of interest in her rival, was also quick to turn it to her advantage.

Irked to see Derek's head bend close to Annalise as he whispered something that made her smile, Marian turned to the countess of Clare standing by her side. "That creature certainly has gall, don't you think? She took advantage of Derek's illness to insert herself into the bosom of the Clavell clan. I gather that she was a good deal more than a nurse to him, but Derek is not to blame. He was scarcely in his right mind at the time, and now he cannot find a tactful way to be rid of her."

The countess soon moved off to spread her tidbit of news and before an hour had passed, the ballroom was abuzz about Derek Clavell's new mistress. Robert was first to catch wind of it, but as he ventured in search of his brother, Derek invited Annalise to dance. Fretting at the passing moments, and the tide of gossip about him, Robert paced until the quadrille was done, then bored through the crowd only to have Derek invite Annalise to dance again. He would have given much to break in on their conversation, for she looked as if she were gazing into the face of love itself.

Oblivious, Derek and Annalise waltzed by him, Annalise's outstretched fingers brushing his sleeve. Impatiently, he waited out the waltz, then firmly claimed Annalise for the next dance. Derek reluctantly ceded her to his brother with a warning look that promised any untoward flirtation would be taken grimly amiss. "And I mean to have the last dance with Miss Devon, brother, so I shall thank you to return her to me promptly."

"All in good time, Derek," Robert replied brusquely, then guided Annalise onto the floor, leaving Derek to idle out the next quadrille.

"Annalise," Robert said only a few moments into the quadrille, "I regret that I must ask you a highly personal question, but as we both have an affectionate attachment to my brother, I believe such an inquiry is warranted. Are you so much in love with Derek?"

Annalise paled, then gathered herself with an effort. "As I told you weeks ago, I have loved Derek for some time. Are you about to suggest that I take the first boat to Tangier?"

He smiled crookedly. "Something like that. I have just learned tonight that your liaison with him is no longer a secret in the community; indeed, it is common knowledge with my brother held to be an innocent victim, and you the vile seductress. While I feel that the real tale runs somewhat in the opposite direction, I would suggest that your departure be immediate, for your own sake."

"And if I refuse?" She was white faced, her outstretched hand stiff in his as he guided her about the floor.

"You cannot refuse if I insist," he said quietly. "After all, I am the baronet . . . but I would prefer that you reach a decision of your own accord. I am genuinely fond of you, and I would not see you hurt. Please believe me when I tell you that no good can come to anyone, particularly to Derek, if you stay at Claremore."

"I shall speak to Derek," she murmured. "If he . . ."

"That's just the point. He won't want you to leave, even if he knows it's for the better. Still, I think that once he realized the danger to your already damaged reputation, he would agree to your departure. Derek is accustomed to going by the rules, once he's convinced of their worth. That is one reason why he made colonel at so early an age." He paused. "It is also why he has always wanted to go into Parliament. He wholeheartedly believes in English law, and any ambitions he has in that direction could be ruined by the wrong connections."

"The wrong connections," she breathed, her mounting temper beginning to color her cheeks again. "I am the daughter of a man as good and worthy as any prime minister who ever rose to power. I am certainly as morally 'right' as Marian Longstreet . . . and if gossip is to be believed, Derek slept with her a good deal longer than he has with me." Unaware of the exciting, seductive figure she made in the rose dress, she glared up at him, her eyes sparkling with anger. "Do you consider Marian an appropriate mate for him?"

"Marian is fitted by birth and training to be a great lady as well as hostess to aristocracy," he replied stiffly. "You may be a lady, but you are not and never will be equipped to manage a household much greater than a parsonage."

"I could learn!" Suddenly, her indignation seemed to ebb. "Oh, Robert, I have never thought that Derek would marry me. I have merely hoped to make his life easier for the short time granted us. When the time is right, I shall know it and leave."

"That time is now . . ."

"I shall have to decide that for myself."

"Very well." Keeping time to the music, he steered her toward a group of chattering women. Their eyes narrowed as she approached. Fans raised and the chatter mounted as their attention riveted on her. Robert led her across the floor past three gentlemen and their ladies. The cold change in their demeanor was unmistakable. Although she held her graceful, erect posture, Annalise began to acquire a hunted look as if she were a rabbit sensing a skirting wolf.

When the dance ended, she had Robert escort her back to the marble fireplace where they had left Derek, but Derek was gone. Quickly gazing about the lavish room, Annalise also missed Marian. The next dance was a gavotte and as Robert arbitrarily swept her out on the floor, she swiftly saw the reason why he had so quickly grasped her arm, for dancing with Marian, Derek had emerged from the crowd. When a buzz of whispers competed with the violins, Annalise felt the stares as if they were claw-marks down her flesh. She had imagined that being an object of scorn as Derek's mistress would be horrible, but the reality was worse than she could have anticipated.

"Robert, take me out of here," she whispered anxiously.

"Not now; our leaving would be too obvious. We must look as if nothing were out of the ordinary and the rumors were mere fabrications. Just look at me and dance."

But Annalise found that ignoring Derek and Marian was impossible. The floor was crowded and Derek had not yet noticed her and Robert, when suddenly she saw him lead Marian from the floor out onto the terrace. Fear gripped her. Why should he want to be alone with Marian if their relationship had ended?

Out on the terrace, Derek looked down at Marian. In the moonlight, she looked like a slender column of pearl and flame. Irresistibly, he felt the old hypnotic pull toward her. Marian had always bewitched him, as if she were Circe lulling men into her power. Only now, he was inclined to remember that Circe turned men into swine. Despite her allure, he realized now that Marian had never brought out the best in him. With her, he was jealous, competitive, inclined to storms of temper roused by her inclination to provoke him, provocation designed to reassure herself of his attraction. With Annalise, he was calm, relaxed, happy, and at peace with the world, yet Annalise was far from dull. She, too, was a flame; cool, yet vivid and with a shimmering intensity of her own. When that flame heated, even Marian might be flung into the shadows. "So," he said after a moment, "it's unlike you to miss a dance, Marian. Is something wrong?"

Marian fluttered her fan somewhat nervously, and he wondered what could have daunted her customary confidence. If she could be presented to the queen without a tremor, why should she be uncertain with him?

"Derek . . . I . . ." She looked up at him beseechingly. "Have you forgiven me for that beastly outburst that parted us? I was beside myself with worry for you, and when you brought up that old question of India, I just exploded." Her lovely green eyes pleading, she caught his arm. "Please say that the quarrel is ended. I couldn't bear it if you went on hating me."

"I've never hated you. I couldn't and you know it."

"Prove it," she whispered. "Prove that you still care for me."

Drawn as ever by her lustrous beauty, he bent his head and kissed her. Unaware that they were observed, he kissed her for some time, his arms winding around her. Blue-black silhouettes in the moonlight, they appeared to be one passionate, indissoluble form. Derek's head lifted briefly, then after an exchange of murmured words, he and Marian turned away from the ballroom toward the boathouse.

Her shoulders curved in shamed sorrow, Annalise shrank back into the shadows of the portico, her hand pressed against her lips. Robert gently but firmly drew her away from the figures on the verandah, back into the sheltering darkness of the conservatory where the Sheraton furniture made shapes like reeds on the watery, shifting light of the polished floor. He closed the Venetian doors behind them. "I'm sorry you had to see Derek and Marian together, Annalise, but Derek has been within her sphere since they were children. Now that he is well, he can run for Parliament. She has always been ambitious for him . . ."

"You mean ambitious for herself," Annalise murmured with a trace of bitterness. "When she thought he was in no position to further her own ambitions, she deserted him."

"Perhaps," Robert conceded, "but Derek is ambitious, too. Unless he returns to the army, the government is the only place where he can advance. He won't get far with scandal clinging to his coattails."

Defenseless, she shrank back from his flat tone. "I only wanted to love him, Robert. Was that so very wrong?"

He hesitated, then shook his head ruefully. "I think Derek might have died without your loving care and support. Certainly, he would not be the man he is today. The Clavells will always be grateful to you . . . but private gratitude cannot erase public scorn. Surely, Annalise, you see how it is."

Annalise saw. In the two figures embracing on the terrace, she saw only too well all the heartache she had hoped to avoid for a little while. Her time with Derek was ended, as surely as if a butcher had bludgeoned a lamb. "I should like to leave tonight, Robert."

"I'll assist you." Quickly, he took her hand and led her away.

Once they were in the boathouse, Marian came into Derek's arms with certainty and a glimmer of seductive triumph in her eyes. He embraced her, his fingertips gliding slowly across her cool skin as their kiss deepened. Marian's kiss was expert and inexpressibly tempting, and Derek's head lifted from Marian's reluctantly, but also with the slight hesitation of bewilderment. Desire still moved him, but there was something missing, as if a fine wine had lost its bouquet from being too long in the bottle. While far from vinegar, the wine was somewhat tasteless, even disappointing. Annalise's lips were like a young wine, fresh and delicate, subtle in their intoxication, yet wildly potent. He missed the violet perfume of her dusky hair, the dark, gilded mystery of her eyes beneath their heavily fringed lashes; the untutored perfection of her lips. Her slender body flowed like honey in his arms, twining about him in a current scattered with snowy blossoms. Yet, the quality that entranced him most in Annalise still puzzled and eluded him . . . the missing essence that made a common wine into a great one. That essence was a tender, generous heart that gave without stint: a heart that had the courage to care for him during the blackest days and risk terrible pain to be near him. Then, as he looked into Marian's ardent eyes, he knew making love to her would never be the same again . . . for he was in danger of loving another woman.

"I'm sorry, I cannot go through with it," he murmured, his hands falling away from Marian's bare shoulders. Her gown was slightly disarranged, her hair beginning to slip free from its pins. She stared at him in disbelief.

"Why not?" she demanded with a trace of uncertainty underlying the note of anger in her voice. "You cannot have become so smitten with that girl that . . ." Her protest faded almost as abruptly as it had begun. Derek's answer lay in his eyes, a certain ineffable distance overlying their confusion. "So you believe you're in love with her," Marian countered, not troubling to hide her bitter derision. "You're wrong, you know, but I'm not going to try to dissuade you now. You'll find out soon enough that Annalise Devon is not the woman to match your ambitions. You'll tire of her and all her soft insipidity. Then you'll come crawling back to me"—her face twisted with real pain—"but I may not be waiting this time. I've had other proposals, you know."

"I know," he answered softly. "You're a beautiful,

exciting woman and I must be daft, but somehow I don't think I'm going to grow sane any time soon.'' He touched her cheek. ''Can you forgive me?''

''No,'' she said briefly. ''I'm not made of the same sort of stuff as the holy Miss Devon, but surely you of all men must have noticed that fact.'' Swiftly, she arranged her hair and dress, then, her pale face strained, she took his arm.

When he and Marian returned to the ballroom, Derek looked for Annalise and Robert, but saw them nowhere. Ceding Marian to her next dance partner, he searched the ground floor, then returned to the ballroom and located Gertrude seated with the countess of Clare on a satin settee. ''Have you seen Annalise and Robert?''

Gertrude gave him a dry look and extricated herself from the countess. She led Derek toward the musicians and his head bowed to catch her words. ''I should be very much surprised if Annalise were still here, given the ugly gossip circulating about her. The local populace has most accurately, for once, come to a shrewd conjecture about your relationship.''

Derek frowned. ''How could they guess? Only Robert and you knew about us.''

Guessing more than she was telling, Gertrude shrugged sharply. ''Perhaps the way you two look at one another when you dance. Anyone within forty feet could have deduced you were smitten with her.'' In truth, Gertrude had a fair idea that Marian had some share in beginning the gossip and she was displeased. Any mud cast at Annalise also spattered the Clavells. She grasped Derek's sleeve. ''Robert has probably taken her home, but you and I must stay for appearance's sake. You owe something to the family, Derek.''

''I owe something more to Annalise if she has been hurt by the gossip,'' he said curtly. ''Will you come with me now, or shall I send a carriage back for you?''

Exasperated, she glared at him. "You're both selfish and foolish, Derek. That girl is but one of many you have known, and she has no place in your life. Let her go now, before there's real scandal. If she should have your child, you can forget any future in Parliament . . ."

But Derek had already turned on his heel and left her standing there. Fool! she thought furiously. He really has no sense of proportion!

Derek arrived at Claremore to find Annalise already gone, and Robert with her. She had not even packed a valise, but left in her ball gown, catching up only a cashmere shawl. She must have somewhere to go, or she would not have left in such a hasty fashion, he thought worriedly as he searched the empty, echoing halls of the house. His pace quickened to a run when she was nowhere to be found. On the stable floor were her hoops, discarded when she had mounted. She and Robert had taken horses for speed rather than a carriage. Conflicting concerns warred in his mind as he saddled his horse. Annalise was an amateur rider, certainly not capable of racing a horse through the dark without severe danger of injury. He was very much afraid she would be hurt, and as for Robert . . . Robert deserved a cracked skull for assisting her to such folly . . . unless Robert had merely made a pretense of disapproving his liaison with Annalise, and in fact, wanted her for himself. He remembered their kiss in the skiff all too clearly. Robert might have run away with her. In a fury of jealousy and anxiety, Derek set out after Annalise and his brother.

Four hours later, Derek was forced to admit he had lost them. Certain they had headed for Brighton, he had taken that road only to realize too late that they must have gone to Worthing to take the dawn cross-country coach to London. He could never catch them before they reached London, and once there, they could easily disappear in the city. Still, he did have one link to them: Robert would need money sooner or later. He could trace them through Lloyd's. Yet, the humiliation of being forced to track them like a dog abandoned by the wayside grated on him. But not for long.

When Derek returned to Claremore, he found Robert waiting for him. He and Gertrude were in the dining room having breakfast. "Damn you"—he stalked toward Robert—"I ought to break your neck!"

Robert hastily stood, waving a placating hand. "Now, don't do anything hasty. Annalise is safe enough. She asked me to see her off to London."

"Which you did with alacrity." Derek jerked his brother up by the shirt front. "Now you tell me where she is, or I'll reshape you into a ruddy teapot."

Robert stoically shook his head. "She made me promise to keep her whereabouts a secret . . . most especially from you."

When Derek drew back his fist, Gertrude sharply intervened. "Enough. I won't have you brawling over that little trollop. The first wise thing she's done at Claremore was to leave it."

Derek rounded on his aunt. "Call Annalise a trollop one more time and it will be the last word you utter in this house."

"You're both better off," rejoined his indomitable aunt. "She knew it, and so do you . . . if you stop ranting for five minutes . . . and put Robert down. His only sin was rather sloppy haste."

Derek gave Robert such a shove into his chair that it skidded backward. "I'll find her, even if I have to make a career of it."

As Derek's face hardened with resolution, Robert straightened with his own share of Clavell determination. "Look here, Derek, you'll never find her"—he rose—"but give up this idea of pursuing her and I'll cede the title back to you."

Taken aback, Derek stood there a moment, his rage

abating into stunned silence. "You'd give up the baronetcy if I give up Annalise Devon?"

"I would," said Robert quietly. "I love you. I want to see you happy and in your rightful place."

"And you think my happiness equates a long life at Claremore with Marian Longstreet," mused Derek, regarding him quizzically, for he knew how Robert disliked Marian.

"Well, doesn't it?"

"I thought so . . . once."

"And don't you now?" pressed Robert with a trace of anxiety.

"I don't know," murmured Derek, turning away as if suddenly lost in his own house. "I feel as if some smug, gaseous monster in the guise of society has stepped on my chest and pressed the life out of me. God knows what it's done to Annalise. She's fragile despite her strength."

Robert clasped his shoulder. "But it's not as if you loved her. She was just a temporary replacement for Marian. It's common for a man to be drawn to his nurse . . ."

Derek removed his hand. "There was nothing common about Annalise, and she and Marian were nothing alike. She gave me everything I needed when I needed it most: tenderness, devotion, affection. She gave me faith in myself when I wanted it most, and temporary is not a word I would ever attribute to her. Annalise had stability and kindness, and unlike the rest of us, she had no vanity. She asked only to be allowed to give, even when it took tremendous courage for her to do so. We proud Clavells are not fit to clean the soles of her slippers."

Gertrude's head snapped up. "Surely, even you don't assume you were in love with this so-called paragon?"

"I think, Aunt," he said abruptly, "perhaps I was . . . and am."

True to his word, Derek left no stone unturned. He went to London where he spent months with the help of a firm of solicitors in search of her. When all their efforts came to a dead end, he racked his mind in search of a name, any name William Devon might have mentioned in connection with London. Then, one night as he was staring out of his Mayfair town house at the rooftops of London, he remembered Hannah Morley, an ex-housekeeper the Devons had employed before going to China. Hoping for a position for her daughter, Hannah Morley had written William just before he died. She had heard there were many marriageable young men in India. The letter had come from Tottenham. By noon, Derek's solicitors were fine-combing the Tottenham hiring agencies. Two weeks later, they came upon the name of Anne Morley, who had been sent to a family in Calcutta. Anne or Annalise? he wondered. Her address bordered on the Hendon district.

Derek soon found Hannah Morley, but not Annalise. "Dear me, no," expostulated Mrs. Morley, "I haven't seen Miss Devon since she was a baby. I've just had the letters from the Reverend Mr. Devon and the Missis, God rest her soul. All the way from China the letters came. I don't believe they had a relative in England left between them, poor dears."

To Derek's disappointment, pressing money on the woman made no difference in her story. Sick with loss, he started to turn away when Hannah clicked her tongue, "Do y'know, there was an old professor friend of the Reverend Mr. Devon's who taught at Cambridge. Sanders or Sanderstown or such. I couldn't say whether he's still there after all these years, but he and the reverend went to public school together. You might try him."

Derek was on the first train to Cambridge. Professor Sanderville might be a long shot, but it was entirely possible that Annalise might hope to elude pursuit in London. Late that afternoon, he found the professor's house just under a mile from the railway station. Locked as tightly as a bank vault with every evidence of being deserted, the house mocked his hopes. Disappointed once more, he rapped halfheartedly at the door of the house across the street. Cornish by his accent, a middle-aged man answered the door. When Derek described the professor and Annalise Devon, the man nodded. "I seen 'em. Left four months ago for India. The professor's a member of some London explorers' society."

Derek was both delighted and appalled. If Annalise had been difficult to find in London, she would be many more times so in India. "Do you know what city they were bound for?" he asked desperately.

"Can't say as I do. Might ask at the university. Anthropology department." The man shut the door, then half opened it. "That Miss Devon's a looker. Shame she's going to a blighty place like India." He shut the door again.

Derek inquired at the university, where he learned that Professor Sanderville was a member of the Royal British Exploration League, and bound for a tour of several southern Indian cities beginning with Delhi. Unfortunately, no one knew his exact schedule, so anyone going in search of him might spend months pursuing Professor Sanderville around India.

Derek left Cambridge in near despair. Back in his London town house, he poured a series of brandies and sat in his bedroom drinking while he watched the stars emerge through the twilight outside his window. Annalise was gone, almost as surely as if she were dead. He could wait the year or so until Sanderville returned to England and hope that Annalise came with him, but that hope was faint. He was certain Annalise would not return. She loved India and the Sussex gossip was too extreme for her to risk humiliation in England again. The professor might or might not reveal her whereabouts.

The twilight was silken, wrapping about the stars like a

jewel-studded veil. He envisioned Annalise, her hair dark as the coming night, her eyes lucent as those stars, with a veil making the loveliness of her face an elusive mystery. She filled the sky for him and made a great, aching emptiness of his heart. To think he would never see her again made the days he had yet to live seem as gray as sifting dust. He did not have to become drunk to know he loved her now. The certainty had been growing within him with each passing hour that knelled his loss. He had taken her so lightly, yet so desperately, as a poet grasps for the phrase that promises the perfect completion of his art. Yet his need for her was not dilettante; in his darkest hours, she had meant his very survival and human dignity. Aristocrat or not, she fitted him as if she were born to love him. And yet, she had never spoken of love. Had she merely pitied him?

The more he sat there and battled the demons of doubt in his mind, the more he remembered Annalise's joyous spontaneity when he made love to her. She must love him; if she did not, she would never have looked at him as if she had discovered a shining miracle.

In return, he had repaid her with a curse of shame that sent her fleeing from him in fear and humiliation. His lovely, crystalline Annalise.

He went home to Sussex.

"I'm going to India, Robert."

Incredulous, Robert stared at his brother. "You cannot be serious! Surely, you see that Annalise has taken the right course in clearing out of the country. What sort of life can she have here now, subjected to the degradation of scandal? She'll never come back."

"That's just it," returned Derek, pulling his boots out of his armoire and dumping them on his bed. "She'll never come to me, so I must go to her."

“But your life is here in England. You can never marry her. Besides, even marriage wouldn't obliterate the gossip. How could she endure that kind of humiliation?’

“She won't have to. I'm going to her on her terms, not mine.”

“You mean to live in India?” Robert was aghast. “What about politics? What about the baronetcy? To me, all the coronets in Christendom aren't worth your burying yourself in Godforsaken India.”

Derek put Robert's hand away with more patience than was typical of him. “The baronetcy has lost its attraction; it's yours. I learned something in the past few weeks. I've never valued highly enough what was given me, only what I've taken. If I go on here at Claremore, I shall only have half a life, just as I came back from India as half a man. Annalise made me whole, but in doing so, she became part of me; a vital part that I don't care to go on living without.” He crammed the last of his clothes in the trunk and summoned his valet to carry the valises downstairs. Quickly, he embraced Robert. “I'll write from Delhi. Good luck with your maiden speech in the House of Lords.”

“But, Derek”—Robert turned in numb defeat as his brother started for the stairs—“what shall I say to Marian?”

Derek did not turn around. “Chin up, and better luck with her earl.”

IX

Sergeants and Serenades

November 12, 1856

"W*ell,* Annalise, do you like Delhi as well as Kanpur?" asked Professor Sanderville as he pulled out a large handkerchief and took off his pith helmet to mop his steaming brow. Against the gay panoply of color in Delhi's busy market, his was a small dun figure dressed in a practical linen walking suit, his appearance of a human mouse belied by an impressive Scots walking stick capped with a heavy ivory elephant head. His shoes, like Annalise's skirts, were covered with red dust, and despite his helmet, his protuberant ears were sunburned from digging in the ruins of The Seven Cities outside Delhi. His small waxed moustache and wealth of mutton-chop whiskers gave him a jaunty air that belied his plodding walk.

Beneath her sweeping leghorn hat, Annalise smiled at him, his alert blue eyes reminding her of William Devon's eager countenance. "Delhi is so large; even the market is huge. I fear I lost all track of our whereabouts as far back as the Street of the Weavers."

Martin Sanderville shrugged. "No matter. We're not due at the commissioner's tea until four o'clock. Even if we do become lost, we have two hours in which to reconnoiter." He strode off again, determined to show Annalise the Street of the Silk Merchants. Patiently, she followed him. Grateful for his efforts to cheer her, she had kept a facade of well-being since they had departed England. Pretending to be intent only upon returning to India after journeying to England with her guardian, whom she let the professor believe was her father's solicitor, she had said nothing to him of Derek. Professor Sanderville seemed to sense that she was grieving for more than her father's death, for if he had any doubts about her stranded circumstances, he asked no questions. Certainly, he was understanding about her total lack of funds and being of a solid merchant family, he was well enough off to insist she allow him to provide her with a modest income for the time being.

Could Sanderville have known just how desolate she really was, he would have been much disturbed. Despite the jostle of the crowds, the bright brass pots that hung from the open-sided bazaar to catch the sun like gold beacons, she was undistracted from the misery she carried like a soul-deadening stone.

Annalise had put two thousand miles between herself and Derek, and still she listened for the sound of his voice. Coming to India was a mistake. Even the greasy smell of the *ghee* in the cooking pots made her think of riding with him outside Kanpur. It had been two months since she left England, yet she felt as horrid as the night she saw Derek kissing Marian Longstreet. She knew she meant nothing to to him, nothing but a passing, ill-considered affair. A mist of tears blurred her eyes. She knew she had no lasting place in his life, but she wondered why he could not have ended their relationship cleanly instead of . . .

Suddenly, with a twinge of apprehension, she saw that she had been so preoccupied that she had lost sight of Professor Sanderville. Like a billow swelling between the buildings, a sea of natives confronted her. Nowhere among the *puggaree* turbans and sari veils was a pith helmet. A sting of alarm spun her around, craning to spy the professor, when a broad, familiar chest in blue and gold lunged into her. "Derek!" she whispered.

"No, miss," replied a baritone touched with a broad Irish accent. "It's myself, Sergeant Conran O'Reilly, at your service."

Her head snapped up so quickly, the brim of her hat flopped back to reveal her startled face. She stared up at a brawny giant of a red-haired man who quizzically grinned down at her with a monkey's homeliness. "Didn't mean to scare you, but the bazaar is no place for a lady to be going about alone, if you don't mind my saying so."

"I had an escort . . . Professor Sanderville," she stammered, feeling like an idiot, "but he seems to have disappeared. He'll be frantic when he realizes I've lost him."

"You seem a wee mite frantic yourself at the moment," Sergeant O'Reilly said slowly. Taking his time looking her over, he offered her his arm. "May I be of assistance?"

"No, thank you," she said quickly, then amended her refusal. "You *are* very tall, and he's wearing a pith helmet. Would you mind . . ."

"Playing the lighthouse, is it?" With a chuckle, he peered about them. In a few moments, he nodded. "Follow me, and don't worry, you can't lose me as quick as you did him."

Still uncertain at being accosted by a stranger, Annalise picked up her topaz skirts and tentatively followed him through the crush. In minutes, Sergeant O'Reilly relocated

Professor Sanderville, who was worriedly searching the bazaar stalls. Sanderville pressed his way through the crowd toward them when he spied O'Reilly's broad hand waving at him. Moments later, he saw Annalise and wormed his way to her. "Annalise"—he relievedly caught her hand—"I thought you had been distracted by some merchant."

Flushing at the memory of the real source of her distraction, she reassured him quickly, "I'm sorry to have caused you concern. I am afraid I simply was not paying sufficient attention to you." She turned to her guide gratefully. "Thank you so much, Sergeant . . . I'm sorry, I've forgotten your name."

"O'Reilly. Conran O'Reilly." He gave Sanderville a tiny salute. "I'm a John Company man, sir. Would you be with that scientific lot down from Cambridge?"

"Indeed, I am," replied Sanderville with another swipe at his brow, "but how did you know?"

"Just guessed." O'Reilly drew himself up with an air of pride. "I'm to be at the commissioner's tea today, too, but if I may say so, sir, the sun's getting high and the bazaar shops are due to close for a few hours. You'll have quite a walk if you left your carriage outside the bazaar on the cantonment side."

"Oh, dear," said Sanderville, pulling out his compass, "we must be going the wrong way." He squinted back into the multicolored, jabbering crush of people about them. "Yes, indeed." He pointed, nearly stabbing O'Reilly with his finger. "The carriage is in that direction."

O'Reilly gave Annalise another appreciative once-over before turning back to Sanderville. "May I escort you, sir? I'm sure you can easily find the way, but I'd like the company," he hastened to add diplomatically.

A gregarious man, Sanderville immediately agreed. With Annalise on his arm, he followed O'Reilly. The professor offered him a ride, and by the time they reached the commissioner's tea, they were well on the way toward becoming friends. Annalise liked Conran immediately. His winsome honesty made her feel comfortable.

Dismounting from the native cart, they were giggling at Conran's story of what the parson told the vicar. A thin-faced old man in pith helmet and linen suit identical to Sanderville's left the commissioner's gate and sneaked up behind the professor with elaborate care. Flipping the professor's pith helmet over his eyes, the old man pounded him on the back until the red dust flew. Outraged, Sanderville whirled around with a bellow. The old man stepped back, threw back his head, and began the undulating trill sometimes heard in Arabia and the Middle East. Sanderville's roar turned to a whoop, and to the astonishment of both Annalise and Conran, the professor began to trill before throwing his arms about the other man, engulfing him. "Jamison, you old mummy's fart!"

"Martin, you old bag of looted relics! Still sunburning your ears, I see."

"Ha! And just look what it has gotten me." Sanderville excitedly pulled from a deep pocket in his rumpled suit a piece of broken pottery. "Day before yesterday. Look here now. . ." The two men were off in another world talking as animatedly as schoolboys as they walked into the commissioner's compound, their heads bent together.

Annalise and Conran looked bemusedly after them. Conran offered his arm. "May I have the pleasure, Miss Devon?"

"Of course, Sergeant O'Reilly." They stepped through the gate toward the cluster of people gathered about several umbrella-shaded tables. In the midst of the luxuriant, varicolored, formal garden was set the vast, white commissioner's residency.

"It's certain I am," O'Reilly began as they walked arm in arm across the lawn, "that as a mere sergeant, I feel the more comfortable in this gathering of high society with a beautiful lady of quality on my arm. My passport, so as to say.''

''And there you see, Sergeant, what appearances are.'' She laid her free hand upon his wrist and smiled up at him. ''Here I was, pleased to be on the arm of a man in such a handsome uniform, thankful for the camaraderie, two pigeons among the peacocks.''

O'Reilly threw out his chest and strutted so much like a pigeon that she giggled. ''Look at that lady in the feathered hat, parading proud by the *jeel*,'' he said with a nod. ''Don't she look like she'd be the better for a bit of bird seed?''

He made her laugh, which she sorely needed to do. He seemed to sense her inner sadness, and on all his many subsequent visits to Professor Sanderville's cantonment bungalow over the next several months, he took pains to lighten her heart. In a short while, it was obvious that he was attached to her and when the time came to leave Delhi, she was exceedingly sorry to see the last of Conran.

Conran was less resigned. ''I'll be seeing you and the professor again, never you worry,'' he said calmly on their last evening together in Delhi. ''What I want to know is''—he bent his head to hers as they strolled the verandah—''will you be glad of it?''

Annalise knew his question was not meant lightly. He was asking her if she was willing to accept his courtship. Her lashes lowered as she considered. She had known the question might be coming, but she was unsure of how to answer him. How could she say she was foolishly in love with a man who had used her, then dropped her like a soiled napkin? Oh, Derek was not so heartless; she knew that. Her place in his life could never have been more than temporary, but seeing him with Marian hurt. If only he had come to her first, and made a clean, honorable break. She was disappointed in him, and that came hard, when once she had considered him the great, brave-hearted hero of her dreams. Now she was a child no longer, and her dreams were no longer inclined to juvenile imaginings. Although a number of men from the army and the commissioner's staff had called upon her, she knew she could do much worse than Conran O'Reilly. He was honest, kind, and loyal, and had a puckish charm that often delighted her. A good man, he was gentle with her as he was with hurt animals . . . and yet, she did not love him. Conran O'Reilly was worthy of love.

"Conran," she said softly, "I cannot lie to you. I have been in love with another man. I should *want* to love you, but . . ."

He laid a finger upon her lips. "Wanting to do a thing is the next best thing to doing it. I'll settle for a bit of wishful thinking, for now; when there's more, I'll know that, the same as you. You go on to Allabad, and we'll see what a bit more time does to the memory of that lost love of yours." He gently kissed her forehead, then walked out to his horse tethered in the drive of the white gingerbread-trimmed house where she and Professor Sanderville were staying. That was the last she saw of Sergeant Conran O'Reilly until one night, a month later, in Allabad.

She was brushing her hair before bed when she heard a band of Indian musicians on the lawn in front of the house the professor had rented. This might not have been so strange, but they were awkwardly playing "Dark Is The Color Of My True Love's Hair." Catching up her peignoir, she went to the window and looked out. Directing the music was Sergeant Conran O'Reilly. A warm glow filled her heart. Perhaps she did not love Conran as she ought, but she did love him now as she had not in Delhi. He made her soul glad, and that was all that even God could ask of her. Perhaps she would never love any man as she had Derek, but she could not have him, and life was too long to be wasted in self-pity.

Wrapping her peignoir about her shift, she strode past the bewildered house servants on the verandah out onto the lawn. Professor Sanderville, who had arrived before her, was waiting in the moonlight under a lemon tree with a croquet mallet under his arm. "Well," Sanderville drawled quizzically when she marched up to him, "do I brain this mad Irishman and send him on his way?"

"No, I think I'm going to marry him." She snagged the mallet.

Conran grinned at her. "What's the matter? Afraid I'll run away?"

With a laugh, she kissed the flat of the mallet, then touched it to the end of his nose. "You may be an Irishman, but you're not dumb."

As the train clacked over the rails, Derek gazed out at the flat, palm and kikar-tree–dotted plain. It had been a stern chase all the way. Departing late into the sailing season, he had met contrary winds and had been held up in Capetown an entire month. The commissioner's secretary in Delhi had thought the professor had gone to Jaipur, and he remembered Annalise well enough. Three weeks later, the commissioner in Jaipur had never heard of them. From Jaipur, Derek had telegraphed Kota, Jhansi, and Agra, and had written several other cities. Negative telegraphic response came within days, and as the negative mail began to arrive, Derek became convinced that Annalise and the professor had gone south. He had been in India nine weeks when he telegraphed Kanpur. His third attempt to a school friend came through and brought an immediate response: PROFESSOR SANDERVILLE AND LOVELY MISS DEVON GONE TO ALLABAD STOP REPEAT ALLABAD STOP TALLEYHO STOP CHARLIE NEVELS

Derek grinned. Good old Charlie. He took the first train south.

He was closing in now and began to wonder just what he should say to Annalise after all these months. He had failed to protect her from censure when he himself had almost totally escaped it. For the first time, he wondered why. Gradually, the suspicion grew that someone close to the family had instigated the gossip. Not Gertrude, certainly; she was far too proud. As for Robert, he could not believe his brother would go to such unsavory lengths to separate him and Annalise. That left Marian, who might be entirely capable of combatting a rival by foul means or fair. Beneath his straw hat, he closed his eyes and pondered. If Marian had begun the rumors, she had done her work well, for they were far more damaging than any gossip about him and Marian. Annalise could never have a place in English society now. Upon their marriage, they would have to either remain in India or emigrate to another of the colonies. He wondered whether she would like Australia.

An abrupt screech of train brakes sent him catapulting into the passenger opposite him. The portly Englishman from Madras let out a belch of wounded surprise. Derek apologized as he pried himself loose, then shoved open the window to cautiously peer out. "Any natives charging us?" demanded the Madras man.

"No . . . the track must be blocked." Despite the lack of charging natives, Derek drew his revolver from his valise. The Madras gentleman's eyes widened. "You don't expect trouble?"

"No more than you, sir." Derek thrust the revolver into his linen coat pocket and quickly left the compartment to go to the rear of the car. Leaning from the door, he saw the engineer and brakeman climbing down from the front end of the train. Derek jumped down to the track bed and strode forward. "What's the problem, gentlemen?"

"Bent piston rod," said the engineer tersely.

"We're all going to have a long walk," was the brakeman's gloomy addendum. "It's forty bloody miles to Allabad."

Derek thought of his fat companion back in the rail car. "How far is the nearest village?"

"Badwali. Eighteen miles southwest of here. You'd be better off sticking to the rail line."

Abandoning the railway men to their injured engine and the barrage of questions now being hurled at them from descending passengers, Derek went back to his own car. Neilsen, the Madras man, was heaving his bulk down to the rail bed. Upon being informed of the difficulty, he swore loudly and with abandon. "I have flat feet," he moaned. "How am I ever going to walk forty miles with arches Hadrian would have hissed?"

"Well, there's Badwali, eighteen miles southwest. We might find a horse there."

Neilsen looked dubious. "We might also find a lot of fanatics out for our pale, shrinking skins. Haven't you heard all the mutiny rumors?"

"Not recently"—Derek clambered aboard to get his valises—"but then, I've been concentrating on other matters. You apparently think the rumors have some foundation."

"The sepoys are now saying that the cartridges they bite when they load their weapons are waxed with animal fat. That we English have found a way to defile them so that they will have no choice but to serve in our armies abroad. Blasted ignorant, superstitious devils. They're as jumpy as Mexican fleas." Neilsen pitched his suitcase out of the window and gave his abandoned trunk a kick. "I'll wager there won't be much left in *that* by the time I get back."

Two hours later, they were plodding through the low brush down a small track they thought would lead to Badwali. Despite the blister forming on his left heel, Derek was still preoccupied, this time about Neilsen's comment on the waxed cartridges. If the tale were true, the natives might have found a cause to unite Hindus and Muslims against the Raj. Such a nationwide mutiny would bloody India beyond belief.

He must find Annalise without delay.

Derek and Neilsen were footsore and weary when they spotted a cloud of dust advancing at their rear. Neilsen swung his coat over his shoulder and hopefully squinted at the cloud. "Think it's a cavalry squadron?"

Derek shook his head. "A squadron would make more racket. Besides, there's something as big as a house under that dust."

The house proved to be an elephant bearing a howdah. At the elephant's mammoth heels trailed twenty guards on horseback, a string of retainers on foot, and baggage wagons. A bejeweled young Indian clad in red and yellow silk hailed them from the howdah. "Hallo! You look jolly well flat. Where's your conveyance?"

"New-fangled conveyance," Neilson told him in disgust. "Damned steam engine dumped us what feels like twenty miles back." Then he ended with a piteous wail, "And my feet are raw."

The young man slapped his *mahout's* shoulder with a horsehair flail. "Put her down. These gentlemen are about to board." He waved to Derek and Neilsen. "If you will be my guests? I am Sadi Wat, prince of Jaipur, and I should be delighted to have your company. Swatting horseflies for two hundred miles has become most boring."

When they had gratefully though apprehensively clambered up on the elephant's back to share the swaying howdah, the prince informed them he was going to Chirmir to be married. "A frightfully pretty girl of excellent parentage, but dimwitted. What a pity I cannot make her a mere concubine." He sighed. "Status has its disadvantages."

Reminded of his own obligations, Derek was inclined to

express sympathy. When the prince produced brandy and regaled them with his misadventures with his English tutor, they spent the journey joking about tutors and public schools, and arrived in Badwali near sunset. The prince apologized for the lateness of the hour. "My elephant alone could cover twenty-five miles in an hour without effort, but my luggage and retainers are not up to such a pace. Now, an elephant race is something to see!"

After sharing a supper of cold pheasant and an excellent local wine with them upon a folding teakwood table set up outside his tent, the prince had a few courtiers ousted from their quarters and offered their tent to Derek and Neilsen. While Derek declined to inconvenience the courtiers, Neilsen agreed readily. "Please," said the prince to Derek, "my people will simply sleep with their friends. It is no trouble."

Derek at length agreed, but sharing a tent with Neilsen's rousing snore proved impossible. Catching up his light cotton blanket, he retired into the village to find an empty shed adjoining a corral. After carefully cleaning dung and mud clods from a corner, he settled down on his blanket. Dawn found him nuzzled by a goat interested in his straw hat. Swatting it aside with the sheared hat, he sat up and stretched his sore muscles. A threadbare mule eyed him suspiciously from the shade of a peepul tree. Limping now from his heel blister, Derek made the rounds of the village. None of the residents had a horse and the prince was not going to Allabad. Unwillingly, he recalled the mule.

At the time, Derek considered his arrival in Allabad with Neilsen straddled behind him on a mule as the crowning humiliation of his life. Burdened with luggage, the resentful mule sat down on the commissioner's drive and refused to budge. The commissioner missed the spectacle, but the secretary and staff all came out to watch the show when Neilsen twisted the mule's tail and elicited an infuriated squeal from the beast. It promptly rose and aimed a kick at his protuberant belly. Dancing away, Neilson bolted for the verandah. "Make it sit, Clavell!"

The mule, of course, did not, and chased Neilsen and the residency staff off the porch. Derek finally lassoed the irate beast with a length of clothesline fetched by a kitchen boy and peace was restored.

He was rewarded by a successful appointment with the commissioner. "Why, Miss Devon and Professor Sanderville took supper with me just this past week," the commissioner told him. "They departed for Kanpur on Tuesday."

So he was close, very close, but if Annalise and the professor were going back to Kanpur, the professor might be about to conclude his trip. Pursuing a lone woman without the professor's official wake to follow would make his search all the more difficult. He had best run Annalise to ground in Kanpur.

Conran's simian face beamed as he showed off his young bride-to-be to his regiment at St. Christoph's on the Sunday when the first banns were posted. Annalise wanted to be married on the ninth of May so Professor Sanderville could give her away at the altar before returning to England. "She's too young and pretty for you, you old war hound," muttered a fellow sergeant to Conran after being introduced to Annalise on the church common after services.

"Don't you wish you'd seen her first," Conran rejoined under his breath. "Tell me again how lucky I am. She's a spittin' little beauty, ain't she?"

As the soldiers in the congregation milled about them with a smattering of drab civilians, Annalise did her utmost to live up to Conran's inflated expectations. She hoped she was good enough for him. Conran was a big man, as tall as Derek, and his heart was as generous. She had also learned he could be as unforgiving as Derek when confronted with a misdeed. What would he say when he learned she was not a virgin? She would not apologize for loving Derek, for in her heart, she was convinced she had done no wrong, but how could she explain that reasoning to the conservative Conran? The only wrong she would admit was in still thinking of Derek, yet perhaps she judged herself too harshly. To banish Derek from her thoughts was impossible three-quarters of a year later. The terrible wound of their parting was still too fresh, too raw to heal.

As she smiled with quiet charm into the faces of Conran's friends, she could not help but imagine Derek among them, tall and commanding in his regimentals . . . but then Derek would never wear his uniform again, never return to India where the ladies were now flushed pink under their umbrellas in the morning's rising heat and the men perspiring in their tight collars. Derek was in another world, as far away as the moon from this cloistered society that moved with such quixotic, stubborn arrogance through the exotic realm of India. India was so unchanging, yet ever changing, somehow akin to Derek and Conran in their mercurial intransigence. Their demands of themselves were as severe as their demands of others. Both were conservative, reliable, and fiercely self-reliant, yet both loved India, with all her fluid mystery.

Still, as Annalise walked with Conran through the crowd, she reflected that the two men were very different. Conran's temper was slower to soar than Derek's but when it did, it could be just as dangerous. Conran was less intelligent than Derek, but what he lacked in scholastics, he made up in wiliness honed to a sharp edge by the roughness of his rearing. A farm boy from County Mayo, Ireland, Conran had a sixth sense about humans and animals that made him extremely perceptive about their moods and qualities. Scarcely had he handed Annalise into his rented carriage and they had ridden out of earshot when he asked her without preamble, "All right now, what's troubling you, dearest girl? You're looking sober as a magistrate who's seen a pickpocket skip free and easy from the docket."

When she made no answer, he peered at her with a trace of anxiety. "You wouldn't be thinking better of wedding me, would you?"

She pressed his hand reassuringly. "No, Conran, If anything, I'm wondering if you won't be disappointed in me as a wife. Hearing the banns read is a sobering experience."

"Aye," he agreed, " 'Tis that, but as for my being disappointed, I fair don't see how I could be." He grinned at her. "You know I don't expect you to do more than boil an egg."

"But I want to be a proper wife to you, Conran . . . in every way," she said softly, the still-low sun slanting beneath her hat to reveal the serious set of her mouth. She paused, knowing she must proceed, yet unsure of how to do so. Finally, she mustered her courage. If he broke off the engagement, she would not blame him, but he had the right to know exactly what kind of mate he was acquiring. "Conran," she went on earnestly, "when I told you I loved another man, I mean that I loved him completely, in spirit and body; I don't regret that fact, but you may. I should understand if you have reservations about going ahead with the wedding."

Conran's face drained. "But that's impossible. You're too young . . . too . . ."

"Saintly, because I am a missionary's daughter? I assure you I am no saint, but a flesh-and-blood creature as are all who walk God's earth. I gave myself willingly, Conran. I knew what I was doing . . ."

"I'll kill him!" he exploded, reining in the horses so hard that they danced in their traces. "The blackguard ought to be horsewhipped!"

"You would need a long whip indeed, to reach to England,"

she said dryly, but refrained from adding that by now her love was probably engaged to someone else. Conran looked too infuriated to bandy the ironies of life.

The sea of Indian humanity swirled and flowed about their carriage as Conran sat immobile, his big body hunched over the reins, his prim Irish mind in a quandary. At length, the driver of a horse-drawn *ghari* began to berate him for blocking the narrow passageway that skirted the Kanpur marketplace. Conran swore back, his face red and shaven jaw jutting as he smacked the horses' backs with an impatient crack of the reins. "Get along there, then," he yelled, passing the *ghari* driver with bare inches to spare, "and be damned to you for a swine-eating dog of a Hindu!"

For the next twenty minutes until they arrived at Professor Sanderville's door, he said not a word. Abruptly, he handed Annalise down from the carriage and walked her to the bungalow door. At the door, she turned and viewed him quietly, the question in her eyes unspoken. "I'll have to think about it," he said curtly, then wheeled and strode back to the carriage. Minutes later, he was gone, leaving behind only the plume of his settling dust.

Two days later, Derek arrived in Kanpur and went directly to the commissioner's residency. Professor Sanderville and Miss Devon were staying in the cantonment with a crony of Sanderville's named Henry Bishop. His heart pounding, Derek mounted his rented horse and rode posthaste to Bishop's residence, where he was told that Mr. Bishop and Professor Sanderville were on a dig outside Kanpur, but Miss Devon was in the library. When the servant started to announce him, Derek stayed him. "Miss Devon and I are old friends. I should like to surprise her." After twenty rupees made the agreeable syce go about his business directing the upstairs maids, Derek slipped into the library and quietly locked the door behind him. He did not want the servant to walk in on what promised to be an emotional moment.

With her slim back to him, Annalise was seated in a chair working at a needlepoint frame by the window's already intense light. The rest of the room, but for the block of sunlight at her feet, was cast in shadow, the comfortable leather chairs and couch somnolent as great, lazing dogs. Derek could see the curve of her left cheek and jaw. Beneath the downy wisps of hair escaping her chignon net, her skin had the softness of creamy velvet, the long slope of her sea-green muslin-clad shoulder a gentle curve. Just to look at her gave him a sense of quick, still delight. This wonder was his; this charming, tender slip of a girl would be his to cherish and protect the rest of his days. No one would ever hurt or insult her again.

He stepped forward, his footfall on the carpet scarcely audible, but she heard him. As if she sensed his presence, she turned swifly in her chair, her attention sweeping up from her needlework. Her face drained as she uttered a little sound of distress, her hand recoiling to accidentally rake the embroidery needle across her palm as she let the needlework fall to lie unnoticed at her feet. Gripping the back of the chair, she gazed at him, her wonder mixed with growing horror. ''Derek,'' she breathed, ''what are you doing here?''

''I've come for you,'' he told her firmly, catching her up to him by the waist. If her first reaction to him was not what he had hoped, her response when he kissed her told him nothing had happened to lessen her fundamental regard for him. Fire was in her kiss when he held her in his possessive embrace; fire that leaped when he touched her. She was like a flaming wand in his arms, bending to him, her throat arched back, her head small with its wealth of hair cushioned by his hand. ''Annalise, Annalise,'' he whispered, ''I was afraid I should never find you. I've been back and forth across half of India. That Professor Sanderville of yours is as flighty as a blind rhino."

"Do you mean you've been following us since Allabad?" she asked in distraction.

"I've been following you since Delhi. I missed you by months, then weeks . . ." Noticing her bleeding hand, he heedlessly blotted it with the end of her needlepoint. She stared down at his brisk efforts as if she were uncertain whether to dart away or object. "Now that I've found you, we're going to be married by month's end, as soon as the banns can be read," he informed her. "Then, by Harry, I'm taking you to Australia where they contend with kangaroos instead of rebel fanatics."

"But Derek . . ."

Giving her no time to argue, he kissed her again, ardently, so that her senses were dizzied. The room swirled, her pulses pounding in her temples like a timpani of drums. When she swayed against him, he murmured, "There, that's better. No nonsense, now. There's no one who gives a damn about us getting married here."

"Conran does!" she blurted, then made a concerted effort to push him away. "I cannot marry you!"

Derek's head lifted abruptly from his pursuit of her lips. "I'd like to know why not."

She braced her palms against his chest. "Because I'm marrying someone else. Sergeant Conran O'Reilly. I'm engaged."

Bewildered, he stared at her, then at her trim waist. "Why the hell are you getting married when you're not pregnant?"

"Because I want to," she replied in a muffled tone. "I like the man."

His temper exploded. "Engaged? You're engaged? Just because you like some blithering colonial popinjay who probably doesn't know his plump arse from an elephant's posterior? Who is he? I'll break his neck!"

Her own temper neared the firing line. "He vowed to do the like to you when I . . . confessed I was somewhat . . . used."

"Used!" He turned nearly purple with fury. "You bandy about the word *used* after what we meant to each other?"

She went stiff and pale. "You were quick enough to turn to your intended, after making love to me!"

Snared in mid-attack, Derek did not know whether to retreat or advance. He decided to advance. "If you're speaking of that passing flirtation at the Briarwood ball . . ."

"Passing flirtation? You took her to the boathouse!"

He looked startled, then said flatly, "I may have taken Marian to the boathouse, but that was as far as things went. I did not make love to her." His tone altered, became cajoling. "I was merely trying to let Marian down lightly, while you became engaged as quickly as a cat after a herring!"

Her eyes flared, their amber lights grown hot. "Well, the cat was far from starved. For all you knew when I left England, I could have been pregnant."

His jaw jutted. "I'm here, aren't I?"

Her own jaw lifted. "You're too late. I'm engaged, and I mean to stay that way."

He gritted his teeth. "Give me one good reason why!"

"Because we're wrong for each other, and Conran and I are right . . ."

"Conran. There's that blasted name again. You would get engaged to an Irishman!"

"I love him," she railed, pressed past all bounds.

"The hell you do!"

"It's not just Conran," she declared angrily. "I won't marry you and be condescended to the rest of my life. I am in no way inferior to your family, and certainly not to Marian Longstreet!"

"Marian's the real rub, isn't she?" he retorted. "Marian meant less and less to me after I met you . . ."

"Oh, yes," she cried, eyes flashing, "so much less that you kissed her the first time you saw her after making love to me. You're as faithless as a cat." She was particularly indignant, for while he was partly right, the social complacency of his family, especially the condescending Gertrude, had offended her deeply.

"I pursued Marian as an experiment," Derek defended himself heatedly. "I wanted to see if I still desired her. For your information, I did, but only superficially." He struggled to elaborate. "The . . . guts had gone out of my feeling for her. All I could think of was you."

"You certainly didn't look like you were thinking of me, standing in the moonlight, arms about her, kissing the . . ." She began to sputter. "But even if you were, it was execrable of you to . . . 'experiment.' You're spoiled rotten. Everything must be your way, and heaven help anyone who defies you. How could you stoop so low?"

"Low?" he railed. "Where does that put you, with your high-handed moralizing? Not a moment ago, you were complaining that we Clavells were too lofty minded for your stomach. At least, for God's sake, be consistent!"

She turned white about the lips. "How dare you bring God into this! The trouble is, you assume you're God's vicar on earth, and everyone else was created when God was loafing. You're insufferable, Derek Clavell! I'm telling you for the last time, I love another man!"

With a snort of impatience, he swept her up in his arms, crossed the room, and deposited her on the settee. Quick as a whistle, he hauled up her skirts, and just as quickly, she squirmed out from under him and began to frantically crawl for the door. Unfastening his breeches as he pursued her, Derek launched himself atop her with the blunt weight of an anchor.

With a squeal of fury, she clawed at the rug, trying desperately to turn over so she could knock him away, but her task was briskly done for her. Derek rolled her over in a trice, and before she could do more than utter a muffled gasp, he was inside her, his accuracy unerring. "Nooo," she yelled, "I don't want youuu. Out, out . . . out." The last wail was markedly less intense than the first, which Derek could not help but note, however high-flown his temper. With Annalise's skirts tossed up about her ears, he applied himself with a will until both of them had lost track of their quarrel and were lost to all but the heady sensation of their joining. Swiftly, inevitably, their passion mounted. Over half a year had passed since they had been together, and they became feverishly determined to make the most of it. Memories of Marian and Conran disappeared into the mists of fiery forgetfulness as Derek's arms locked about Annalise, his face buried against her cheek as his body drove hard into hers. Her arms wound about his neck, she moaned with pleasure under his onslaught, whispering her mounting, long-parched need for him. All Derek's pent-up impatience in pursuing her across India edged his frustrated desire. His lovemaking was forceful, almost merciless as he wordlessly asserted his dominion. Annalise climaxed before Derek in a wild surge of ecstatic movements. With a muted cry that mingled with her own soft sound of pleasure, Derek felt his body shudder as he found effortlessly sweet release that fountained like a burning rain.

For some minutes, Derek lay entangled with Annalise in the creased wreckage of her skirts, his breath coming hard as her breasts quickly rose and fell beneath him. "Derek," she managed to say at last, "you must let me up. The servants . . ."

"To the devil with the servants," he retorted. "I'm not letting you go until you agree to see the last of the Irishman."

"I cannot, Derek. I am committed to him." She twisted, trying to get free of him, but his arms clamped about her.

"You cannot love him, Annalise; not as you do me. You could not have responded to me as you did if you preferred another man."

"You are vain . . . and presumptuous, Derek," she breathed. "You made love to me in England when you preferred another woman. Do not mistake love for lust."

He brushed her tumbled hair from her cheek. "I only thought I wanted Marian. She was like a bad habit I was too blind to break. By the time I discovered my mistake, you were gone."

"I won't hurt Conran as you hurt me, Derek. Besides, you would have to give up Claremore if you married me. We should be exiled if we went to Australia."

"Do you think I would have come this far if any of that mattered?" His voice lowered. "I want you . . . and only you. It's time you knew just how much." His lips covered hers, taking her breath as they gently clung, shaped to hers. The kiss they shared was like liquid fire, reigniting their desire for one another. When his lips lifted, she turned her head away in a last attempt to evade him, but it was already too late when his touch at her breast was molten as he slowly unfastened her bodice, baring the creamy flesh beneath her camisole. The satin ribbons loosed, fell away, as his fingertips grazed the pink peaks beneath the thin cotton.

She caught her breath. "Derek, don't . . . we mustn't . . ."

"Don't fight me, Annalise," he murmured. "We've both wanted this moment for a long, long while."

And so it was: a long moment in the golden sun streaming across the floor while the pool of her snowy lace petticoats gilded beneath his brown, masculine hand as her undergarments sifted to the floor. Her black hair fell over his broad shoulder as her bare body was lowered to a satin settee, there to be brushed by his dusty jacket flung across the pillows. For a long, long while Derek and Annalise made love, his pillage of her sweet and langourous. He kissed every curve of her slim, sleek body, then lightly kissed the corners of her mouth and closed eyelids where her long lashes fringed across the subtle roses of her cheeks. "I treasure you," he whispered, his body long against hers. "How could I have believed so long you were a child when you were blooming like a white lily before me. You are as fair as Sheba was to Solomon. Do not go into some faraway land where I cannot find you. Stay . . . stay with me for all our lives. Love me, Annalise, whose name is a timbrel within my very soul . . ." His head lowered to hers again, his caress sweeping her from shoulder to slender thigh as he kissed her lips, her throat. Her head arched back as she languidly offered her breasts to him and let him feast as he would, her arms entwined about his neck.

The moment his desire was ripe, she yielded all her body when he took her, and yet . . . kept her soul for her own. For Conran. Where once she had given Derek everything, she kept a little apart, seeking protection for her still-wounded heart. He noticed nothing, for her body betrayed no slackening of response to him. Her fire blazed high, brighter than ever for the loss he had not yet recognized, for Annalise had made of her breaking heart a burning pyre of her love for him. The licking flames carried them both to a clouded, molten world of blind passion where naught could survive but unbearable longing. Assuagement was brief, and final. When the throes of desire ebbed, Derek sensed that something between them had altered. An iron door had closed, although Annalise's eyes were still lambent with love. "You're going back to him, aren't you?" he whispered roughly.

"Yes," she said simply. "He loves me like a trusting child. I have already given him pain by honesty; I will give him no more by lies and deceit."

"Tell the mother's son free and clear that you love me. Is that a lie?"

"My loving you makes no difference, Derek. We were never meant to be together. We come from different worlds. To wed me would cost you everything. One day you would regret it."

He was silent a moment. "So you think you were meant for Conran?"

"If he'll still have me."

"He'd be a fool if he didn't." His voice altered, roughened. "Does your commitment include making love in the back of a carriage?"

She glared at him, her temper rekindling. "How dare you ask me that when you molested me when I refused you not an hour past. My relationship with Conran is none of your affair."

"You're mine by previous right if you want the legal niceties. Besides, I can give you a hundred times more than he can. He's a measly sergeant; I even outrank the bastard!"

She pushed him away angrily. "He's not a bastard. He's the kindest man in the world, and you'd like him if you weren't such a gold-plated snob."

He glared at her. "Now, who's bandying names . . . and I'll like whomever it suits me to like. I don't like your poaching Irishman."

She caught up her petticoat and jerked it on. "Put your clothes on, *Signor* Casanova. You've outstayed your welcome."

He began to cram on his pants. "I've wasted six bloody months chasing after you and this is the thanks I get. How could I have considered marrying a complete idiot."

She whacked him with her hoops. "You think anyone's an idiot who doesn't agree with you. You're so self-centered, you could be used for a spare carriage wheel."

He rounded on her. "Hit me with those hoops again, and I'll apply them to your backside!"

She levelled the hoops again for another swing that was narrowly averted by a soft but determined knock at the library door. "Memsahib . . ." There was a nervous pause. "The O'Reilly sahib is here and wishing to speak with you."

The angry flush drained from Annalise's face, leaving it chalk white. Then, at the mocking delight that erased the surprise from Derek's features, her anger rekindled. "Tell the sahib I shall be delighted to receive him in a few moments. The gentleman with me is just leaving."

"The hell I am," purred Derek.

With a furious glare, she dragged on the rest of her clothes, then stood impatiently tapping her foot while Derek took his sweet time donning his own. "What's the matter?" he teased. "Afraid he'll take up with the cook?"

"You are insufferable," she gritted. "I'm afraid he'll kill you." Then, as he was finally dressed, she spun on her heel and opened the door.

Conran strode into the room, his somewhat tense smile at Annalise fading at the sight of her rumpled hair and Derek's skewed cravat. Crimson suffused his face to the roots of his hair. "This is the gentleman I was telling you about," Annalise addressed him stoically. "I have informed him that he has come all the way form England on a fruitless mission. He is, however, unwilling to retire gracefully."

"He is, is he?" grated Conran. He turned on Derek, his thick brows beetling over his normally genial face. "I've got three inches and as many stone on ye, laddie. Do I need to administer a ballet lesson?"

"Try it," snapped Derek. "You'll find yourself doing pirouettes."

Seeing Conran advance on Derek, Annalise hastily darted between them. "I won't have any fighting! The matter is closed." She turned her mutinous face up to Derek. "Is that clear?"

"For the moment . . . but we're not finished, you and I." He measured Conran cynically. "She loves me, though she can squall like a cat till kingdom come that she doesn't, and I think you know it. If you can be satisfied with second best, that's up to you, but personally, I wouldn't stoop to another man's leavings."

Annalise barely ducked in time as Conran's fist crashed into Derek's jaw. Derek staggered, then swept her out of the way even as he retaliated with an accurate left hook. Conran sailed into the couch, skidding it across the floor and sending the pillows flying. "Stop it!" Annalise cried, grabbing for Conran's arm as he surged up from the couch, but she might as well have tried to stop a launching catapult. His momentum carried her into the center of the fray, where she was promptly shoved out again. "Rachid, help!" she called wildly for the houseman as the two men traded blows. When Rachid somewhat reluctantly arrived with nothing but a *punkah* fan, she let out a stifled sound of exasperation and went for the musket mounted beneath the trophy tiger. After grabbing the gun by the barrel end, she belabored the pugilists with a hearty energy that startled them more than it hurt. "Stop it, I say!" she railed at them when they paused, panting, to stare at her. Although by no means short, Annalise looked diminutive holding the long musket, and the effect was ludicrous, had either man been inclined to laugh. "I shall brain the first man to touch the other," she warned. "Now, both of you, out!"

Slowly taking in the shambles about them, the two men came to the grudging conclusion that they were wrecking an innocent man's house. Conran eyed Derek, then looked at Annalise with steely resolution. "I was coming to say I hadn't reconsidered my proposal. I've no objection to getting married if you haven't."

"A more winning offer a girl never had," scoffed Derek sarcastically.

"Considering the state of the two of you when I walked in, 'tis a wonder I'm making any offer a'tall," retorted Conran grimly.

"Well, you needn't," intervened Annalise, upset. "Neither of you need make me an offer. I'm really not sure I want anything to do with either of you. You're a pair of ill-mannered boors! How shall I ever explain the state of his furniture to Mr. Bishop?"

Conran raised a brow. "It's furniture you're worried about? What of . . ." He paused warily when she brandished the musket. "See here, girl, I'm willing to overlook . . ." He hesitated again when the musket made another warning jab. "All right, I'm going, but the devil knows whether I'll ever come back again."

"The devil take your favors, Conran O'Reilly," Annalise flashed back. "If you don't love me now, you may take yourself back to County Mayo, for all I care."

"That's telling him," encouraged Derek gleefully.

"And as for you"—she rounded on him—"this is all your fault. If you hadn't barged in here like a pirate with his pistols cocked, there wouldn't have been a fight in the first place. Now I'll thank you to leave!"

One look at her flaring eyes and trembling but determined lips told both men they had, indeed, worn out their welcomes. Sheepishly, they departed, leaving Annalise to kick the leg of the settee and burst into tears.

Although Conran was inclined to sulk for a week and leave Annalise vanquished by her own guns, he was less inclined to leave the field clear for Derek. After inquiring after Derek's identity from the commissioner's aide, he was somewhat chastened to learn Derek was not only a hereditary baronet, but a colonel. If nothing, Conran was accustomed to respecting his military superiors and taking orders:

however, after some argument with himself, he soon rallied to the fray. Derek, *huzoor* or not, was in for a fight if he presumed to march away with Annalise as his booty.

As for herself, Annalise was hard put to explain the library's smashed furniture to Mr. Bishop, but Professor Sanderville, having guessed something of her predicament, fortunately took Bishop aside and fabricated a more or less accurate excuse that left her reputation intact. This was to be her last respite, for both Derek and Conran took pains to be at every social gathering she was likely to attend for the next month. That she would speak to neither of them dampened none of their determination. Derek managed the advantage when he caught her alone at an officers' ball to which Conran had not been invited.

Never at a loss for nerve, Derek reconnoitered the ballroom floor until he spied Annalise momentarily left alone by Professor Sanderville. While Sanderville went after punch, Derek made a direct attack. Approaching Annalise from the rear, he sidled up to her, flicked her dance card from her fingers, and promptly filled in three places before she could manage to retrieve the book from him with any decorum. "Give that back," she hissed vehemently. "I'll not dance with you now or ever."

"But you must, or make a scene, for I intend to claim my rights," he informed her calmly.

"You have no rights. You forfeited them the afternoon of your brawl with Conran. The both of you are behaving like spoiled children coming to blows over a toy."

"Rest assured, I am in no wise playful. I mean to marry you, and if you weren't being the miffed diva, you'd stop making such a fuss."

Reflecting the icy crystal beadwork encrusting the white ball gown the professor had purchased for her, Annalise's eyes glittered pure resentment. "I shall marry whom I choose, Derek, and you may rest assured, the man is not you."

When she moved to walk away from him, he caught her hand. "The first dance is mine . . . or shall I start a nice noticeable row?"

She glared up at him. "If you think to win my favor by this beastly way of treating me . . ."

He grinned impenitently. "I can think of far more beastly ways of treating you privately. It's our unfortunate luck that we happen to be in a crowd."

Gritting her teeth, she allowed him to lead her out onto the floor. "Derek, you're merely upsetting Conran and me," she muttered as he swung her into the polka. "Please go home and leave us in peace."

"I like to see Conran upset; it does wonders for his beefy coloring."

"He's a good man, Derek," she said tightly. "He doesn't deserve this. It's enough that he's disappointed in me as a prospective wife . . ."

"Disappointed?" Derek took umbrage instantly. "The big ape's lucky you gave him the time of day"—his mood abruptly changing, he added darkly—"or is it the time of night?"

"I'm not sleeping with Conran," she said stiffly. "I should think you, of all men, ought to know that. I may have been a trusting fool once, but never again."

"So it's still pique over Marian that has you in an uproar," he returned unsympathetically. "You're positively pea green."

Tears of angry hurt almost came to her eyes. "You're vile. When I saw you together on the terrace at Briarwood, you had forgotten me entirely. I was dispensable."

Seeing her evident pain, he grew serious. "If that were so, why would I come all the way to India to find you?"

"You're only here because you feel some obligation to me," she replied in a stifled tone. "You also feel guilty."

His defenses sprang up again. "Believe me, guilt over Marian never crossed my mind. After all, I've known her a great deal longer than I've known you, and mere obligation would not elicit more than a trip to London from me."

Her eyes, large and dark, turned up to his. "Then why did you follow me here, Derek?"

"If I told you," he said softly, "would it make a difference?"

"I suppose not," she answered even more quietly than he. "I am under obligation to Conran. If he still wishes it, I am bound to marry him. After all, none of this muddle was of his making."

He sighed. "You've a Quaker's passion for the niceties. Simply tell him that you have a prior commitment."

"As you had with Marian Longstreet," she observed a trifle dangerously. "Precisely how did you go about telling Marian you had second thoughts?"

Thinking better of relating his exact words, Derek hedged. "I simply explained that I no longer felt the same way about her as I had when I left England. After all," he added with a somewhat eager carelessness to cover his awkwardness, "people change."

"Yes," she replied gravely, "they do. I am not the same near child that I was in Sussex. I can make a good and faithful wife to Conran if he will still have me . . . which would be a wonder, considering the hurt he must have suffered at finding us together at Mr. Bishop's. I only hope I can make it up to him."

"But you would marry me if you were free of Conran?" he inquired intently.

She eyed him warily. "Not necessarily . . ."—her eyes narrowed—"and certainly not if some disaster were to befall him."

He turned innocent. "I shouldn't hurt a hair of his head."

"Good," she said flatly, "for if you did, I should know it, and despise you."

He gauged her resolution. "You genuinely care for the man, don't you?"

"I do. He deserves a far better wife than I, but I shall do my utmost to make him happy."

"He's a lucky man," Derek said softly. "I envy him."

She looked directly into his eyes. "Enough to meddle?"

"I promise"—he drew a swift line across his heart—"I'll not hurt him. And now"—he drew her closer to him—"will you attend the races with me this Saturday? He cannot have made his decision by that time."

Firmly disengaging herself, she shook her head. "I shall go nowhere with you until Conran has made up his mind."

The wedding was held at St. Christoph's church. A simple affair with only Conran's and Professor Sanderville's friends attending, the wedding ceremony was over in less than an hour. Derek stayed only minutes after the ceremony, just long enough to see Annalise's white, resolute face turn away from the altar. Her eyes met his without faltering, but with a pain that transmitted itself as if she had struck him. She loves *me*, he thought furiously. Yet she's marrying Conran O'Reilly because it's the "right" thing to do.

Only Derek knew that he was everything to Annalise or she could never have given herself to him. She was not the careless sort, who could go from man to man. She gave herself for life.

She's *mine*, he wanted to scream at Conran, but it was too late. Suffocating in his own frozen silence, Derek turned his back on the couple at the altar and left the church.

Annalise watched Derek go as if he were tearing the heart from her breast. I promised Conran, she warned herself bleakly, that after this day I would not think of Derek, and I must not. I lost him once and thought I should die of it . . . but I lived, and I must go on living now.

Conran looked sober as they descended the church steps. She wondered what he was thinking as they hurried through the parting wedge of uniforms and the few civilians with their ladies. The open barouche loomed up, burdened with their luggage. "To the train station," Conran ordered the carriage driver in a hail of rice that resembled a blizzard of snow falling about them. Annalise shivered in spite of the heat.

I wonder if the rice is an omen of ill luck, she wondered as the carriage jostled through the crowd. Professor Sanderville came forward to take her hand; after him, Mr. Bishop, his portly face flushed with the heat. Then the faces of the well-wishers began to dwindle away into a pink blur that gradually faded among the golden *mohur* trees.

X

Storm Clouds Gather

"*I hope* you don't mind sitting up all the way to Delhi, dearest girl," apologized Conran. Then he added sheepishly, "I couldn't afford the sleeper fare."

Annalise could see he was thinking of Derek and all the comfort she might have enjoyed had she married into the Clavell enclave. She was thinking too much of Derek not to sympathize with his dolorous turn of mind. Annalise patted the train seat beside her and laughed at the clay-colored cloud of dust she raised. "Come, sit down, Conran, and don't trouble about luxuries. Papa and I rode all the way from Szechwan to Canton by ox cart, and in much the same fashion from Calcutta to Kanpur. I vow I should not know what to do with the niceties of travel." When he gingerly sat down beside her, she patted his sleeve. "Tell me about Meerut and what sort of lives we shall lead there."

Cheered by her falsely bright expression, he ventured to

describe Meerut. " 'Tis hot this time of year, but not quite so hot as Delhi. Ordinarily, most of the women and children will be away at Simla in the north enjoyin' the pines and cool mountain air, but the cooler weather has lasted unseasonably long this year, and you may get to meet several of the wives if they have tarried in Meerut."

She listened with determined interest as he told her of the myriad teas, dinners, races, and various entertainments of Meerut, but gradually, her dispirited memories of Derek increasingly took hold. He had looked grim and more than a little desperate at the wedding before striding out of the church door as if intent on drowning himself. She was dismayed to perceive his grief was not merely wounded pride, although much of that had been evident in his attempts to dissuade her from marrying Conran. They had quarreled like fishwives with heated emotion sweeping away all logic.

She realized now that their last fight over Marian and his snobbish family was the first time Derek and she were realistic with one another. When they first became lovers, they played roles: she, the virginal nurse and Derek, the wounded hero. On a deeper level, they needed each other to face life. They tried to bridge the social gap that separated them with their bodies, but even their most tender lovemaking could never overshadow their different worlds forever. Idealistic about each other, they wanted to be perfect for one another, when they were merely human.

Conran never tried to be anything but human, although Annalise sensed he was now trying to be Derek for her. He would be utterly miserable in being anyone but himself, and she could only blame herself for this change in Conran.

Still painting a picture of Meerut for her, Conran's words seemed to run together as her mind refused to give her peace. Conran must learn that she cared for him, and that she did not wish him to take Derek's stead.

She turned slightly in her seat to listen more intently to Conran, for she thought he had begun to sense her entire attention was not devoted to him. At the rapt expression on her face, he began to take heart, not realizing that her attention was a shade too fixed and determined. "Where will we live, Conran?" she asked when he paused for breath.

"I've rented a tiny bit of a place near the barracks," he told her with a slight blush. " 'Tis modest, but clean as a scrap of new-whittled twig. I've managed a cook, too," he added proudly.

"A cook!" Annalise was genuinely admiring. "You needn't have gone to so much expense, Conran. I don't need to be waited upon."

"I'll not have you lifting a finger. You're a lady, and meant to be treated like one."

"No, lad, I am but a minister's daughter, and cook as well." An affectionate smile curved her lips. "You needn't feel as if I am made of glass. I assure you, I'm constructed of much more durable stuff."

"That may well be, but I can afford a cook," he returned adamantly. "When I come home in the evening, I want you all to myself."

Despite his assurances, Annalise was worried that he was burdening himself with extravagances on her behalf, but she knew better than to press the point. Where Conran's pride was at stake, she had best tread lightly. Once she saw the household accounts, she would know well enough how their financial matters stood. Pride or no pride, she would not let him ruin himself with an exaggerated style of living. In striving so hard to please her, he was attempting to become Derek's sort of gentleman, but at least he was falling back into his natural brogue when he was at ease, and not being so careful to speak as an Englishman. She did hope that he would relax with her, for she wanted to make him happy.

"Conran," she began, when there was a lull in the conversation, "did you know that Papa and I lived in such a place as you describe in Canton? We were most content there. I think I shall be very glad to live in your little house in Meerut."

He lit up. "The windows are lined with boxes of marigolds, and there's a well . . ."

The miles streamed by as the train made its way toward Delhi. Night fell, and the engine sparks flashed in the darkness like glowing splinters from an anvil that streaked away to be swallowed up in the night. Annalise had given up trying to sit upright. Fatigued from the hasty preparations and strain of the wedding, she dozed fitfully with her head against Conran's shoulder. He felt so comforting, so big and safe, that she had the same sense of protected well-being that her father had always given her.

In her half-dream state, she could imagine a great wall of water rushing toward her. The water was jade green, shiny as glass, moving to envelop her as if she were a butterfly about to be captured beneath a vast, weighted dome. The sun rose behind the water, gradually rendering it ablaze with gold. She saw the dome was a pearl of amber about to inundate and petrify her, and when she opened her mouth to cry out for Derek, the resin filled her mouth and choked off her desperate cry.

Conran's hand at her shoulder quickly jostled her awake. "You were having a nightmare," he told her abruptly when she peered at him drowsily. The expression in his eyes told her she must have called aloud for Derek, and she flushed with the shameful realization that he must have guessed that she still loved Derek . . . and would go on loving him for years, perhaps for a lifetime.

"I'm sorry, Conran. I didn't mean to disturb you," she murmured penitently. Still asleep, the passengers about them were sprawled like discarded feed sacks in their hard, wooden seats. Nowhere was there a spare space, and bundles were piled high against the windows. Even the top of the train was crammed with passengers and luggage as if ragged blackbirds were nesting there. Outside the windows that were open to combat the heat, the rattle of the wheels made a deafening din that daunted no one from sleeping, and the engine cinders stung Annalise's cheeks. In the moonlight, Conran's cheeks were black with soot while the whites of his eyes caught the moon glow as if he were a frightening demon from scrolls she had seen during her childhood in China.

"See here," he said suddenly in a harsh voice she had never heard him use before. "I know well enough that Derek Clavell was far more than a suitor to you, but I think I have a right to know he'll not stand between us on our wedding eve. Just what are your feelings for the man? Would you rather it was him here instead of me?"

Her eyes widened with startled pain as his fingers dug into her arm. "No, Conran, honestly!"

"Good, because I won't have it, do you hear?" His rough voice softened. "Mind, I don't half blame you. By all accounts I've heard in the army, he's a brave and gallant gentleman. Too many of Clavell's kind are gentlemen in name only, but he's a true one, according to the men in my regiment who've served with him. If you have to be in love with another man, I'd as lief it was him, but if I ever lay eyes on him again, I'm likely to beat him to a pulp."

Gazing at Conran's sulky face, Annalise said nothing. Conran was too honest to dislike Derek, but too much in love with her to keep from hating him.

Nestling her head against Conran's shoulder, she tried to get some sleep.

Dawn's first light spilled across her eyelids even as a gunshot sharply cut through the train engine's regular racket. A man perched on the train top above them shrieked, then lost his balance and fell off the train. Stunned, but unwounded when he landed on the swiftly passing plain, he struggled up and stumbled frantically after the train, the sifting rays of the sun gilding him just before a second shot rang out, spun him about, and flung him into the dust. Women inside the train cars began to scream, clutching at their husbands and children.

"What can the matter be?" gasped Annalise who, still half-asleep, clasped her hat as she gripped Conran's arm.

He peered cautiously from the window, then seeing a band of horsemen bearing down on the train, jerked back his head. "Sepoy cavalry! Dammit, they're attacking us. Bloody mutiny!" Quickly, he shoved her to the floor. "Keep your head down!" The high-pitched whine of a new Enfield bullet whistled overhead, and crouching over Annalise, Conran dug into his carpet bag for a pistol. He swore again with feeling as he shot at a lead horseman and missed. "Blast, I'd give a month's pay for my rifle!"

Annalise shrank against him as splinters spat from the window frame. Terrified passengers cowered against the train sides and along the floor. Annalise felt her whole body shake. Mutiny! Derek had long predicted an outbreak of violence. Was all India soon to be ablaze? Only a few men were pulling out weapons; most passengers were mercantile families, as unused to violence as pet spaniels.

Suddenly, the train gave a surging lurch, then seemed to slam into a mountainside, skidding sideways and pleating like a deadly accordion, its wheels reaching the abrupt end of the rails where a length of track had been torn up. Metal screamed and twisted, drowning out the screams of the passengers trapped within it. A grinding crash pitched Annalise forward against Conran, his body buffering hers as it hurtled forward, then wedged violently between a twisting series of seats. Conran cried out. The train car crushed, spilling its passengers forward in a frantic heap. Her arms outstretched in a futile attempt to stop her forward slide, Annalise struck hard against the sharp metal corner of a steamer trunk. Sparks of red light danced across her eyes, then vanished into an overwhelming darkness.

Derek carefully opened a second bottle of brandy, then left the dark-panelled study to woozily stumble back to his rooms in the guest wing of the commissioner's mansion. Give it to the veterans of John Company; they kept the best liquor and went to the devil in style in this hellhole of a country. He stared out of the second-story window and sipped his potent drink. India might be beautiful, but it stank with decay. Things were rotting everywhere: plants, animals, people. And just as fast as everything died, it bred. Derek envisioned Annalise in his arms, white and serpentine. He imagined himself inside her. Loving her.

God, why could he not stop loving her? She lingered in his mind like a cancerous disease that he wanted to cut out, yet when he tried to tear her away, she became a lovely, night-blooming flower, seductive and impossibly irresistible. He hated her, he loved her, he adored her. Just like mute, huge Conran adored her. They were both pitiable, and she refused them both the love they needed most from her. Conran, who would never possess Annalise no matter how many times he bedded her, had her; while he, himself, who had possessed her, would never have her again.

I wish I had her soft, swanlike neck in my grip, he thought wildly. I want to strangle her . . . I . . . want to kiss her. He took another swig from the bottle and bathed his face in moonlight that turned the city outside his window into a Scheherazadean fantasy of splendid palaces and minarets. After a few moments his grip tightened on the bottle, then he hurled it in a long, violent arc toward the door. The bottle smashed, spraying out from the door in a glitter of glass upon the floor. The door still dripped when it opened a fraction to reveal a wedge of the commissioner's somewhat wary face. "My lord, may I come in?"

Derek let out his breath in a short, explosive sound of exasperation. He was in no mood or condition to converse with anyone. Controlling his impatience with an effort as he stepped through the glass, he swiftly opened the door. "Yes, of course, Commissioner. What was it that you wanted?"

The commissioner entered the room and paused near the door as he eyed askance the smashed glass. His grim attention turned to Derek's rumpled clothing and hostile stare. "Shall I return at a more convenient time?"

Derek sighed and ran his hand through his hair. "An hour from now, I shall be an hour drunker than I am. Best you state your business while I am still somewhat steady afoot."

"I thought you might like to know that the Delhi express has not reached Delhi on schedule," the commissioner informed him. "There is no communication along the line. I just received a telegram from Usjal that the train is eight hours late."

Derek's attention focused sharply. Eight hours. Engine breakdown? Bridge out? If the devastation he had long feared had come to pass, Annalise and Conran had ventured into the heart of it. Alarm was quickly overcoming his irritation. "Is there word of any trouble?"

The commissioner shook his white head. "No, but I suspect there is. Only a few months ago in Meerut, eighty-five sepoys were sentenced to ten years in prison for refusing to bite the cartridges of their new Enfields. There was quite a stir of resentment among both the Hindu and Muslim civilians over the matter. Commissioner Lawrence told me privately that he's been stockpiling arms and food in the Lucknow residency against the possibility of mutiny. He's not a man to shy at shadows."

Derek jerked on his shirt, then caught up his boots as he

dropped onto the edge of the bed to don them. "May I purchase a horse from you, sir? I may not be able to return the loan of one."

The commissioner shook his head. "I'll give you a horse. Just get back here as quickly and safely as you can. If there is a mutiny, I suspect the telegraph wires will be cut at any moment. Meet me in my study and I will give you a personal letter for the Delhi commissioner." Leaving Derek to his dressing, the commissioner went to call his syce to round up a mount.

Derek's intoxicated stupor had been wiped away with the stinging astringent of anxiety. He imagined Annalise fallen prey to the myriad horrors of war and its hellish butchery. To drive the English from their home, the sepoys, knowing that failure meant bloody reprisal and harsher repression, would turn to massacring every white person in India. His only hope was that somehow, Conran would be able to protect Annalise.

Annalise awoke amidst a haze of yellowish gray smoke that lay like a mist over a spilled river of bodies wedged into the bottom of the train. The metal seat legs formed shoals with crumpled human forms banked high. Death was everywhere, its sonata sung by a whine of flies and shrill cries of mutineers gloating over the booty they were still wresting from the corpses. When anyone was found alive, there came the quick, sickening plunge of a knife. Occasionally, a rifle barked, but not often, for the sepoys were intent on conserving their shells. Blood hazed Annalise's vision and she forced herself to stifle a groan at the splitting pain in her head. Through the rosy haze, she saw a sepoy dressed in scarlet going through the bodies heaped in the train door. Another sepoy was pawing through corpses a few feet behind him. Panic-stricken, she closed her eyes, trying to shut out the certainty that they would kill her when they found her. The first sepoy turned over one body, then another, working his way toward her. The sepoy's puttees came closer as he bent over an elderly, white-linen-clad man and rifled his pockets. Snatching a gold watch and chain from the bloodstained vest, he turned to throw aside a child lying across Annalise's arm. Fervently, she prayed the child was dead. She felt the child's weight abruptly lift, then drop again as the sepoy turned to Annalise. Presuming she was dead, he jerked up her head by her hair. After a moment, he let her head fall with a sickening crack on the metal floor, then moved on to his next victim.

Suddenly, there came a shouted command in Hindi outside the train window. The sepoys swore, then reluctantly scanned the remaining bodies on the train. The first sepoy left the train, but the second tarried. Swiftly, he stooped and rifled the coat of yet another man, then stuffing his pockets with pound notes, he hurriedly stepped over the still forms in the aisle. His blocky form was a brief silhouette against the sun's glare in the doorway as he descended the train.

Annalise heard the Hindustani commands growing angrier as stragglers were slow to abandon their booty. She was shivering despite the heat, and although something heavy lay painfully across her legs, she dared not move. After what seemed like forever, there was silence outside the train. The silence inside the train was a horror. Eventually, beyond the windows came the hiss and squawk of vultures. The shadows arrowed long, plum streaks across the increasingly orange light while the sun rose as if biding its time.

Painfully, Annalise pushed upward from the floor and struggled free of the heavy body that pinioned her. Turning over to push it away, she saw it was Conran, his back bent at an impossible angle. His open, glazed eyes were staring at her as if in gaping reproach. You brought me to this, he seemed to say. We were damned from the start.

"Oh, Conran," she whispered, tears starting from her eyes, "I'm so sorry." She cradled his big head in her arms and closed his eyes. He looked relaxed with his eyes shut, almost asleep. She could not help but wonder if God had let him die to save him from something worse. She would have done her utmost to make him happy, but his sudden death was like a prediction that she would have failed. Her tears of mourning fell upon his face and ran like quicksilver in the dawn, making her long to keen over him as an Irishwoman from his own land would have done. It's far from home you are, my lad, she grieved, with a wife who loved you too late, and not enough. Slowly, she pulled a loose coat over his eyes, then steeling herself, rifled his pockets. There was nothing, no money left by the ghoulish sepoys to help her back to Kanpur. Without money and unable to speak more than the simplest Hindi, her chances of making her way through the rebellion-torn countryside were worse than none. She felt as doomed as Conran.

Coming to her knees, she looked out of the window. A few dark heaps lay on the glowing, sun-drenched plain; most of the bodies must still be inside the train. Choking down her fear and revulsion, she worked her way back through the train car to the section where the sepoys had been interrupted. She found a gold signet ring and wallets of pound notes, also a reticule with a small jewelry pouch. Just as she started to take it from the dead Englishwoman, she realized she was making a grave error. Both her clothes and her money, not to mention her lack of Hindi, would give her away as English to the first passerby.

Quickly, she gathered her skirts and went back to the first native car. Here, there were moans among the bodies, for the sepoys had stopped short of murdering their own kind. She looked about for water, but the car was first-class and none of the passengers had demeaned themselves by bringing waterskins aboard. She hurried back to the third-class car and found a full waterskin. Wherever she heard a sound or groaned cry for help, she offered water. Soon there were cries everywhere in the carnage. She emptied the waterskin, then went back to forage for a second. A man was sitting up, holding his bleeding head. At his feet was a dead child, a woman slumped over its small form. Pity filled Annalise. "May I help you?" she called softly to the man as she advanced with the waterskin.

Still only half-conscious, he glared up at her. "*Feringhi* bitch!" he hissed malevolently. "My family was killed because of the likes of you! Stay away from me. Stay away!"

Distraught, she left him and returned to the first-class Indian car. So much death everywhere, so much grief . . . and more would come if the mutiny spread. Who was really to blame, besides the combination of native superstition and resentment that had been stirred up by the English? Heaven knew the native customs and rights had been ignored, and India rightfully belonged to the Indians, if one could call the melange of races and religions Indian, but the butchery that would come out of revolt and its repression would carry little hint of justice. As an Englishwoman alone and unprotected, she would stand no chance of surviving in the countryside.

Crumpled across the aisle, a bejeweled Hindu woman whimpered as Annalise started to step over her. Quickly, Annalise stooped to help her. A cast mark looked like a small, black fingerprint of death on the woman's forehead as Annalise slipped an arm underneath her armpit to help her up. "No," the woman gasped in Hindi, then added brokenly in English, "I am hurt . . . my chest . . ." Quickly, Annalise lowered her to the floor again. "Do not leave me," the woman whispered. "Kali, the goddess of death, walks . . . this place. I do not . . . want her to find . . . me . . ."

Annalise gave the dying Hindu woman comfort until the

sun was well up, when the woman's head dropped sideways against the floor and her breath ceased to rasp amid the groans in the car. Everyone in the English cars was dead, but a few natives were bestirring themselves. With a muttered, "forgive me," Annalise swiftly stripped the woman of her jewels, then went back to the poorest native car and stripped another woman of her ragged red sari. She pulled off her own clothing before someone ventured back to investigate, put on the sari, and concealed a native money pouch containing the rich woman's jewels beneath it.

Heading back to the English car to bid a last farewell to Conran, she hesitated as she passed through the car containing the malevolent Hindu and his dead family. His face suffused with grief, he scarcely glanced up at her as she hurriedly passed by him. Suddenly, his head lifted, his eyes narrowing as he recognized her behind the sari's drape over her pale face. Fury twisting his countenance, he spat at her feet. "Excretion of a pig!"

She shrank back, fearing that he would attack her, then hurried through the car. Upon reaching Conran, she could not find his pistol. The gun must have been flung from his grasp when the car derailed. She bent over him, searching for the weapon, and finally spied it several feet from Conran's body, which was wedged between an iron seat leg and the rail-car side.

As she stepped forward, a hand grabbed her sari at the back of her neck. The red cotton ripped from her head when, panic-stricken, she lunged forward toward the pistol. The Hindu grasped the rough fabric and swiftly tried to reel her in, jerking her off her feet. Her falling weight toppled him almost atop her. Gripping one iron seat support after another, she dragged herself along the floor. The sari ripped with a sickening sound. Gasping, Annalise kicked at him as he clawed at her. His free hand shot for her throat even as her fingers inched toward the elusively gleaming gun. Making a muffled cry of terror a split second before his hand closed on her throat, she futilely grabbed at the weapon. With her left hand, she struck hard at his face, then when he failed to release her, hammered at his unprotected nose. As he cut off her breath, the Hindu's nose began to stream, making darker splotches of crimson on her red sari. Her vision was blackening about the edges, her starving lungs rasping for air. Gathering all her strength, she pronged her fingers for his eyes and dug with all the mercilessness of desperation. With a shriek, he let go, trying to protect his eyes. Her fingers closed on the gun and in a hard overhead arch, she swung it down, splitting his scalp. Stunned, he fell atop her. For good measure, she swatted him twice more until his body went limp. Gasping for air, she pushed his body away with an effort and crawled out from under him.

Picking up her sari skirts, she fought her way from the rail car and out into the murky orange-gray daylight. The plain loomed away, blank and lifeless as a desert, but for patches of dry palm trees with shriveled fronds, and a few train passengers stumbling from the cars. Seeing three of them headed south along the train track, she fell in some fifty feet behind them. If she kept her distance, they would make no effort at conversation. Sometime before dawn, the train had spent several hours on a siding in Aligarh, which could not be too far away.

Catching the torn sari high about her face, she turned back for one last look at the gleaming brown and red serpent that sprawled broken-backed across the plain. In its bowels lay Conran, who had loved her. She would spend her life mourning Conran, whose heart was as big as his great, gentle hands. Conran had known only how to give, but never to take. And she had not even been permitted time enough to give him a decent burial. If she stayed with the train, she would die. That murderous Hindu would not be the only grief-stricken native aboard who would seek vengeance for those innocents killed. They would care nothing that among their children lay her dead, childlike Conran. Tears streaming down her dusty face, she stumbled along the shining thread of the track, the single strand binding her to bitter life.

"I wish to accompany a cavalry squadron north along the rail line," Derek adamantly told the Kanpur commissioner for the third time. "If there's trouble, we had better find out about it. You've still had no answer from Delhi. The telegraph may well be cut."

The commissioner stubbornly shook his head as he sanded and folded his quickly scrawled note. "Here, for the Delhi commissioner. I must refuse the regiment; if there's trouble, it could be cut off, and I've no men to spare. You are it, my lord. Word of mutiny should drift to Kanpur quickly enough. I won't risk the residency defenses unnecessarily." He turned to his attaché. "Mr. Pease, please send in the *badahur shah's* emissary. He has been kept waiting long enough," he added pointedly.

Forced to subside for the time being, Derek impatiently paced by the window as the *shah's* emissary was admitted to the imposing, teak-lined office of the commissioner.

The emissary, dressed in the green and gold of the *badahur shah's* household, bowed abruptly. "Mr. Commissioner, my master sends his respects. I have come this day from Delhi to advise you that the *badahur* has wearied of the English presence in his dominions. He requires that you leave. All property which has been illegally maintained by the English within his domain hereby reverts to the custody of the *shah*." There was more, equally calculated to rouse the ire of the commissioner, who was not in a good mood to begin with.

"Absurd," the commissioner bit out, taken aback. "We

have no intention of going anywhere, or abandoning our property. You take a good deal upon yourself, sir. . ."

The emissary's eyes beetled dark over his sweeping moustachios. "We take back what is ours, and is long overdue. We are now recovering the north. Meerut will be ours, along with Allabad and Lucknow. You would be wise to surrender now to evade the needless slaughter of your women and children. Once surrounded, you can easily be starved out. We are millions to your paltry few thousand."

The commissioner found the summary arrogance of the man stupefying. His sorely tired temper fired. "To the devil with you, sir! I'll be damned if I turn over so much as a farthing to you! Get out, and take my refusal to the *shah*. If he wants Kanpur, by God tell him to come and take it!"

The emissary turned on his heel and stalked out. Derek wheeled on the commissioner. "So they have cut the train line, sir, as well as the telegraph. This rebellion has been long in coming, and if the Muslims and Hindus are united, we are in grave jeopardy. The *shah's* messenger was not speaking from mere bravado."

The commissioner dropped into his chair. "Well, this cracks it. The north up in arms while we're cut off here. Few of the residencies are designed for defense. We've nothing between us and the rebels but a few regiments of questionable loyalty. . ."

"And complacency, which has stood you in such good stead in the past," finished Derek ironically. He leaned over the desk. "Well, do I get my squadron or not?"

The commissioner eyed him flatly. "You do not. I'll need every man here."

Derek's jaw tightened. "Then good luck to you; you'll need that, too." He left the commissioner pawing through his desk drawers for maps and yelling for his attaché.

Derek thought and thought hard as he strode through the residency toward the great front door. He stood little chance of survival if he ventured into the north alone. An Englishman would be fair prey to any rebel band. Still, Annalise must be found. If she were still alive, she would be in dreadful danger. How could he reach her?

As he came to the broad verandah and sharply beckoned to a syce to bring his horse, he saw the emissary mounted on a massive black stallion trotting through the wrought-iron gates . . . and thought of a way to find Annalise.

The emissary of the *badahur shah* smiled grimly. The commissioner was a fool, and his like would soon be wiped from the face of India. The English never knew when they were beaten. Sometimes such ignorance turned the tables upon their foes, but this time they stood no chance. Before the year was ended, the rule of the Raj would cease to exist in India. He urged his stallion to a gallop. Soon he would report to his master. The *shah* was an old man, bewildered that his people now looked upon him as a leader, but his advisers would not be pleased to hear that yet another English commissioner refused to be sensible. How should he phrase his report . . . ?

He had no time to come to a decision, for in the next instant, his horse pitched him *puggaree* over boots. Stunned, he lay in the dusty road, lifted his head, and saw his stallion struggling to its feet. A rope camouflaged by dust was strung across the road. Bandits! Swearing, he fought to his knees and reached for a pistol, only to gasp and clutch at his neck as a garrote settled. His knuckles whitened as a black shield shuttered across the palm trees and clay-colored grasses beside the road. He never even saw the man who throttled him into unconsciousness was the same who had glowered at him in the commissioner's office.

Derek swiftly dragged the emissary into the weeds and stripped him, then bound him hand and foot with his belt.

Fortunately, the man was a tall Sikh of a like height and breadth as himself, but the breeches were a trifle short. Derek changed into the Sikh's clothes and stuffed the breeches into his own boot tops. Hastily, he wound the gold sash about his narrow waist, thrust in the Sikh's broad knife, then snatched up the pistol from the dust. His own horse was better than the Sikh's; a shade too good, so he did not trouble to shift the Sikh's tack, but mounted the black stallion and pounded off northward toward Delhi.

Disaster had struck Annalise, he knew. The emissary would not have been so cocksure or so quick in coming to Kanpur had he not had some certainty of having the English on the run in the north. He only hoped that Conran could protect her long enough for him to find them.

XI

The Search

Ready to drop from exhaustion, Annalise stumbled along the track until she reached a road she thought might take her back to Aligarh. Distraught with their own sorrows, the small group from the train who trudged along the railway quickly blended into the mass of southbound refugees who were beginning to clog the roads. She wound the sari higher about her face and tried to remain alert. Although she understood little of the Indian dialects, the wild chatter and forlorn faces of those about her said the train attack was but one debacle in a series of horrors. While her skin was light for an Indian, no one paid any mind.

Ghari carts lumbered by, laden with household goods. Threading between them were peasants afoot with bundles and children shambling with fatigue. Everyone's brightly colored clothes were dust dulled, and their feet yellowed by rising clouds of grit. Annalise was parched, but dared not ask for water from one of the *ghari* carts with their huge clay pots. If she could only last until nightfall, she might find a stream or unguarded well in one of the villages. Dazedly, she slumped down by the roadside to rest for a few moments. In minutes, she was asleep, a small puddle of scarlet in the grass. A goat cropped nearby, nosed the sari spilled over her hair, and moved on.

Derek rode hard as far as Villipah, then had to ease up as his horse was beginning to strain. He stopped at both the train stations of Jedipur and Meerulpore; at both, Annalise's train had been on schedule, but when word of its failure to reach Delhi was telegraphed back along the line, all following trains had been halted. The tracks were choked with rail cars. Now that the telegraph line was down, no one knew what had become of the last train to Delhi. Past Meerulpore, he began to encounter refugees on the Grand Trunk Road. "Hi, you there," he called in expert Hindi to a merchant struggling along with his large family, "what has happened up ahead?"

The merchant eyed him suspiciously. "How is it that a servant of the *badahur shah* does not know of the northern troubles?"

"I have been in Kanpur for the past week," explained Derek easily. He leaned over his horse's crupper. "May we hope that the rule of the Raj is coming to a swift end?"

The merchant spat in the dust. "A curse on you and all your kind. All you can think of is fighting while the peaceful man starves. All Delhi has been ransacked by the sepoys; the streets are in riot, and the residency besieged."

"What about the train from Kanpur?" questioned Derek urgently when the man shifted the heavy bundle on his back and started to prod his family along.

"I do not know and do not care," responded the merchant sharply. "Kanpur is yet seventy-five miles from here and you detain us."

Derek bowed slightly and tossed him a few rupees. "My apologies. May fortune smile on your journey."

The merchant shrugged as one of his children darted forward to pick up the money. "You may have better luck with a train from Meerulpore. No trains are leaving from the station at Jidda." So saying, he herded his family down the road.

Leery of questioning anyone else, Derek rode warily into Aligarh. The city was in riot, the sepoys ganged up and firing on the residency, the central market a shambles. He picked his way through the crowds milling in the street. Occupants of the upper floors of buildings along the route leaned out to shout encouragement to the rioters. If Annalise and Conran had left the train and encountered a melee like this, their position would be desperate. Working his way through the crowd was difficult despite his prestigious uniform, so Derek steered for the side streets, and after some hours, reached the far side of the city. The comparative quiet of the Trunk Road was a relief after the shriek and babble of Aligarh. Two miles beyond the city, he cut over to the railroad and followed the track northward.

Near dawn, Derek found the demolished end of the track. In the murky, gray half-light, the smashed serpent of the train lay broken-backed across the plain, its passengers spilled like bloody entrails across the rails and yellow dust. He felt his stomach lurch as he slid from the stallion's back, then picked his way through the bodies. With his sleeve over his face to evade the stench, Derek groped through the corpses with fear wrapped about him like a shroud. He quickly found the two cars that contained the English passengers.

"Please, God," Derek whispered passionately in the dreadful silence, "don't let Annalise be here. Don't let me find her butchered like these poor wretches . . ."

In time, he found Conran. His back twisted like the

train's, the Irish sergeant lay midway through the second rail car in a spilled heap of bodies. Like a dam, he blocked the flow of death, and it was piled high as the seats at its crest. His hands shaking, Derek turned over each body in the car; none was Annalise. He started on the second car, and there, near the end, found the leghorn hat in which he had seen her so often; its new rose ribbon was trampled in the blood dried on the floor of the train. Gripping the hat, he stared down at it as if one of the vultures outside had roweled at his brain. Reality had become a violent, futile slash that spilled the life from his hopes, screamed at him that Annalise was dead. She was lying somewhere amid these broken bodies, and he shrank from finding her, was sickened by the very idea of finding her.

Only he had to find her. He had to know she was dead, and all his hopes with her.

One by one, he examined each body in the train, a ghastly task, as the sun began its climb. Under the searing glare of noon, he came to the last body and studied the strange Hindu woman's face as if reassembling its features. Here would be the amber eyes that had the dusky glow of fireflies on a summer eve; here, the lips that curved like the velvet petals of a lush empress rose. Here, here was his love, as carelessly torn from life as if cut from it by steel shears.

Here was a stranger, remote as the Himalayan snows. Tears seeped from his eyes as he mourned the dead woman, his mind dull and gray. After some time, he forced himself to laboriously think. If Annalise was not among these corpses, where was she? Had the sepoys taken her? Beautiful or not, she was of no use to them, as their religion forbade defilement by raping a *feringhi* woman. The dark pall over his mind began to lift. There must have been survivors among the natives; possibly she had gone with them, and yet . . . they, like the sepoys, would want no part of her. She might have been spirited away by some savage genie.

His thoughts bleak, he mounted his horse and retraced his route south. If Annalise had somehow escaped, she would try to find her way back to Kanpur. Alone. In a country shrieking for English blood.

Annalise awoke at dusk, her limbs leaden from exhaustion. She was not the only one who had settled by the edge of the road for the night. Small groups huddled by fires for miles across the flat plain. The new moon hung low on the horizon, a silver ghost in the pall of dust still sifting up from the earth. A dove called from a copse of peepul trees darkening a few yards away. She gathered her sari about her and rose to her feet; bare and bruised from the long walk. She did not have time to think of sandals. In Aligarh, she would buy sandals with the jewels she carried, for she hesitated to use English pounds. Just now, her stomach was knotted with tension and lack of food. She knew the groups clustered by the campfires would give her nothing. The poor were common as houseflies in India, and treated with the same dismissal.

Heading for the copse of trees, she reasoned that a stream of some kind must have marshalled their outcrop. There was a rivulet, scarcely a brook, that trickled through the trees that cast long bars of shadow across the dank grass and mud. Looking warily about her, she crept to the stream, knelt, and cupped her hands to drink. The water was tepid, and slightly rank. With a cool pragmatism derived from the horrors of the train, she hoped there were no bodies lying upstream. As she dipped her hands again, her peripheral vision caught the whisper of a shadow, then others, low and striped against the grass. Swiftly, she rose, her heart pounding. Hyenas, skulking in the wood, were creeping near. Filled with fear and disgust, she retreated back the way she had come. If the hyenas grew brave enough, they would attack.

She wished she had brought Conran's pistol; something told her she was going to need it before long.

She slept near the largest group of refugees by the wayside, their firelight barely dappling her. From time to time, she caught a few words of Hindustani, a smattering of argument, then the fading whine of a child. The ground was hard and the dawn came slowly, but she was too tired to do anything but sleep. The sari over her face stirred with her sometimes fitful breathing, then settled as the dawn brought a hush of still air. A twitter of sparrows sounded from the grass, and overhead, a solitary northbound crane sailed its kitelike shape over the yellow earth.

Awakening, Annalise peered upward at the great, hazy sun rising somnolently beyond the crane. Cranes were omens of good fortune. Why could not Conran have known the lax, lazy birth of this day? If any man deserved fortune's sweetest smile, it was he. She missed him terribly. They might have had years together, grandchildren . . . and yet the thought returned that Conran's death was a judgement. To save him the unhappiness of a wife who loved him too little, fortune had taken him too soon.

Famished and dispirited, she reached the outskirts of Aligarh by evening of the following day. It had been a hellish journey, her only water from scum-covered irrigation ditches, her only food a mouthful of sour rice from the garbage pit behind a burning village. The city outskirts were hushed after two days of rioting, with the few people in the streets either beggars with nothing to lose or thieves prowling after scraps from unbarred shops. Glad of the ragged sari which dismissed her as a beggar, she kept close to the walls. Night fell quickly, with smoke from scattered, guttering fires spilling upward into the darkness. A fresh blaze flared up from near the center of town and she followed its light to the marketplace. Here, the streets were no longer empty. Bands of men cruised the shadows like sharks nosing out prey, and here and there, a single remora or two stole past her. In the main streets, mobs were gathering, brave now that they were cloaked by the night. Chilled with fear, she peered upward at shop signs, some of them ripped from their supports and dangling like unbaited hooks. Her empty stomach rebelled at smells from the marketplace of smashed fruit overripened in the day's heat. Even the rancid scent of *ghee* and urine could not stifle her ravenous appetite.

Frowning in desperate concentration, she tried to remember the streets once casually pointed out to her by Professor Sanderville. She took one wrong turn after another, but eventually her patience was rewarded when she caught sight of a wooden sign cut like a huge red ruby on a corner marked as the Street of the Jewelers. Only a few shops with steel-grated windows and doors remained undisturbed by plunderers; the rest were gutted caves of smashed display cases, their rich pillows and carved furniture vanished. She rapped at one barred shop door, then another; there was no answer. Fearful of attempting to trade rich jewelry for food in the market, she persisted. If she displayed a jewel to the wrong person, she might well be robbed or killed.

Another two shops produced no sign of life, but finally, at her rap on a shop door near the end of the street, a balding head popped out of a window overhead. "Begone," the merchant hissed. "Can you not see we are closed?"

"I wish to trade precious gems for rupees," she softly called upward. "You would do well to talk to me."

Startled by her English, he peered at her more closely, then catching sight of her ragged sari, he glared down at her and swore. "Begone, or the street guards will hang you for a thief!"

In answer, she raised her arm from beneath the sari. A glitter spilled halfway from her slim wrist to her white elbow. The merchant hesitated, then shot a sharp glance down the length of the street. "Stay," he muttered. "Wait. I will come." Then shutters closed abruptly.

Annalise huddled against the wall and waited in the murky silence. Another fire had been set ablaze, this one only a few streets away. In the reddish glow, she heard shrieks and smashing glass, then the battering of a door. A woman's sobs rose above the racket. Only hours ago, I was crying like that for Conran, she thought bleakly. To remember him striding through the marketplace as she had first seen him, proud and tall, was like a terrible slash across her memory. To remember Derek's distraught, twisted face, when she told him she would marry Conran, was a scar upon her mind.

The shopkeeper unlocked the door and jerked it open just far enough for her to sidle through. Suddenly, she was shoved violently forward from behind and trampled to the floor as two men thrust their way into the shop. The shopkeeper stumbled back, carried by the momentum of their weight as they charged him. Squealing in near mute, stupefied fear, he scrambled back toward the curtained door that led to the steps up into his private quarters. A knife flashed upward, a hand spun the shopkeeper into the curtain, entangling him. He bleated once as the knife flashed down, then made a shallow, gurgling sound as it descended again.

Uttering a stifled cry, Annalise bolted toward the door. A hand caught in her sari, then her hair, ripping it from its half-fallen chignon. "No!" she screamed as the blade darted toward her throat. She managed to block the blow with her arm, the knife grating off the bangles. Whirling about, she plunged her fist into her assailant's stomach as her free hand clawed frantically for his eyes. She felt hair tear from her scalp as he lost his grip, then tried to grasp her hair anew. She flailed out again and this time connected with his nose. He yelled and let her go, a freshet of crimson spilling down his face. Swearing in Hindustani, he pursued her across the room as she ran for the door. The other man, intent on smashing the few shop cases for their jewels, ignored her.

Head foremost, she barreled into a crowd of perhaps ten men pouring into the shop. One of them grabbed her, while three more attacked her assailant with bludgeons. When he tried to ply his blade, one of the men shot him point-blank in the stomach with an old flintlock pistol. He sat down abruptly, his hands clasped over his belly, then toppled over in a heap. Five more men shoved the torn curtain and shop proprietor aside and charged up the steps after the dead thief's partner. They dragged him shrieking down the stairs, then out into the street along with Annalise. The group was a motley crew, mostly fat and balding, apparently a merchant band of vigilantes. Amid the shouting and shoving, someone produced a rope, slung it over the shop's awning rod, then shoved the tearful thief's neck into the noose already fixed to the end of it. A few heartbeats later, they strung him up from the awning, strangling and kicking. In horror, Annalise stared at his bulging eyes and frantic, gaping mouth. For a long while, he struggled, his face purpling to a black gargoyle mask, his feet inches off the street, then he twitched to silent, dreadful immobility.

Then, to Annalise's shocked horror, two of the men jerked her forward as another unstrung the noose from the thief and rehung it from the awning. "No," she cried out, "you cannot mean to kill me! I have done nothing!"

Shocked by her English, the men halted and stared at her. She had little Hindustani, but enough to follow something of the magpie chatter that broke out. "She is an *amah*," ventured one of them, "who has lost her employment as a nursemaid with the *Angrezi*."

"No," put in another, holding up her arm and running back the sari veil to show the rich bangles, "she is one of the thieves. They used her to lure old Amahl into opening his shop."

Most of them were inclined to agree she was a thief and proceeded to string her up. Annalise protested wildly. "No, no, you don't understand! I *am* an *Angrezi*. English. I had nothing to do with those men . . ."

Unable to understand her, they glared at her in some alarm. An argument broke out. Most of the men wanted to hang her, but two who seemed to be leaders were less eager. "What if she is *Angrezi?* What if the *Angrezi* come back after the revolt is done and punish us for her death? They will not see that we were only protecting ourselves and our property. . ."

One of them pulled the sari back from her head. "See, her skin is light. She may be *Angrezi*."

Annalise nodded swiftly. "I am the widow of Sergeant Conran O'Reilly of the 3rd Cavalry."

Catching the gist of her last words, they looked at one another. "Send for the magistrate," one suggested.

"Faugh," said another. "No magistrate is going to judge a beggar woman when the whole market is put to the torch."

"Then we'll take her with us," said one of the leaders flatly. "If we don't find a magistrate by morning, we'll hang her and be done with it."

Using the noose to bind her arms, two of them towed her after them. "Say your prayers, woman. Magistrates are as scarce as hen's teeth tonight. You are unlikely to greet the sunrise."

Derek reached Aligarh two hours before dawn. In the light of the full, setting moon, the city looked like a worn-out whore sprawled over the plain. Smoke hung in a pall about her parapets, while mist curled from the river choked with bodies in an unhealthy miasma. He was hungry, weary, and dejected. Nowhere in the crowds streaming from Meerut and Delhi had he seen any sign of Annalise.

Finding her was an impossible task. Children tottered in the road, wandered from parents sleeping by the wayside. In dusty lumps, they lay like stones on the ground. In the darkness, he evaded a goatherd driving a band of chalky shadows along the road. The city gates were unguarded, their great hinges creaking like arthritic bones. He rode into the heart of the city where the mobs of the night were beginning to disperse. The residency was a quiet, burnt-out shell, its walls pockmarked from gunfire. There was no food left in the market's abandoned stalls where awnings flapped in the fitful air. He dismounted by a stone well and lowered the bucket, only to hear a stolid thump in place of a splash when it struck bottom. Something was likely dead in the well. With a sigh, he pried his half-empty canteen from the stallion's saddle and pressed it to his lips. Brackish water ran into his mouth. A man furtively hurried by, made a hasty bow when he saw the *badahur's* uniform, and scuttled off into the darkness. A jumble of rioters surged into the marketplace, torching the awnings and stalls. He saw silhouettes dancing and capering with the weight of fatigue from a night's revels dragging at their heels. Tiredly, he remounted, and with the casualness of no longer giving a damn, rode through the rioters' ranks as if they were nonexistent.

"*Huzoor!*" cried a voice on the outskirts of the mob. "*Huzoor,* you must give heed!" A man ran forward to seize his stirrup. "We have caught a murderous thief and you must come to render judgement."

Derek shook him off. "I am on a mission for the *badahur shah*. I cannot trouble with your affairs."

The man danced up and down with impatience. "You do not understand, *huzoor*." He looked about him to make sure the rioters were paying no heed, then hissed, "The thief is *Angrezi, huzoor*."

Derek abruptly halted the stallion. Not only were the rioters beginning to show an interest in him, but the unlucky

Angrezi was as good as dead if he refused to look into the matter. He disliked the situation; he had enough trouble on his own, and if someone caught a flaw in his Hindustani, more than one *Angrezi* might be executed. "Very well," he said curtly, "but be quick to show me this thief. I cannot tarry here."

"Very well, *huzoor,* but do not blame me if the thief is already hanged."

Annalise struggled violently as one of the vigilante merchants slipped the noose around her neck and tossed the end over an awning rail. "Let me go!" she cried desperately. "I had nothing to do with the thieves!"

Understanding her no better than before, the merchants ignored her. They had by now settled the argument that she must be a thief, for otherwise, what would a ragged beggar woman be doing with the rich jewels of a high-caste Hindu? *Angrezi* or not, she was out of luck. They began to haul on the rope.

Annalise gasped, her feet sliding across the ground as the rope cut off her last moan of panic. The noose tightened abruptly, and her bursting brain dimly registered the sound of hooves as she started to swing off the ground. A *tulwar* sliced a sharp curve through the air with a whistle as a tall Hindu in the green and gold uniform of the *badahur shah* leaned from the saddle to sever the rope. She saw the Hindu's eyes widen as he looked down into her terrified face. "God's . . ." he started to swear, then with an expression of vast relief, turned his back deliberately on her and curtly addressed the merchants. "You have indeed caught an *Angrezi*. You were sensible not to execute her outright. I will take her to the commissioner in Kanpur and see that she is dealt with."

"But *huzoor,*" one protested, "there is no need for you

to trouble yourself. She was used by the thieves as a lure. How else would she come by these baubles?" So saying, he grasped Annalise's arm and displayed the bangles.

"Did you see this with your own eyes?" demanded Derek.

"No," the man assured him, "but she was inside the shop and it is clear..."

Derek turned from him to Annalise and spoke swiftly in English. "Give your reasons for being in the shop, and quickly. These lads are in no mood for chitchat."

She stared up at him in astonishment, then stammered out that she had meant to trade the jewels for food. The thieves had just burst into the shop before they could be stopped.

"Did you steal the jewels in the first place?" he demanded first in Hindustani for the sake of the vigilantes, then in English. "Tell the truth," he added. "If they sense you're lying, you're gallows bait."

"Yes," she faltered, "I took the jewels, but the woman was dead. I only hoped to . . ."

He cut her off. "Then you will go with me to the commissioner for judgement." He turned to the men surrounding them. "This woman is in my diplomatic custody. I have business with the *Angrezi* commissioner in Kanpur. He will see to her."

Relieved to be freed from a complicated business and eager to go home after a long, harried night, the merchants agreed after a mercifully brief debate. Annalise was near fainting from exhaustion, hunger, and fear. They pushed her at Derek. "Take her, but give us the jewels she carries for our trouble in holding her for the commissioner."

He dickered with them for a few minutes to keep from seeming too eager to claim Annalise: minutes which dragged interminably for Annalise. Eventually, they settled for half the jewels and good riddance. He seized the rope binding Annalise's wrists, and hauling her after him, rode off through the dwindling crowd. He kept up a quick pace through the city that she was hard put to match. Finally, stumbling with fatigue, she fell to her knees and cried out, "Stop, for pity's sake! What do you take me for, a pack animal?" Although he reined in, his horse jerked her over onto her face. Wretchedly, she curled into the dirt and began to weep, her tears streaking tiny, clear rivulets through the dirt on her cheeks.

"Get up, woman," ordered Derek bluntly in Hindustani as he slid off his horse. Going to her, he bent down and hauled her to her feet. In her ear, he whispered urgently in English, "You must last until we're out of the city. We're not out of this yet."

"I cannot go on any longer," she returned desperately. "I walked all the way from the train . . . on no food . . . all night . . ." She sagged forlornly against him. "Conran is dead, Derek. Dead . . ." Tears streaming afresh, she sagged back into the dirt. There she huddled, like an abandoned bundle of rags, sobs shaking her whole body.

Glancing about, Derek noticed a few idlers watching them. Although he longed to comfort Annalise, to give her solace now would invite suspicion. He dragged her to her feet. "Pull yourself together," he hissed. "If you break down now, you will get us both killed. Delhi is in flames and Aligarh no longer has a commissioner. We must get to Kanpur to be safe."

Her battered mind dully comprehending him, she stood in mute despair as he swung back onto his horse. The tether jerked her forward, and feeling as if she would drop at any moment, she followed him down the street.

The city seemed like an endless nightmare as the sun crept above the horizon. They cleared the southernmost gates as the sun cleared the parapet walls, slanting through the sullen billows of smoke that hung like soiled wood over the rooftops. A half mile from the city, Annalise collapsed in the road. When Derek tried to rouse her, she did not move. Her head lolled against his arm. Senseless, she lay like an exhausted child against his shoulder.

The road was beginning to grow crowded with the day's refugees. Derek scooped up Annalise and took her to a thicket of weeds. Her lips were cracked from lack of water, her bare feet bruised and covered with bloody scratches. The long lashes he had loved to kiss delicately shielded her eyes from his intent gaze. He lay down beside her in the tall grass where he held her limp body close to him. He had been in the saddle over thirty hours, but she was with him again. His aching body cried out for a few minutes' rest, for the peace he had always known in Annalise's presence, but she was in need. She would soon wake and his water bottle was nearly empty. He kissed her cheek softly, then covered her face with her sari so that she appeared to be one of the bodies abandoned by the wayside. Then he set out in search of food and transportation.

Two hours passed before he found a farm that had not been ransacked for just the sort of supplies he wanted. The rest of Annalise's bangles went for a few *chupattis*, goat's milk, and a skinny, big-shouldered white mule. There was no woman at the farm so he could not purchase a change of clothing for Annalise; that lack troubled him, for her ragged, bloody red sari and his uniform were a dramatic contrast. They would draw attention, and he feared he might be called upon to intervene in yet another awkward situation. He could not simply dress as a native, for he did not look like a farmer, and he had not the beard of a tall Sikh. He would just have to continue in his official capacity.

When he went back for Annalise, he found he had another problem: she was gone. There was a furrow parting the grass where she had lain, as if she had been dragged away out of sight of the road. His water bottle lay untouched in the grass beside his blanket roll. His heart pounding and his gun drawn, Derek followed the furrowed track along the road to a stand of bamboo lining a small stream. Annalise was lying by the stream, trying to drink from it. Upstream, there lay a dead, bloated sheep lodged among the rocks. He ran to her and jerked her back. Crying out, she struck feebly at him. "I need water, Derek . . . I must have water . . ."

"Not this water: it's fouled." Lifting her slightly, he pointed out the sheep. She stared at it, then weakly put her hand across her mouth as if she wanted to retch. He pressed her to his chest and whispered into her hair. "Hold out just a little longer. I know you've had a brutal time, but I am here now, and I shall take care of you. This time, you won't have to look after me." He kissed her forehead. "Lie still. I'll be back in a few minutes."

When he returned, he gave her the last of the brackish water from his canteen, then the goat's milk, letting it drip slowly from its clay container into her parched mouth. Although she made a face at the taste, she drank greedily, lifting her head to reach the rim. "How long has it been since you've eaten?" he asked, smoothing her hair.

"Three days. I thought I should never reach Aligarh." She caught his hand. "Have you been to the wreck?"

He nodded. "And seen Conran. I'm sorry." Then he added more quietly. "I may have been jealous of him, but I liked him. You married a good man."

"Yes," she whispered. "He was a good man. He died trying to protect me."

"I thought you were dead, too," Derek said softly. "When I couldn't find you . . ." His voice growing husky, he caught her to him. "I thought I had lost you when you married him, but I didn't know the meaning of loss until I found Conran in that smashed train car and you weren't there. I love you beyond breathing, beyond life. Never leave me again."

She gazed at him sadly, her fingertips grazing his cheek. "I can never be yours, Derek; I knew that when I married

Conran. You and I are meant to travel different paths. Conran's death changes nothing. Certainly, you could never have been friends. Even if I had not come between you, the social chasm would have been too great. I cannot live in your world, Derek, any more than Conran could have done."

Derek smoothed the sari back from her hair. "Conran's poverty has no bearing upon us. I love you. Annalise, if the last few days have taught me nothing, they have shown me that life without you, on any level, would be empty."

"You feel an obligation to me; that obligation intensified when you thought I was dead."

He threw up his hands. "Women. Their logic defies description. Were you deaf when I told you I loved you?"

"You didn't tell me until just now."

He hesitated, registering her observation. "Surely, I mentioned it earlier."

She shook her head, her eyes as level as a justice's on a royal bench. "No. Desire was mentioned liberally; love never . . . And why not; both of us knew there was no point to it."

Taking her hand, he took a deep breath and stood up, drawing her with him. "My profoundest apologies, madam. I have been sorely remiss."

"And generally a jackass," she added stringently.

He winced. "Agreed . . . more or less. You left Claremore like a witch out of Hades; how could you expect me to rectify the situation? Besides, you are going to marry me. You love me. Why should you be perverse enough to marry someone else?"

"I am guided not by perversity, but by common sense. We should never be happy together if we were married."

He spread his hands in exasperation. "We were deliriously happy at Claremore until I was stupid enough to cast a second glance at Marian."

"That happiness couldn't have lasted," she said stubbornly. "You . . . would patronize me. I couldn't endure that."

He gripped her slim shoulders. "I would love and cherish you. You would be the center of my life. What more do you want?"

She shook her head. "I shouldn't be the center of your life. You would always be looking outward." She hesitated. "Besides, I shouldn't want to be the center of your life. I'm not that selfish. I want . . . balance. Can you understand that? Conran offered a sort of balance."

"You can say that of a man you didn't love? What sort of equality would Conran have ever known from you?"

"But I did love Conran," she said softly. "Not enough, perhaps, but I loved him. He was the dearest man in the world."

"He worshipped you like a graven image. He would have gilded the very Irish potatoes he fed you, and the real prick is"—he glared at her indignantly—"that you never would have disillusioned him. You would have gone on the rest of your life playing the paper saint." He caught her up by the hand and dragged her after him.

Stumbling, she nearly ran into the mule. Already cantankerous, it tried to kick off her head. Derek jerked her out of range. "Watch where you're going. If you're headed off for another miff, this is no time for it. In case you haven't noticed, the countryside is rife with mutineers and riffraff . . ."

She balked. "In case you haven't noticed, *I'm* riffraff!"

He threw her up on the mule. "Stop being difficult. Riffraff hasn't the stuffing for it."

Athwart the mule, she glared at him. "I haven't had breakfast yet . . . or supper or lunch or . . ."

He tossed her a *chupatti*. "Haven't you heard? We upper classes eat on the run."

XII

On The Run

They reached Kanpur by midafternoon of the next day. The unseasonal coolness was ending, the usual sweltering summer beginning to hold customary sway. Annalise had wilted in the saddle, her sari hanging like the molting plumage of a scarlet bird. She looked the part of Derek's prisoner, so no one interfered with them. "In case anyone inquires," he had told her on the road, "you're mute. You have not enough Hindustani to give simple orders to a cook."

Derek had a natural gift for languages and his command of the northern Indian dialects was superb. Urdu rolled off his tongue as easily as French, and he spoke Hindustani as well as he did English. Unlike Aligarh, there was a jostle of activity in Kanpur. The cantonment was in flames, Mr. Bishop's tiny bungalow long incinerated, like the parsonage and Derek's house. Annalise anxiously watched the fire leap high over the *mohur* trees. She wondered if she would find Dr. Bishop and Professor Sanderville.

With no defenses, the cantonment must have been easily overrun. A billow of black smoke rose near the commissioner's residency. Derek eyed the sooty cloud narrowly. "The residency must be still standing, or there would be more of a fire. Let's see if the residency garrison has kept a path clear to the mansion."

They rode down one street, then another, their way blocked by crowds of jubilant citizenry and pilferers. One woman danced by in an English ball gown, her earrings and bangles jangling. Two men carrying a piano mowed a wide path through the crowd and Derek and Annalise fell in behind it, listening to the curses of those it thrust aside. Their slight hopes of reaching the residency disappeared when the crowd thickened near the grounds. A gang of sepoys had set up an artillery piece, but the occasional shots were falling wide of the main house. Some of the sepoys were mounting an attack, their leader exhorting them to drive through the makeshift barricades. While Derek and Annalise watched from behind a wall flanking the residency, the infantry charged, scattering from their ramming formation as shots from the residency crumpled those in the foreground. After a few minutes, the sepoys fell back in a grayish mist of gun smoke. For the most part, the wounded lay where they fell.

Sipping weak tea from little clay cups bought from a passing hawker, Derek and Annalise crouched behind the wall most of the day. The frontal assault occurred repeatedly, with the Indians simply filling the breech each time it was emptied. Finally, in the face of such losses, their interest in mass suicide tapered and the attacks came more sporadically.

During the long afternoon, Derek debated several ways of gaining access to the residency, hopefully without being shot from either side. Dusk seemed to hold most promise, when both sides would be interested in cooking fires. Then, as the sun was casting long, smokey shadows over the lawn before the residency and Derek and Annalise were gathering courage to make the dash, a disturbance began along their wall to the left. Derek stood, casually stretched and yawned, then mounted his black stallion. From that vantage point he could see someone with authority had taken over conduct of the siege. A detachment of sepoys were clearing onlookers from the wall and stationing sentries with disturbing regularity. Derek had a decision to make in a hurry.

"Come, woman," he announced loudly in Hindi. "We have tarried here long enough." Without a backward look, he turned away and rode slowly back into the city. Annalise scrambled to keep up.

While reconnoitering that night, Derek was stopped by a three-man patrol as he approached the residency. After they cheerfully gave him directions to the nearest whorehouse, Derek decided further investigation would be extremely risky. The next day, the sentries were still posted and a second gun had been brought up, although its accuracy was still dubious.

Intent on discovering the options for himself and Annalise, he went to the telegraph office, which was open though guarded by armed mutineers. The civil servants inside continued to take messages, frustrated by sepoy censors and frequent line breaks. A listener sympathetic to their overworked plight soon had only to nod in agreement while the clerks recounted their troubles. All the while gossiping with the operators, Derek sent a telegram, inquiring after the health of a fictitious grandmother in Delhi. He thought gossip, although highly risky, more prudent than direct telegraphic inquiry to all the surrounding commissioners. What he found was discouraging. Delhi had fallen and Meerut was expected to surrender any day. There was no word of Aligarh, but he knew the situation there. Lucknow was still holding out. There was no word from the south, only that rioting had broken out in Allabad.

His face was taut as he went back to Annalise, who crouched over a begging bowl in the market. He motioned her to follow him. Away from the market, they mounted and headed toward the east gate. Riding close to her, Derek spoke quietly. "Did you make anything?"

"What?"

"Your begging bowl."

"No, but I thought I looked the part. Why are we leaving?"

"You heard the gunfire last night?"

"It woke me up twice."

"It was meant to harass the residency to keep them awake . . . and the perimeter sentries are still in place. That detachment of mounted sepoys on the east side of the market were there the whole time I was in the telegraph office. I think they're a flying column, kept ready to counter any sortie from the residency. Someone," he concluded, "knows how to run a siege. I think we had better try for Lucknow, although it chafes me"—he slapped his thigh hard with his quirt—"to leave those poor devils in the residency here."

"You don't think we'll be any better off in Lucknow, do you?" she asked him quietly as they rode under the still-unguarded, big east gate.

"No, but we've little choice short of trying to make it to the south, and I don't want to risk that."

"With me, you mean." She gently touched his shoulder. "You'd stand a much better chance traveling on your own."

"Perhaps"—he smiled—"but I'd have far less pleasure out of it . . . rather like missing a leg."

She colored slightly. "You don't need me, Derek; you never really did except when you were ill."

"I've needed you all my life," he said softly. "Marian was

a showpiece, but you're a necessity; I didn't realize that until you had left England. Conran was not alone in loving you."

She looked at him for a long moment. "I loved you from the first moment I saw you, I think. You were the perfect picture of a hero, and you never did anything to mar that image, except when you turned to Marian. I saw you as ideal, not human, and that was my grave mistake. You still see me as your nurse . . . some sort of ministering angel. I am no angel, Derek, but a real and frightened person. If there is rebellion throughout India, where can we go? We've been lucky, but our chances of surviving on the road are nil. You speak Hindustani, and might stand some chance alone, but never with me. You would do better to go to Lucknow alone, and let me manage on my own. Enough rupees could get me through. . . ." At the expression on his face, she dwindled off. "No, I thought you would not hear of such a plan."

"And if you were to conveniently disappear, I should spend my life looking for you and not go to Lucknow at all. So don't harbor any ideas," he warned tersely. "Whatever happens, we will meet the future together. As for idealizing you, I have seen you try to face down a mule and fail, and that is a humbling weakness in your character, my love. If I want to protect you, that is my problem and not yours, so don't try to solve it for me." Noting that they were unobserved, he gripped her shoulders and kissed her firmly. "The same can be said of loving you. You will be the mother of my children or Robert can be responsible for the family line. I shall marry no woman but you, Miss Devon, so reconcile yourself."

She pulled away from him. "I don't believe that, and even if I did, I shouldn't be harassed into wedding you. You've a good heart, Derek Clavell, but a pigheaded streak as broad as Sussex itself. Go home and marry a blueblood like yourself, if you must be married, but forget me. I certainly mean to try to forget about you."

"You won't succeed," he replied flatly, "any more than I could forget about you, so shall we stop arguing about nonsense, and be practical? We suit one another. You won't let me bully you, and I won't let you cajole me. Lord knows we both hold grudges like elephants. You'll be throwing Marian up to me until we're gray, and I'll bray about Conran, but I've seen worse matches than us buried in their dotage."

She sighed. "You are blind to reality. Where should we live? We certainly cannot return to England, and India is exploding like an overheated kettle. Besides, what's the point in arguing a future neither of us is likely to enjoy?"

"We can still go to Australia," he supplied briskly, then with his eyes brightening like a boy's, added, "and I'll corner the gold market."

She laughed. "You're like Papa, always pursuing new frontiers."

"And you're Papa's daughter, aren't you?" He grinned knowingly, his dark eyes amused. "You'll like Australia; it's full of soft, woolly lambs. You can mother them until we produce our own brood."

She arched an ironic brow. "You don't think it's in slightly bad taste to make such proposals to a recent widow? You know I haven't the slightest intention of going to Australia with you or anywhere else."

"I'll wait," he replied calmly. "You know the old proverb, 'All things come to him . . .' "

"Who knows when to leave well enough alone," she finished briskly. "I shall go with you as far as Lucknow; shall we leave it at that?"

He shrugged. "As you like. I am your slave, madame."

"You defer to no one, not even yourself," she retorted. "I remember your dragging about on one leg in the house in

Kanpur. You demand excellence of yourself and everyone else.''

He studied her perfect profile above the graceful draping of the tattered sari. Annalise would have been a beauty in sackcloth, so mere rags became her well; they would not have suited Marian, and for the first time, he saw why not. Where Annalise had unconscious pride, Marian had arrogance, much like himself. He had always disliked himself to some degree; now he knew why.

But upon hard reflection, he knew he loved Annalise for far more than her looks. In her gentle heart, she had as much compassion as she had courage. He was not exaggerating when he proposed to have no woman but her; she was the only one who could touch his heart with such warmth and tenderness. But he had to admit that she now had the added attraction of being a challenge.

By midafternoon, Annalise was slumped in the saddle. They had gotten little sleep the previous night, and had crossed the Ganges, an exhausting and terrifying ordeal for Annalise, who was unable to swim. After several days and at least two nights in the saddle, Derek was bone weary himself. Annalise made no complaint, but he knew they had to find a safe place to rest before the dash into Lucknow, which Derek hoped would be safe in the capable hands of Commissioner Henry Lawrence. When they passed the village of Nanjul still thirty miles from Lucknow, he made a fateful decision. ''We are going to stop here for the night.''

''Won't it be dangerous?'' she asked.

He shook his head briefly. ''The villagers are a mixture of Hindus and Muslims, but one of my old *rissaldars* is headman here. I would trust him with my life . . . and yours. Still, the less the villagers see of you, the better. Keep your sari over your face for the time being.''

Derek boldly confronted the first villager they met, a dottering *sadhu* with a scorpion tattooed on his forehead.

"Greetings, old one. Can you direct us to the house of Mohammed Afzul?"

The old man stared at him, then his eyes narrowed shrewdly, dispensing any impression of his senility. "What business has a representative of the great *badahur khan* with so humble a man as our *cotwal,* Mohammed Afzul?"

"With all courtesy, what business is that of yours, old one?" returned Derek pointedly.

The old man affected a humble posture. "I mean to give no offense, but Mohammed Afzul is greatly respected in the village of Nanjul. We hope that he is in no difficulty."

"None that I know of, old one. Where does he live?"

The old man waved to them. "Come with me. I will show you." Hobbling along with his gnarled cane, he led them to a stucco house no different from the other simple, blocky dwellings that surrounded it. Swings of twisted hemp hung from the trees, and in the dried mud streets, children darted back and forth at play. Few adults were outside in the heat, but a sharp-featured, middle-aged woman with an earthen jug approached them from the direction of the river. Her eyes widened at the sight of Derek's official tunic, then she quickly lowered them as if she had noticed nothing. "Marja," called the old man. "We wish to speak with Mohammed Afzul. Is he at home?"

She eyed the old man warily, then looking over Derek once more, nodded. "He has just awakened from his afternoon nap, old one. Whom shall I say is calling?"

Annalise, who had enough simple dialect to follow that much of the conversation, almost smiled. The woman sounded like a Mayfair maid.

"I am Kasim Karas, sent by the *badahur khan* in Delhi," Derek told her. "My felicitations to Mohammed Afzul. We were old comrades in the army of the Raj."

Marja's lean face showed no welcome as she quickly took in the Scorpion's alertness at this scrap of information.

"Come," she said flatly. "I am sister to *cotwal* Afzul. Our house is yours." She turned on the *sadhu* as he started to follow them. "We shall enjoy privacy, old one, and you have important matters to attend. My brother will be most unhappy if he holds the elders' council tomorrow night and your plans for the new sluice to the pottery works are not ready."

The old man shrugged. "I did not vote for the pottery works."

"But the plan was carried and accepted by the council. Your duty is to the majority," Marja told him abruptly.

"Who are you, woman, to tell me my business?" the Scorpion demanded.

She glared at him. "Who are you, old man, to lurk about looking for gossip to prate to your cronies? Begone, or I shall tell Mohammed Afzul that you are too lazy to be worth the dole he gives you."

The old man's jaw projected. "The money the village gives me for my services to Mohammed Afzul's predecessor. You owe me respect, woman."

She shrugged eloquently. "I owe nothing to an old viper who would strike my brother in the back if he had not long ago lost his fangs."

Seeing the Scorpion turn scarlet and prepare to launch another angry attack, Derek swiftly intervened. "This bickering accomplishes nothing. I would see Mohammed Afzul before the sun sets and night hides all our faces . . . and grievances."

"Well said, my friend." Round-faced, stocky Mohammed Afzul himself stuck his head from his hut door and scratched his rump amiably. Sleepy-eyed, he grinned at Derek. "You are long in coming, *huzoor*. Too much wine and too many women slow a man abominably."

With an answering chuckle, Derek threw his arms wide and embraced him. Several villagers, having heard the spat between Marja and the Scorpion, had come out of their huts. To the Scorpion's disgust, they looked impressed to see their headman on such intimate terms with one belonging to the court of the great *khan*. He shuffled off with a muttered curse at Marja. "May you shrivel like your female parts. No wonder no man will have you, adder tongue."

Marja merely sniffed, and shot his departing back a disgusted look. Clearly, his insults were nothing new to her.

Mohammed Afzul drew Derek and Annalise inside the house. The whitewashed room was comparatively cool, its thick walls shielding out the sun. Bright red, blue, and purple rugs flowered on the floor, while at the windows, heavy shutters were open to reveal hard blue blocks of sky. Marja, spotting the Scorpion still lurking about the house, abruptly closed the shutters. The house instantly grew stuffy. Mohammed Afzul cocked a brow at his sister. "You make too much of that old man, Marja. Why not ignore him?"

"Even an old scorpion wears a sting," she retorted, then her glance softened. "You believe good of everybody until they steal your drawers."

He laughed, then pinched her skinny arm. "I grow angry only when they try to steal you."

She made an impatient sound that did not hide the pleased gleam in her eye. Quickly, she drew out cushions and went to put on a pot of tea.

With a motion to Derek and Annalise to do the same, Mohammed Afzul dropped on a cushion. "So"—he picked up a *tulwar* and split a coconut before tossing it to Marja to grate on their dinner mutton—"why do you travel in the guise of an envoy of the *badahur*, my friend? The last time I saw you, you were still wearing the colors of the Raj." Noting Derek's wary glance at his sister's suddenly alert stance, he added, "We can talk in front of Marja. Her tongue is only loose when she wishes to bait scorpions and toads." He shot Marja an admonitory look when she gave him an empty scowl. "You will remember that my friend's business is his own?"

She grunted and began to grate the coconut, each scrape a hint of her annoyance.

Derek crossed his long legs lotus style and leaned forward. "The lady and I are in flight for our lives, as you may well have guessed, old friend. The colors of the Raj are the color of blood in these evil days."

"I am no great friend of the Raj," warned Mohammed Afzul, "so that days that are dark for the *Angrezi-log*, are bright for the people of India. Still, I have warned my village to make no demonstrations against the Raj for the sake of their own safety. We have not participated in the slaughter, and no one here will harm you."

Marja grunted again, and this time, the sound was dubious.

"Marja is right, Mohammed Afzul," said Derek. "Despite your authority and prestige among your people, no one can be certain of anything now. Of course, taking no part against the Raj will not guarantee against the Raj's revenge, should the mutiny fail. *Angrezi* women and children lie among the dead. This will not be forgotten if there is a reckoning."

"You are honest, my friend, so I will be honest with you. It is wise to take precautions, but none shall touch you in my house, unless he kills me first," replied Mohammed Afzul firmly, then continued with a wry smile. "There is no man who is my equal in the village with a *tulwar,* so I think many would swallow their dislike of the *Angrezi-log*, if they had to contend with me first."

"I ask only to stay the night, my friend. Tomorrow, Annalise and I will venture into Lucknow to see if there is any chance of finding refuge in the residency."

Mohammed Afzul shook his head negatively. "The residency is surrounded and not designed for defense. There are rumors that Commissioner Lawrence died on the fourth day of the siege. I do not think those in the residency have long to live."

The news of Commissioner Lawrence's death was a severe blow. Derek considered him the best of the company's commissioners, and knew him as the best friend India had among the English. If the residency fell, the last island of safety in the north would sink in a sea of blood. Derek's gaze went to Annalise. Fatalistic about his own chances, he was more concerned about her than himself. He squeezed her hand. "If we are to die, it will be good to spend our last days among friends, Mohammed Afzul, but we do not wish to put your family at any risk by harboring us if matters have gone so awry in Lucknow. Perhaps it is better that we leave."

Mohammed Afzul did not answer. "Who is the woman with you?" he asked in Hindi. "She is a beauty, even for your tastes."

"She is my wife," answered Derek in English, and waited for Annalise's explosion. She would not likely realize that a Muslim could be as stuffy as the English about a man's traveling with a woman unrelated to him.

As expected, she shot him a fierce look that promised a sharp argument in private. Not wanting Mohammed Afzul to note her anger, Derek ignored her, but noticed Marja's sharpened interest. Marja quickly averted her eyes, then pointedly concentrated on the water coming to a boil. She poured the tea, then placed the tea things on a tray and set it on a low table in their midst. Mohammed Afzul poured. "Then it is settled. You will both stay with us until the mutiny is ended one way or the other. It is not safe for you to venture abroad any longer. Delhi has fallen, you know."

"We cannot subject you and Marja to such danger, Mohammed Afzul. You might be killed if Annalise and I were found here. I had planned to take Annalise into the jungle to wait out the mutiny if Lucknow appeared hopeless."

Mohammed Afzul calmly blew on his tea. "If you stay

with us, our friends will not know you are *Angrezi* providing all goes well, and your friends will be our friends if the mutiny sputters and dies like a matchlock on a damp day. I am not such an idiot as you think me, my friend. India is not bound to win her freedom by sheer numbers. You *Angrezi-log* are a stubborn lot, and as you say, much angered by the mass slaughter of civilians. If the mutiny is settled in India's favor, Marja and I will send you to the jungle quickly enough, but for now you must stay with us. I will hear of no other course." He smiled rakishly beneath his broad moustache. "That I also like you, is of no consequence."

"You are a good friend, Mohammed Afzul," Derek said quietly. "You may be sure I will remember that fact to your advantage one day."

Mohammed Afzul nodded genially. "I know your capacity for generosity, *huzoor*. You saved my brother's life in the Kyber. You may consider me repaid in advance." Sipping his tea, his big brown eyes fixed on Annalise. "Your wife is very pretty, although it is impolite of me to say so. When did you marry, *huzoor?*"

Derek glanced at the uncomprehending Annalise. "Not long enough ago to regret it."

Mohammed Afzul laughed. "You must take to the jungle for your privacy during the heat of the afternoons when everyone is napping but the children. We have only curtains here to shut out the . . . noise." He cocked his head. "And the Scorpion. Despite what I say to Marja, she is right about him. He may be old, but he carries a stinger yet, and has no love for the *Angrezi-log*. He would betray you in a moment, so you must take great care that he suspects nothing." He nodded to Annalise. "I take it that your lady speaks only English, so we will tell everyone that she is in *purdah*."

Derek disagreed. "Annalise would be a prisoner if we visit *purdah* upon her. Why not garb her in the white of bereavement and say she has taken a year's vow of silence for the recent death of her father? That way she can come and go as she likes. We can teach her Hindustani and Urdu at leisure.''

After some further discussion, the details of Derek and Annalise's stay were worked out. Marja's chief objection was dietary. ''How can I possibly cook for unbelievers, Brother?''

Derek translated for Annalise. ''We will purchase our own pottery in the village and cook for ourselves,'' Annalise told Marja, regarding her in her gentle manner. ''I hope we shall not be a great inconvenience to you.''

At Mohammed Afzul's translation, Marja's answering expression stated that they would be far more than an inconvenience. ''You will sleep over there,'' she announced flatly. ''As we have no extra bedding, you will need to buy that as well.''

Mohammed Afzul arched a brow at his sister. ''Until that time, Marja and I will loan you our bedding. We wish you to think of yourselves as family.''

Marja sniffed.

By evening, Derek and Annalise were settled in the house. Derek's extended stay was to be explained to the villagers as his being a friend of Mohammed Afzul on personal leave from his official duties. ''This will add greatly to my prestige,'' Mohammed Afzul explained exultantly. ''I have had a little difficulty in persuading my villagers not to take part in the mutiny. Old Scorpion, for one, is particularly against the *Angrezi-log*, but he has not found effective support. Still''—he sobered—''although my people are ordinarily a quiet lot, you would do well to be wary. If any one of them were to learn that you are *Angrezi*, it would go ill with all of us.''

The men were alone in the house, the women having gone for water, and Derek and Mohammed Afzul sat just outside the house door to take advantage of the cooling breezes of the approaching sundown. "I would not lead you and your sister into danger, old friend," Derek said quietly. "Perhaps it would be best if Annalise and I left tomorrow."

Mohammed Afzul glowered. "Will you insult me? You have long been the good friend of my brother and me, and I owe you a life. Both Allah and I would be greatly displeased if you were to go away. Besides, I have had no one to talk to about the old days of soldiering for the Raj. Who in this place is my equal and battle brother but you?" He grasped Derek's shoulder. "I should not only be angry, but very disappointed if you left . . . so the matter is settled." He gave Derek's shoulder a shake. "Eh?"

Although still dubious, Derek nodded in grudging surrender. "You win. We shall see how it goes for a few days."

"A few days?" Mohammed Afzul laughed shortly. "Very likely a few months. You hold the peoples of India in low regard if you think we cannot sustain a simple revolt."

Mohammed Afzul was right. The mutiny dragged on for months. July and the heat of summer came upon them. Annalise spent much of her time indoors despite the heat, helping Marja with household tasks and learning to do them in the Indian manner. Unaccustomed to Indian ways, she felt vulnerable to exposure out of doors, even if she were mute. Annalise especially loved working at the small handloom, which was the only one of its kind in the village. Marja was proud of it, saying frequently the loom came from the ends of the earth. Annalise wondered what Marja meant until she noticed a small brass plate on the bottom: Rotweillen S.S. Amsterdam, Netherlands. She smiled, and the next time Marja noted the source of her wonderful loom, Annalise commented, "I see what you mean. Your translation is quite correct. Netherlands does mean land at the end of the earth. I've sometimes wondered," she mused, "why the Dutch chose that name for their country. As you know,

Holland is right across the Channel from England. Come to think of it, they are on the other side of the world, at the ends of the earth from India."

Marja said nothing about Annalise's tact, but the next day while washing clothes at the river, she casually commented to the other women that the *huzoor's* wife was beginning to handle the *Dutch* loom with some facility. As this was practically the first bit of information volunteered by Marja about her guests, especially the young, pretty one, the women were all ears. Marja did not say much more, except to comment that the girl, for all her ragged clothes, must have married below her station as she had little ability at any common household task. The loom was a wonder. Scandal hung in the air, and after that, as Annalise moved through the village, the women paid more attention to her waistline, expecting a bulge, and paid little heed to her awkwardness and unfamiliarity with village ways.

Marja, who had eyed Annalise's tattered crimson sari askance from the first, finally spoke her mind on that subject one day when the two of them went alone to the river to wash clothes. "You look more like the colonel sahib's prisoner than his wife," she said flatly. "The lowest beggar passing through our village dresses better than you."

Applying herself to scrubbing the white cottons over the rocks until they turned snowy, Annalise said nothing. To infer Marja's comment was an exaggeration was redundant. She had only her old crimson sari to wear when the white one was dirty, and no opportunity to purchase another one. No one had gone to the market in Lucknow since the mutiny had begun. As sister of the headman, Marja took great pride in her own attire, and had an extensive varicolored wardrobe complete with many gilt baubles and bangles.

"Suppose I lend you a sari: a white one, old, but of fine cotton."

Annalise sat back on her heels for a moment. Marja was a businesslike woman and not given to wild generosity. Her brother and the village's many children were the sole recipients of her astringent benevolence. Marja had spoken only three words of English to her in two months. Her Hindustani and Urdu lessons were delivered in the old Spartan style, and once she had even rapped Annalise's knuckles. Despite Marja's acerbity, however, Annalise liked her sturdy independence and peppery wit, and she suspected Marja knew it. "I should be honored," she replied at last, then drew a small sapphire ring from her finger. It had belonged to the woman aboard the train; Annalise had no jewelry of her own. "Will you wear this while Derek and I are with you, as a token of our friendship?"

Marja pondered the carefully worded offering. The token was not an outright gift, which would have been offensive. Also, the ring's value far outweighed that of the sari, and such a gift would have belittled her own offer. Marja accepted the ring with a terse nod, then admired it for a moment, letting the sun glint off its facets. "You have been clever in learning Hindustani and Urdu. We will now speak Urdu in private." She flashed the ring again, momentarily preoccupied with its glitter. "You will not attempt to speak with anyone else, mind you; your Urdu is not that good."

After that day, Annalise and Marja passed as friends, but her relationship with Derek was less simple. As time wore on, Mohammed Afzul became concerned that Derek and Annalise's extended stay might arouse gossip among the villagers. When a widower in the village died in August, both Derek and Annalise attended the funeral. Afterward, Derek bought his house from his relatives for a fair sum, and installed himself there with Annalise. He let it be known that he and his wife had a liking for the village and contemplated taking up permanent residence there. This was not to the liking of the old Scorpion, who resented the glamour that Derek brought to Mohammed Afzul's position. While he dared not malign an emissary of the *badahur khan,* he lost no opportunity to decry Mohammed Afzul behind his back. Annalise was no happier than Marja with the situation.

One day, as she sat weaving just outside the door of their new house, some of the children of the village began to hang about to view the bright colors growing on the loom. Accustomed to Annalise's welcoming smile, they began to ask questions about the weaving. Unable to speak to them, she took one seven-year-old girl up into her lap and began to show her how to ply the loom needle back and forth through the cotton threads. Delighted with the ease of her task, the child was adept, and reluctant to give up her place to the next child who begged for a turn. A squabble soon broke out.

"You have been forever at the loom, Nani," complained the applicant, her eagerness making an exaggeration of the time. "Give someone else a chance."

Annalise put down the first little weaver, and took up the next one. To forestall further outbreaks among the other children waiting a turn, she began to pantomime a story about a sly cat and a mischievous monkey for them. Derek returned from clearing a new field with Mohammed Afzul to hear the children's delighted laughter carrying down the path to the house in its grove of peepul trees and palms. Quickly putting his hand on Mohammed Afzul's arm, he laid a finger against his lips. The two men crept closer to see Annalise, now standing before the children to put on her mime play. Behind her, a young girl plied the loom, its shuttle clicking in time to Annalise's dancelike gestures. Gracefully, Annalise imitated the stealthy cat as it circled the monkey who had boldly drunk the cat's milk. The monkey, cornered after much vain capering and fearful of losing its life, offered to milk the cow for the cat's food. The cat agreed, then for revenge, scratched the cow while the monkey was milking it and caused the cow to send the monkey flying to the moon. Unfortunately, the monkey had toppled the milk bowl and the cat was left to mourn its vengeful loss. "If we kill all the *Angrezi-log,*" asked a pensive little boy, "will we be sad like the cat?"

Annalise tilted her head to show that his suggestion might be a possibility.

Puzzled, then slightly angry, he jumped up. "I'm tired of stories. Let's do something else."

The seven-year-old Nani caught her hand. "I will teach you to dance. Hasim will be Vishnu and I will be his wife, Lakshmi. We will do the wedding dance, and everyone else will be our courtiers."

"No," interrupted the boy, objecting to slavery, "I wish to be Vishnu's elephant avatar. The monkey king will come to kidnap Lakshmi and I will trample him."

Nani sighed. "You are always so tiresomely fierce. Can we not simply have a beautiful story?"

"Your stories are never stories," he retorted. "Everyone just stands about and tried to look 'beautiful.' It is all very silly."

Eventually, the argument was settled in the elephant's favor and the dance-play began. Annalise learned the graceful part of Lakshmi as though she had rehearsed for it all her life. Slender as a curving willow, she wound her way among the children, shadowing Nani's every gesture. Her fingertips tapered as expressively as a *gupta*'s, her eyes large and laughing above the sari veil drawn over her face.

Among the peepul trees, Mohammed Afzul caught his friend's rapt expression and smiled. "It is rare to love a new wife," he murmured, "but a good thing. Your Annalise is as lovely in spirit as she is in the flesh. You are a lucky man.''

''The pity is that I did not recognize my good fortune sooner,'' said Derek quietly. ''I should be greatly grieved if I should ever lose her.''

''How can one lose a wife?'' responded Mohammed Afzul with a pragmatic lift of his brow. ''In my experience, death rarely comes as a convenience, and to have a woman in the same house with Marja would be a living hell.''

Derek laughed at his friend's resignation. ''Perhaps you should find Marja a man and let her move into a house of her own.''

Mohammed Afzul snorted. ''The village men know her too well. I have tried to bribe three of them to wed her and failed. As for moving away, she refuses to live apart from me and all her relatives. I think she is afraid of losing her authority in another household.'' He glanced up to see that Annalise had noted their presence. Instantly ceasing her dance, she blushed, her long lashes sweeping down shyly across her burning cheeks. The children came to a fumbling halt, then sidled off toward the wood. Mohammed Afzul waved gaily to her. ''You must not be so modest. Truly, you should have been a court dancer.''

Turning an even deeper shade of scarlet, Annalise started to make him an answer, then remembered the children. Turning an even deeper shade of scarlet, she stood very still as the men approached her. Mohammed Afzul swiftly nudged Derek and said in Urdu too rapid for Annalise to follow. ''In truth, she is a jewel . . . and tongue-tied, to boot. You are indeed fortunate.'' Chuckling to himself, he trotted up the path toward his house.

Wearing the simple cotton clothes of a peasant farmer, Derek looked down at Annalise, his wrists looped over a digging stick braced over his shoulders. His shirt open to his waist and skin damp with perspiration, he was tanned to the darkness of a native and smelled of cloves that he chewed in the mornings after cleaning his teeth. His teeth flashed white as the *puggaree* wrapped about his head. "Mohammed Afzul tells me that I am a lucky man to have so docile a wife," he said in Hindustani in case the children were still in earshot, then swiftly ducked his head and kissed her lightly. He grinned when she ducked back, her eyes startled. "Come now, we must at least pretend to be fond of one another."

"I have never said I was not fond of you," she murmured, not looking at him. "I merely said I would not marry you." She went quickly to her loom and began to gather up her skeins of brightly colored cotton.

He followed her. "Is that not hypocritical, under the circumstances?"

"Not at all," she flashed back, her cheeks brightening again. "Women often do not marry men they... of whom they are fond." She made a sling of part of her sari skirt and hurriedly scooped the skeins into it.

His fingers gently but firmly closed on her arm. "Why are you so afraid of me? Have I touched you more than once in these last months? Today's slight kiss was the first we have shared... no, not even shared, for you did not return it."

She clutched the skeins to her. "You look at me as if we were still lovers. You never let me forget that you want me. Am I to have no peace?"

"None," he replied flatly, "for you give me none. We were meant to be together, Annalise. You know that."

She tired to pull away. "I know nothing of the sort. How could you tell Mohammed Afzul and Marja that we were married?"

"I told you. They would not understand our being together if we were not." His eyes glinted mischievously. "I think it a very wise custom."

"Well, I think it was vile of you. You took complete advantage of the situation."

His eyes darkened beneath his slight frown. "You have learned shame since we were lovers. Once you gave yourself to me as naturally as spring jonquils bloom. If I have stolen that innocent delight from you, then I am indeed vile. But I wonder"—he cocked his head—"how much of your indignation is due to shame, and how much to your woman's jealousy."

She hesitated, then answered him honestly. "I do not know, but I hope I am not governed by spite. I am moved that you came so far to find me, and I am grateful that you saved my life in Aligarh and have since protected me, but I can feel no other way toward you than I did when I married Conran."

"Why not? Would you repeat a mistake twice?" He gripped her shoulders. "Admit it, Annalise; you realized you should never have married him before you were halfway to Delhi . . . didn't you?"

She averted her eyes. "Why do you say that?"

"Because you have cried your eyes out every night since he died. You didn't love him enough for that much grief. There has to be another reason."

She glared at him angrily. "What other reason could there be?"

"Guilt. You wanted to be a virgin for him and you weren't. You wanted to love him and forget me, but you couldn't. You expected a miracle to happen in the space of two days, and if not that, two years . . . only you didn't have two years with him, did you?"

"Stop it!" she cried. "You've tried everything from charm to browbeating me into bed with you . . . well, I won't make love to you again, Derek. I don't . . ."

Before she could finish, his mouth plummeted down on hers. He kissed her long and hard, and well before he finished, she stopped fighting him. Her body weakened, grew pliant against his, her lips softening under his onslaught, until he ceased to force her, binding her to him instead with the starved hunger of his kiss. "Annalise, I need you," he whispered at last, all of his renewed hope shining in his eyes. "If you never gave yourself to me again, I should go on loving you no less deeply. I cherish you . . . yet have not the words to give you ease and win your trust. Once, when I lived in darkness, you were my light, and having beheld the warmth of that light, I cannot bear to be without it. My days are as cold as my nights, beloved. Each time you turn away from me, ice touches my heart, and I die a little." He kissed her again, softly, his lips clinging to hers so tenderly that she could only yield to him as a flower that wanes in the shade seeks the sun.

When he lifted his head at last, he whispered, "I do not seek to give you pain, but only consolation."

She bowed her head. "I fear I no longer know how to bring solace to anyone. Since Conran's death, I have been at a loss, as though I were somehow emptied by his passing. Perhaps we are much alike, you and I. His smile once lit up my world when I thought it forever darkened. Now that smile is gone, his great kindness and gentle heart gone . . . so violently." She lifted her head. "I shall always miss him."

"Missing him is well enough," he said quietly, "but punishing yourself is another matter. You could not give to Conran what you had already given to me. One day you would have yielded him a free part of your heart, but God saw fit to take him first. Now, you must let yourself heal. Conran, of all men, would want it so." He tilted her chin up. "The sun always rises, Annalise, if you will not hide yourself from its warmth. God does not deny light to any of his creatures. Only those who choose to live in darkness do so."

This time, when he kissed her, she clung tentatively to his

lips like a poised butterfly. Only the titter of the children secreted in the wood caused her to break away in startled alarm. One of them waved reassuringly to her. "Kiss him again, Lakshmi, and see if he turns into an elephant!"

That night, the moon rose over Nanjul like a huge silver shield, the stars sprinkled about it like sparks from the great anvil of the night. Annalise lay in the darkness of her room alone on the simple *charpoy*. She could hear the rustle of palms and the soft *chiuu* of the cicadas outside the window. Some palm fronds brushed against the side of the house with a dry rasp that undertoned the crickets' high song, and somewhere, a ginko scuttled. She could smell the smoke from Derek's cigar, sifting across the moonlit wedge in her open doorway. The shade swung against the unglassed window with tiny clicks in the restive breeze. It was hot, but not so hot and still as most nights, and they had dined later than usual.

She could not sleep. If Derek chose her over Claremore, he would come to resent her, and perhaps even hate her in time. They were as far apart as ever; he, the baronet, and she, the pauper's daughter, and that knowledge gripped her heart like a cruel, icy fist. She longed for him, ached for him, but they were destined to live apart. When the mutiny was done she would go back to China as she had resolved. The revolt had made life in India impossible, for the memories, if naught else. The tears came again, hot and unceasing, as they had for so many nights. She had no idea how long she lay there, attempting to stifle her sobs, when suddenly, she felt Derek's hand on her shoulder. She stiffened, ready to fight him when he picked her up, and light sheet and all, carried her to the doorway of their house. The night air was slightly cool on her wet cheeks as he set her down, then cradling her against him, sat with his back against the doorjamb. Smoothing her hair, he crooned to her an old Hindu lullaby that softly echoed the night sounds, his clear baritone carrying out over the clearing to rouse an owl. At long last, she slept, curling into his arms. It was all he asked.

As the weeks passed, Annalise's grief ebbed. Each night, Derek held her in the same way, and sang her the same songs, seeming to know that for the time being, she needed the predictability of his actions. She came to enjoy and look forward to being cuddled each evening, being soothed by his calmness and peace, being sheltered by his arms. This was a good man, asking nothing from her but the chance to hold and comfort her, yet she knew him to be a man with a need for love and tenderness, too. Finally, one night he kissed her gently, and she responded to him.

"Lise, Lise," he whispered, his face against her soft cheek, "I have longed for you so, and yet I would not frighten you, or touch you unless you wish it. Once I took you by storm, and you bent to me, but then the storm passed, and you stood free and solitary again. You were never a woman meant to be alone, yet I have learned that love alone will not bind you to me. Be mine again, for a little while, so that we may remember the sun while the night throws its shawl over us. Let me be all that you desire me to be, for if you wish it, I would change myself like molten metal to whatever shape you wish."

"You cannot change, Derek, and you know it," she murmured. "I would have you no different than you are, for there is much in you to love. I have never sought a saint, but only a man to love me and hold me dear. Where once I loved a hero, I now love a man, yet such a man as I have rarely known. My father was such a man, and Conran . . . but they are both gone forever. I would not lose you to bitterness, and for a little time, I will be yours as you will." She touched his lips. "You must not ask for more, Derek, for I cannot give it. Promise me."

"I promise nothing," he breathed. "Give yourself freely or not at all. I cannot promise to give up . . . what I will not, not so long as I breathe. As for bitterness, you owe me nothing. Not faith nor virtue, nor grief. And you are not, and never will be mine, but your own. Whatever you give, you may take back again: I own you not. But this night I claim, if you will it. Come to me, Lise . . . come." His lips brushed hers, then clung with the gentle certainty that she loved him.

He carried her into the house and set her down by his floor pallet. Standing there, their bodies molded together, he slowly covered her throat and temples with kisses. She pressed her face against the curve of his jaw, felt the subtle grate of stubble stroke against her delicate skin. "Annalise," he breathed against her ear, "I have waited so long for this moment. When I thought I had lost you, I nearly went mad. Can you know how I love you? May I show you . . . ?" His lips brushed hers, then lingered long and sensuously, drinking of her as if he were assauging the long, burning ache of his desire . . . passion so long denied could only mount as his fingers slipped to her sari, felt soft flesh beneath the thin, white cotton. His breathing quickened like her own as his lips traveled to the cleft of her breasts, seeking the slow trail his fingertips made when they unfastened her bodice. Having waited so long, Derek hurried no part of their pleasure and rediscovery of one another. The buttons came undone one by one, silkily releasing the young curves of her breasts, until he slipped the bodice entirely from her and slid his fingers beneath the ripeness of her. "You are lovely as the Song of Solomon. Even a king weary and beleaguered by the harsh weight of his office might turn poet with such beauty before him. What must a battle-torn soldier feel when gifted with such sweetness?" His touch feather-light, he caressed the undercurves of her breasts wonderingly. "Even if your body were dross instead of the poet's dream that it is, I would love you, for your heart and mind are easily as fair as your form. What sweet genie brought you to me on that long-ago day when the monsoons had swept this land with rain like the tears of a goddess?" His hands curled into her hair, he drew her to him, his lips grazing first her mouth, then the arch of her throat, before trailing downward to even more tender flesh. When his tongue lightly teased the roses of her breasts, she sighed, then caught her breath, arching against him.

"Soon," she whispered. "Come to me soon, for I hunger for you, my love. You have become my sun that makes radiant all the black and lonely nights, as if you were a splendid star come to visit this midnight earth. Make me forget all my winter dreams for the summer that now wraps me round and warms me in its burning light." Twining her arms about his neck, she drew his head down to her. "Come to me, sweet soldier, and we will make a memory for all the lonely nights to come."

His arms tightened about her, his lips lowering to the crests of her breasts. Annalise made a little sound in her throat as he grazed sensitive flesh. He bent her back, his fingertips sliding along her bare spine, and she shivered with sensation despite the heat of the night. The shade rustled at the window, making an echo of their quickened breathing, and outside, a large lizard stirred, its tail making a quick serpentine trail through the dust.

Derek's hands curved to Annalise's tapering waist, stopping just above the sari wrapped about her hips. A flick of his fingers undid the fold securing the sari, and it twined slowly to the clay floor to finally pause gracefully as if she were a pliant work of art. Derek's lips locked with hers, and they sank to the pallet, his body arching over hers. Because of the heat, he was naked but for a loincloth, his body tanned to burnished mahogany. His muscles were hard, his limbs long, and when he covered her, she almost felt overwhelmed by the maleness of him. He stroked her surely, as if she were part of the clay. . . part of the earth itself, and he knew the shape of her like his own body. His hair brushed her belly and lower as he sought the source of her, first with his hands, and then with his lips. When he first touched her womanhood, she gave a startled gasp, then waited, tense and uncertain as his mouth found her. Slowly, her body seemed to melt, turning into a flowing liquid as if she were a river of fire. Here was the source of life, that Tigris and Euphrates of all creation.

Derek was perspiring, his skin damp against her own, his mouth hot against her heat. Swiftly, he cast aside his loincloth, then returned to his sensual feast. Her sex felt swollen, as though she were ripening fruit about to burst against his tongue. When he prolonged her pleasure, she moaned as a scorching sensation rippled through her, then cried out as another swept over her, and at its crest, he entered her, his sex swollen as her own. Hard, and starved for her, his body thrust against hers so strongly that she felt herself moving with him, against him, craving him and all the force he might care to loose. His rhythm grew quick and hard, his breath coming against her neck in heated gasps. The fire built in them both, flashing suddenly and with a blinding heat. Derek's hands knotted in her hair almost painfully, but she scarcely noticed it in the flaming holocaust of passion he had created about them both. "Lise!" he cried as his body shuddered against hers at the peak of their ecstasy. When they lay spent and still, he whispered in husky exhilaration, "You're like no woman I've ever . . . I'll never have enough of you."

But you must, she thought sadly. You must have all you desire of me now, in this little time we are together. When we part again, it will be forever.

The moon rode high, its luminous disk paling their bed. Through the long night they made love, finding one another again and seeking the heart of their love that seemed so ever elusive. A soldier and his maiden, they might have sprung from the entourage of Alexander when centuries ago he had sought to bring India into his empire. Love, unlike the face of nations, had changed little in all that time, but for one instance: a woman might not so easily be taken with a sword.

XIII

Alexander's Wake

The dawn came with a furling of mist over the *jeel* fringing the fields. The dry palms were saffron in the gauzy light, the mallards and teal kiting low over the bronze, burnished water. Annalise stirred fitfully against Derek's shoulder. In her dreams, she had seen again the train wreck, and the thief's dancing toes as he had been strung up to the shop awning. In macabre procession, she saw a line of thieves that stretched as long as Alexander the Great's army when he had so long ago come to conquer India. Then the grisly view faded away and left only the dawn, smooth and limpid as a silken veil thrown over the north country.

Annalise lifted her head to gaze down at Derek. He was still asleep, his arm thrown over his eyes to shield them from the light. His naked body was coppery in the sunrise, his beard stubble needled black across his lean face. He needed a haircut, and the moustache grown to assist his disguise was thick across his upper lip. She loved to look at Derek's mouth when he was sleeping. Awake, his lips could curl in arrogance and anger, freezing her heart; but asleep, he looked like the caring, compassionate man he was beneath the hard-bitten, lofty aristocrat and soldier.

She leaned over him, her long, raven hair sweeping his chest, and kissed him gently. His eyelids flickered, and he smiled. "Did you sleep well?"

She laughed. "Not at all, I think, thanks to you. You are a man of indomitable energy."

He wrapped his fingers into her hair and drew her down to him again. "I was inspired by your angelic charms. Kiss me again so that I will know you are no dream sent to beguile me from weeding the west field today."

With a giggle, she kissed him, then amusement faded as the kiss lengthened, heated. A little time later, she lifted her head with a dreamy distance in her eyes. "How foolish of me. Now we shall not rise for at least another hour, and Mohammed Afzul will accuse us of shirking our duties."

His arms tightened about her. "I was weaned on duty. Let it go hang for a while. I've more pressing interests just now."

Feeling the growing rigidity of his manhood against her thigh, she smiled at him with lazy mischief. "I've an idea to distract you further, sir." Then, with the long, loose sweep of her hair, she began to brush him as if he were a great, drowsing cat. The tickling caress of her hair made him laugh a little, but his eyes soon narrowed with desire. By the time she reached his naked groin, he was fully aroused and eager for her.

"I should not have thought myself capable of making love to any woman after last night," he said huskily as he tugged her beneath him. "You're like some wild, potent elixir in my veins, stirring me to excess. I can never have enough of you . . ." His lips brushed hers. "I want to die of you . . . still without surfeit. Love me, Lise . . . love me yet again until we are as dazed and delirious as we were in the night . . ." He brushed his face against her hair, slipping it away from her bare breasts, finding their glory beneath the soft, black stream. His tongue flicked her, teased her, made her gasp as the peaks of her breasts bloomed. With a purring sound, she insinuated herself between his thighs, arched and stroked against him, feeling the length of his sex powerful against her belly. Rolling over and over until they had left the pallet behind and only the cool, dusty clay was against their backs, they curved together. Derek poised, then sank into her, his eyes closing in ecstasy as her snug sheathing received him, her slim body fit to him. His hips moved in slow syncopation, luring her into becoming one with the pulsing, feline rhythm that soon conquered them both. She clasped his hips lightly, then with a tightening grip as she guided him deeper within her. Her lips parted beneath his searing kiss, her legs locking about him. Fiercely, he gave himself to her pleasure, reveling in the low, husky sounds that emerged instinctively from her throat. Her hands slid up his back to grip his shoulders. "Now," she whispered. "Now, Derek . . . now."

Then he lost himself in the liquid warmth of her, the boiling surge of his desire mounting until her nails were digging into his flesh, their tiny, stabbing needles bending with the pulse of his driving body. They were both lost to the haze of the morning, the rising heat that brought droplets of perspiration to the flexing surfaces of flesh. When the moment came, Annalise arched high to reach the pinnacle with him, her muted cry sounding lonely in the sun-misted air. Derek shuddered against her, muscles tightening fiercely, then, he relaxed as if his body were releasing a long sigh.

Long minutes passed before Derek stirred slightly. "I think I shall forget weeding altogether today," he murmured with a note of sleepy satisfaction against the mass of her hair.

In answer, she tickled his ribs, and when he pulled away with a laugh, she swung her long, shapely legs out from under him and swiftly got to her feet. "Marja is far more difficult to please than Mohammed Afzul. If I do not appear directly for laundry, she will never let me hear the end of it."

He grabbed her ankle. "Marja can go hang. She has a foul temper at the best of times. If you stay a little, I will bring you breakfast in bed."

She laughed and tugged at her ankle, almost losing her balance. "My lord, what will the servants think if the master of the house comports himself like a lusty lackey? Let go, I say! Fie on you for a lazy fellow!"

He grinned slyly, drawing her toward him. "I'll show you lazy, you impudent wench . . ."

In the house of Mohammed Afzul, Marja was already warmed to her day's spite. "I say send the *Angrezi* colonel sahib and his wife on their way," she argued, speaking of Derek and Annalise. "There is talk in the village, thanks to their staying so long. No courtier of the *badahur khan* would willingly choose to stay in such a moth-eaten place. The colonel sahib goes out to work with you like a field hand, and his woman insists on helping the women with their menial tasks. She should keep to her house."

Mohammed Afzul sighed. "There is no suiting you, Marja. If the memsahib were to keep to her house, you would complain that she is good for nothing. Besides"—he thought of the news that had reached him last night—"they will not be here much longer. I have heard that Sir Henry Havelock sahib is bringing a force to relieve the Lucknow residency. He is only a day or two away from us."

Her eyes narrowed. "Then the council must be fearful that he will fall upon our village for it undoubtedly lies in Havelock's path."

"Havelock is interested in keeping his forces together to attack Lucknow, not squashing flies like us." He fell silent as she continued to rail. He had indeed had trouble with the council, but not of the sort that Marja anticipated. The council wished to join with the other villages of the north at sniping at the column and wearing Havelock's forces to a nub, so that the English effort would fail. India for the Indians; that was their stance. Feeling had risen against the *Angrezi-log* in the last months, as first Delhi fell, then Kanpur. The insects were astir. The smell of power and distant, conceivable victory was in the air. The *Angrezi-log*, taken off balance in their overconfidence, were being overwhelmed. Mohammed Afzul was beginning to worry that he could not keep his people in rein. Old Scorpion was doing his effective best to oppose all his pacifistic efforts. "You are the creature of the *Angrezi-log*," he railed. "We should hold a new election." Naturally, the Scorpion expected to be elected, which was ridiculous, for despite his insidious influence, his venom had made him generally mistrusted for years. Mohammed Afzul sighed, his distant gaze fixed vaguely upon his sister. Over and over, she kept complaining. Truly, he should marry her to the vindictive old *sadhu* and let them work their tiresome wiles upon each other.

Finally, he rose, and with Marja's complaints bouncing off his back, headed for the door. Derek was nowhere to be seen. He waved off Marja's final harangue and walked toward the fields. Derek would show up for work soon enough. He could hardly blame him for lingering with his lovely bride. A woman like that could distract a man for years. His own first wife had been a pretty thing until the typhus had carried her off. His second wife had been a plump comfort, but she had run away with another man during his second hitch with the company's army. Technically, they were still married, but if truth were to be told, he did not want another wife. Marja was trouble enough. When he reached the maize field, he began to jerk out the weeds, pretending they were his nagging sister's hair.

Marja kept muttering to herself after Mohammed Afzul had gone. Preoccupied with the dishes and her complaints, she did not notice the old *sadhu's* scorpion brow cocked near her outside window. He had been listening for quite some time, long before Mohammed Afzul had taken himself off to the fields. He was particularly alert to her talk to Mohammed Afzul of Derek, Annalise, and the *Angrezi-log*. So, he said furiously to himself after a time, Mohammed Afzul had been harboring a pair of *Angrezis*. At last, having found the chance for which he had been waiting, he hurried off to inform the village.

Derek reluctantly joined Mohammed Afzul in the fields when the sun was only an hour past the eastern horizon. The heat had already created a shimmering haze about the green sprouting maize, and the work quickly grew backbreaking. Their loincloths tucked high, Derek and Mohammed Afzul worked one part of the field and then another. Derek wiped dripping perspiration from his brow. He had ridden on cavalry maneuvers until the sweat from him and his horse puddled on the ground, but he was unused to menial labor even after months at it. He was beginning to have a very fair picture of the exertion exacted of the gardeners at Claremore. Winding his *puggaree* tighter about his brow, he straightened to rest his back. Marja was a distant figure across the *jeel*. She would be coming to bring them lunch and a gourd of water. He pictured Annalise scrubbing the clothes at the river, her white hands wet to the wrist in cool water. He wanted her to touch him with those wet hands, caress him with their calm certainty. She had always instinctively known how to excite him physically; in the same way, she could soothe him when he was troubled and weary.

He was troubled now. Time was ticking by with no word of relief to Lucknow in sight. He suspected Mohammed Afzul knew more than he was telling, but feared to share the news. When Marja arrived, he accepted the gourd gratefully, then left her and Mohammed Afzul for the river that fed into the *jeel*. He wanted nothing to eat in the heat; his appetite was bent on Annalise.

He found her kneeling by the river. She had set the laundry aside and was winding up her hair in preparation for a cooling bath. Silently, he stood among the palms and watched her. Unaware of him, she gracefully disrobed, and with her body like a white, lissome wand, stepped into the water. Her hair soon spun out like a long, dark serpent in the slowly swirling water, her back pale and straight. She cupped the water in her hands, pressed it to her face to let it fall in silver rivulets down her arms and breasts. She dipped her head back into the water, letting her body sink back luxuriously with a smile of soft delight upon her lovely face.

Derek felt a sense of immense calm come over him. This exquisite, gentle creature was his to cherish for the rest of his life, if he could only persuade her to marry him. He must heal that pain in her heart before he could truly claim her for his own. Above all she needed tenderness now, as well as his protection, and now that the world had turned bloody about them, all his strength and wit would be needed to preserve her from danger.

He pulled off his *puggaree* and loincloth, then padded silently down to the river to join her. The heat was close about them as was the whir of insects. The reddish, baking rocks were like molten ovens underfoot. Small scraps of brush and bracken protruded from the cracks in the stone, and a drowsing lizard scuttled from his path. Startled, Annalise sank up to her shoulders and whirled about when she heard the scrape of gravel at the water's edge. Seeing him naked, her eyes widened momentarily, then filled with soft delight. "I did not think to see you again until the evening," she said quietly. "I have whiled away the morning thinking of you."

"As I, you," he murmured, wading out to her. He caught her fingertips and drew her to him, with water and perspiration beaded on his brow. Dipping her hands, she filled them with water and bathed his face, letting the water spill down. He buried his face in her palms and kissed them, then with water dripping from his lashes, lifted his head and kissed her. Their faces were cool, tranquil in their sylvan setting. Their bodies flowed about one another like silver water, their arms encircling one another with the fluidity of the current. Jade-green water swirled about them, its eddies rusty brown with wafting plant life near the stoney shore. The sun sifted down in slanting golden bands through the overhanging *mohur* and peepul trees that bowed with no stirring of leaves in the stifling heat of the coming noon.

Clasping her sleek, wet head between his hands, Derek looked long at Annalise. "I love you," he whispered, "more than you can imagine. My life would be as dust should I ever lose you again. Say that you will stay with me . . . and trust me but a little. I swear upon my mother's name that you should never regret it."

She met his eyes with ineffable sadness. "You ask of me more than I can yield you."

He tilted her silky head up. "What if you have my child within you? It's very possible, you know, considering the times we have lain together. Would you expose him to the shame of being without a father?"

She eyed him with a trace of mischief underlying her gravity. "Are you so very certain that any first child of yours will be a boy? If I should have a daughter, you would have two helpless females to protect."

"I am serious, Annalise. What if you become pregnant?"

"Then I shall bear your child and gladly," she answered levelly, "but I still should not be willing to be your wife." She lifted a fine brow. "You would not know what to do with a wife, Derek."

A faint look of startled offense crossed his hard features. "Why not? A wife is no different than any other woman."

"Ah, but she is. A wife would prevent you from seeking the beds of other women. She would tie you to home and hearth, and like a hound, you would chafe at the restraint." She shook her head. "You would never be happy with just one woman, Derek. Marian might look in the other direction if you dallied abroad, but I should never forgive it."

He eyed her. "You are very fierce today, for the mate of a tame hunting dog."

She laughed in spite of herself. "You are far from tame, and our mating is but momentary. . ."

"Is it now?" He kissed her firmly. When she went pliant in his arms, he grinned and teased her delicate earlobe with his teeth. "I wander, madame, only for want of petting. Shall we tarry awhile? I've time before I must rejoin Mohammed Afzul at uprooting his tiresome weeds."

"I feel as if I were entertaining a doctor who must directly be off on a summons," she teased. "Will you take my pulse, sir?"

He tested her wrist. " 'Tis a trifle slow, miss, for my liking. Shall I quicken it?" His fingers slipped between her thighs, and she let out a startled squeal that quickly turned to a sound of delight.

"You are very naughty, sir, but I cannot fault the success of your method."

His free arm closed about her, his other hand continuing its ministrations. "Squeal again; I like it."

She giggled. "Perhaps you should seduce an opera singer."

"I am quite satisfied with the present company. Your

range is excellent." So tempting one another, they drifted into the main current of the stream and downward with its flow toward the mouth of the *jeel* where it was thickly shrouded with vines and waterlilies. "There is an old tale of Krishna and girls of his village that is most delightful," Derek observed after a long series of rapturous kisses that left them both tingling. "It goes like this. Krishna, the blue cowherd from the land of Braja, had come upon the pretty maidens from his village all bathing in a stream. He stole their clothes and climbed a tree to see them better. Krishna teasingly invited them each to follow him into the tree and give him a kiss in exchange for their clothes. The laughing ladies obliged, but the last and prettiest countered the invitation by suggesting that she would give Krishna far more than a kiss if he would join her in the water. Stripping off his clothes with alacrity, he descended the tree and jumped into the stream, only to find that the mischievous lady had eluded him and was on the bank putting on his clothes. Krishna was obliged to don the lady's attire to follow her back to the village to the great amusement of the inhabitants. Of course, Krishna wound up married to his quick-witted seductress."

Annalise laughed with delight. "What a fine story. Did Mohammed Afzul tell it to you?"

Derek shook his head. "Ahmed told it to me after he had been in my employ for two years. Apparently, he decided I was not as stuffy as I seemed."

She arched a brow. "Indeed, he might come to such a conclusion, judging from the number of concubines in your *bibi gurh*."

He eyed her calmly. "What do you know of my *bibi gurh?*"

"No more than anyone else, but everyone kept rather a close tally. Four, I believe it was, at last count."

"I got rid of the concubines . . . what a delightfully archaic term . . . when Sarah Quill moved into the house."

"That means you did without them two whole days before I arrived. You must have held quite a send-off party."

"If I had known I should never see them again, it would have been more of a party," he retorted unrepentantly. "What a pity you cannot cite a similar experience. Had you known the pleasures of a single life before abandoning it, you would be highly unlikely to complain."

"*Abandonment* is the word. I believe you led a very loose life, indeed. Scarcely a knot in the whole scheme of your existence. Along with the *bibis,* half the women in the cantonment were in love with you."

He dunked her. "Enough impertinence, you water sprite. I've a mind to make love to you, despite your pricking tongue." He wrapped about her, and bent her back. Reclining among the ferns sweeping thickly down the bank, they became one, their bodies intertwining as if they were part of the luxuriant life there. How easy it was for them to see that India was the cradle of creation, its verdancy going back to ancient times when the world was new and few men walked the earth. Oldest of the old were India and Egypt and Persia. Here, lovers had met, and loved, and given birth to generations, until the world was peopled, thick with disease and war. Yet through it all, the lovers continued to come together, and the beauty they created surpassed all the hatred and death.

Derek kissed the water droplets from Annalise's jetty lashes, his hands warm and certain upon her body. Their loving was languid, almost somnolent, the pulse of their bodies throbbing as they joined. He buried his face against her neck, his body slowly surging into hers, its sweet rhythm as old as time. She clasped him to her, yielding herself almost completely. She wanted to trust him, let her soul flower within his embrace with her, yet something held back: some tiny kernel of apprehension that seemed to make no difference in her physical response. As though she had been mated to him from origins primeval, her body responded to him.

His hands slowly swept down to her hips, rejoicing in the youthful womanliness of her, her slenderness, her fragility. She was so strong to be so soft, her heart bold, yet gentle. This was the woman of his boyhood dreams. Now the boy was a man, the certainty of his vision unchanged. This was the woman he wanted to marry, and he would have pursued her to Hades to claim her if necessary. He forged deep within her, praying he would get her with child. He wanted some tangible bond between them, some forging of their powerful yet transparent link. She would not willingly bring shame and hardship upon a child. She would marry him . . . unless she conceived of marrying someone else. He had little knowledge of her past life; in England, they had talked mostly of himself and he felt a twinge of guilt. Who could she anticipate as a husband but him?

With renewed fervor, he applied himself to his delightful task until their loving flowered, bloomed like a rich, exotic orchid in the deep, dark heart of the forest of differences that separated them. A golden mist of fertile pollen swept about them, with bees humming low across the bracken. Their desire peaked, fell like a shower of sparks amid the golden pollen. Annalise arched against him, her body an ivory willow, pale and luminescent in the greenish glow of light. In that moment, she was *his,* he knew it . . . until he suddenly knew who she might choose as the father of her child.

"Professor Sanderville!" he blurted, nonplussed.

"What?" she murmured, stirring beneath him.

"You mean to marry Professor Sanderville!"

Annalise was taken aback, for she had not thought of it. Still, in theory at least, the proposition would work well and divert Derek, for he was still far too sure of himself. Although she could not take his suggestion seriously, she still had no intention of marrying him. If she became pregnant, she would go back to China and let it be assumed that she was a widow; after all, she was. Her eyes opened, limpid, golden, feline slits of complacency. "Why shouldn't I marry Professor Sanderville?"

"He's *old* . . . three times your age," replied Derek, startled and beginning to grow angry at her apparent imperturbability. "How can you possibly consider . . . ?"

"So long as I did not interfere with his celibate bachelorhood, Professor Sanderville would not hesitate to marry me. He is a chivalrous man."

"He's also a man. He would stay neither celibate nor chivalrous for more than a fortnight if . . ."

She smiled benignly at his suggestion. "I trust him, whereas with you . . . well, you are a proven libertine."

"Libertine? Where did you find your education? In a home for the sedentary?" Affronted, he started upward.

She gently restrained him. "Darling, I do not propose to shackle you with responsibilities . . ."

"I *want* them," he protested heatedly. "Why on earth can you not see that I would make a perfectly normal husband?"

As Derek's argument with Annalise continued on the riverbank, Mohammed Afzul rose in the distant field to resume his labors. Always a difficult woman to convince of anything, Marja, who stood nagging over him, was particularly intractable about her now unwelcome guests. "They will be the death of us," she continued to assert to her brother. "We must be rid of them."

"Marja," he declared, fed up, "I have heard enough for one day. Either go home or help me in the field. I have work to do." He rose, brushing the bread crumbs from his clothes.

Marja snorted. "Call your *huzoor* from his dalliance with his wife if you want help. What good is he of late? He can scarcely take his eyes from her long enough to put on his sandals, far less be of any use as a laborer. These *Angrezi-log* have no stomach for work in this heat."

"Why should the colonel sahib love to grub in the heat and dirt any better than I? No one with any sense wants to do farm work in India." He turned his back on her and began to pull at the weeds.

With a final glare at him, Marja gathered up her basket and headed back to the village. The dirt street was empty but for the Scorpion who stared at her fixedly when she arrived at her house. No sooner had she entered the door, when she saw six of the village women waiting for her. "What is it this time?" she asked irritably. "Why do you always come to me with all the complaints you wish to relay to my brother?" She plopped her basket down on the dirt floor.

No sooner had the wicker struck the ground, than one woman picked up the heavy wooden bowl beside it and swung it in a hard arc level with Marja's throat. Her eyes widened in shocked alarm, but she was not quick enough to duck. The bowl caught her across the windpipe, spinning her to the ground. She choked, her breath coming like a saw blade drawn across a rough board. Women grabbed her under the arms and one of them strung a length of hemp through the pot hook on the wall. Looping the other end of the hemp into a noose over Marja's neck, they hauled her to her feet. She was still gasping when the hemp jerked her off her feet to strangle her. Within minutes, her desperate, agonized jerking ceased. She hung lax, a dark, empty sack of a figure, against the whitewashed wall.

* * *

Derek sighed and took Annalise in his arms. He was never able to get anywhere arguing with her. In her mild, calm way, she was as obstinate as he. Yelling certainly never did any good. She was smiling at him now, and he was unsure whether she was teasing him when she expressed the possibility of marriage to Professor Sanderville. "You don't mean it, do you?" He peered at her narrowly. "Sanderville may even be dead by now."

"Don't borrow trouble," she reminded him gently. "We do not know that I am pregnant; neither do we know that Professor Sanderville is dead. We do know that we cannot stay here much longer."

"You're probably right"—his dark-eyed gaze was unswerving—"even if you are changing the subject. I think we should head for the jungle before the week is out. Mohammed Afzul has talked us into staying too long, as it is."

"He has been a good and loyal friend to us," she murmured, resting her head back against his arm. "I pray we have not brought trouble upon him. The old Scorpion grows vehement these days."

Derek kissed her. "He will have trouble enough if I do not soon rejoin him in the fields. The crops will be ready for picking before long, and he will have no one to help him once we are gone. Still, he has managed before." He nuzzled her ear. "What a delicacy you are . . . well worth my missing lunch. Marja sends the same *chupattis* and rice every day." His lips browsed from her ear to her lips again, and there he lingered. Her sari was spilled about them, sodden against the bracken, and his loincloth was tangled with it. The wet cotton was deliciously cool in comparison with the white glare of sunlight beyond the shade of the *mohurs*, and Annalise was pale as a lily beneath its dappling. She seemed to glow in the small pools of incandescent light.

Slender and beautifully made, she was silken in his arms, her skin soft as a fawn's. Desire came upon him once more, and he entered her as smoothly as a sigh, his body fitting to hers with the ease of certainty. For the moment, she was his. While he did not share her faith that God would provide for tomorrow, he was grateful for the present.

Her lips were nectar, her body flowing with his, and their loving became a single stream of passion, its currents growing swift as their bodies quickened. The heat weighted them like a dream, making their urgency seem isolated and apart from them. The sensation was both lulling and vehement, as unreal as a dream, and as real as their perspiring skins and uneven breathing. When the moment came, they felt a pleasure sharp as a knife made of mist, and when the child's face appeared before them, they were more startled than if the knife were real.

The child was Nani, her small face awed at seeing them naked together. For a quick moment, she did not speak, but only stared, then found her voice, which emerged like a lamb's bleat. "You . . . you must go," she whispered frantically. "They have killed Mohammed Afzul and his sister. You and the sahib will be next if they find you, memsahib. They have guessed you are *Angrezi*."

Derek swore, then swiftly grabbed his loincloth and wrapped it about him. He threw Annalise's wet sari at her. "Quick . . . we must get to the boats and take to the *jeel* before they find us. It's a small lake, but promises more safety than the road."

"Many thanks, Nani," Annalise told the child. "You have done bravely. . . but now you must go lest they suspect that you have warned us." The child scuttled off as Annalise swept on her sari. Annalise's fingers were sure with the wrapping, but fumbled with the last tuck. She wanted to ask Derek where they could possibly go after leaving the *jeel*, but held her tongue. There would be time enough for questions later . . . if they lived.

Derek caught her hand, and keeping to the shelter of the jungle, ran with her out onto the spit of land that served as a landing stage for the village. Swiftly, he slit the underbellies of the boats on the shore. After handing Annalise into a narrow, piroguelike boat, he gave it a shove out from the bank and threw himself athwart the gunnels, then into the boat. Just as the bow cleared shore, a mass of village men, their clothing dappled with the blood of Mohammed Afzul, boiled from the jungle. Derek dug in his paddle while Annalise caught up the other one and plied it with all her strength. The men had gotten hold of Mohammed Afzul's old musket, and one of them fired. Unused to the gun's weight, he aimed too low and the bullet spat off the water. In the half minute it took him to fumble with reloading, the canoe had forged beyond the shallows where the men were swarming, but a few plucky swimmers with machetes in their teeth gave pursuit. One of them grabbed at the stern to catch the slamming blade of Derek's paddle in his teeth. He sank in bubbles of bloody water. The next assailant was brained in the temple. His ear bleeding, he let go of the boat and flailed backward to evade the next vicious chop of the paddle.

Annalise was less lucky. A man succeeded in grabbing her paddles, nearly unseating her and tipping the boat. Crying out, she raked at his eyes with her nails and shoved his *puggaree* down over them so that he was momentarily blinded. Surging forward, Derek struck him. His hands went lax on her paddle, stretching upward like the claws of a dead chicken as he sank.

The paddles flashed, the sun glinting on the barrel of the reloaded musket ashore. There was a black puff of powder, then a second bullet whistled past Derek's ear. The marksman was learning quickly, but fortunately, not quickly enough.

The boat slid out of range when the last bullet slapped the boat just above the waterline. The other men had taken to the boats on the shore and filled the air with foul oaths as their launches bubbled and sank beneath them. Annalise's face was flushed, her slim shoulders straining at her paddle as they cleared the shoreline. The *jeel* calmly stretched out before them, as impervious to the men screaming in its shallows as a crocodile to warts.

Night fell slowly, the afternoon laboring on like a woman striving to heave a child from her womb. The villagers had gathered on the bank, sporadically hurling curses out across the *jeel*. The *jeel* was surrounded by a thin chain of people who brandished weapons as if they had encircled a tiger. Several of the ruined canoes had been hauled into the village for repairs. "Can we fight clear?" questioned Annalise softly.

"Not with paddles," answered Derek grimly. "My weapons are all ashore, probably divided up among our former village friends."

"They'll try to come at us tonight, won't they?"

"Probably, but then they won't be able to see us any easier than we can see them. We stand some chance of getting away."

A slim one, Annalise's mind echoed silently. The *jeel* was not large enough to spread out their attackers so thinly that she and Derek might be sure of penetrating their circle. She was hungry, although she barely noticed it. What was a missing lunch when one was likely to be missing a head by midnight?

The villagers lit torches after sunset, and the *jeel* became a ring of fire. Annalise shivered although the night was not cold. "They'll be coming soon."

Derek said nothing for he was thinking. They stood more of a chance in the water than in the boat, for the boat could not near shore without being seen in the torchlight. Around the stony banks were patches of greenery, some of it knee-high. "Can you swim, Annalise?" he asked suddenly.

"Not a stroke. I never had any opportunity to learn in China."

Her voice was faint with shame, but he had thought as much. Few Englishmen, and no women in his acquaintance, knew how to swim. "It's all right; don't worry about it. I'll do the swimming for both of us. Just hang onto my shoulder like you did the horse's tail crossing the Ganges."

To her credit, Annalise asked no questions, far less made any objection. Drowning presented fewer fears than butchery by a band of irate natives. The marsh crocodiles that populated the *jeel* must also frighten her, but she gave no evidence of it. He loved Annalise for many reasons, but not the least was her courage, and she was showing each moment that she had more grit than he imagined.

Unfortunately, the moon was as bright as the one the night before, when they had made love by its silver light. With the machete at his hip, Derek sliced up the fishing net on the bottom of the boat, and used it to lash the paddles erect, so that the boat still looked as if it held passengers. Then he eased over the far side of the boat and motioned Annalise to follow him. Swiftly, she entered the water and put her arms about his neck. "Lie back on your back and put your hands on my shoulders," he whispered, "and don't talk. The water carries sound."

Silently, he swam through the darkness toward the thinnest point in the ring of lights. Twenty yards from the boat, they saw the black silhouettes of two boats moving toward them, the gunnels outlined by torchlight. Annalise caught her breath as Derek submerged briefly, swimming underwater several yards to the right. White bubbles flurried dimly by their heads as the boats slid past with paddles feathered. When his lungs were ready to burst, Derek headed for the surface, and Annalise tried to muffle her desperate gasp as their heads broke water. He dug in hard, hoping to gain as much distance as possible from the invading boats before their occupants realized their quarry had eluded them.

The minutes sped by like a matter of seconds until the bowman in the lead boat let out a cry of angry frustration upon seeing the upright paddles. "They're gone," he yelled, then whipped around in the boat to scan the shore. In a moment, he spied the route Derek and Annalise must have taken to bore through the circle of torches ashore. His finger jabbed toward the thin spot. "There!" He and the others began to yell at their comrades on shore, but the babble of voices was confusing. The torches ashore began to cluster in order to hear and discuss what was being said, and thin spots began to appear throughout their ranks. "No, no!" shouted one of the boatmen. "Do not leave your posts!" As he was disregarded, the next fifteen minutes was pandemonium, made worse by the villagers' awareness that their quarry must be making the most of it.

Derek had shifted course before the bowman had fixed upon it. Now he had his choice of points to penetrate and he bored for the north shore in hope of reaching the jungle. With Annalise in tow, he was tiring, for he was trying to make the best speed possible. Finally, they reached the shallows and he tried not to rasp air into his winded lungs. Bullrushes grew heavily about that portion of the shore, and carefully parting them, he and Annalise worked their way through the mud to see figures just ahead running back and forth, frantically trying to spy them in the darkness. Torches swung high, flaring off the bullrushes and casting long black streaks across the water. Derek clasped Annalise close to him, and they both ducked as a torch swooped over their spot. Grabbing Annalise's hand as soon as the torch passed over them, Derek dragged her after him and they bolted for the shelter of the trees. For a few moments, they were not noticed in the melee, then old Scorpion's sharp eyes spied them. "There they are!" he shrieked. "Get them!"

Fast as Derek and Annalise were, they were not fast enough. A torch appeared from either side as they made the trees. The first man swung his blazing torch at Annalise's face, her wide eyes reflecting the reddish glow. Derek grasped the shaft of the flaming brand with both hands, wrenched it from the man's grasp, and fed him the pointed end. Before Derek could wheel, the second attacker was on them, *tulwar* raised high. In an inspired effort, Annalise crumpled to the ground and rolled into the man's ankles. He went down with a shriek and Derek trod on his neck with a muffled crack. Grabbing up both torches, Derek flung them to the left, shouting "This way!" Then, grasping Annalise's hand, he sprinted off to the dense undergrowth to their right.

The distraction was sufficient and dawn found Annalise and Derek crouched beside a low wall next to a burned-out plantation house. The sight of the charred ruins and the smell of burnt hair that still hung around Derek brought back to Annalise visions of the flames in her face. She shivered and huddled close to Derek, both of them wet from a morning rain. Having eluded pursuit all night, they were in a quandary as to what to do when the ground began to rumble beneath their feet. Derek gingerly peered over the wall.

"What is it?" Annalise asked.

"I should say the cavalry has arrived." Almost as his last word was uttered, a mounted assault of red-coated British lancers and loyal 12th Native Cavalry launched into the clearing. One rider jumped the wall as Derek swept his *puggaree* off his head and shouted, "Welcome to Nanjul, you sluggards! What took you so long?"

The rider responded by wheeling on him and charging with lance poised. Startled, Derek swore, and sidestepping, grabbed the lance and jerked the rider head over crupper to the ground. The lancer rolled as he hit, coming up with sword drawn and giving Derek a wicked slash toward the head.

Derek impatiently warded him off. "Enough of that, Captain, or I'll jerk your rank when we get to Lucknow . . . if it's still standing. That *is* where you're bound, isn't it?" When the lancer hesitated, Derek added, "Former Colonel Derek Clavell, at your service." He swirled his *puggaree* at Annalise. "This is Mrs. Conran O'Reilly, widow, formerly of the 3rd in Kanpur." He waited a moment as the lancer goggled. "Cat got your tongue, Captain? When you start a cavalry charge, you can expect to scare up almost anything."

"We were just trying to clear the way for General Havelock's forces," stammered the captain. "We had no idea you were here."

Derek's teeth flashed wolfishly white in his dark face. "If you hadn't shown up this morning, we wouldn't have been. The locals were about to turn us into fricassee." He clasped the lancer's shoulder. "By God, I could kiss you, Captain."

Then, to the lancer's horror, he did.

XIV

Havelock

"*You've* had quite an adventure, Mrs. O'Reilly," growled Sir Henry Havelock over dinner that night. "But then, it's to be expected, traveling about with the likes of Colonel Clavell." He winked at Derek. "The colonel and I go back a long way, and I know. Where there's trouble, you'll find Derek Clavell."

"I should have been killed more than once on this journey, if not for Colonel Clavell," Annalise defended her lover, who impishly sidestepped the compliment.

"I believe you were in a similar predicament when we first met nearly three years ago," Derek quipped. "You lead an extraordinarily precarious life, Mrs. O'Reilly."

She laughed, too relieved to be alive to argue. "That's true enough. My hair should be white by now. I despair of ever living long enough to kiss my grandchildren"—she shot a mischievous glance at Derek—"but then Colonel Clavell is bestowing enough kisses for us both."

Havelock laughed delightedly. "If I hadn't arrived when I did, I'd have had to settle a duel. That lancer had his back up." He leaned over the table. "Tell me, Derek, what are you doing out here, so far ahead of the army?"

When Derek told him, Havelock pursed his lips. "I didn't know that you'd resigned your commission. The army has lost a good commander. I can tell you, we're short of men now. What do you say to temporarily joining my staff until we settle this Lucknow mess? You're not likely to get far as a lone civilian until the mutiny is put down."

Derek thoughtfully toyed with his wine. "I hadn't planned to rejoin the army, sir." He glanced up at Annalise. "What do you think?"

She flushed. "I'm sure my opinion cannot matter. You must follow your own course."

Havelock shrewdly eyed Derek, then her. "Your husband was a soldier, Mrs. O'Reilly. You must have some idea of what such a commitment entails."

"Conran was devoted to the army, sir. I'm sure that had he been given a choice between his bride and his profession, he might well have chosen his profession."

"Mrs. O'Reilly is probably right," said Derek, "but whatever I decide, I do not propose to remain a soldier once the mutiny is done." His eyes rested on Annalise. "I have other plans."

Annalise felt chilled, although she met his gaze levelly. Derek might mean to marry her, but he also might still hope to return to Claremore, and that, she could not bear. She did not believe he was truly committed to giving up Claremore forever to take her to Australia. Australia seemed especially far away now, though it had never been real to her.

The terrible events of the past two days swept through her memory, and she suddenly felt fatigue overtake her. Brushing her hand across her brow as if to banish remembrance, she rose. "I beg your pardon, gentlemen, but I am very tired. I should like to retire now, if you don't mind."

Derek immediately got up from his chair. "I'll see you to your tent."

Accompanying her through the small encampment to her tent, set apart from the others near the picket lines, he observed quietly, "You seem subdued tonight. Do you feel unwell?"

She shook her head. "I am well enough, though exhausted. Only when I think how close we came to death today. . ."

"I know. And our friends' fate was horrible. The mutiny has been cruel, and will get worse." He did not add that if Havelock were cut off behind enemy lines, they all would die horribly. For now, they were unspeakably lucky to be alive, and he longed to take her into his arms. "Annalise," he said softly, "I want you tonight, but if you prefer to be left alone, I will not trouble you."

She looked up at him when they reached the tent, a small canvas affair big enough for two cots, although it held only one. "I want you to hold me tonight. I dare say that once we reach Lucknow, we shall have little enough privacy." She glanced at the pickets pacing about the far side of the tents. Their ears pricked to every sound from the surrounding darkness of the jungle beyond the encampment, they were oblivious to Derek and Annalise. Quickly, the lovers ducked inside the tent, and even more quickly, their lips met. Fevered by the release of the harsh tension of the last two days, they undressed one another, and Derek lowered Annalise to the *charpoy* without lighting the lantern. She was silk beneath him, twining about him luxuriously, her skin damp from the heat. His lips clung to hers as his hands found her bare smoothness. "I've longed for you," he breathed against her throat. "You're like a dream of passion, your eyes rivaling the very stars that blaze across the sky tonight. Touch me, breathe into me all your being, until we soar together higher than we've ever gone. I love you . . . I love you . . ."

Turning over to lie atop him, she became like the sky's canopy, cool and nearly weightless in the welcome breeze that drifted beneath the rolled-up tent skirt. She lifted her arms, her hands twining into her hair to let it fall about them. Raven black, her hair tickled slightly, its sensuous sheen in the glimmer of the new moon as luxurious as the sultry night itself. She bent forward gracefully and touched her lips to his, then trailed down his body until his breathing quickened, and he plunged his hands into the black, silken stream that flowed over him. She flicked his nipples delicately with her tongue, then kissed them as if she were deeply kissing his mouth. Only when his nipples became hard, sensitive pebbles did her lips trickle lower to his groin to find the flowerlike stem of his sex, already rigid with desire for her. Then, shyly, curiously, she tasted him, and delighted at his startled gasp of pleasure. Slowly, tentatively, she enveloped him with her mouth, until he groaned softly and arched beneath her. "Ah, Annalise," he whispered, "you are becoming altogether too knowing . . . you make me wild for you . . ."

Finally, when he could bear no more, he drew her up across his body and slowly sank into her, his sex filling her so completely and with such heat that she let her head fall back in celebration of the sheer ecstasy of his entry. His hips began to rotate in sensuous rhythm, seducing her to move upon him, and gradually her motion quickened with a fluid, musical lilt. He drove deeply, making her gasp and arch, her breasts rising pale from the stream of her hair. She uttered a muffled cry as her moment came, swift and intense; then another swept her and she bit her hand to keep silent.

His neck cording, Derek pulled her onto him and drove deeply inside her, their pleasure winding, coiling, striking again and again as if it were a sweet, magical serpent whose hypnotic sway had been broken at last. When at last their desire was satiated, they lay together, their skins shining with perspiration in the glimmering moonlight which set the tent aglow. The breeze had stopped and the night was close, as close as their bodies entwined on the *charpoy*. The toes of Annalise's bare left foot brushed the ground and her hair spilled from the edge of the *charpoy* like a falling night. "Never leave me," whispered Derek. "I should not want to live if I lost you."

She looked down at him sadly, and his face twisted at her silence. "You still haven't forgiven me, have you? Marian still stands between us."

"Marian and a thousand other things," she answered softly. "Not until I saw you together, did I realize just how quickly and cruelly our love affair could end."

"It hasn't ended . . . and it needn't end!" He gripped her arms. "I love you more than ever . . . can't you see that?"

"And I love you," she murmured. "I shall always love you, but I can never marry you. When the mutiny is done, you must return to Claremore and put your life together again. I have decided to go back to China."

"China!" Disintangling himself, he sat up. "China is on the other side of the earth!"

"So is Australia," she reminded him.

"But in Australia, we could be together." A note of pleading entered his voice. "Listen, Annalise . . ."

She stilled his lips with his fingertips. "You promised you would not press me, Derek. Remember?"

Upset, he ran his hands through his hair and twisted away. "I remember the days we spent at Claremore until Marian came between us. It can be that way again."

"No," she replied gravely. "It can never be that way again. I can never be the innocent I was again. And if I were to go with you, one day, you would see me as a millstone around your neck."

"To be fair, Annalise, you must let me be the judge of that. Since we returned to India, you have allowed me no choices. I find myself tagging after you like an unwanted pup on a string."

"I have hurt your pride then."

"To say the least."

"Your pride is very important to you, isn't it?"

He started to retort, then his eyes narrowed as he caught her drift. "Pride is not more important to me than you, if that's what you infer."

"I think it is," she said softly. "Somehow you have mixed up pride with honor, and honor should run deeper than a cause to duel. Honor implies faith and commitment. The marriage vows decree 'for better or for worse' and 'forsaking all others'; that means not only other lovers, but all relationships which would damage the marriage. You are a baronet, but I shall never be a baroness, even if you should crown me in Canterbury Cathedral. Your whole way of life would undermine any marriage between us." When he started to protest, she waved a weary hand. "We must talk of this another time, Derek. I fear I am exhausted."

He sighed, then enfolded her to him. "You are stubborn, for such a gentle creature." His lips quirked in the darkness. "I fear Professor Sanderville will find you an unruly wife."

Her head lifted quickly. "You sound as if you don't believe I would ever marry him."

"Oh, no," he assured her calmly, "I believe you readily enough, and I should not want to propel you into another hasty wedding that we might both regret. One husband was quite enough for me this year." He regretfully gave her bottom a farewell pat. "I should like to make love to you until you fall asleep, but I fear I must go to my own tent. The officers' mess will break up soon, and I'm sure enough lively conjecture must have arisen about us already." He kissed her lips lingeringly. "Good night, my little love. May all your dreams be of Australia."

In spite of herself, Annalise laughed. "I shall imagine serving you mutton each and every evening."

Moments after dressing, he was gone, and she found herself wide awake. Australia.

Havelock's convoy moved out before dawn. In the dark morning's misty air, syces scurried to and fro with tack and fodder for the horses, while the sepoys hastily wolfed cold vegetables and *chupattis* for breakfast. The tents emitted pie wedges of lantern light and an occasional saber could be heard sliding into a sheath. Dressed in her sari, Annalise waited in her tent until Derek came for her. "You'll be traveling with the women. We're not the only refugees Havelock has picked up during his trek; I counted nearly fifteen gathering by the supply wagons. If we collect any more," he added with a glum note, "you may have to share your tent."

They were underway within the hour and made quick time while the slight coolness of darkness lasted. Dawn was an explosion of heat and within the crowded women's wagon, the air was stifling. Annalise soon felt faint, and the rocking of the wagon sickened her. Pale and sticky with perspiration, three children lay with their heads together on a grain sack, while Annalise had taken a baby onto her lap. Whimpering fitfully, the baby wilted against her breast and she thanked heaven she had no child of her own to be crazy with worry about. The mothers looked harried and hot. She was glad Sarah and Timmy Quill had left India the year before. She had grown extremely fond of them both, and Timmy was as dear to her as her own child might have been. So many innocents must have been slaughtered in the mutiny. Thanks to the unseasonably cool weather that had lasted well into spring, civilian families had been slow to begin their annual pilgrimage to the highlands of Simla, where they might have been safe from the uprising. Hundreds of them had been caught in the debacle. As the day wore on, some of the women told Annalise of the horrors that had been taking place throughout northern India.

That night, Derek told her their scouts had reported getting into Lucknow would be touch-and-go, retaking the city doubtful. Lucknow residency compound was a series of now half-ruined buildings separated from the city only by its fences, lawns, walls, and makeshift barricades. The main bungalow was a lavish three-story, verandahed home combined with company offices, and undoubtedly crammed with refugees. They were now twenty miles from Lucknow and would reach the city tomorrow. The fighting would be bloody hell.

And there were no more refugees. Any *Angrezi-log* within proximity of the city were either well hidden in the jungle or dead.

Derek and Annalise lay together in her tent for some time. Clasped in his arms, she slept fitfully from time to time from the sheer exhaustion of the two previous nights without sleep and a day of rattling about in the wagon with fretful children and frightened women. He cradled her close, not knowing when he would be able to hold her again. Oddly enough, he thought of Conran. Somehow, he felt he owed Conran a debt. If Annalise was ever to be his, he must prove himself as worthy of her as Conran had been. Conran would expect him to see her through tomorrow and whatever dangers the days afterward might bring. Only courage and tremendous luck would bring them through, and he did not know quite what to expect of Havelock, who was a good commander but conservative. Tomorrow would tell.

He left her well before dawn to join the other officers for a brief meeting in Havelock's tent. The sentries had been doubled during the night, and everyone's nerves were on edge. "We'll have to hack our way through," Havelock told them. "If we're overwhelmed, we'll be massacred to a man. Keep the women and children at our center, but don't sacrifice your position for them. Battle is no place for civilians, and they'll have to take their chances like the rest of us. We dare not leave them behind."

As Havelock called the meeting to a close, Derek grimly contemplated his words. The general was right; civilians were a severe liability in a fight. When a man's mind was divided between the fight at hand and those he needed to protect at his back, he was half a fighter and often made mistaken compromises. On the other hand, knowing massacre of himself and those he loved was the only alternative to victory, he would fight like a cornered rat.

And for that day and more, rats they became. The city of Lucknow was a distant, ghostly glimmer in the pearl-gray dawn when Havelock's single battery of artillery opened fire on the central gate. By midmorning, they cleaned the walls of defenders, then bored through the gate. For Annalise and her companions in the wagon, the mounting heat and din of battle created a hellish combination of terror and anticipation. There were not enough men to guard the baggage train outside the city, so they followed the army into the narrow streets. First, the guns would clear a street, then they would forge through it, combating any stubborn defenders they met. Counterattacks were many and furious. Once a saber slashed through the canvas of the wagon cover and a child wailed piteously until his distraught mother jammed a hand over his mouth. Dust from the skirmishing together with the toppling rubble of buildings on either side made visibility a plaster-choked cloud. Annalise cradled a small girl to her breast and sang a lullaby to her that seemed to calm the others although they could hear little of it.

The hours dragged on, and the *ghari* moved in fits and

starts. For long periods, it would stay in one spot, then heave forward at an alarming rate, only to falter again after a time.

Finally, at sunset, after they had been waiting for some time without budging, Derek stuck his head in the canvas flap at the rear of the *ghari*. "We're digging in here for the night. Stay in the wagon and keep your heads low; there are likely to be snipers on the rooftops." He gazed at Annalise for a long moment, as if drinking in the fact that she was unharmed after a day in which he had seen nothing but butchery, much of it hand-to-hand. Her eyes went lambent with love and relief at the sight of him as she clasped the child more closely to her breast. Before she could speak, Derek was gone.

For the next few days, she saw him only for brief minutes at a time, and her nerves were raw. Each day, she waited out the hours as if they were seeking to tear her heart from her breast, for as Havelock's force neared the residency, the fighting grew worse, and more desperate. Shrapnel tore through the canvas of the *ghari* and killed one woman. Screams could be heard from the *ghari* behind them, and several women panicked. "Please, you must stay where you are," Annalise told them quietly. "God is with us for now and always." Two women refused to listen and bolted from the *ghari*. From the flap, Annalise saw one of them shot down as she ran toward a crouching British soldier.

"Stay back!" The soldier desperately waved to the second woman. "Go back to the *ghari*." His last words fell on deaf ears, for a bullet caught her in the throat and splayed her on the cobbles.

Though Annalise quickly closed the flap for fear of frightening the other women, she caught a brief glimpse of the residency, its frayed Union Jack hanging laxly under the September sun. Amid a mass of several whitewashed buildings, the residency fit in snugly with the rest of the city.

Grain sacks and piles of brick and plaster had been stacked before every opening to form redoubts across the lawn from the residency to shield the mutineer's guns.

Suddenly, explosively, the *ghari* lurched forward and rumbled toward the residency at an alarming speed. Gunfire cracked about them like the high-pitched whine of furious bees, rising to such a din that Annalise felt the *ghari* was the hive itself. The *ghari* jolted over debris and bodies in its path, then entered the comparative quiet of the residency compound where piles of furniture and debris had been piled up to reinforce the flimsy defenses. Derek wrenched open the *ghari* flap and motioned them out. Annalise, the last to leave the *ghari*, nearly fell against him, for she was burdened with the baby of one of the women killed only hours before. For a moment, he caught her close to him, his eyes darkening as if he longed to kiss her, then he waved the small, frightened group into the residency.

"Derek, are you all right?" she asked him anxiously as soon as they were inside the doors. He was covered with dust and blood that caked stickily on his clothing, his face streaked with perspiration under a nearly sodden *puggaree*.

He smiled reassuringly. "I've had a nick or two, but nothing serious. Still, I wouldn't like to take that stroll through the city every day. We lost a good many men"—he lowered his voice—"too many to fight our way out again, unless the troops here at the residency are mostly intact, and that's doubtful."

Her eyes widened. "You mean we're trapped here?"

He nodded. "I wouldn't be surprised. Those pandies are a determined lot. They would have overrun the place already, if they weren't hesitant to launch a full-scale attack."

They looked about the residency proper. Through shattered blinds at the windows poked rifles from gaunt, tired-looking men stationed about the large, dingy rooms. Dust streaked the sunlight streaming in through the blinds and sifted to the torn, dirty carpeting covered with broken glass beneath a chandelier tinkling wanly overhead. As they walked through the residency, they saw that the rooms facing the streets looked much like the first one. With hope renewed, civilians, dressed in bits and scraps of clothing that included curtains, crowded the halls, hoping for some word of rescue. Some of them in tattered evening dress, women carrying food and water wove their way through the crowd, where without exception, discipline was steady. No hysteria ran through the halls, but disappointment was evident in many faces when the worn condition of Havelock's troops was noted.

Taking Annalise's arm, Derek led her to the ballroom, where as he supposed, the noonday meal was being issued. Annalise slowly ate the few pieces of warm bread given her and washed it down with thin, watery gruel. Her stomach, tense from the ordeal of the last few days, almost rebelled. If Commissioner Lawrence had not long ago predicted the mutiny and stored supplies within the residency walls, the defenders would have been shortly starved out.

"I think we had best pretend we're enjoying a picnic," Derek observed to Annalise as they settled themselves on the floor.

No more had Annalise tucked her feet beneath her sari skirts than a clear, sardonic voice cut through the gloom. "My, haven't we gone native."

It was Marian Longstreet.

XV

Old Times and Old Friends

Annalise felt dismay seep into her very bones. The last person, the very last, she wanted to see was Marian. At least, she had a slight inkling from Derek's face that he felt the same way, for he was all sobriety as he took in his former fiancée. Marian was wearing a grimy beige muslin dress torn at the hem. Her hoops were gone but her innate hauteur remained starched as ever, and she was still beautiful, still dashing, hardship having defined the strong, fine bones of her imperious face. "What are you doing here?" Derek's voice had a blunt edge.

"How civil of you to ask," Marian retorted ironically. "It was you who practically left me at the altar."

"You were the one who ended our engagement, Marian"—a glint on her left hand caught his eye—"and isn't that a wedding ring you're wearing?"

She made an offhand swoop with her hand. "Rodney

Overton proposed a month after you left England. He's been sick with dysentery three weeks now."

"And he brought you to India." Derek lifted a sardonic brow. "I believe you always wanted to see India."

She shrugged and brushed back a tendril of wayward red hair from her perspiring brow. "I thought he meant to stay in England. Halfway through our honeymoon, he announced that he had bought a plantation and meant to inspect it."

"I imagine the rest of the honeymoon must have been lively," observed Derek dryly.

"Indeed." She gave him an amused glance, then turned her attention briefly to Annalise as she continued, "So, tra-la, here we are. Poor Rodney always feared this climate would kill him, but he didn't think it would finish him so untidily." A genuinely regretful shadow crossed her face. "He is a love; so attentive."

"And rich." Derek gave her a crooked smile. "You'll make a very handsome widow, Marian, if anticipation of that event is any indication."

She gave him a slow smile. "I believe Miss Devon is in mourning, unless that white sari indicates a very different state of affairs."

"I married Conran O'Reilly, a sergeant in the 3rd Cavalry," replied Annalise quietly. "He was killed *en route* to Delhi."

Marian studied her a moment. "And you genuinely mourn him." She ran her fingers through her hair again, then glanced back at Derek. "Did you know your brother, Robert, was here?"

He was startled, and horrified. "Robert, here in India?"

"Not only in India, but here at the residency. He came over just before Rodney and I, in hopes of persuading you to come back to Sussex. Your giving Claremore to Robert in trade for Miss . . . Mrs. O'Reilly was a bit rococo of you, darling."

Annalise stared at her, white faced. "Derek officially gave up Claremore for me?"

"Didn't you know?" Marian laughed shortly. "He virtually shouted his renunciation from the Sussex rooftops . . . only to come all this way and find you . . . attached to another man. What bad luck."

Derek got to his feet. "Where is Robert? I want to see him."

"I believe he's upstairs. They're employing the better shots as snipers. I dare say he won't thank you for getting him into this, Derek."

"Oh, that's my fault, too, is it? Why couldn't you all just have stayed at home where you belong?" He headed for the stairs.

Marian eyed Annalise's distraught face as her gaze followed Derek. "I take it you've been giving Derek a hard time."

"Everyone in India is having a hard time, Miss Long . . . what is your married name? You never mentioned it."

"I am Lady Sheffield now, Mrs. O'Reilly." Marian trilled out the last as if she were a mocking bird.

"Please don't employ my married name as if you were insulting me, Lady Sheffield," returned Annalise, "for when you do so, you insult my husband's memory. He was a man of great integrity and courage."

"Undoubtedly, those qualities made Derek quite fond of him. As old soldiers, they must have enjoyed telling each other stories of war and women. I wonder what Derek said about me."

"No more than he said of me, Lady Sheffield," replied Annalise coolly. "He is a gentleman of great discretion."

"Ah . . . so Derek is a gentleman while Sergeant O'Reilly was merely a man. I take it that even you presume you have overreached yourself, Mrs. O'Reilly."

Growing angry in spite of herself, Annalise retorted, "I am grateful to have been loved, Lady Sheffield, and to have loved in return. I believe the latter state is unfamiliar to you.''

Marian turned crimson, and sweeping her skirts about as she rose, flung back curtly, ''Do not pretend to read my emotions at this moment, Mrs. O'Reilly. I am sure they run hotter that you can imagine.'' She strode off, her gait as determined as a man's.

Annalise looked after her for a moment, then pensively out of the window at the tranquil gardens walled by the buildings blocking out the city. That Derek had already given up Claremore was deeply troubling, yet she was also filled with relief and exaltation. He loved her more deeply than she realized. Australia had not been merely some fanciful myth he had concocted to persuade her to return to England with him. Somehow she had never believed he would end his ties with Claremore. She was sure if the mutiny had not broken out, he would have long ago returned home. And yet he had stayed to look for her, even when she was in Conran's protection.

She felt suddenly confused. Everything that had once seemed so clear was jarred out of focus. She had decided that Derek was to return to Claremore while she went back to China. A hideous choice, but necessary . . . or was it?

She pressed her hand to her brow. She must not let temptation get the better of her; nothing had really changed. She and Derek were no more suited to one another than ever, for Derek's pride would always come between them. But how she longed for him. When he made love to her, she was transported into another world: a world of sweet tenderness so different from the destructive reality about them. Derek was a good, kind man, but she could not disassociate him from the imposing magnificence of Claremore. How often had she listened to her father's sermons on vanity. Sometimes she feared her inclination to love pomp and luxury more than Derek's. Life had been very easy in many ways at Claremore . . . but all the same, she had been alienated there by Marian's supercilious behavior, Aunt Gertrude's coolness, and Claremore's overwhelming magnificence. While Derek had never been unkind, he was one of *them*: that upper crust that never crumbled, even in the face of chaos. Marian was as certain of her superiority as ever, despite the horrors reigning outside the residency. And even in rags in the village, Derek had looked like a lord. There was no blending him into the commonweal.

She sighed, then rose and began to walk toward the infirmary; perhaps she might be of some use there. She was certainly of no use to herself.

The makeshift infirmary was lined with *charpoys*, and between them, the sick and wounded lay in the aisles. Annalise was startled to see Marian tending a young, brown-haired man at the far end of the room; he might well be Rodney Overton, for she could not imagine Marian wanting to be bothered with a hospital's drudgery and stench. Still, even as she watched, Marian moved on to another patient.

A battered, weary-looking man in a bloody apron was coming down the aisle. Obviously the doctor in charge of the infirmary, he regarded her incuriously, despite her sari. She saw that he was in the last stages of exhaustion, and from his few comments to the patients on either side of him, probably even too worn to talk. She touched his arm as he passed. "Doctor, I am Annalise O'Reilly. May I be of some assistance to you?"

"Are you Hindu?" he asked bluntly as he took in her sari.

"Welsh." She smiled. "I have been living in the countryside these last months."

He arched a gray, wiry brow. "And came out of it in one piece. You must be a stalwart soul."

"I owe my life to Derek Clavell, and my husband. I lost Conran at the offset of the mutiny."

"Have any experience at nursing?"

"I sometimes assisted my father in Canton, also in Kanpur."

"He was a doctor."

"A missionary."

One of those, his ironic look said. "I am Dr. Neville." He waved toward Marian. "See Lady Sheffield there. She's my chief nurse. Not much knowledge of medicine, but the stomach of a Cossack." He started to move on, then added as an afterthought, "Oh, and don't go washing your hands every hour. We've barely enough water ration for drinking." He shambled down the aisle.

Annalise stoically approached Marian, who looked up wearily from the man whose chest she was rebandaging. "I was told to report to you, Lady Sheffield. I have offered my services as a nurse."

"I thought a virtuous miss like you would show up sooner or later." Marian had regained her temper. She even looked amused, with that quixotic touch of irony she had shown upon their earlier meeting. She waved at the ward. "My house is your house. Take your pick of the patients. They're all in miserable shape or they wouldn't be here. No one who values his life wants to come near the place. We've no medicine, and less sanitation. Any questions?"

"No questions . . . oh, just one." Annalise had moved toward the next bed, then turned her head. "Which patient is your husband?"

"Why? Planning on seducing him into your web?"

"I dare say I'm not the only spider around here," retorted Annalise mildly.

Marian laughed. "Indeed not. I am reputed to have left husks of men all over England, but that's rank exaggeration. Rod is the one on the left next to the arch. You can practically smell him out from here.'' Her eyes narrowed slightly in warning. ''Mind, I am the one who changes his diapers, so don't get any ideas.''

''Goodness, is it affection or acreage that inspires that proprietary tone?''

''Experience. Missionaries' daughters are unexcepted where Rod is concerned. He has an eye for a pretty ankle, and that sari shows yours off rather too well. The last thing he needs just now is the excitement of conquest.''

''My walls don't fall all that easily,'' said Annalise mildly, ''and I haven't your knack with lowering the drawbridge. One castle at a time is my motto.''

''See that you remember it, my dear Guinevere.'' Marian turned back to her bandaging.

Annalise found Marian was right about the patients. Most of them were in dire condition. The heat in the infirmary was intense, particularly now that it was high noon, and outside, the battle was still raging. She could hear Havelock's artillery combine with that of the residency's in response to the mutineers' guns, rattling the windows' scanty remaining glass. Inside, they were out of linen for bandages and using women's crinolines as gauze, wrapping it layer upon layer. Rodney Overton was too ill to be glad to see a new face. He was a long, willowy man with auburn hair and an attractively elegant face that somehow reminded her of an Irish setter. She disliked his color; he was pale with fever and dehydration.

More than ever, she missed her father's calm manner with people, and more than that, she missed his staunch faith in God. She often had doubts that God's will was in evidence in the world, but William, never. She could envision him now in this woebegone place. Oddly enough, more than any of the other six nurses in the infirmary, Marian Longstreet reflected William's dapper nonchalance in the face of disaster.

The afternoon wore on, until finally Marian ducked over

her shoulder. "Shift's up. Come on, let's find Derek and Robert. We'll have a celebration party tonight."

They found the men with the snipers. Outside the upper-floor windows, the sky had turned purplish with the onset of the rosy, sinking sun. Smoke lay over the shot-divotted square between the residency and the rest of the city, while above it the minarets and onion domes glowed with a pearllike iridescence in the twilight. Derek looked bored. Clearly, he anticipated many more days like this one, spent picking off anything that moved, as if they were ants crawling over a layer cake. "I say we keep score," said Robert, winking at Annalise in her sari. "Whoever wins treats us all to a proper bash in Delhi when the fighting's over."

"We're having a proper bash tonight," Marian informed him. "I've been hoarding rations for just such an occasion."

From the wan look on Robert's face as he rose to briefly embrace her, Annalise knew that a rise in morale was in order.

"We're stuck, you know," Robert commented as they went out to the rear terrace with their meager picnic. "You and the old man haven't brought us enough reinforcements and supplies to hold out more than a few months, Derek."

"Thank benevolent God for that much," returned Derek. "The defenders in Meerut were wiped out to a man."

"And woman," added Marian. "Don't forget we weak and useless have a stake in the fray. I should much sooner polish my marksmanship than clean up excrement in the bowels of this place. Don't you agree, Annalise?"

Faintly startled that they were on such familiar terms, Annalise smiled reservedly. "I am no markswoman and never have been . . . Marian. I shall leave that arena to you and the brothers Clavell."

"What a demure wench you are," observed Marian. "One wonders how you had the stuffing to come this far, but then''—she smiled sweetly at Derek—''Derek has enough stuffing for the ruddy elk.'' She turned to Annalise. ''I shall invite Professor Sanderville to dinner if you like. He's been having a fine time observing the butterflies in the garden. Perhaps he will deign to present us with a monarch *en grillé ce soir.*''

''Professor Sanderville is here?'' Annalise's face lit. ''I should be delighted to see him!''

''Done,'' said Marian. ''Robert, why don't you run along and find him. We shall stay on the terrace.''

When Robert went off through the rose garden on his errand, Marian turned to Derek. ''Well, tonight should be like old times. Everyone all sweetness and daggers.''

He gave her a mild glance. ''Speak for yourself. I could wish your Rodney were coming. Why spare the weak and wasted?''

''Rodney will soon be up and about,'' she retorted. ''He's made of stronger stuff than he looks. Annalise . . .''—she darted a seemingly negligent glance at her rival—''how long were you married?''

Annalise flushed slightly. ''Less than two days.''

Marian gave her a sage nod. ''At least Derek need not fear your vintage has turned to vinegar.''

''Let up, Marian,'' put in Robert. ''You've enough vinegar stored to pickle Scotland.''

''I believe it's Ireland, dear boy. Reilly with an *O*.'' She linked her arm in Annalise's. ''Don't take me seriously. I merely pretend to be vicious. Actually, I'm a lamb, but Robert would have me served as chops.'' She grinned wickedly at Derek, then abruptly changed the subject.

''Poor Rodney's going to be sorry he missed this celebration. He hasn't had anything but gruel for ages. I shall have to take him a truffle.''

Annalise's eyes widened. ''You have truffles?''

"And a smoked ham," said Marian smugly. "If I hadn't been born a lady, I should have made a damned fine pirate."

They settled in a spot overlooking the garden and spread cushions from two armchairs and a sofa on the dusty floor of the verandah. Annalise sat on Derek's right, Marian on his left. The twilight grass was dry, the roses papery from the heat, but a breeze had come up; although Annalise longed to lie down and let it flow over her, she lacked Marian's earthy nonchalance. Aside from her one barbed comment at their first meeting in England, Marian had been far less outspoken there. The siege seemed to have changed her. She was more casual, as if she had either given up hope or the dangerous situation fitted her love of excitement. Derek must have noted the change, too, for he was watching Marian intently, less with a lover's interest than that of a clinician. "How much food have you hidden away, Marian?" he asked bluntly. "This is quite a display."

"Eat heartily, then, milord, for there's little more where this came from. We've all been eating scraps for months. The sepoys can hold out forever. As for us, well . . ."—her shrug held a touch of fatalism—"I never wanted to grow old and lose my looks."

If those sepoys break through, you'll lose more than your looks, thought Annalise. In coming to Lucknow, they might as well have reached an island in a sea of horror. At any moment, a sudden tidal wave of mutineers could overwhelm them.

Robert appeared suddenly, not with Professor Sanderville as she had hoped, but with Jane Witherton. "I was unable to locate the professor, but after leaving him a message, I encountered Miss Witherton emerging from her quarters. Annalise, I believe you know Miss Witherton."

Annalise extended her hand. "Jane, how good to see you again. I hope your parents are with you."

"My parents are both dead, killed in Kanpur when the rioting broke out," responded Jane quietly.

"I'm very sorry to hear that." Her compassion rising for the young Englishwoman, Annalise rose and took her arm. "Please, do sit with us. We have not yet begun to dine."

"You're very kind." Jane looked startled at the spread of food on the white patch of linen. 'I had not thought there was so much food in all of the residency." She sank to her knees as if longing to snatch a handful of bread, but inbred good manners held her back. "How delightful," she said simply.

The picnic party by kerosene lamplight was more muted than she expected. For the first quarter-hour, everyone devoted themselves to eating. Marian had even found cutlery and plates. Derek tried to draw Robert into an argument about the relative merits of tiger hunting in India and wild pig sticking in the Black Forest. Unresponsive at first, Robert caught his brother's intent of relieving the general sobriety, and began to discuss the differences in red and gray foxes when riding the hunt. Jane had never ridden after foxes, but she *had* ridden after wild dogs south of Kanpur, which added another dimension to the conversation. The scene resembled the ghost of a dinner party in Sussex.

We're all ghosts, Annalise found herself thinking. We're living on memories of a time gone forever and trying to keep our world together when it has been blown apart. Her heart clamped hard and painfully within her as she watched Derek's animated features. He seemed to be back in the world at Claremore as surely as if he were drinking a stirrup cup with the master of hounds.

Jane, too, was watching Derek. Annalise felt a flash of jealousy, then realized Jane's attention was not fixed on Derek but on Robert. Her gaze was not flirtatious, but assessing. Like Marian, she had been changed by the mutiny. Even when Robert engaged her in conversation, her manner was subdued.

Annalise wondered if she, too, had changed. Everything seemed more immediate now, for after tomorrow, none of them might be there.

"You're looking thoughtful," Derek murmured in her ear. "Are you frightened now that we're cooped up in here with Havelock?"

"Yes," she answered honestly. "Our backs are to the wall. There's nowhere else we can run now, is there?"

"Nowhere. Reduces things to essentials, doesn't it?"

Her lids lowered. As much as she wanted him, she knew in her heart that she would never have him.

The evening went well. Everyone seemed relieved to have some respite from the fighting for a time, and when Professor Sanderville arrived, Annalise felt a great wave of relief and joy. "I feared you might have been killed, sir," she said as she rose to embrace him. "How fortunate that you left for Lucknow immediately after my wedding."

With a trace of tears making his blue eyes glisten, he enfolded her in his arms. "I was greatly grieved to hear of Conran's death. The dispatch I received stated that you had also been killed. How glad I am to see you well!" He kissed her cheek, then grasping her hands, held her at arm's length to study her face. "You've had a hard time of it, yet your sweet beauty remains intact. You remind me of a rose growing from the ruins of an ancient abbey. By the grace of God, such fragile persistence may outlive destruction."

Then he caught sight of Derek and stretched out his hand to clap him on the shoulder. Dawning recognition of Derek's deep love for Annalise shaded his voice as he said huskily, "You went after her, did you not, sir?"

Derek smiled. "Like a terrier, but I did not catch up with her until Kanpur." He described how Annalise had made her own way to Kanpur, and the frightening events that led them both to Lucknow.

Professor Sanderville's arm tightened about Annalise's shoulders. "Saved twice in the nick of time. You have more lives than a cat, child."

As she laid her head on Professor Sanderville's shoulder, Annalise felt a sudden intuition invade her mind. This is the moment, Annalise, she told herself. Derek is lost to you; you have known that since you left Claremore. If you would make your separation from him a quick, clean one, now is the time to do it. For a moment, she was silent, then she forced herself to speak before her distraught heart could intervene. "I should like you to sit beside me, Professor." She indicated the place between her and Derek. Both Derek and Sanderville looked startled, but to prevent an awkward moment, Sanderville took his seat as she requested. She served him herself from the remaining ham and rice, then turning all her attention upon him, saw to it that he wanted for nothing. She was so absorbed in pretending indifference to Derek that she missed Robert's discerning eye.

But Marian, who had paid no more attention to Robert than Annalise, spied her chance. She leaned against Derek's shoulder and offered him a stale cracker smeared with jam. "Dear Derek," she murmured huskily, "your little widow is smitten with an older man. How provoking."

Picking through the dried fruit on his plate, he ignored her, but she was not to be dismissed. "Why bother with Annalise when we might amuse one another, if only with trivial gossip?" she whispered. "I may be married, but I am not dead." She bent her head close to his. "Perhaps I should remind you of just how lively I can be?"

"You don't like to lose, do you?" he murmured back. "Why not just chalk me off as part of the price of vanity? I had the impression that you were genuinely fond of Rodney."

"Fond, but not frozen in stone like a medieval mourner.

Rodney won't be out of his sickbed for another several weeks at least; I don't see why that time should be spent in pious fasting''—she smiled intriguingly—''and dreary abstinence.'' Her gaze slid to the preoccupied Annalise. ''Why not? Perhaps your lady's heart will beat faster once she sees that you refuse to be tethered to her like a penitent to his rosary. You persist in seeing her as virtuous when she is not . . . entirely so. Perhaps you should see one another as you are, rather than as dubious saints.'' She smiled into his narrowed eyes. ''You always loved me for my sense of reality, remember? Nothing can be more real than this place. Tonight we dine, tomorrow we die.'' Her lashes lowered demurely beneath his penetrating gaze. ''You still find me attractive, for all that I am unlike Annalise as darkness the dawn . . . and the coolness of night can be a great relief when a man has spent too long in the sun.'' Boldly, she touched his cheek, and this time drew Annalise's hot-eyed gaze. With a little chuckle, she turned away. ''You'll come to me . . . in good time, but don't linger too long. Rodney is important to me in a way that you may never be.''

Robert noted his brother's fascinated but ironic gaze and had little difficulty in discerning that something was missing in Derek's expression. Sipping an acceptable port, he studied the interaction around him, and several things became clear. While Derek may have once been infatuated with Marian, he was not now. All his attention was on Annalise, whose attention was on Professor Sanderville. Even Jane, whose interest Robert would have much preferred to be upon himself, was more intent on Derek. Derek was larger than life to them all, a heroic figure, and therefore, a trifle unreal.

Marian was real enough; the sulfurously seductive look in her eyes that she bent on Derek said that trouble was brewing here; when and if Rodney rose from his sickbed, vengeance for either real or imagined causes might explode.

If Robert did not intervene.

But how? Robert arranged and rearranged the pieces of the puzzle in his mind, and finally arrived upon a single, simple answer. Derek had come to India with one woman on his mind, and that woman was not Marian but Annalise. He had given up his entire heritage and splendid prospects for Annalise; therefore, he ought to have her hand in marriage as compensation, at the very least. He also thought he had Annalise figured out. Robert was not in the least fooled by Annalise's too-determined preoccupation with the professor. She was attempting to separate herself from Derek, whom she adored; that much he knew from seeing them together at Claremore. She had married one man to be free of what she considered to be a fatal attachment to Derek; she was entirely capable of marrying another man for the same reason, and quite pointlessly. *Ergo*, Annalise ought to have Derek.

Marian ought to have Rodney.

And he himself ought to have pretty Jane, at least for the endurance of the siege.

That left Professor Sanderville to his shovel and archaic bits of dusty history, which was only appropriate, as Professor Sanderville was a dusty sort of man, as far as Robert was concerned.

"Miss Witherton," he said after thinking a few minutes more, "although we have spent little time together, I must say that I have rarely encountered so courageous a young woman. I cannot tell you how sorry I am that you have lost your parents; that you still grieve for them is evident, for you seem highly distracted tonight. May I be of assistance to you in any way?"

A trifle startled, Jane shifted her attention from Derek, her blue eyes widening. "I am so sorry. I did not realize that my preoccupation must have seemed negligent. I must confess that I was thinking of your brother, and not my parents' sad fate. I had the honor to know Colonel Clavell in Kanpur before he left for England. Everyone in the cantonment respected him; we greatly regretted his being wounded in the Kyber."

"I am sure Derek would appreciate those sentiments." Robert produced his most engaging smile. "You are very kind to think of him."

Jane flushed, fearing her interest was too evident. As Robert supposed she would, she changed the subject. "I believe you have recently acceded to the baronetcy at Claremore. You must have a great deal of responsibility."

He nodded seriously. "Particularly now that I am severed from all communication with England. I left Claremore in the keeping of my solicitor and steward, but can now give them no instruction . . ." He went on speaking of Claremore for several minutes, and at her evident interest, described the estate at length. Soon, his Clavell charm had her fascinated, but just as he thought he had her entire attention, he caught her stealing another look at Derek, who was watching Annalise and Professor Sanderville with grim frustration.

Swiftly, Robert changed tactics and shifted his conversation to Annalise. "Mrs. O'Reilly, I have heard my brother's description of your husband. I gather he was a formidable fellow."

Annalise looked up from the cracker she was spreading for the professor. "Conran was a trifle frightening in appearance, I admit," she replied softly, "but he was eminently kind. He could have soothed the smallest swallow and taught it to trust him. I was very sorry to lose him."

Robert shot a look at his brother. Derek's face was pensive, and Robert realized he had liked Conran O'Reilly. Continuing to gauge Derek's expression, Robert murmured, "I hope your grief will be soon ended, Mrs. O'Reilly. Life is often sweetest in times of greatest difficulty. May I walk with you after dinner? We have had no chance to speak together since you left Claremore.''

At Jane's discomfited expression and Robert's flirtatious inference, Annalise was taken aback, for she clearly remembered Robert's kiss on the river at Claremore. She glanced quickly at Derek's narrowing eyes, then turned her attention back to Robert. ''Yes, of course, if you like, but . . .''

''Good,'' Robert inserted quickly. ''You have not yet seen the rest of the rose garden, which flourishes despite the daily strife we endure. I'm sure the professor knows the many varieties which grow here.''

The moment his reference to the professor left his lips, he could have bitten his tongue, for Annalise quickly turned to Sanderville. ''Will you join us, sir? I should welcome a small lesson in horticulture.''

Sanderville, who had been paying little attention to the conversation and less to its undercurrents, smiled wryly. ''My only forte is antique pottery, I fear, Annalise. Besides, I have promised Lord Annandale that I will accompany him to General Havelock's quarters. Perhaps Miss Witherton knows something of roses . . .''

Jane could not miss Annalise's hopeful look. Hesitant at first, the former belle relented. ''Yes, I should very much like to come. We have had little opportunity to enjoy pastoral pursuits here. Some touch of gentleness would be welcome.''

''Mrs. O'Reilly's gentleness is well known,'' said Robert, deliberately misunderstanding Jane's inference. ''I fear Claremore will never be the same, now that she is gone from its gardens.''

So, willy-nilly, Annalise was obliged to accompany Robert and Jane. As they promenaded about the garden, Robert's reasons for inviting her were bewildering, for she had thought his interest in her ended before she left Sussex. Certainly his favors were democratically bestowed, for he flirted with Jane as much as he did with her. Although Jane was subdued at first, she rallied in the face of unexpected competition. The whole scenario was slightly unreal, in the face of Annalise's sari, Robert's grimy clothing, and Jane's torn, soiled dress that dragged the ground for lack of crinolines. They chatted so calmly of roses and acquaintances in common that they might have been back in London rather than a battered garden cratered and blasted by sepoy artillery. In the rapidly fading twilight, the garden was thronged with ghostlike figures as tattered and bedraggled as themselves. Hoping to capture some vestige of cool, peaceful breeze, much of the residency had turned out. The dim light leached most of the color not only from their clothes, but the roses as well. Jane confessed she could not tell one variety of flower from another.

"Like the light, we are stripped to essentials," Robert commented. "If the siege endures, there will be little left for the mutineers."

"Many of us are in despair. The death of Commissioner Lawrence four days into the siege was a blow," Jane told Annalise quietly. "We all had the highest hopes of General Havelock's escorting us out of here. Now we are still trapped."

"You must not lose hope," Annalise responded gently. "God has not forgotten us."

"But what if he declines our prayers as he did the poor wretches in Kanpur," put in Robert.

"How did you get word of Kanpur?"

"We use pigeons." His pensive expression took on a grim edge. "We picked up that trick from the mutineers. Of course, there has been little news, with all of it bad. I am beginning to think we might be better off living in ignorance." Then, noting the women's faces, he apologized. "I'm sorry. I didn't mean to put a damper on the evening.

We are fortunate that General Havelock broke through, of course. We may be on tight rations, but we are fairly well supplied, and with Havelock's help, should be able to hold out for another several months.'' He smiled at Annalise. ''Certainly, Derek was particularly lucky in finding you.''

She laughed softly. ''He was particularly persistent; that is one of his most endearing traits.''

Robert caught her hand. ''He *is* dear to you, isn't he . . .'' then seeing Jane's intent expression, quickly added, ''as a friend.''

''You are also dear to me, Robert . . . as a friend.''

Robert cast a sly glance at Jane. ''A man cannot have too many friends, particularly when they are as brave and lovely as you ladies.''

''Oh, I think a man can have too many friends,'' said Jane levelly, ''and when those friends are women, he may find himself in particular difficulty.''

Robert laughed. ''You may be right, but I am an amiable sort of fellow. When a lady smiles at me, I am apt to smile back. Of course, if the right lady smiled, I should be the epitome of faithfulness.''

''That should put you on a par with the average dog,'' dryly observed Derek, just behind him.

Not having heard his brother come up to them, Robert turned unabashedly to see both Derek and Professor Sanderville. ''I beg to disagree. Dogs drool; I am merely effusive.'

Then he grinned at his brother's ironic face. ''So you've finished with Havelock. What has he to say for our prospects?''

''Very little, but he does not think we are doomed. The mutineers lack the nerve to make a concerted attack, so unless they wear us down, we can hold out for some time. Of course, their sappers are making a concerted effort to beaver under our walls, so the enemy isn't sitting on his hands.'' He jerked his head toward the city. ''I would suggest we go into the residency now. It is too dark to be entirely safe out here."

Annalise took Professor Sanderville's arm. "I wish to speak to the professor, but we shall come in directly."

For a moment, Derek looked as if he might countermand her, but then reconsidered the impulse. "Very well," he said briefly. "Just don't be long."

After Derek had gone with Jane and Robert, Annalise turned to Professor Sanderville. "Sir, I must ask you a great favor, if an unlikely one. I hope I shall not insult you by being direct."

Sanderville patted her arm. "I shall be happy to assist you in any way I can. What is the difficulty?"

Annalise lowered her eyes a moment, then looked at him levelly. "As you may have guessed by my behavior in Kanpur, I formed an unfortunate attachment to Colonel Clavell when in England, and returned here to break off the relationship; I had hoped my marriage to Conran would end all possibility of its resumption. Unfortunately, that has not been the case . . ."

When she faltered, he finished for her. "You fear your own weakness for him."

"Yes," she admitted simply. "I love him. I should not, but I do."

He studied her a moment. "I fail to see the problem."

She flushed at being forced to explain. "His rank separates us as finally as the void between earth and moon. We can never be happy together."

"The earth and moon have gotten along amicably for eons; why should you be any exception?" Sanderville's peppery brows furrowed quizzically as he took her uncertain hand. "What do you fear? Clavell's money and social status?"

"I fear their effect upon his character," she answered in a troubled tone. "I fear his vanity may be too much touched by ambition and the manner in which his fellows see him. 'All is vanity,' William Shakespeare says, and I fear he is right."

Sanderville nodded. "The old bard was wise, but he was also a cynic. Perhaps Clavell has more depth of character than you think."

"Perhaps, but I do not believe he would let anything stand between him and his pride: even me."

Sanderville was silent for a moment. "What do you expect of me, child?"

"I want you to pretend that you yourself . . . love me. That you are ready to marry me." At the change in his face, she added hurriedly, "Certainly, you would never need to go so far as a proposal, and I would not ask you to make a pretense of courtship, if I were not desperate."

He began to sputter. "It won't work!" he concluded finally. "Besides, he'll never believe it. I'm old enough to be your grandfather."

"It worked once," she reiterated stubbornly. "He gave me up to Conran, and as for age . . . well, you would not be the first man who found a younger woman attractive."

"I was not thinking of my attraction to you, but the reverse," Sanderville countered dryly. "He will certainly never believe you are mooning after me."

"I shall make him believe it," she said resolutely. "He may persist in seeing our connection as one of convenience, but my reasons do not matter, so long as the fact remains."

"He'll probably shoot me," Sanderville observed morosely. "He already looks frustrated enough without having to contend with another man." For a time he said nothing, then a curious gleam entered his eyes and he smiled at her oddly. "All right, I'll do it. Shall I kiss you publicly at high noon tomorrow and watch him turn blue?"

"No, we must be subtle," she reproved, too relieved by

his agreement to ponder his motives. "We should take a week or two at least to become interested in one another."

"At least," he agreed dryly, then diverted her. "What of Robert Clavell? He seemed rather smitten with you tonight, but then I could not tell whether it was you or Jane who held him entranced. Derek may be persistent enough, but Robert appears to have a fickle mind."

"Robert is a harmless flirt. Truth to tell, I think he is more interested in Jane."

The professor tucked her arm in his. "I wonder. Somehow I have a feeling that Robert is less harmless than he looks."

She laughed. "As Marian would say, Robert is a pussycat. I can deal with him."

The professor shook his head soberly. "I have seen Robert in action these past months . . . and more tractable cats roar over bloody kills in Africa. Derek Clavell wears the same claws. You would do well to tread carefully."

She regarded him worriedly. "You aren't reconsidering, are you?"

Sanderville smiled at her crookedly. "For you, my dear, I would charge into the jaws of death . . . just remember that at age sixty-six, I am not so quick on my feet."

XVI

The Courtship

S*anderville* escorted her into the residency, then left her alone at the entrance of the women's quarters. As Annalise started to open the door, a hand brushed the back of her neck. Her nerves on edge after Havelock's rip through the mutineers' ranks that day, she stifled a sharp cry and whirled about, her back pressed against the doorjamb. A tall figure emerged from the shadows. "Derek," she whispered, shaken, "what are you doing here?"

"I had to see you," he said softly. "I want you with me tonight."

A shiver of remembrance ran up her spine. To lie with Derek was to lie with excitement, and danger . . . and forbidden delight. To lie with him was to surrender herself utterly to love forever denied. He was taking her into his arms. She must not succumb to him, for seeing Marian again had made her recall all the vast social void that lay between them. Yet the darkness of desire in his eyes was already flowing about her, overwhelming her like a lulling, irresistible dream.

He kissed her, his lips grazing hers like a subtle, stirring breath: an invitation to ecstasy. His fingertips glided along her spine, subtly tightening when she made a last effort to elude him. As his kiss slowly deepened, she closed her eyes. It was so simple not to think . . . only to feel, to have his arms enfold her and stir the slumberous coals of her passions. Her lips parted beneath his, her head slipping back so that her hair fell silkily across his arm.

"Love me, Lise," he whispered, nuzzling her throat. "Love me tonight . . ."

She must fight to keep her sanity, keep him at bay, or she was lost, yet it was so hard to keep struggling. She was unresisting in his arms; only some tiny fragment of her mind was pushing him away. She must get away.

And then he was kissing her again, taking her assent for granted, picking her up and carrying her down the hall to a still, silent room that was as black as velvet, as close as his hands slipping her sari away and sliding across her bare skin. She felt the thick, perspiration-damp fur of his chest brush her breasts, and hardness at his groin as he opened his clothing. Then he was kissing her again, all over, loving her with his lips and his hands, and finally his sex—warmly entering; and then, slow, sensuous thrusting. She wound herself about him, for the moment not caring that she should not be with him, should not be giving herself to him, when all she wanted was to give, and give, and give. She wanted to arch back and feel him all the way to the secret heart of her. She opened to him, giving way to sensation, her fingertips brushing through his hair, then tightening, grasping, as he took her into a roseate, glowing place where heat and light came together. A place where she was submerged in him, reveling in being beneath him and feeling his hard-muscled weight upon her, his sex deep inside her. His body shuddered, his breath coming in a long, husky rasp as their joining brought them to a single, mindless explosion. The light was blinding, delicately needling behind her closed lids and throughout her body, centering at the base of her belly. She felt an almost unbearable heat and weightlessness that melted her body into his, lifting her with him into another place, another time where they would always be joined together.

And yet, they were already separating, although his lips were still pressed to hers. Like an ebbing tide, the glory went, and her spirit seemed to close in upon itself. This love was never meant to be, her mind warned, its hard logic pressing past all the barriers she sought to erect. To love this man completely, she must accept him completely. She must bear the burden of his pride as well as his integrity.

And she could not.

Derek noted her stillness. His lips parted from hers, hovered as if he longed to kiss away her fears and reservations. His eyes were dark, beckoning her to linger and give him hope that he was not losing her irrevocably. "You know, don't you?" she whispered. "You know that nothing has changed. I cannot stay with you, Derek. This must be the last time we come together."

Filled with denial, his eyes held hers. "You love me, Lise, just as I love you. There can never be an end for us. Despite every reason you find to fight me, you still come to me as naturally as the rain falls upon this land. This year, and the next, as long as the earth spins through time, you will be mine."

"You are wrong, Derek," she whispered. "I belong to myself, and to God. God will not let me go against my conscience . . ."

"You give heed not to God, but your own fears," he said abruptly. "After all this time, you have never learned to trust me. What must I do to convince you of my loyalty? Give my life for you? I will; you know that."

She touched his face. "It is not your life that I seek, Derek, but your understanding. I cannot ask you to be what you are not. I cannot ask you to give up your inheritance."

He sat up and distractedly ran his hand through his hair. "I already *have* given up Claremore. It doesn't mean a tinker's damn to me without you."

Slowly, she rose and wrapped the sari about herself. "I shall not always be young and desirable, Derek." She held out her hands, palms down. "This face, this body will one day be lined. My hair will turn to gray as surely as the winter whitens the meadowlands of Sussex, while Claremore will be unchanged. One day you will regret your choice."

He sighed with a trace of impatience. "Life is full of possibilities. If someone falls asleep on guard duty, we may not live to see tomorrow's dawn. If the monsoons fail to come in time, we may run short of water. If the wind blows too hard, we may all fly away." He caught her hands. "I do not mean to make sport of your reservations, but we must live for today, not tomorrow or yesterday, particularly now that none of us knows if tomorrow will ever come."

Gently, she disengaged her hands. "I cannot do that, Derek. God exacts a reckoning for tomorrow as well as today. I will not bequeath my mistakes to my children."

He let out a short sound of exasperation, then smiled up at her wryly. "You will have us both grandparents if the siege holds long enough." He got to his feet. "Come, let me at least escort you to the women's quarters. A night's rest may ease your troubled mind."

After seeing her back to the women's wing, he kissed her again, slowly, as if he feared it might be for the last time. "Say that you will not make a final decision just yet. Give me a little time . . ."

"No," she answered softly, but firmly. "I am only

human, Derek, as you know all too well. If I persist in making love with you, I shall only weaken in my resolve. Please, please allow me the freedom to make my own choice."

He kissed her gently. "Very well, but I promise only that I shall not use devious methods of persuasion." His fingers tangled in her hair as he drew her head back for a second, lingering, sensuous kiss. "I shall be direct, Mrs. O'Reilly."

Her troubled eyes grew lambent as amusement took her. "Fie, sir, I confess I should not know how to live without a wolf at my door..."

As his lips grazed hers again, her eyes closed with a sense of languid surrender, then suddenly a peripheral glimpse of color startled her from her reverie. Her eyes opened, widened as she saw Marian watching them ironically from just inside the door. Annalise pressed at Derek's chest until his head lifted. "What's wrong?" he muttered dazedly, then noting her intent eyes, turned and caught sight of Marian, who smiled at them with a touch of self-mockery.

"Time for bed, children." Gathering her shift more tightly until it revealed the lush curves of her body, Marian turned and glided back into the women's preserve.

"Good night, Lise. I must go up to the roof to relieve the guard," Derek whispered with a final kiss. "May all the angels sing thee to sleep."

She held him to her for a moment, then reluctantly left him. Behind the canvas partition of a *chik*, the bare halls and rooms of the women's quarters were chalked in moonlight, and she saw Marian ahead of her, winding between women and children sleeping on the floor. At length, Marian found her space, and beckoned. "Here, beside me," she whispered. "Tomorrow, we will get you a straw tick."

Annalise settled on the floor. The bare boards were hard but cool, and she felt grateful to have the long day ended and a bundle of rags for a pillow. No one had gotten much sleep while Havelock's forces were fighting their way through the city, for at any moment, they expected to be annihilated. Now, all was silent and peaceful, but for the stirring of the sleepers and the occasional whimper of a child. Within minutes, she was nearly asleep, until she sensed a stealthy movement at her side that abruptly cleared her drowsing senses. Marian had put on her dress and was slipping out of the room. That woman! thought Annalise tiredly, suspecting mischief. I don't want to get up again. She debated a moment, then quickly arranging her sari, stole after the shadowy figure moving silently ahead of her.

Marian went directly to the residency roof, where the balcony overlooked the city. Spaced at some distance from one another, a dozen men with rifles stood and sat at intervals behind the columned balustrade surrounding the residency proper. Marian slipped from one to another, and directly approached Derek, whom she knew from his height and *puggaree*. He straightened abruptly when he saw her. "What are you doing up here?"

Annalise shrank back into the shadows behind a column. She could hear very little of the conversation, but she could see well enough. While she felt ashamed of spying, she did not trust Marian in the least, and while she desperately wanted to trust Derek, she remembered too well the pain that had come from doing so in Sussex. Marian had put out her hand to touch Derek's face. He did not embrace her, but neither did he pull back. Annalise heard Marian's soft, husky murmur, then Derek's lower tones. He shook his head negatively after a few moments, and Marian's voice rose with a trace of anger.

"Why not? Annalise has made it clear that she does not want you; she even married another man. Do you lack all pride?"

He laughed ironically. "What do you care? You married Rodney quickly enough when I left England."

"I love Rodney as I once did you," Marian retorted. "You were entirely different when you returned to England after being wounded in the Kyber. Your mind was not on me; it had already drifted to that mealy-mouthed church mouse." She glared at him. "I really cannot abide her, Derek. She pretends to be too virtuous, even though all the while in England, she looked at you with fire enough in her eyes to melt your father's coronet. She was after your money, and the title; now that you lack them, she wants no part of you."

"You're wrong there," returned Derek coolly. "If I were a plowboy, she might have me . . . but as far as she is concerned, a baronet can drop into the nearest well."

Marian frowned. "That doesn't make sense, and even less, now that you've given up the baronetcy."

"Annalise seems to feel my abdication makes no difference. She has fixed on Professor Sanderville as her ideal."

"Sanderville!" Marian's eyebrows shot up. "He's practically in his dotage!"

"But he *is* convenient. Annalise would dote on the devil himself if he kept me at bay." His eyes narrowed. "Look, Marian, don't ask me to make sense of her thinking. I am as much in the dark as you. The wench loves me to distraction . . . just as I do her, but she'll have none of me as a husband. Naught I do will change her mind."

"Then let her go, Derek. There are women enough to love you. I ought to know; I was one of them." She wound her arms about his neck and kissed him. "Try and forget me, if you can," she murmured. "It may be over between us, but some memories never die." She kissed him a second time, then with a reluctant smile, turned toward the stairs.

Annalise glared after Marian with a sulfurous glint in her eyes. No one, even Marian, would have described her at that moment, as mealy-mouthed. Although she had heard nothing of their conversation past mention of Sanderville,

Annalise had seen enough to fire her temper for a year. She did not wait to accuse Derek. How could she? After all, she had rejected him.

But still, he had not precisely fought Marian off, and Marian was a married woman.

Ready to give vent to her anger, she went after Marian, but was startled to see her turn away from the women's quarters; instead, Marian went to the infirmary, and directly to Rodney Overton's *charpoy*. After smoothing his brow with the greatest show of affection, Marian leaned down to kiss him. His hands clasped in hers, she settled down beside the *charpoy* and began to talk softly to him.

After a moment of hesitation, Annalise drew back to the door. She had no more right to upbraid Marian than Derek. In fact, she had no right to Derek at all. Pain began to wash away her anger, particularly at the sight of Marian's tenderness with her husband. How could Marian pretend to love Rodney so, if she did not? Was she telling the truth; did she genuinely care for Rodney?

Bewildered, Annalise backed away before she was seen and returned to her own sleeping place. Marian's embrace of Derek still filled her with pain, but then she had brought that pain upon herself, had she not? She had forsaken every tie to him because he was excessively proud, the one characteristic Marian accused him of lacking.

Over the next few weeks, the battle raged relentlessly. Annalise soon became a staunch admirer of the hardy souls who held the residency despite the continued battering of the mutineers. As the days slowly dragged by, to the nagging persistence of the sepoys' guns, Professor Sanderville played his role of Annalise's suitor to the hilt; in fact, to the point that she began to wonder if he remembered his role was pretense. Robert was equally devoted, until Derek began to be on edge. After Derek's daytime duties on the firing line were done, he and Annalise had several arguments. On one such night, his saturnine face in the moonlit garden was twisted with frustration. "I'm sorry, but you are driving me to distraction, Annalise . . ."

"Oh, don't let her do that," came Robert's gay baritone behind him. "When you're smitten, you're the absolute devil to live with."

Annalise and Derek both turned abruptly. "This is a private conversation, Robert," Derek informed his brother flatly. "You're unwelcome at the moment."

"Am I unwelcome?" Robert questioned Annalise with a knowing grin. He appeared to have grown certain of his position in the last few weeks and this was not the first time that fact had irked his brother.

Annalise smiled up at him with grave politeness, as careful as he to keep her attentions in balance. She did not wish permanent animosity to grow between him and Derek. "I am always glad to see you, Robert, and you need not apologize. Your brother and I were about to end our conversation."

"It's a relief to see that you're speaking," Robert said blithely. "You two seem so much at odds these last few days that I had begun to wonder. Making up?"

Derek gave his brother a disgusted look. "Mrs. O'Reilly and I are on perfect terms. Don't you have sniper duty at noon?"

"Too hot," retorted Robert amiably. "I traded with another fellow today. By the way, I met Havelock on the terrace a few minutes ago. He's looking for you . . . says it's important."

"Likely story," muttered Derek. "If he isn't, I'll be looking for *you*."

Robert grinned unabashedly. "You'll have no trouble finding me; I'll be with Annalise."

With a final scowl that promised a reckoning, Derek strode off in search of Havelock.

"Robert," murmured Annalise as her velvet gaze followed her beloved's back, "why do you persist in pretending an interest in me when you have none?"

"Ah, there you are mistaken," Robert assured her with a wicked grin. "I have the utmost interest in you, possibly only slightly less than has Derek."

She went to sit on a broken wrought-iron settee beneath a golden *mohur* tree and settled her skirts. "I believe you are altogether too bored and are playing at mischief. By courting me, you provoke everyone: Derek, Marian, Professor Sanderville . . . even Jane. Ah, yes, Jane."

"What about you? Are you angry with me?"

"I know you too well. You may have no liking for Marian, but you love Derek dearly and would see him have whatever he wants in life . . . in this case, whether it be wise or no. Too, I believe you are out to make Jane jealous. I have caught you watching for her reaction to your games from time to time. Why, though, do you harass Professor Sanderville?"

"Because I believe that by encouraging him, you may cause more difficulty than you wish. A jealous suitor is not only a barrier to Derek, but an enclosure about yourself. You will never make me believe that you would marry that old man, dote on you how he will."

"But he has never asked me to marry him, and you cannot be sure what I would do if he did."

Robert eyed her with a trace of concern. "You wouldn't accept him, would you? Not just to be rid of Derek."

"The last thing I want is to be *rid* of Derek, and I certainly don't wish to hurt him," she said softly. "I merely wish to set him free."

"Well," said Robert, "don't blame me if you throw a net

over the lot of us. I think the professor is serious about you."

"Only Professor Sanderville knows the extent of his interest," she said mildly. "I am sure he is in complete possession of his faculties."

"Really?" Robert's eyebrow raised, then he nodded in the direction of a shrub facing the battered residency porticoes. "Then why is he watching us with binoculars?"

Startled, Annalise swiveled her head to catch the sun's glint on a pair of field glasses from the shrubbery. A white pith helmet abruptly disappeared among the leaves as if it were a stopper sucked down a drain. "Good heavens," she whispered, appalled, "what can he be thinking of?"

Robert gave her a broad, mock-salacious grin. "The connubial delights of matrimony, no doubt."

She whitened and caught up the parasol Jane had lent her. "Do be serious!"

"Have you ever known the professor to be anything less than serious?" Robert turned, and sticking his fingers in his ears, deliberately made a face at the shrubbery.

Annalise swatted his shoulder with the parasol, then hurried off to the shrub. Robert's chuckle followed her. Doffing his cap to the professor, he strolled off.

"Is he gone?" queried Professor Sanderville in an irate voice as soon as Annalise bent over his portion of the thicket.

She cast an impatient look over her shoulder. "Entirely gone." She tugged him up by the coat collar. "Whatever are you doing in the bushes?"

Periscoping upward, he gave her a reddened, flustered look. "I was looking for butterflies."

"Then where is your net?"

"I forgot it," he responded lamely. "The excitement of the chase . . ."

"Poppycock," she said in a soft bewilderment. "You were following Robert and me. Whatever for?"

He gulped and straightened his tipped helmet. "I'm in love with you."

Her eyes widened with a touch of concern. "You mean you're pretending to be in love with me . . . as we agreed."

Flushing even redder, he shook his head slowly from side to side. He looked for all the world like a boy caught with his hand in the cookie jar.

"Oh, dear," said Annalise in a choked voice. "You don't mean it."

This time, he nodded up and down as if speechless with embarrassment.

"Oh, dear." Annalise's dismay became acute. "Please, you mustn't do this; it isn't part of the plan."

"Your plan; you never asked what I thought of it. I wasn't certain before you married Conran, but now I am. I love you . . . madly."

She helped him from the shrubbery and brushing him off, peered anxiously into his face. "You've been out in this heat too long; it's making us all lightheaded."

"I'm not so dizzy that I don't know my own mind." His tone held a touch of truculence as he brushed her hands away with dignity. "I'm quite all right, just taken a bit off guard, that's all."

Her eyes widened with horror. "You mean you've followed me before this?"

He drew himself up. "Only for two weeks. What do you take me for, some pathetic urchin?"

Annalise stumbled away from him back to the settee. He was on her heels. "I hope you will do me the courtesy of giving me an answer."

"To what?" she muttered dazedly.

"To my proposal. Obviously, I wouldn't make a confession of love without honoring it by a proposal."

She sat down hard with stunned desperation in her eyes. "I cannot marry you . . ."

"I realize I am some years your senior, but that should make no real difference in the long run. You need a protector. Who is better suited for that office than I?" His voice rose as he asserted his case. "Certainly not that young coxcomb who was just pressing his attentions upon you . . . and even less, Colonel Clavell, whom you have told me you wish to escape." He went to his knees and clasped her hand. "Say only that you will listen to my proposition, and I shall be a happy man."

In any other circumstances, Annalise would have been inclined to laugh, but as it was, he seemed so terribly in earnest that she could only pity him, and despise herself for not earlier realizing his inclination. She tried to let him down gently. "Truly, Professor, I do not think we are at all suited to one another . . ."

His grip tightened fervently on her hand. "I have had no chance to prove myself to you. My years do not make me a dotard. On the contrary, I can be as ardent a suitor as you could wish." Flashing a look over his shoulder as if to make certain he was unobserved, he clasped her in his arms.

Unable to believe he had not seen Derek coming swiftly toward them from the residency, Annalise tried to protest, but the professor's whiskery jaw scraped hers as he planted an eager kiss upon her lips and held her fast.

Too startled to be angry, Derek clasped the professor by the shoulder. "What is going on here, sir?"

Professor Sanderville shook him off with dignity. "Colonel, you intrude. Mrs. O'Reilly is my intended fiancée."

"But I never told you . . ." Annalise began.

He cut her off with a level stare. "Why, have you not given me every reason to hope during these last weeks?"

"Sir, I never meant . . ." Confused and distraught, she broke off, unsure of what to say.

"Truly, madame, you leave me to assume that you have led me on," asserted the professor angrily. He turned on Derek. "Have you any claim upon this lady, sir?"

"I have," Derek replied steadily, then stared fixedly at Annalise. "She is to be my wife."

Annalise's uncertainty was swiftly doused. She turned on Derek like a harried animal. "I am not! You have no right to make any such statement!"

Before Derek could give rebuttal, Professor Sanderville slapped him in the teeth. "Sir, you have insulted this lady. She may not have me, but I will not see her set upon by every Tom, Dick, and Harry who wishes to claim her. You are a cad, sir. I insist you meet me upon the field of honor."

"What?" Dumbfounded, Derek stared at him.

"I am calling you out, sir," the professor said succinctly, grim faced and tight-lipped, his fleshy jaw rippling.

Still dazed, Derek placed his hands on his hips. "You're out of your mind."

"You need not add insult to injury, Colonel. Will it be pistols or sabers?"

"Neither one," replied Derek flatly, his eyes narrowing. "I have no intention of fighting you."

"But you will, sir," Professor Sanderville warned, "or be considered a coward. I shall expect you in the rose garden at dawn with your second." He stalked off.

Derek peered after him. "Was I hearing things or did that old fellow just call me out?"

"He did," breathed Annalise in stricken amazement, "but it was all so quick. Surely, he cannot be serious."

"If he is, he's a lunatic," said Derek grimly. He started after Sanderville. "I'll have a talk with him and straighten all this out."

For a few moments, Annalise was too stunned to take action, then catching up her sari skirt, started after him. "No, Derek, let me talk to him. You were simply a witness to his embarrassment. After all, he must really be more angry with me for denying his suit; he may believe I have been playing some heedless game with him."

Derek swiveled. "Well, haven't you? You've been using him to keep me at arm's length these past weeks. He should be furious with you."

She ducked her head penitently. "I thought he saw me as a daughter, that he . . . but it doesn't matter now what I thought, I suppose." She looked after the professor, who had hurried up the residency steps. He encountered Jane, who caught at his arm, then stepped back, stunned, after he uttered a few terse words. "Oh, dear, I hope he's not telling everyone of his decision to fight." A crease of worry furrowed Annalise's smooth brow. "Perhaps I can persuade him to see Dr. Neville. He cannot be in his right mind." She started off after Sanderville, then whirled. "Surely, you do not mean to meet him as he demanded?"

"I can hardly refuse. It is a question of honor, isn't it? His, as well as mine." Before she could remonstrate with him, Derek turned on his heel and left her standing there, alone and suddenly terrified.

XVII

The Duel

As Annalise and Derek had feared, the entire population of the residency had turned out for the fight. The murky dawn light made visibility difficult, and the two men who had squared off jaw to jaw in the rose garden were almost ludicrously ill matched. No remonstrance had been able to dissuade the professor from defending his offended honor. His mutton-chop whiskers giving him the look of an irate badger, he had brought a newly sharpened ancient saber from the arms collection in the residency billiards room. Upbraiding Derek fiercely, he stalked back and forth before him and demanded that he fight. "Choose your weapons, sir! We have tarried too long at this business."

A head taller than the professor, and a head taller yet in his *puggaree*, Derek folded his arms across his chest and shook his head. "I have no quarrel with you, sir. If you have one with me, we must settle it in a manner befitting gentlemen, and not ruffians."

The professor let out a yelp of anger. "You dare insult me further, and before witnesses?" A fearful murmur went up from the crowd, and Robert, who had insisted upon being Derek's second, stepped quickly forward to intervene as the professor thrust his saber under Derek's nose. "You will give me satisfaction, sir, or I will peel your hide by inches!"

Annalise, who was anxiously standing behind the professor, caught at his arm. "You must desist," she pleaded. "The fault is mine, and not Derek's. Won't you let me apologize?"

"I will not," Sanderville stormed. "I will have it out with this fellow or know the reason why." He thrust his chin out and raised his voice. "You will fight me, sir, unless you wish to be known before one and all as a rank coward. I faced far better men than you in sporting trials at Oxford. Meet me with your fists if you have no braver option."

Flushing at the smart of Sanderville's blunt insinuation, Derek tried to keep his patience. He had already endured far more public insult from the professor than he would have tolerated from any other man and his exasperation was mounting. Nothing he said would dissuade the old man, but he could not, and would not, let his temper fly. As the second ranking officer in the compound, he had promised Havelock he would not risk his own life unnecessarily. Besides, he would not risk harming Sanderville; both he and Annalise were fond of the old fellow. "Come, sir," he said quietly, "will you not play a game of chess with me? Our minds are more equally matched than our muscles. There is no need for a bloodletting."

"A chess match?" Sanderville laughed bitterly. "I should say not. There, I should have you upon your knees in earnest. No, you have insulted me at a young man's game and I will have appropriate retribution."

As bewildered and dismayed as Annalise, Robert tried again to intervene. "Professor, surely some other way must suffice . . ."

Seeing Sanderville's adamant, truculent expression, Derek cut his brother off. "It's no use, Robert; the professor has made up his mind." He looked at Sanderville for a long moment in the growing morning light. "Sir, I shall not fight you and that is final, rail how you will."

"Ah, I think you will," snapped the professor, taking a broad swipe at Derek's sleeve. A snippet of fabric wafted to the earth as a gasp went up among the crowd clustered twenty yards away. Annalise let out a cry and Robert firmly thrust her aside before she could throw herself between the two men.

Although startled, Derek stood breathlessly still. "Leave off, sir," he warned, his brows knitting.

"Coward!" Sanderville cried loudly and deliberately. "Fight me or I shall whittle you to a toothpick." He stamped forward, on guard, and took another accurate swipe that opened Derek's jacket from shoulder to elbow.

"No!" cried Annalise. "Please don't hurt Derek!"

Robert caught her arms and held her.

"You must stay out of this," he muttered fiercely into her ear. "You have gotten Derek into it, but you don't stand a chance of getting him out. You can only make things worse by interfering."

"But the professor is going to kill him!"

She struggled fruitlessly, and Robert bore her away to the sidelines, where he addressed a solidly built gentleman. "Hold her fast, sir, lest she be hurt. If she continues to fight, carry her back into the residency."

The man nodded. "Done. I'll keep her safe enough." He jerked his head a bit worriedly as the pair squared off in the center of the ring of onlookers. "Your brother has himself in a fix. Why doesn't he swat the old man with the flat of a blade, send him head over heels, and be done with it. If I were him, I wouldn't stand there and let myself be called a coward."

"It's lucky you're not him," returned Robert tersely. "If you think my brother a coward, why not call him out yourself?" He strode back to Derek and Sanderville.

Marian, who had been standing with Jane, came up to Annalise. "How could you let it go this far?" she demanded. Her normally cool, patrician features were distorted with anger. "The professor is acting like a tyrannical child. He should have been your responsibility."

"I don't control him," protested Annalise. "How could I know he would take the bit in his teeth?"

"I had the impression, as did everyone else, that you knew the professor altogether too well," Marian grated. "He has trailed you about like a stud stallion ever since you came here. I never noticed you being out of control of him before."

"Do you think I want this?" Annalise bit out furiously, tears coming to her eyes. "I love Derek! But you all made it so impossible . . ." At Marian's chilling expression, she did not bother to explain. "What difference does it make? He belongs to you and your kind of life. That's what you want, isn't it? Isn't that why you're playing dog in the manger now?"

"I want to see him happy! He could have been so if you had not imposed such ridiculous standards of reverse snobbery upon him. Now his pride is being torn to ribbons over you, and he is just letting it happen! Is that what you wanted?"

Marian's words echoed and reechoed in Annalise's mind. She never wanted to see him humiliated! But Marian was right. Derek let Professor Sanderville publicly trample his pride—the pride she considered so overbearing and unswerving—because he refused to humiliate an old man.

Annalise watched in growing panic as Sanderville continued to slice bits of jacket from Derek, who refused to either retaliate or run away. Where was Havelock? she wondered frantically. Why didn't he come to stop this travesty?

Annalise felt her strength go out of her. She had been wrong about Derek, fearfully wrong. Now Derek might be killed because of her mistake. "Please," she murmured faintly to the man who gripped her arms, "let me go. I shan't try to run away."

"Sorry, ma'am. I was asked to keep you secure, and that's what I'll do." His grip tightened until he realized she was unsteady on her feet. Bending over her shoulder, he asked with some anxiety, "Are you all right?"

Marian too, noticed her pallor. "My God, are you going to faint?"

Annalise's eyes opened quite clearly. "Don't you think that would be a good idea?"

Jane instantly caught her drift. "Yes, do it! Do it now, before the professor misses his mark! He's going to draw blood in a moment!"

Annalise dropped like a rock and Jane let out a noisy shriek. "She's taken ill! Mrs. O'Reilly has taken ill! Oh, help! Help!"

Derek instantly started for Annalise, but the professor as quickly blocked his path, sword to his throat. "Leave her be, sir. The lady's faint is too well timed to be credible." Then, to Derek and Robert's astonishment, he broadly winked. Robert frowned in puzzlement, but Derek, desperate to reach Annalise, was quicker to fix on the most obvious intent of the professor's gambit.

"Why, you old fox," he breathed. "You set on me just to bring her into line."

Sanderville emitted a fearsome growl and took a roundhouse swing at his tall adversary. Derek let out a yell and clutched his arm. "Leave off! You've wounded me!" Beneath his breath, he hissed, "Watch what you're doing! You've drawn blood, you conniving old bully!"

Sanderville grinned and drew back his saber for another slice.

In view of Sanderville's bewildering behavior and maniacal glee, Robert was unconvinced of his good will. He clutched Derek's sleeve. "For God's sake, duck! He may be crazy!"

Fortunately, Derek took his advice, and Sanderville's next slice split Derek's *puggaree* instead of his scalp.

In a panic, Annalise wrenched at the man supporting her. "Stop, Professor! Please don't hurt . . ."

The words were knocked from her as the first shell of the day barreled from the sepoy artillery. The ball screeched past the residency roof and into the crowd. Shrieks of fear and pain went up with a billow of dirt clods and smoke. "Damn," swore the man who lay half atop her. "They've found the range at last."

The crowd scattered in all directions to escape the field of fire. Stunned, Annalise lay there until her head cleared and she saw Marian stumbling through the smoke. "Are you all right?" Marian called, then not waiting for an answer, gripped her under the armpits and helped her to her feet.

Annalise pushed hair from her eyes. "Where's Derek? And Robert? Are they safe?"

In answer, another ball whistled its eerie cry and splayed its brutal path into their midst. The shock knocked them to the ground again, and this time they stayed put, covering their heads with their hands. Dirt sprayed them, and through the rising yellow-gray cloud, people ran and screamed in fear. Through a gap in the smoke, Annalise saw Derek struggle dazedly to his knees, then spy her and Marian beyond the unearthed rosebushes razed by the last shell. The sepoy artillery crew paused to correct its aim to hit the residency, and Havelock's gunners sent an answering shell screeching toward enemy lines. Reaching Annalise and Marian, Derek jerked them up by the arms and steered them to the trenches dug on the far side of the garden. Through the smoke, they heard Jane calling shrilly, "Robert, Robert Clavell, where are you?" Seeing them, Jane waved to prove she was all right, then stumbling over the crumbled, uneven ground, resumed her search for Robert. As soon as he had seen Annalise and Marian to safety, Derek turned back to retrieve Jane.

"Give it up and come to the trenches," he ordered. "You'll get your head blown off out here."

"No, I must . . ."

Derek picked her up bodily and carried her from the field to where Annalise and Marian were waiting. "I'll find him. Just stay put." He dumped her unceremoniously with the two women, then hurried off again.

They noticed the incline of his body as he adroitly dodged the two craters, then another shell crashed into the ground just short of the residency and the shock of the explosion knocked him off his feet.

Half-stunned, and his head aching, Derek crawled to where he and Robert had been standing when the first shell hit. Robert was lying on the ground, clutching his blood-soaked knee, his teeth chattering with reaction. With an effort, he lifted his head from the ground when Derek reached him. "I can't feel my lower leg," he muttered, white faced. "I think my kneecap's shattered."

Derek examined the wound, then, his face haggard with concern, ripped the sleeve out of his own shirt and bound it as a tourniquet above Robert's knee. "Lean on me." Eliciting a shivering groan from his brother, he dragged Robert to an upright position, then pulled him to his feet. Stumbling underneath the weight, he headed down a gravel-strewn garden path toward the trenches. Sanderville, who had been half-buried beneath the debris from one of the shells, had dug himself out, and scurried after them, his short limbs jerky with alarm.

They converged simultaneously on the women and tumbled in a heap in the bottom of the trench. "My God," exclaimed the professor, "I'm sorry now I didn't dig deeper instead of protesting my age with each shovelful."

"As I recall," gritted Robert, a sweat of pain on his brow, "it was I . . . who first left for water."

"We will all have a chance to dig deeper if they knock the residency flat," commented Derek as flying glass sprayed the bushes over their heads and scattered in glistening shards on the ground. "Where the hell are Havelock's gunners?"

Havelock's gunners were in fact providing a steady thunder, each skillfully manned gun firing three times a minute, pouring their meager supply of shot and shell into desperate counter-battery fire, trying to silence the sepoy gun which had found their range. The cheer which rose from the gun emplacement before the residency and the blessed silence that followed were testimony that they had succeeded.

Carrying Robert between them almost as one body, the professor, Derek and Annalise lurched to the infirmary, where other wounded were being carried. The ones able to walk stumbled along as if they were in a daze, and Annalise picked up a child who was blindly wandering, its face covered with blood from a head wound. Jane was on Robert's far side, her shoulders bent beneath her share of his weight, and once tripping on an uprooted rosebush, she almost pitched headlong. Professor Sanderville relieved her. "My shoulders are broader than yours, Miss Witherton," he advised her quickly and propped Robert up to a more comfortable angle. They ducked inside the infirmary building with Marian in the lead. The hall was crowded, the traffic streaming all one way, and inside the infirmary proper, the wounded were beginning to collapse in the aisles and block all further flow. Dr. Neville was hurrying up and down, stepping over bodies, bending over others, his much-washed apron already blood soaked.

Experienced from many a foray on the battlefield, Derek lowered his brother to the floor and began to tend to him himself, for it was evident that Dr. Neville had his hands full. Having given his *puggaree* to Annalise to bind the child's head, he tore off his other sleeve to bandage Robert in an effort to stop the bleeding. Jane contributed part of her skirt, then cradled Robert's head in her lap. "Is the kneecap shattered?" Robert demanded shakily.

"Completely," was Derek's grim answer. "You'll be lucky to keep the leg."

Robert let his head fall back into Jane's lap and looked dazedly up at Marian who was studying him with a clinical frown. "Suppose we let bygones be bygones while you ferret up a bottle of brandy. I think I shall need it shortly."

Her expression softening, Marian crouched by his side and took his hand. "Will sherry do? I reserved half a bottle in case the sepoys broke into the residency. I thought I might die with some dignity if I were drunk."

In spite of his pain, Robert laughed in rueful derision. "Sherry couldn't make a chipmunk drunk, far less hardened soldiers like you and me."

Marian rose and dusted off her skirts. "How about sherry and a whalebone corset stay to bite on? That's my best offer."

Robert nodded, then winced as he tried to move his leg. "Done. Just don't dawdle."

Marian was off in a flurry of skirts. She paused momentarily to kiss Rodney as he passed her in the aisle, then she hurried up the stairs. Her husband came directly to the small group clustered about Robert. Hunkering down, he addressed Robert. "Sorry, old man. What rotten luck."

Robert regarded Rodney's russet cavalry whiskers and handsome, ruddy features. "God, you look disgustingly healthy for a man just done with dysentery."

With a rakish grin, Rodney snapped his suspender straps. "Fit as a fiddle. The trots wasted two inches off my waistline." He patted Robert's shoulder. "Never you mind. I owe my life to Marian and Annalise. With a pair of efficient nurses like those two, you'll be up and about in a month."

"In a month," Robert said grimly as he tried to sit up, "we'd all jolly well be out of here or we'll be fine, fat cannibals feasting on one another."

Derek firmly pressed his brother back down. Robert was shivering. "Stay put. You're in no condition to be moving about."

"But I feel fine in spite of this deuced leg," protested Robert.

Derek cranked back one of his eyelids. "You feel fine because you're going into shock. No sherry when Marian returns."

Robert made a skeptical face. Anxiety he was attempting to hide was etched in the lines of his pale, perspiring face. "That's hardhearted, brother. Do you think I've nerves of steel?"

Annalise wiped his brow. "Derek is right, Robert. You will have to do without alcohol, but I shall assist the doctor in the surgery. Dr. Neville is competent, and with any luck, we should save the leg." Her eyes dark with compassion, she motioned to Derek to keep Robert quiet, then rose to fetch Neville. "I shall return when Dr. Neville is ready for you. Meanwhile, he has need of me to help with the rest of the wounded."

Robert stared wistfully after her departing back. "I might have known a missionary's daughter would have no truck with good, sound liquor." His head fell back as if it were beginning to be too heavy for his neck. "Gad, my head seems to be floating off . . . either that, or you've all gone swimming." He tried to lift his head again, then gave it up, and after a time began to mutter phrases mixed with incomprehensible words.

Rodney shook his head, then worriedly craned after Annalise. "I hope she manages to persuade Dr. Neville to take your brother out of turn, Derek. He's loosing blood too quickly to linger here waiting."

Jane was white faced. "Surely, you do not think he will die?"

Professor Sanderville noted Derek's somber expression. "He might, and speedily. That knee is in splinters. To think of saving it is optimistic."

Derek was silent. He dreaded the impact of an amputation upon Robert, who was as active as himself. A man might conquer the pain of atrophied and scarred muscles to return to full mobility, but a missing limb was a missing limb.

Marian returned with the bottle of sherry, then left to give nursing assistance to the wounded now cramming the aisles. "At this rate," observed Professor Sanderville, "the infirmary will be overflowing. The sepoys must be bent on grinding us to a pulp today."

A half-hour went by, then another twenty minutes before Dr. Neville and Annalise reached Robert. Dr. Neville knelt down by his side and inspected the knee. "That leg will have to come off."

Noting the tightening in Derek's face, Annalise intervened. "Please, Doctor, don't you feel there might be some chance of saving it? I'm sure that Robert would rather risk his life than lose his leg."

Derek agreed. "Mrs. O'Reilly speaks for both Robert and myself. Robert would . . ."

Dr. Neville abruptly cut him off. "I simply haven't the time for proper sutures today. There are too many wounded waiting who may die if they are held back from attention while I work on your brother."

Annalise spoke up hurriedly. "I have often seen you suture, Doctor." She faltered shyly, then added, "If I could clear out the bone fragments and complete the sutures, would you handle the cauterization and set the bone?"

Dr. Neville frowned dubiously. "Embroidery is one thing, Mrs. O'Reilly, but if you have never sewn on human flesh . . ."

"I can manage, Doctor, if you will only allow me to try."

Neville eyed her white, determined lips, then directed his gaze on Derek. "You are the patient's closest relation, sir. What is your decision?"

Derek's lips set in a straight line. "We'll try it. I can assist Mrs. O'Reilly."

Neville nodded tersely. "Very well. Set him up on the table over by the south window. The light is getting better and the sun should be coming in soon. You'll all be needed to hold him still while Mrs. O'Reilly stitches. I rather doubt if she can accommodate a twitching patient on her first effort." He produced a long tweezers, a shard of glass wrapped in a white square of paper, a pocket skein of catgut, and a hooked suture needle. "I want you to clean the wound of bone splinters, then irrigate it with boiled water . . . Miss Jane, hold the teakettle. I can spare a little carbolic.

"Use the glass shard to cut away truly mangled flesh," Neville continued, "but leave as much as you can. Use the catgut to tie off any blood vessels you can find and stitch what flesh you can back together. What else . . . oh, I'll send someone with clean lint if we can find some. Good luck, Mrs. O'Reilly."

Rodney stood by Robert's shoulder while Derek sat on the wounded leg and Professor Sanderville took the other. Annalise took a deep breath, then delicately inserted the tweezers into the wound. Robert groaned, his face and neck beading with sweat. Her own damp face beginning to show smooth diamonds of perspiration, Annalise bit her lower lip as she stiffened to avoid flinching. The tweezers dug in again and Robert jerked against the combined weight of the men holding him down. "Please, keep him still," Annalise whispered, "otherwise, I may accidentally sever another blood vessel." She worked on Robert for some time until all the splinters and small gobbets of flesh were cleared away, then began taking tiny stitches to suture the wound. Robert tried to thrash, his neck cording against the pain as his struggles proved futile.

Derek watched Annalise's small, set face as she concentrated upon her work. He could see that she was afraid, and desperately uncertain of her ability, yet stitch by patient stitch, she closed the severed blood vessels. Finally, her skin waxen, she waved to Dr. Neville. "He's ready for you."

The scream that issued from Robert's throat when the wound was cauterized chilled all their hearts. The stench of burnt flesh mingled sickeningly with all the infirmary's other foul and bloody smells, and momentarily, Annalise flinched away from the sight of the red-hot iron being pressed against Robert's leg. Derek caught her elbow to steady her. "Hang on," he whispered. "You've done your part. Let's just pray his famous Clavell luck is still with him."

Robert was unconscious by the time Dr. Neville finished setting his leg, and Neville was not optimistic. "Well, that is the best we can do for him. We can only hope to avoid gangrene." He turned to Annalise. "Let me know immediately if there is any sign of the wound turning putrid."

"I will, sir," she replied quietly.

Derek gave her shoulders a brief squeeze of reassurance. "I must go back into the breach, but I am sure Jane will stay with Robert until nightfall."

Jane looked up from Robert's face, her eyes wide with concern. "Of course, I shall be glad to be with him. Annalise must be freed to assist the other nurses." She blotted Robert's damp brow with her handkerchief, then grimaced when it came away soiled with the dirt from the shelling. "Surely, there is water for the wounded? Robert is likely to turn feverish."

Annalise escorted her to the water barrel. "Only four dipperfuls per patient per day." Out of the corner of her eye, she saw Derek wave to her as he left the infirmary. She turned toward him, her heart in her eyes.

Please, God, keep him safe, she prayed silently as she gave him an answering wave. I have held apart from him too long. Do not let me lose him now.

Then he was gone, leaving in his wake the milling of desperately hurt and frightened people. The compressed heat of the infirmary suddenly became stifling. She felt dizzy with the scent of blood and waste from those helpless wounded who soiled themselves where they lay.

But it was the responsibility that affected her more than the heat and stench, she realized, steadying herself against the water barrel. The magnitude of what she had done began to dawn, and her hands trembled. It was an appalling realization that she, untrained, inexperienced, was one of the best surgeons in the residency, for no one else was available. How could they possibly hold out month upon month with daily casualties that threatened to overwhelm them? Where did everyone find so much courage? Jane was as pale and intimidated as herself, and Jane was unused to the rigors of the infirmary. For her to volunteer to stay with Robert had required courage, and for the first time, Annalise found herself genuinely admiring the lofty Miss Witherton.

And not only Jane, but Derek, had drawn her respect this day. When he let himself be publicly humiliated, refusing to risk harming an old man in a duel he would have won handily, he had proven himself to be more than the man she thought him. Not only had Derek shown generosity and compassion, he was flexible enough to soften his stringent code of honor and compromise his pride. Professor Sanderville was his inferior socially and physically, yet Derek had faced him without ridicule and left him his dignity. He had not even defended his refusal by belittling his opponent. Derek had let himself appear smaller in order to make Sanderville appear large, and then revealed a fundamental depth in him she had not suspected.

The realization had sprung upon her, full force. If he had not belittled Professor Sanderville, whom he respected, he would not belittle her, whom he loved. She had never wanted to be aught but his equal, and now inadvertently, he had shown her she would never be less.

She had been wrong in thinking Derek a blind snob, Annalise thought suddenly. Because she so resented Marian, she had put Marian's sneering traits upon him as well . . . and yet, like Jane, Marian had courage, and was indomitable under fire. Despite her fierce resentment of rivals, Marian was not entirely the vile, shallow creature Annalise had thought her.

In the same manner, Derek might not be perfect, but he was admirable . . . and eminently lovable. She closed her eyes, a fervent prayer rising from her heart. Out of fear and blindness, she had wasted so much time in running away from Derek. If God would only grant her time to prove her love to him. Surely, just one more day . . .

The hours wore on, and fresh bloodstains blotched over the old ones on Annalise's worn white sari. For much of the day, she worked at Marian's side, silently complementing her skills. Finally, at day's end, Marian turned to her. "I owe you an apology," she said evenly. "You're a good nurse and a strong woman. I could want no more in a sister."

Startled, Annalise was silent for a moment, then held out her hand. "I do not know whether we can be friends, but I hope so. I have come to admire you, Lady Sheffield"—her eyes twinkled—"whatever I might have once liked to think."

Marian laughed. "You're as honest as I am; that is rather more like a sister than I would like. Suppose we simply declare *pax* for the time being and see how it goes." She linked her arm in Annalise's and, their days's work done, they walked over to Jane, who was trying to recushion Robert's leg. Stirring fitfully, he opened his eyes.

"How is the patient?" Annalise asked softly.

"Irritable," gritted Robert, "and damned uncomfortable, but also damned glad to still have a leg that can ache like blazes." He smiled weakly up at Annalise. "I gather I have you to thank for that."

Annalise laughed. "Thank my mother; she taught me how to sew."

"Where is Derek?"

"Sniping on the roof," said Marian gleefully. "I took him some water, and at last count, he had dropped a mutineer for every bullet spent. When I accused him of exaggeration, he gave me a demonstration. The man is a dead shot, no pun intended. He dropped three of the blackguards, as neatly as sitting partridges, while I watched. I think he's evening the score for you, Robert."

"Good for him. I wish I were at his side. I feel like such a waste, lying here."

"Resign yourself," said Annalise. "You will not be moving for a month."

"If we last that long," mused Robert grimly. He tried to shift his leg and gave a faint yelp of pain. "What time is it?"

"Time for you to go back to sleep if you can," replied Annalise. "You need all the rest you can manage."

Robert let out a short sound of exasperation. "Why not? Have I anything else to do?"

"He always was a good patient," affirmed Marian dryly. "I don't envy you, Jane." She stooped to inspect Robert's bandage.

"Will you excuse me?" inserted Annalise, leaning slightly over her shoulder. "I promise to be back by the next shift."

"Don't bother," said Marian. "You've been on duty for twelve hours. You may as well have some sleep."

XVIII

The Farewell

Annalise met Derek coming down the stairs. "How is Robert?" he asked.

"As well as can be expected," she answered softly. "He's in more pain than he admits, but his strength seems to be holding." She touched his arm. "I know you are eager to see him, but could we steal just a few moments to talk?" She faltered. "I have so much I want to say to you."

He studied the mysterious depths of her lovely eyes. Fatigue marked her pale face, while her slender body was fighting off weariness. "Don't you want to rest?" he questioned gently. "Surely, anything important between us can wait a little longer."

"No, I'm afraid not. The most important thing has already been put off far too long. Is there somewhere private we can go?"

He took her arm. "The roof; it was almost deserted when I came downstairs."

Slowly, they mounted the stairs. As the last slanting rays of sundown cut across the open doorway to the roof, Annalise saw that Derek was as weary as she. Like her, he had gotten no sleep the night before, between guard duty and the impending confrontation with Professor Sanderville. His face was covered with reddish dust, his skin burnt to a deep mahogany by the day's unrelenting sun. Even without his *puggaree*, he looked dark enough to pass for an Indian. The mauve twilight dusk fell quickly as they darted across the roof and found a niche secure from the sepoy guns still trained on the residency. Annalise let herself sink down into Derek's arms. He kissed her softly, then smoothed her bedraggled hair back from her brow. "What's wrong, my love? Your face is troubled."

She was silent for some time, not knowing quite how to begin. Finally, she said simply, "I am sorry, Derek. I have made a great mistake in believing your pride dearer to you than anything else. You might have humiliated Professor Sanderville as a foolish old man, even killed him today, but instead, you endured his insults and accusations beyond the point where most men would have fought. Once, I ran away from you because I believed you too proud"—her head lowered, her long lashes flickering downward—"but I am not running anymore." Then she looked at him levelly. "I haven't looked over my shoulder in so long . . . I haven't dared. Now, I'm unsure whether you're still there."

His lips curved quizzically. "Let me get this straight. You're telling me you want me now . . . because I behaved like a coward."

"Exactly," she said softly. "But then man has always held woman to be incomprehensible."

His lips hovered over hers. "Bewitching, bewildering . . . and fascinating." He kissed her lingeringly, as if she were some long-awaited and unbelievably sweet dream come true. The kiss deepened, lengthened until its slow, fevered honey overtook all her other senses. Her head slipped back against his arm, she sighed, a childishly beatific smile curving her lips.

"I should have thought you would make me plead just the slightest bit. After all, I have given you a very difficult time. You're owed a little groveling."

He laughed. "Old soldiers never test their luck. I've waited too long for you to quibble now." He kissed her again, taking his time, savoring each delectable moment. A little dazed, he finally lifted his head. "I cannot believe it," he breathed. "Truly, I had given up hope. I cannot imagine that so simple a thing as my consideration for an old man could affect you so completely. I should have offered to hold his hat while he carved me into a plate of hors d'oeuvres."

"I'm very glad you didn't. I was terrified for both of you." Her eyes darkened gravely. "If a fight had resulted, I should have been completely at fault. I had no idea that the professor would take his courtship so seriously when it began in so false a manner. After all, I made it clear in the beginning that I merely wanted to discourage you."

Derek was silent for a moment, his eyes pensive. "Do you know, I think the old boy played out your charade to suit his own ends. He may have foreseen that I would refuse to fight him, thereby either winning your admiration or frightening the living daylights out of you. If so, he judged us both correctly."

Her eyes widened. "Why, the sly old boots! I shouldn't wonder. He's been behaving like a perfectly sane man since that aborted duel. In fact, he has been treating me like a comfortable armchair. If he is a man foresworn, he certainly is amiable about it." The more she considered the idea, the more its likelihood was apparent and comic. She burst out laughing. "Why, I feel like an idiot! Which is precisely what he must have intended."

"But if I had answered his challenge," observed Derek dryly, "the story might have ended quite differently. He could have ended up with a saber through his gizzard. I must remember never to wager with the man. He's too adroit a gambler."

Annalise sobered, her lovely face shaded by the quickly fading light. "I might have brought about a tragedy today. . . but no matter how fortunately the situation ended, I am ashamed to confess that Professor Sanderville knew you better than I." She paused, distress touching her eyes. "I love you desperately. How could I have been so mistaken about your character?"

He tipped her chin up. "Because I once gave you grave reason to doubt me when you were deeply vulnerable to any hurt. I should not have kissed Marian, but for a few, foolish moments, I surrendered to impulse because I felt free of responsibility to you. I was too new to that responsibility, too selfish to understand that your unselfishness was not to be taken for granted. I have counted the cost since, and it has come hard." His fingertips caressed her cheek. "Today, I came to understand why you are so precious to me. I wanted Marian, but I want you far more, and when you assisted Dr. Neville in Robert's surgery today, I knew why. For all your gentleness and hatred of war, you were there when Robert needed you. You were afraid and uncertain, yet you reassured him quietly and did your utmost to help him. In saving his leg, you may well have saved his life.

"If I have gained any serenity," he continued, "I have gained it from you. You have both courage and modesty: rare traits to find together." A wry, self-deprecatory smile crossed his lips. "Also, as an honest woman, you are a level to my flamboyant character."

Her own smile teased his. "What a practical lover you

are . . . but how can you call me honest when I deceived you for so long with Professor Sanderville?''

His arms tightened about her. ''Deceived me? What can an angel, albeit a mischievous one, know of deception? God grant you never learn to feign your love for me, for I have been as distraught as any jilted suitor. Had the professor been twenty years younger, I should have skewered him cheerfully.'' He kissed her, his lips tracing a flame that darted through her entire being. ''You have led me a merry chase, and now, my sweet love, you must pay.'' He picked her up and carried her down the stairs. In minutes, they were isolated in the tiny room where they had first made love in the residency. Through the broken windows, the mauve and copper light sifted like a diaphanous drapery across the cool, bare, parquetry floor. The gilded molding framing the faded ivory panels on the walls caught glints of bronze that played through Annalise's dusky hair as it spilled free into Derek's hands. He wrapped the dark tresses about her throat as he kissed her deeply, his arms encircling her, his body melting into hers. ''I love you,'' he whispered, ''more than I ever dreamed possible. Please, never abandon me again to fear of losing you.''

''I shall not,'' she answered quietly. ''I am yours, now and forever. You have taught me to trust in you, and I shall never forget the lesson.'' She kissed him then, softly and with all her heart, offered him all he would have of her.

''Lise, Lise,'' he murmured as he sank with her to the floor. ''How long I have waited for this moment . . .'' His lips grazed her throat, her shoulder as he bared its whiteness. Slowly, he undid the tiny fastenings of her bodice, releasing her full, high breasts to the searching heat of his mouth.

She sighed, winding her fingers through his dark hair, letting his lips graze where they would until the roseate crests he sought bloomed with aching delight. ''Oh, Derek,'' she whispered, "hold me now for all the moments I have thrown away. Love me now as if we will never love again."

For a moment, he hesitated, startling her, then as if he were in reality making love to her for the last time, his hands sought her as a blind man might, as if he were rediscovering her both anew and in farewell. His fingertips were sensitive as moth wings, grazing her earlobes, then the nape of her neck, and down her spine where the bodice had come undone. The bodice slid to the floor, leaving her slim body bare to the waist. Slowly, he unwound the sari still twined about her hips and let it slip free. Like an ivory goddess, she was naked to him, her jeweled eyes glowing in the semi-darkness as she wound her arms about him. His clothing soon joined her upon the floor, and naked, they serpentined together, his skin dark against her pale flesh.

She arched against him as his caresses made her senses swim. They might have been floating in a sea of longing, the wavelets slowly growing, rising to lap against them. Silken sensation swept over their bodies, curling, foaming as he lifted her above him to enter her in a single surge, and then the sea caught fire, its incandescent light sweeping high. The tides of their passion rose as Derek's hands slid over her, knowing instinctively how to make her cry out for him, plead with him to take her *there*, to that high, flame-encircled place of splendor where the starry constellations streaked across the night sky and set it ablaze. The sensual rhythms of their lovemaking mounted, soared, and she cried out against his lips as the starlight seared them, wrapping around them like a lustrous, lambent cocoon of spinning lights. Then, all at once, the stars went white-hot against the inky blackness and Annalise's choked cry echoed about the small, gilded room, bringing the night of their passion cascading down, down like the sweep of her heavy hair against Derek's chest. His face buried in her neck, Derek let out a muted sound that interwound with hers as if they were a single spirit woven together with blazing ecstasy.

Slowly, the starlight faded, leaving them drifting in the mists of somnolent time. The tide of passion ebbed, slipped away to a tenuous thread that never quite disappeared, never quite left them separate. Annalise slowly grazed her cheek against the dark fur of Derek's chest, felt it tease and caress her until she laughed softly. "How I have missed you. You are like a great bear who terrifies me with his fierceness, yet is unbelievably gentle when I reach out to him."

His lips curved. "Was I so gentle when we made love?"

She chuckled. "No, you were delightfully ferocious. You must have me for your dinner every night."

Seeing the gay light in her eyes, he sobered, and when he spoke, his voice was grave. "We shall not be together every night, sweet. Havelock has given me an assignment."

Instantly, her gaity faded. "Is it dangerous?"

He smoothed her hair. "You've heard the artillery in the distance outside the city for the last few days. Havelock believes that a relief force is on its way to Lucknow under command of a General Campbell. As I speak Urdu and look the part of a Muslim, I am to meet Campbell's troops outside the city and lead them to the residency."

She paled. "But that is suicidal! How will you get past the sepoys?"

"By mingling with them . . . temporarily. I leave just before dawn three days hence." He paused. "So as you see, I had a second reason for not fighting Professor Sanderville."

She nodded in understanding. "You could not risk jeopardizing your mission."

"Unfortunately, the mutineers must also know Campbell is on his way and will make an extra effort to seize the residency. You will be in as much danger as I." He wound her hair about his hand and drew her down to meet his lips.

"Promise me that you will take care. When I leave you behind, I leave all my heart and hope."

"I shall be here . . . waiting when you return," she breathed. "I should wait a thousand forevers for you, only . . . *do* please come back to me."

He kissed her softly. "I will try . . . so long as I breathe." His fingers traced her lips as if he were memorizing them. "Watch over Robert for me."

"You need not fear. I shall take the best possible care of him . . . and Marian."

He smiled crookedly. "That's a large promise. Even I couldn't keep Marian leashed . . . but you're right; I still care for her . . . as a friend."

"I think she could be a friend to me as well, if I gave her the chance."

His eyes narrowed slightly. "I wouldn't be too sure. Marian has her good points, but she is a natural predator. I once loved her boldness as well as her beauty, but I learned even as a boy not to trust her too far. To be kept guessing is well enough when one is a child, but unpredictability taken too far can become fickleness. I do not envy Rodney"—he kissed her nose—"but I think Rodney envies me."

A dubious smile crossed her lips. "That is surely your imagination. Marian has his whole attention."

His arms wound more tightly about her. "If I am ever jealous, you are ever modest. Robert may have been playing at love with you, but Rodney has not Robert's playfulness. He may have guessed that Marian's body may be his, but not her mind. For once, playing upon a man's jealousies has not gotten Marian the results she wished. I think he has begun to regret marrying her."

Annalise frowned. "Whatever makes you believe that?"

"Nothing tangible, but there's something in his eyes when he looks at her: a disillusionment that appeared a little while after we arrived here."

"Perhaps he sensed she was still interested in you."

"Interested? If she had thrown herself at my head any harder, I should have been challenged by Rodney rather than Professor Sanderville."

Annalise's frown deepened. "But I got the distinct impression that she loved him."

"I think she does, but she still loathes losing to you. You're happy; she's not . . . but then she has always been too dissatisfied to be happy. I represented some impossible aura of perpetual excitement to her. Life with me was to be some carousel of adventure, and yet she could not abide the idea of leaving Sussex and her established domain. I don't think she ever adjusted to the irreconcilability of her ambitions."

"Certainly, she has had adventure enough to last a lifetime here at Lucknow. Perhaps it has ceased to be such a need for her."

"Perhaps, but all the same, I would not rely too completely upon her good will." He kissed her lingeringly. "But enough talk of Marian. I don't want to waste a moment of the time we have left." His lips shifted to her temple, trailed to her earlobe, then the hollow of her neck. "Have you ever heard of the *Kama Sutra*, my shy dove?"

"Never," she murmured between kisses.

"You might be interested to learn that Indian mythology and religion is highly erotic. The *Kama Sutra*, for instance, is a book which highlights virtually endless and intricate ways of making love."

"Indeed," she breathed, her eyes seductive beneath their long lashes. "I must confess that I am a near illiterate when it comes to South Asian culture . . . not that I am interested in a professional lecture. Suppose you detail the *Kama Sutra* . . . more directly."

"Gladly, ma'am. Suppose we begin with the basics so wholeheartedly supported by you industrious missionaries."

He drew her down under him, his lips slowly molding to hers.

After a long moment, she winged her arms out and about his neck. "Revelation."

The next few days went by too quickly for Annalise and Derek. As often as possible, they stole away together, but their separate responsibilities often kept them apart and plagued by exhaustion. Despite their fatigue, they made love feverishly, aware each time might be the last. The *Kama Sutra* was soon abandoned, their fertile imaginations taking over their passionate inclinations. Love-swept, they lost all sense of time in one another's arms, knowing only that time was stealing away.

The intensity of their relationship was not lost on the others, particularly Marian, whose interest in Derek quixotically rose as she sensed his interest in her was gone, finally and forever. One morning, she accosted him in a deserted hallway when he was *en route* to Havelock's quarters. Her long, white fingers brushed his sleeve as he passed. "Darling," she murmured urgently, "I must talk to you while we have a moment alone. Rodney is already with Havelock. He tells me you are to undertake a perilous mission now that there is a possibility of being relieved by General Campbell."

Derek nodded soberly. "I leave tonight."

She clasped his shoulders. "Come back to me. I couldn't bear to lose you now."

Gently, he detached her grip. "Marian, you are a married woman now. Whatever was between us is gone. You have Rodney and I have Annalise."

"But she . . ."

"She is to be my bride as soon as her term of mourning is done."

Marian's green eyes narrowed with a flare of temper.

"How can she be such a hypocrite? I know damnably well that you have been bedding her . . . and quite regularly of late. She has not used her *charpoy* in the last three nights. Besides, she has made it eminently clear that she does not wish to marry you. What of Sanderville . . . *and* Robert? Both of them probably have as much claim to her as you."

"Marian, you of all women should have no right to chide Annalise for changing her mind," he said quietly, "and as for our being lovers, we *were* lovers before she ever met Conran. Sanderville, Robert, *and* you have nothing to say about it."

Marian's face twisted with pain and anger. "You never loved me. You used me . . ."

He gave her an impatient, little shake. "Stop it, Marian. I loved you, madly. You left me, not the other way around, but it's just as well. Once Annalise came into my life, there was never really any other woman for me. I will always remember you affectionately, but our time together is done."

She slapped him, hard, then raised her hand to claw at his eyes. As he swiftly started to fend her off, she abruptly changed tactics to a silken, menacing purr. "You're wrong about our being done, Derek. You'll come back to me. Just wait and see." She flicked back her skirts and strode off.

Derek watched her determined figure with some trepidation. With Marian on the warpath, Annalise was too innocent of feminine battle tactics to anticipate Marian's ploys. And whatever happened, he had no choice but to complete the mission for Havelock.

Somehow, though, he felt uneasy. He had best ask Sanderville to watch over Annalise. While Marian often made promises she did not keep, he had an idea that this was not one of them.

He bade Annalise farewell at dusk in the small, gilded room. She was there before him, waiting in her simple, ragged sari, her hair hanging in a sleek skein down her back. Although there were bruises of fatigue beneath her eyes, he thought she had never been so beautiful. She seemed smaller and younger than she was, yet somehow ageless, as if she had already become a memory to him. He was unable to rid himself of the sensation that he would never see her again, and when he sank to his knees to kiss her, it was with a sad wistfulness of longing, a deep hunger never to be satisfied. She came into his arms with the trust of a child and the fire of a woman. Silken soft, she nuzzled his throat, the hollow of his neck where his shirt had opened. Her hands slipped under the loose cotton and brushed his nipples, her lips parting beneath his as his arms tightened about her. "Lise, we've only a little time," he said huskily when he finally lifted his head. "I've asked Robert to make a place for you at Claremore if anything happens to me. You will be able to live comfortably for the rest of your days with income from the estate . . . wherever you like."

"Please," she said softly, "don't speak as if you are never coming back. I have so much fear in my heart tonight . . . and so much love." She touched his lips, her eyes dark with pain and need. "Kiss me, my beloved. Let me feel your heartbeat against my breast, so that in this long night, I may remember it and believe we shall both see the dawn. I love you with all my being . . ." Her voice faltered, and he took the rest of her words away with an agonized kiss. The coming night seemed to close about them with a deceptive tenderness that banished the promise of morning. Her sari parted easily beneath his caressing fingers, letting them glide softly over her bare, flushed skin. The gauzy fabric slipped from her shoulders to slide to the floor where it lay like a soft, filmy cushion to capture the spill of her dusky hair. She curved against him, her lips pressed against his in a growing tumult of anticipation as she felt the hardness of his sex against her thigh.

He let her slip back to the *charpoy*, his lips trailing between her breasts to her navel, his tongue teasing as he moved lower, then lifted her to him. Her back arching, she sighed as he found the secret heart of her femininity, his caresses stirring her to wanton rapture. Her fingers tangled in his hair, knotted as liquid heat coursed through her body like a play of summer lightning. The probing of his tongue became unbearable, causing her to open to him, beg him with small, uncontrolled whimpers in her throat to enter her, fill her . . . and when he succumbed to her pleading, to cry out in a soft, husky voice, "Now, yes . . . now. Please, I want all of you inside me . . . loving me." Transported by desire, she wrapped her legs about his hips, trapping him sweetly where he most wanted to be.

He surged within her, his body moving like a powerful sea tide, drawing her out with him, farther and farther from the safe shore of gentleness into a growing whirlpool of violent, mindless sensation. The tide rose, its spume enveloping them both as it swirled about them in a roseate cocoon of desire. Annalise moaned, took Derek deeper, until the sheer size of him within her, forging to the center of her urgency, answered her spindrift longing only to make it wild and chaotic once more. Their passion was like a storm, with brief lulls and ebbs between its overwhelming gales. Lightning played across the sky, caught the tips of high, white waves of desire that were almost frightening in their power, then let them crash down to engulfing abysses of creamy foam. The surging of Derek's sex within her quickened, grew ever more intense until she writhed beneath him, her body arching desperately against his in overwhelming need. The quicksilver moment of passion's peak came, and came again, to repeat like a shiver against scalding glass. Derek's release cascaded in a molten lava flow, hurrying to meet the sea.

For a long while, they lay entwined together, then made

love again, and again, until they were spent with exhaustion and satiety. The molten sea's roar became an echo reluctant to fade until finally it was gone, leaving only a lull of apprehension in its place. "I must go now," Derek whispered at last against Annalise's perspiration-dampened cheek, "but I shall come back. You won't change your mind about marrying me in the spring?"

"Never," she murmured. "I shall wait for you forever if necessary. Only do take care. I should want to die, too, if anything happened to you."

"See to Marian," he said, as he reluctantly rose. "Rodney's going with me."

"Rodney? But he speaks neither Urdu nor Hindustani."

"The other volunteers are no more expert . . . and as you may guess, there were very few of them. Havelock wants a second man along as insurance in case one of us fails to reach the relief force."

She sat up, gathering the sari about her. "Can you trust Rodney? After all, he must know that you once meant to marry Marian."

"I should trust him far sooner than Marian," was his dry reply. "In her current mood, she is as reliable as an adder."

"Why did you first fall in love with her, Derek?" Annalise asked softly.

He fastened his trousers, then pulled on his loose shirt. "Her gallantry. . . and unpredictability. She can be the worst and the best person to have at one's back in a pinch. Even Marian doesn't know which way she will react in advance." He caught her chin gently and kissed her parted lips. "On the other hand, I love you for your faithfulness. If I were ever against the wall, I know precisely that you would stay by me."

He finished buttoning his shirt and Annalise handed him his *puggaree*. Wondering to himself if it would make him a more accurate target, he wound the scarlet cloth about his head. There was much he was not telling Annalise about the danger of his mission, and he imagined Rodney was as reticent with Marian. To reach the relief force, they must negotiate the city beyond the Alam Bagh. He would have felt safer had he not been obliged to take Rodney along, for Rodney had little practice at pretending to be a Muslim. Derek had taken the time to teach him a few simple phrases in the Urdu dialect and something of the manner of a Muslim, but he was unsure whether Rodney would remember his lessons when under the enemy eye. If they were caught, they would most certainly be hacked to death.

He drew Annalise up to him and kissed her lingeringly. "Until I return with Campbell," he whispered.

"Until then," she echoed him softly. "May God guard you and keep you safe. I shall pray for both you and Rodney." She stroked her cheek against his, then kissed him once more. His arms tightened about her momentarily before he reluctantly released her. . . then like a shadow among her memories, he was gone.

Her distraught gaze on the door through which Derek had passed, Annalise sank to the floor and as if she were still in his embrace, hugged her arms about herself. Tears welled in her eyes, but did not fall. Derek would expect her to be strong, and strong she must be. There would be time enough for weeping when she was no longer needed by those about her. Still, she felt cold despite the close, mildewed heat of the small room. The walls seemed to press in on her, as if attempting to crush her soul. The gilding became grotesque, reflecting the decayed lavishness of India that seemed suddenly suffocating to her. This land, old when Alexander the Great first came to conquer it, was as deadly as it was beautiful, and yet she had come to love it almost as much as she did Derek. So much blood had been shed here, yet India was a land of perpetual birth and luxuriant life, both in its myriad, polyglot peoples and its vast, pungent rain forests and sweeping plains. Here was the cradle of the world . . . and the cradle for her future with Derek. By God's grace she would have his children someday and they would grow old together, whether here or in Australia. She liked the idea of Australia; it was a new world with fresh, fertile ideas: a world free of the ancient, rotted hierarchy of caste that was as evil and complex in England as it was in India. Their children would have a beginning in a sturdy culture made vigorous by energetic, new bloodlines . . . if Derek and she survived long enough to make that prediction possible.

The next few days would tell the fearful tale.

XIX

The Campbells Are Coming

Derek and Rodney went over the rear residency wall after midnight. The night was moonless, the shadowing of the wall pitch dark as they cast a rappeling line down it, taking care to avoid the torch glare from beyond the sepoy guns. The rope bit into Derek's hands as he slowly lowered himself a foot at a time, then landed soundlessly at the base of the wall. Across the narrow street was a facing of shops and houses, deserted by the court hangers-on of the last King of Oudh, Wajid Ali Shah, since the beginning of hostilities. Only a cat slinking along the parapet of the opposite wall broke the stillness when it knocked a crumbling tile loose to strike the dirt near Derek's feet a few moments after he reached the ground. Forcing his startled heart to still, he gave the rope a signal twitch and tightened the line for Rodney, who was more awkward than he at the descent. When Rodney reached the base, Derek twitched the rope a second time and Professor

Sanderville hauled it back up to the top. The two men faded into the darkness of the closely clustered buildings.

On her infirmary rounds that same night Annalise stopped by Robert's *charpoy* to make certain his fever had not risen. His wound looked clean and there was no swelling about the joint. With luck, he would regain his health if not the use of his leg. He was sleeping easily, and as she smoothed his ragged cotton sheet back in place, she felt a presence behind her. Turning, she saw Marian staring coldly down at her. "Is it true that you are going to marry Derek?" Marian demanded bluntly.

"Yes. We hope to be married in a few months," answered Annalise softly. She pitied Marian, for there was pain mixed with anger in Marian's face. Her hair was like a rising flame about the rigid whiteness of her skin, and her hands were clenched tightly at her sides.

Heedless of Robert, Marian said tensely, "You must be mad to think you can make him happy. You were right to run away in the first place. Why couldn't you have just kept going?"

"Derek is a finer and more honorable man than either you or I once thought him. I was late in coming to know that, but now that I do, I mean never to leave his side. He sees me as his equal, no matter what you may think . . ."

"But you're not his equal. While your poverty may have been genteel, your behavior was not. I know you were sleeping with him at Claremore. Where is the honor in that?"

Robert opened his eyes with an exaggeratedly weary sigh. "How can a man get any sleep with the two of you going at it like a pair of peevish pouter pigeons?" With an effort that whitened his face, he pushed himself up to a sitting position. "You're hardly one to decry anyone's behavior, Marian. After all"—he lowered his voice—"you did not go to your marriage a virgin. Annalise loves Derek, while you used him to please yourself and your unending vanity."

"I loved him deeply enough," retorted Marian, her face twisting. "Do you think I found it easy to give him up? I was right in refusing to come to India, as this hideous siege well shows, but why should Derek ruin the rest of his life for one mistake?" She stooped and gripped the edge of the *charpoy*. "Give Claremore back to him, Robert. Give him another chance to see that marrying this . . . mission wench is impossible." She looked fiercely up at Annalise. "There, look at her face. She does not want him to have his birthright, for she knows well enough that living at Claremore would show just how ridiculous her ambitions are."

Robert laughed easily despite his pain. "I would gladly give Derek Claremore, but he won't have it . . . and Annalise is the least enterprising young lady I have ever known." His eyes narrowed. "You were the ambitious one, Marian. You wanted the baronetcy more than Derek. Why should you give a damn now whether he inherits or not, now that you have Rodney?"

"I love Rodney," Marian asserted, "but I love Derek, too. I want him to have his due."

"Are you certain it's love, or are you just being a dog in the manger?" retorted Robert.

Looking as if she longed to slap him, Marian hissed, "Your sudden nobility is sickening and suspect, do you know that? No wonder you want Derek to marry Annalise. So long as Derek marries Annalise you are well off. You have the baronetcy *and* Claremore."

Robert flushed with anger. "Don't attribute your greediness to me. I want my brother happy, whatever. And that 'whatever' happens to be Annalise."

"You hypocrite . . . you . . ."

"Stop it," cried Annalise softly. "Both of you, please stop it. I won't hear you tear each other apart. You are both very dear to Derek and should remain so." She touched Marian's arm. "Say you will be Derek's friend, whatever he decides. Surely, my becoming his wife should not sever your long affection for him."

Marian stared at her. "Do you propose to share him like a mutton pie? A slice for you and a slice for me?" Her lips curved contemptuously. "Truly, you are generous."

"Love shared grows only greater," murmured Annalise. "While Derek has taken me into his heart, I do not seek its ownership."

Marian's face twisted. "I do believe you are genuinely modest . . . and gullible. You do not know the first thing about fighting for a man. You simply talk of sharing friendship. Don't you know that I don't wish to be your friend? That I hope you disappear from the face of the earth!" She turned on her heel and left the infirmary.

Robert looked up at Annalise. "I think she means to have the whole mutton pie."

Derek and Rodney followed the main road beyond the Alam Bagh for two hours after eventually slipping by the sentries at Lucknow's gate, but they saw no sign of Campbell's campfires on the plain. The road was rutted and walking was difficult with wait-a-bit thorn scrub on either side. In the dim starlight, they could barely see eight feet in front of them. Finally, they decided to turn south and some time later, Rodney grabbed Derek's arm. "See that flickering light? It must be one of Campbell's fires!"

"Then where are the rest of them? The fire seems too close," began Derek, then saw the glowing worm of a gun match lighting up the face of the Hindu blowing on it. Forcibly, he dragged Rodney to the ground, and seconds later, a blast of cannon-fired grapeshot whistled over their heads. An excited jabber of Hindustani and Urdu followed the shot. "Wonderful," Derek whispered grimly. "We've walked into a road barricade of sepoys from Lucknow!"

Giving Rodney a shove toward the side of the road, he rolled after him. They hit the thorn almost as one, then scrambled up, and ignoring the wait-a-bit's long spines, darted through the brush. A second volley of grapeshot crashed, and they bit the dirt once more, their arms protectively covering their heads. As soon as the cannonade of grapeshot ceased, they bolted up and ran. In a matter of seconds, they were out of range and over the ridge, where the stars seemed to fall into the earth. Beyond them was a blanket of campfires: surely Campbell's force, at last. Behind them came the jingle of bits as several sepoys took to their horses in pursuit.

They bounded down the hill, regardless of thorn bushes and rock. They had a fifty-yard head start when Derek halted and jerked a long, cylindrical object from underneath his loose shirt and jammed it on its stick into the dirt. Black shapes loomed on the ridge, obscuring starlight, and he struck a match. Rodney caught a brief glimpse of a fuse igniting a rocket's sparks. Angled low, the rocket flared, then with a hissing shriek, snaked up the hill into the riders. Horses whinnied and reared in fear as their riders landed in the thorn, where cries and curses bit the night. Startled yells answered from English sentries and a hullabaloo broke loose in the camp.

Derek and Rodney took off again, but several riders remounted and plunged off after them, their horses crashing through the brush in hot pursuit. Derek whirled and lit a second rocket, holding this one in his hand. Whistling like a banshee, it sped toward its targets, and this time, by sheer accident, it connected with a horse. Screaming, it went down, pitching its rider headlong. A second horse stumbled over him and crashed to the earth. A lone rider still forged on toward them, hoofbeats resounding on the hard-packed earth, growing louder. "This one is yours," muttered Derek, thrusting a magnesium flare at Rodney. "I'll try to drag him off his horse if you miss."

"I'll go you one better!" Rodney lit the flare's fuse and dropped it in the dirt. Taking his knife, he swiftly hacked off three palmetto fans from the scrub and stuck one of them upright in his *puggaree*. As the blinding white light filled the night, he danced wildly in front of it with the palms in his outstretched hands, all the while screaming, "Kallliieeeeee!" at the top of his lungs. The effect was demonic, as if a feathered devil from hell had burst from the earth. The rider's mount reared inches from his quarry, with the terrified sepoy struggling to keep his seat. Derek rose from the scrub, reached up, and neatly jerked him from the saddle. His knife rose, fell, and then there was a ring of silence about the macabre figure that had frozen in front of the still-glaring flare.

Seeing riders from Campbell's camp approaching on the run, Derek hurriedly jerked off his *puggaree*, then ripped off his shirt. Beneath it were borrowed regimentals from the 3rd Cavalry. As he jerked at his white cotton breeches, Rodney croaked, "Hurry, man, or they'll shoot me for Sunday chicken!"

His urgency was in vain. An English sergeant and two subalterns rose up from the night like avenging angels. Under their pistol bores, Derek halted with his breeches half down over his regimental trousers, while Rodney, embarrassed, raised his outstretched arms and dropped his palm "feathers" into the dirt.

"Now who would you fine chickadees be?" demanded the sergeant, sounding much like Conran O'Reilly.

"Former Colonel Derek Clavell and the Earl of Sheffield," retorted Rodney calmly, "and we always dress for dinner."

XX

The Betrayal

Dawn rose with a rosy gold cast that gilded the parapets and minarets of Lucknow, and cocks sang about the city like clarions of the coming fray. Pinched between the residency force and those on the plain, the sepoys alternated their batteries to train both on the residency and the streets leading to it. At intervals throughout the city were pockets of resistance, with heavier forces installed along the canal and main avenue that connected to the road from the Alam Bagh. All the able men inside the residency were on duty. The women were divided between the infirmary and supplying water and food to the firing lines. Annalise and Professor Sanderville had helped Robert install himself in a rooftop sniping niche. With his wounded leg heavily splinted and extended before him, he readied his new Enfield and stuck a paper hat upon his head to fend off the swiftly growing glare of the rising sun. Perhaps twenty yards from him was the door that led into the residency proper, and to his left was Professor Sanderville with an ancient matchlock. The professor had on his pith helmet and periodically swiped at his brow with an impatient gesture to blot the perspiration running into his eyes. At one point, he sighed to Robert, "If only this thumping siege would end. I feel like a boy bound to a teacher who never knows when to stop droning his lecture."

Robert smiled in sympathy. Indeed, in their bizarre hats, the two of them looked like a pair of children who had stolen a day from school and found its entertainment not at all to their liking. The professor's disgruntled face was red as a lobster's, his normally wiry mutton-chop whiskers drooping from the heat. The rooftop was a blaze of reflected light, the men wilted at their posts, and the door to the stairs was a black block of shadow exposed to the rifles of sepoy snipers on roofs surrounding theirs. "The next few days will tell the tale," murmured Robert. "Either Campbell's men will break through and overwhelm the besiegers or we're done for, sooner or later. I cannot imagine another relief force being sent where two have failed."

"That's a pessimism I would expect from a man my own age," returned Professor Sanderville. "You young scrubs are supposed to be ripe for the fray."

Robert shook his head. "Like you, I've had enough. We've been here for months with no end in sight. I don't know about the rest of the men, but I'm in the mood to fight like a savage out of sheer boredom." His eyes narrowed as he scanned the city. "Where the hell *is* Campbell's artillery? It's nearly noon . . ."

The words were scarcely out of his mouth when a crack of gunfire and thumping artillery fire sounded well to the rear of the sepoys beyond the Alam Bagh. Campbell had arrived, and cries of anger and alarm went up from the sepoys as plumes of smoke issued forth from their cannon redoubling the assault on the residency. Here and there, a man dropped among the sepoy barricades of grain sacks to lie under a pall of heat and smoke while Robert and the professor fired repeatedly in mounting exultation. "Ta ra ra boom de ay," Robert sang through clenched teeth as he dropped a sepoy. "You'll never get through the day, you sons of bitches."

Robert was wrong, for the battle went on not only that day, but many more and often into the night. As the rattle of gunfire and artillery sounded outside during that long week, Annalise sent up silent prayers for Derek and the other valiant Englishmen attempting to break the siege. She, Jane, and Marian had drawn relief detail instead of their usual duties in the infirmary. Under the hazardous flare of gunfire, they took food and water to the men based at the residency upper-floor windows and roof ramparts.

It was a hot and dusty afternoon when Jane and Annalise reached the top floor with its sniper-lined windows. "Keep your heads low," a codger in knickers warned. "The bullets are flying like nasty bees."

"What are we having for lunch?" another fellow inquired jovially. "Pheasant under glass?"

"Roast sepoy," tossed back Jane. "Admittedly a little on the rare side, but the chef is in a bit of a rush today with preparations for tonight's victory feast."

The two women separated and began to make their rounds, handing out mealie cakes and cups of tepid water. Around them the wall plaster powdered in pocks as the bullets sang.

The dust lay in a thick pall over everything, even the men, and perspiration made brown rivulets on their faces. Little glass was left in the windows, but the air was still, leaving scant crosscurrent to cool the room. Carefully, Annalise handed out the rations, one to a man, while Marian did the opposite side of the room. Although the sun was high, there was little lull in the fighting, and the flying bullets were as lethal as ever, singing their wicked whine about the walls and tearing into the plaster. As Annalise stooped over one man, a bullet struck the chandelier overhead, shattering a mass of crystals and sending shards of glass flying. Annalise flung her arm over her head and sucked in her breath as she felt tiny stings of glass splinters sting her shoulder, then spray her forearm and hand.

The man pulled her down. "You'll want to keep low, ma'am. Those pandies are fit to be tied today and they're firing at anything that moves." Quickly, he picked the splinters from her skin, leaving tiny pricks of blood in his wake. "Best shake out your hair, too."

She did so, then thanked him and handed him his ration. "Best shake it out," she teased.

Annalise ducked low to hand a man his lunch and he whistled nervously. "They're making it hot for us today. I hope it's because they're scared witless."

Annalise smiled. "But of course, *we're* not. All of us are made of iron with monstrous teeth, and have nothing to fear. How long do you think it will be before General Campbell's boys break through the lines?"

The man stroked his beard thoughtfully. "By midafternoon. I'll wager on it."

"My ration of mealies against your watch fob?"

Knowing who she was, he looked startled at her willingness to gamble. Then, realizing she meant to take his mind from his fears, gave an unsteady laugh. "Done . . . and I'll throw in the chain as well."

"I shall see you at dinner then," she promised gaily, and went on to the next man. She had finished her side of the room when she turned to encounter Jane crossing the floor to meet her. A high whine seared through the windows' shadow pattern on the wall and with a brief, strangled cry, Jane crumpled. Ducking and dropping her basket, Annalise ran to her aid.

A bloody blotch stained Jane's left shoulder, but she was conscious when Annalise anxiously bent over her. The gentleman in knickers swiftly joined them. Jane was white faced with alarm, but her eyes, though wide, were steady. "That will teach me to strut about like a vain peacock."

"You're going to the infirmary," Annalise promised determinedly as she tried to rip a bandage from Jane's petticoat. Exposed by Jane's tumbled skirts, the hoopless cotton lay spilled like snow across the sun-baked floor.

The knicker-clad gentleman caught the petticoat from her and gave it a firm rip. Taking another wad of fabric he gave her, Annalise applied it to Jane's wound, which had passed through to her back. "You'll be all right, I think," she murmured. "The bullet has gone through the fleshy part of your shoulder. I don't think it caught any bone." She inserted a hand beneath Jane's armpit. "Will you help me, sir?"

"Certainly." He nudged Jane confidingly as he assisted her to her feet. "Why, you scarcely weigh more than a cricket bat." He looped her arm about his shoulder, and still pale from reaction, Jane caught Annalise's arm.

"Don't tell Robert," she pleaded. "He already thinks I'm an idiot."

"I won't," Annalise promised, leading her from the room. "But you know, he must find out sooner or later."

"Better later... when I've had a chance to redo my hair."

Annalise and Knickers helped Jane into Robert's vacated *charpoy* in the infirmary, then the cricketer doffed his cap and headed back upstairs. Jane opened her eyes weakly. "Blast," she said. "Blast and damnation. Now I won't be able to wear off-the-shoulder dresses."

Carefully shielding her from the eyes of the curious

wounded man in the next cot, Annalise tore the shoulder from her dress and began to bathe the wound with a little of the water from the *chatti* beside the bed. "There's no privacy in this place," complained Jane. "Why can't I go into the women and children's ward?"

"Because the doctor is tending to gunshot victims first and as most of them are men from the firing line, this is where he will be most likely to give you immediate attention. Are you in much pain?"

"Not much. I suppose I'm still stunned . . . because the wound is just beginning to ache." Jane's eyes widened slightly in apprehension. "I've seen operations. There won't be anything to kill the pain . . ."

"Don't worry," Annalise reassured her gently. "The wound is clean, so Dr. Neville won't have to probe. The procedure should not be too difficult."

Jane spotted Marian coming into the room from the women's ward. "She's coming this way. I hope she isn't meaning to extend her condolences. I feel like a fool."

"Bullets are exceedingly dramatic, Jane. You needn't assume you've stepped down in life."

"How are you, Jane?" asked Marian urgently as she came up to them. "I just heard what happened. You look dreadful."

"Thank you. I'm so flattered," said Jane dryly, then her demeanor softened as she noted Marian's real anxiety. The strain of working under fire was telling on all of them. "Really, I shall be all right. I'm just a bit dizzy."

Marian propped a pillow beneath her head. "Here, you'll want this. I'll see if I cannot speed Dr. Neville along."

"Oh, don't," said Jane apprehensively. "I am in no hurry for surgery."

"Well," Marian returned dubiously, "if you're certain . . ."

"I'm certain. Why not run along with Annalise back to

the line, only do be careful; it's like walking into a hornet's nest."

Marian eyed Annalise reluctantly for a moment as if she were attempting to think of a reason to withdraw her company. Finally, she acceded, her eyes scathing. "Very well, come along, Mrs. O'Reilly. Let's not dawdle. Those abominable sepoys are making it hot for our boys today."

Annalise gathered up her baskets with a farewell smile for Jane. "I shall return as quickly as possible. Just lie still, and if you need anything, ask for Mrs. Conroy. She is heading up the nursing staff today."

Jane nodded. "Thank you, but I probably shan't need to bother her. My wound hurts surprisingly little."

"Oh, it will wake up," Marian assured her. "Just don't suffer in silence too long."

"Jane has proven to be quite a trooper," Annalise confided to Marian as they mounted the stairs to the supply dispensary.

"Indeed," returned Marian ironically. "I had thought her to be rather empty-headed upon our first meeting. First impressions can be misleading."

"That is very true." Annalise studied her gravely. "I must beg your pardon, for I fear I was misled in my first assessment of you. In these last months I have come to greatly admire your courage and self-sufficiency. I do hope you and Lord Sheffield will have many happy years together."

"I imagine you do," retorted Marian, "for then I should be well out of your way. Do not hope to soften me into friendship, Mrs. O'Reilly. I may be out of Derek's life, but that does not mean that I believe you will fill it admirably in my place. You will hold Derek down and call the iron chains with which you bind him, love. I thought you first refused him because you genuinely cared for him, but now I think you sly. Derek cannot resist a challenge. You learned that in observing his pursuit of me. You have made him want you for the moment, but in future years, he will come to regret his foolish choice. Then, I promise you, you will regret the match, for money alone will not prevent your life from becoming a hell. I have known him longer than you; he will cease to be faithful to you, and in the end you will wish you were dead."

"You may have known Derek longer than me, Lady Sheffield, but you do not know him as well," returned Annalise boldly. 'Derek is capable of infinite love and loyalty, as you would have discovered, had you not abandoned him for Lord Sheffield. Time there was, when Derek could speak only of you and I was nothing to him. I cannot regret that time has passed, but now that it has, I shall be a good and worthy wife to him, as I believe he will be a fit mate to me. I shall follow him wherever he wishes to go and give him all that he will have of me." Her usually serene eyes flashed. "You have no need to hate me, Lady Sheffield, but to wish Derek well, as I do. Love him, as I do . . . but from afar. Do I make myself plain?"

"I do believe you are warning me to keep my hands off your man," drawled Marian. "That's fair. I should hate to think I am at odds with a jellyfish." Her tone turned ominous. "But be warned, I can fight to the death as well as any man, so do not assume you have won the battle. *En garde*, madame; this is one fight I mean to claim."

Annalise made no response. In the quietest part of her heart, she was sure Marian could not come between her and Derek. Watching Marian now was like seeing the crescendo of a brilliant pyrotechnical display; there was a good deal of flaring light, but little heat. Marian had already lost, could she but know it. Her defeat was in Derek's eyes, his voice, his tender devotion. He would be making love to no more Marians: of that Annalise was certain, but Marian would never believe it until Derek himself made it clear to her . . . and yet, he probably *had* made it clear to her. Marian's entire behavior suggested it. The more Derek told her he had ceased to care for her, the more she tried to erase that fact. Marian could not believe that a man who had loved her all her life, finally had come to see her only as a friend. Annalise pitied her, but pitied Rodney more. How must he construe Marian's behavior, when she had made her discontent so evident?

She let Marian precede her up the stairs, then together they filled their baskets with mealie cakes at the supply dispensary. Most of the other women had finished their rounds, and Annalise was anxious to see that the men in her charge did not have much longer to wait for their rations. When she was done, she turned to Marian. "I must be growing weak, for my basket feels no lighter."

Marian eyed her lissome curves coolly. "I could wish you would turn into a hag from lack of food, but undoubtedly you would waste too attractively. At times, I feel you have been sent to punish me for my sins, and there have been many from the look of you. You are altogether too fetching for a missionary's daughter."

Annalise laughed. "Shall I thank you for the compliment?"

"Certainly not, for it was ill meant. Do not think to soften me with sweetness. No woman loves another for her looks when there is a man between them."

The heat in the stairwell to the roof was stifling but there was little sound of gunfire from the outside. Gingerly, Annalise opened the door to the roof. As the door crack widened, the shots began to sing, with a crackle of response from the men on the roof. Ducking low, the women darted from the door to the line of men crouched behind the wall while the bullets sprayed about them. "Hold off, it's lunch time," sang one of the sharpshooters, and the responding fire from the English died down. After a minute or two, the mutineers also ceased firing. "No one wants to fight in the heat of high noon," a young subaltern advised Annalise as she handed him his corn-bread pattie, "but still, you had best take care. They're nervous today." He pointed out the smoke from Campbell's invading troops who were gradually nearing the mutinous sepoy lines. "We'll have them in a tightening vise, and just like a dentist pulling a bad tooth, will wrench them out and crush them."

Annalise looked out over the city rooftops which were laid over with a pall of smoke and dust. Only a half-dozen buildings overlooked the residency and someone had built a wall of rubble on those parts of the roof directly in their fire. The sun filtering through the haze created a fierce glare against the white plaster, and only bright colors and figures moving against dark shapes were visible. Although the sun mirroring off gilded domes and minarets hurt Annalise's eyes, she continued to peer out into the city in futile hope of seeing some sign of Derek. Even if he succeeded in reaching Campbell, leading the troops back into the city must be perilous work, for the pandies were stubbornly holding Lucknow street by street. Often, she had imagined him killed in some pile of rubble or cornered and outnumbered in some derelict building. Feeling her heart beginning to hammer from anxiety, she bent low and hurried along the line, the perspiration beginning to run down her temples and the sari sticking to her ribs. She could hear Marian calling out jaunty greetings to the men.

Professor Sanderville was the last man in the line and he looked spent from the heat, his pith helmet pushed to one side from being pressed against the parapet. He had on a pair of smoked spectacles, which he promptly tried to loan her when he saw her squinting in the glare, but she refused. "I have no need of hitting a target as you do, but only finding my way about. You will directly have a headache if you remove your spectacles."

Sanderville laughed ironically, "I shall melt first." He pawed through the basket and seized a wizened mealie.

"The dregs of the rations again," he sighed with a morose look.

Annalise patted his shoulder. "If we are still here tomorrow, I shall do you the favor of doling out the food from your end of the line first. I should not wish you to become as lean as one of your Egyptian mummies."

He gave her a rueful smile. "I am already a mummy. This infernal sun had dried me to a turn. At least the fellows attempting to rescue us sometimes have the advantage of fighting in the shade."

"I hope Derek is safe," she murmured, looking out over the city. "The battle directed against Campbell's men has been so intense these last hours."

Sanderville nodded. "Caught like rats in a trap, the pandies are, but they're large rats and fighters to a man. So far the battle has run in their favor, so let us hope we can press them hard enough to turn the game." He squeezed her hand as she started to withdraw the basket. "Put in a prayer for us, my dear. Perhaps your father has credit with God."

Across the parapet, Robert hailed her. "Is anything left of lunch? My belly is sticking to my backbone."

"Belly, sir?" she teased as she crossed to him. "How familiar of you. If this were merry old England, I confess I should be shocked."

He laughed as he pawed through the basket. "You are perhaps the least shockable woman I know. In your quiet way, you reduce all the horrors of this war to pitiable stupidity." His tone changed as he came up with only a few broken mealies. "What, no biscuits, no toffee, no jam? What sort of tea do you serve here, madame? One can scarcely call it luncheon, for it would barely serve to divert one of my hounds at home."

"I am sorry, but the rations are getting low. Perhaps tonight I can make up the difference to you." She knelt by his leg and examined the bandages. The linen was still white, with no trace of bleeding. "How is your leg, Robert? Are you still in pain?"

"Oh, it hurts like blazes, particularly in the heat," he replied between bites of mealie, "but I've grown used to it . . . just as I've grown used to the idea of your marrying Derek."

Her attention centered gravely upon his face. "Is our marriage so difficult an idea to accept?"

"It was at first, I admit, but then I've come to admire you in more than looks." He paused, his expression sobering. "When Derek marries you, the family will be gaining a great lady. If some of us are too stuffy to see it, then it will be our grievous loss." He chucked her under the chin in a brotherly fashion. "Just keep that pretty head high and your eyes on Derek. He'll give you enough love to found a new dynasty, if necessary."

"I shall remember that."

"Remember, too, that I'm very fond of you. I always have been, but I had to do a bit of growing up to realize it. For what it's worth, I wish I had met you first, but the truth is, I would have wasted the opportunity. I shan't be so foolish with Jane."

"She is very much worried about you."

"Good; it keeps her from flirting, which she does altogether too easily to have it matter to her. For the time being, I prefer Jane to be in a serious sort of mood about me; that way, when I propose, she'll take notice."

Annalise laughed. "Oh, she'll notice. She's practically sewing your name into her handkerchiefs."

Robert's smile broadened into one of self-satisfaction. "Then I had better let her suffer for a few weeks. She's been indulged too long by the cantonment beaux . . ."

"But then," intervened Annalise smoothly, "Jane isn't one to endure the disagreeable. The residency gentlemen cater to her as much as you ignore her. She just might decide that enough is enough."

Robert eyed her. "My vanity is not blind, Mrs. O'Reilly. Jane sees to it that I am duly notified when I grow too puffed. I propose to ask her hand on the day the siege lifts. What say you to that?"

"I wish you all luck, sir, and I shall be the first to congratulate you." She gathered up the basket. "Now, I must take my leave, for I see that Marian is beckoning to me."

Keeping low, she darted across the parapet to Marian, who greeted her perturbedly. "The sepoys have shifted one of their gun positions and the door to the stairs is exposed to a crossfire. You had better let me go first, but stay close."

Annalise was startled. Although Marian's gallantry was highly unpredictable, it was unlike her to extend it to someone she detested. Without waiting for an answer, Marian caught Annalise by the hand and headed across the parapet to the door. Instantly, the sepoy rifles picked them out and shots sang out at their heels. "Damn, damn, damn," swore Marian, zigzagging at each epithet. Her grip was firm, nearly dragging Annalise off her feet. Suddenly, Annalise skidded on gravel and went down. Marian wheeled in anger as much as fear. "Get up!" she shrilled, then her face twisted as if she were enduring some kind of terrible conflict. She backed away toward the door, her lips drawn back over her teeth like a snarling dog's. "You fool," she hissed. "You little fool. You shouldn't have trusted me, when I cannot even trust myself . . ." Spinning on her heel, she catapulted for the door, swung it wide for a brief moment, then slammed it. Behind her.

For a few seconds, Annalise was stupefied with horror. She was locked out of the residency. Marian had left her exposed to the sepoy guns! Throwing herself forward to the ground, she rolled forward toward the door, then abruptly stilled as if she had been shot. A shot spat inches from her head, and another over her neck. Squeezing her eyes shut, her heart drumming out a fierce song of terror, she forced herself not to move. She heard Robert cry out, then answering yells from the other men. At first, she thought he was calling to her, then caught a note of elation in his voice. Clearly, they had not noticed her; their attention was riveted on the pandy line beneath them. She wanted to scream for help, but feared that any man who came to her aid would be shot as well. The rooftop about her was still being peppered with bullets and her heart threatened to burst from fear.

A shot whistled past her cheek and another creased her arm. She felt a sharp sting, then a seepage of blood down the curve of her elbow. Please, her mind screamed, *please*, somebody, help me! But overhead the sky was a merciless blue as hard as lapis lazuli.

Then, suddenly, she saw a black crack appear at the door rim; it slowly widened and in its wedge, she saw Marian's taut, apprehensive face. Marian was intent upon discovering whether or not she had been killed. Her eyes wide with pleading, she lay like a pinioned butterfly, and Marian's lips parted in a gasp of torment. Her green eyes filled with turmoil, Marian stared at Annalise as if she wanted to deny her existence, then her pale face crumpled. She threw herself forward from the doorway toward Annalise and extended her hand to her. In that moment, three sepoy guns sang out and a bright red splotch appeared at Marian's breast. Pressing her hands to her side, she pitched headlong to the rooftop, her bright hair tangling with Annalise's dark tresses. Her lips parted, she gazed at Annalise in stunned confusion. "I should have . . . let you die . . . should have . . ." A cough shook her, then left her drained. Her face waxen, she tried to lift her head with a mingled expression of bitterness and relief. "So easy . . . murder, but . . . so hard."

Then her head went lax, her outflung hand curling up like a child's.

Torn between shock and pity, Annalise stared at her beautiful, dead face. Rodney, she thought dazedly. Poor Rodney.

Robert's harsh voice cut across her thought. "Annalise! Marian!" Then came the scrape of his crutch.

Oh, no, she realized. He's trying to come to us. I must stop him! Without even a second's hesitation, she threw herself away from Marian and toward Robert, digging her sandaled feet into the rooftop so that she could crawl toward him. "Stay where you are!" she cried as she worked her way through the singing bullets. "Marian is dead!"

She saw him hesitate where he crouched, his back to the balustrade. His face taut, he extended the crutch. She flailed out, grabbed the crutch, and he hauled her in, scraping her shoulder mercilessly on the rooftop gravel. His arms went about her, holding her momentarily close as she let out a gasp of reaction and relief.

"What happened?" he demanded.

She hesitated, then murmured, "I fell . . . and Marian was shot trying to save me. She was killed instantly."

Something in her tone made Robert study her face dubiously. "That was noble of her."

"It's the truth," Annalise replied levelly. "She was killed trying to save my life."

He searched her eyes, and then nodded. "All right. Your story will stand . . . although I dare say you would have said the same thing if she had tried to bury a meat cleaver in your skull. Rodney will take this hard, and Derek little less so."

"I know," she whispered. "I dread telling them."

"Well, you'll have your chance, I'll wager." He pointed to the sepoy line on the street below them. The line looked thin in places, but not yet broken as Campbell's troops assailed them. Suddenly, a band of English and loyal native troops with a tall, familiar figure at their head appeared at an intersection of narrow streets feeding into the square.

"It's Derek!" cried Annalise.

"And there's Rodney. Someone's lent him a uniform." Robert sighed in relief. "I was afraid they hadn't even made it to Campbell. Thank God!"

"Yes," agreed Annalise fervently. "God *has* looked after all of us today." She craned to see the action in the street below and Robert hurriedly pulled her down.

"Let's not press the Divine patience. The Lord has enough on his mind with our lads down there."

Derek squinted up at the parapet, and for a moment he could have sworn he saw Annalise and Robert gazing back down at him, but then they disappeared and his attention was driven back to the fierce battle at hand. The sepoys were barely visible through the dust, but they were manning their guns handily enough. From his vantage point in the last house he and Rodney had cleared of snipers, Derek had determined the extent of the sepoys' siege works on this side of the residency. Two six-pound guns were of particular menace, situated behind a rude barricade in the middle of Residency Row, their muzzles directly before the residency gate. But, he had noted with a savage grin, despite the size of the makeshift ramparts, their military engineering had left much to be desired. The siege lines extended almost directly east and west from the gun emplacement, an arrangement which was about to cost them dearly.

Now he peered around the street corner at the back of the two six-pounders. The stone facade above his head chipped and splattered as a ball ricochetted away into the square behind him. He sat suddenly, pressing his back against the hot stone. God, that had been close. He swallowed twice, trying to moisten his dry throat. The loyal sepoys at his side were a blur of wide, white eyeballs in sweating brown faces. One sprang into focus, a fierce moustachioed *havildar* with a new slash on his face which was going to be a magnificent scar, if he lived. The *havildar* grinned widely at Derek and murmured, "Time to earn our pay, sahib."

Derek gripped the sweat-soaked, sharkskin handle of his saber and grinned back, "Right you are, messmate." Standing, he waved his saber, shouting at the men behind him and at those crouched behind the building across the street, "Come on lads, do you want to live forever?" With that he turned the corner and charged up the street, his loyal sepoys pouring after him, heading for the guns two blocks away.

Snipers dropped many of the charging troops but the mutineers were caught off guard by the sudden rush and no infantry had been drawn up in deadly rows across the street to protect the guns. The gunners, hearing the charge behind them, made mad work of turning their guns around, and before the charge had covered half the distance, both cannon crashed, a heartbeat apart. Derek would always remember the unreal clarity of the six-pound iron ball coming directly at him, seemingly suspended in space, and the enormous whoosh as it passed, an arm's length above his head. Lucky, he thought, breath rasping in his throat as he pounded toward the gunners who were frantically reloading. Sometimes, it is better to be lucky than good. Had the guns been loaded with grapeshot instead of roundshot for battering the residency walls, he would have been perforated and the entire troop decimated.

The gunners were trying to rectify their omission and had already rammed home the cloth sacks filled with the grape-sized leaden balls when Derek's men were upon them. The artillerymen's short swords were no match for the charging bayonets and sabers, and they were soon all down, gutted among the rammers, rods, and paraphernalia of their trade.

Derek leaned against a wheel of the western gun, gasping for breath. "Come lads, spike them around. Quickly now! Aim them east and west along the ramparts." His order being quickly obeyed, the boom of each cannon was followed by the horrible departing buzz of the grapeshot flinging down the length of the ramparts, bloodying and mutilating the surprised mutineers.

A cheer went up inside the residency as Derek's men broke through the line and began to roll it up, the flank curving around and behind the pandies. Desperate, the mutinous sepoys fought like trapped rats, but some of them began to scatter, forging their way back into the city streets to filter away and run for their lives. Derek slashed his way into the line with his saber and a brown face went down before him, face split in mid-scream. His saber slid through sleeve fabric, ripping it away before coming down again to spin another pandy into the dust. Rodney was behind him, yelling at the top of his lungs. "Come on, boys! Let's take them! We have them on the run now!"

Several sepoys, out of ammunition, began to swing their rifles overhead like bludgeons, and one of them caught Rodney on the side of the head. Nearly unconscious, he went down, but Derek caught him under the armpit and dragged him up from the melee. "Thanks, old man," muttered Rodney, swaying against him. "Another second, and I would have been trampled. Why won't these bloody beggars give up?"

"Because they'll be slaughtered to a man," returned Derek briefly. "Look around you."

The sepoys had been decimated, with the remainder of their line in fragments. The few who tried to surrender were cut down without mercy. Here was revenge for Meerut, Delhi, and the women and children who had been massacred at Kanpur. Here was the retaliation that had been gathering for months. A plume of smoke drifted upward from a smashed gun as Campbell rolled his artillery into position. Inch by precious inch, the ground before the residency was taken, until the dead lay in heaps, and the victors stood exhausted over the field of battle.

Shouts of glee rose from the residency, and shouts of triumph pierced the very clouds. The bars on the great doors of the main building crashed down, and the doors flung wide. At the head of his men, Derek shambled wearily into the residency. Instantly, a crowd of cheering people surrounded them. Through the thrashing hands and open mouths, Derek saw Sanderville trying to grasp his hand. A jolt of fear went through him. "Annalise!" he yelled desperately. "Is Annalise safe?"

Unable to hear him, Sanderville frowned and cupped his hand behind his ear. "What?" he shouted. "What did you say?"

"Annalise! Where is Annalise? And Robert?"

Beside him, Rodney repeated the question, but the professor waved vaguely up at the sky and Derek could have wept from frustration. Then suddenly, the professor glanced behind him and smiled. His arm stretched out and pulled two newcomers into the tightly packed group. Derek saw Annalise's lovely face with tears shining on it. Her hair had spilled free about her shoulders and her eyes were dark with longing. Behind her was Robert. With a laugh of sheer release, Derek pushed through the cheering, exultant crowd and swung her into his arms. His head bent to hers in a passionate kiss, and in the churning sea of Englishmen and women, they were a still, certain center.

Annalise closed her eyes, feeling only Derek's lips warm on her own in the jostle of the crowd. Here was her haven; here, her future. Whether that future lay in Australia or the far ends of the earth, she cared not. At last, she was with Derek, and nothing mattered but loving him. Sunlight streamed across their faces, and she opened her eyes. High, high into the serene cobalt sky, a hat was flung above their heads. Sanderville's pith helmet came into focus, sailing upward like a gay, jaunty kite over a "Hip, hip, hurrah!"

Postscript: The relief of the Lucknow residency sounded the knell for the sepoy mutiny. General Colin Campbell withdrew the besieged occupants of the Lucknow garrison from the city in good order, leaving behind him a future linking force to continue fighting at the Alam Bagh. He returned in December and completed the final retaking of the city on March 21, 1858. The remainder of northern India soon returned to English hands. The East India Company had accomplished well their policy of divide and conquer. Ironically, the mutiny, known to native Indians as one of their first battles for independence from England, led to the consolidation of the English colonial empire in India. India, once a patchwork quilt of tiny regal states, became too unified a nation to be ruled by the company. With the end of the mutiny, the entire subcontinent became part of the British empire under the direct rule of the crown. Not until the leadership of Mahatma Gandhi did consolidated India peacefully achieve independence from England.

Two weeks after the mutiny ended, Annalise O'Reilly was married to Derek Clavell in St. Christoph's Church, Kanpur, India, and went to happily reside with him in Perth, Australia. Together, they produced five children and the lucrative Clavell Merchant Marine Shipping Line, which still operates at the writing of this account of their romantic adventures.